Holloway Falls

Neil Cross is the author of *Christendom*, *Mr In-Between* and *Holloway Falls*. His next novel, *Always the Sun*, will be published by Scribner in Spring 2004. He lives with his wife and two sons.

To Ethan and Finn

I wish the stairs were endless

Acknowledgements

To anybody interested in the frontiers of New Age folly, I recommend Damian Thompson's *The End of Time*. From this fine and funny book I borrowed much of Rex Dryden's theology as it appears in Chapter 5. If it stinks, that's probably because it originated with Paco Rabanne.

Like the end of the world, *Holloway Falls* was a long time coming. Happily, many hands helped to make light work of it.

Not only did David Godwin's commitment and enthusiasm never flag, his willingness to re-read slightly different versions of the early manuscript exceeded the limits of human endurance. For this I will never be able to thank him properly, or indeed apologise. I'm similarly indebted to Tim Binding. He determined to get the best out of me, whether I liked it or not and, annoyingly, he was never wrong – not even about me thanking him for it, in the end.

To those I've worked with (so far) at Scribner – Rochelle Venables, Joanna Ellis, Alex Heminsley, Neal Price and James Kellow – thank you for making a new boy feel so quickly at home, and for caring about this book.

To Jeremy Palmer: thanks for the years of close reading, large bar bills and the free exchange of ideas, most of them stupid. And to Jon Parker, who knows all the right words to all the right songs, not to mention a thing or two about books.

But the greatest debt by far is owed to my wife, Nadya Kooznetzoff. Her patience never strained and her nerve didn't crack – not even when I gave superabundant cause for both. Anyone who knows her will tell you she was always out of my league. And they'd be right. She still is.

Holloway Falls is from both of us, with love, to our sons Ethan and Finn.

Part One

Nowhere Forever

We're just going to leave you now, okay?

> *Robert Grimson, leader of the Process*
> *Church of the Final Judgement, taking*
> *leave of his remaining followers, Boston*
> *Common, 1975*

There are certain people who have that ability ... Cops by nature are sceptical. They don't like to talk about this stuff, and it doesn't make it into the reports most of the time for obvious reasons.

> *Police Chief Robert DeLitta, following the*
> *death of Dorothy Allison, a professed*
> *psychic credited with solving more than a*
> *dozen murders and locating more than fifty*
> *missing children*

Sufficient unto the hour is the evil therein

> *pub graffito*

1

Andrew had done his research.

Although he knew the odds on successfully faking suicide were not good, one night he caught a train to the south-west coast of England and fabricated his death by drowning.

He thought of pupae and butterflies. Time lapse. Reversed.

Before that day came, there had been much to do.

His father had left him £25,000, which Andrew had transferred straight to a building society. He imagined a fungal mound of greasy cash in a damp basement corner; but he no longer cared about that and from the account he arranged to withdraw £9,000.

He and Rachel were affluent in a way that privately rather embarrassed him. She worked for the natural history department at BBC Bristol. When the weather was fine, she walked to work. Andrew was deputy head teacher at a south Bristol comprehensive. He earned less than his wife and didn't mind. In addition, Rachel received an annuity from her grandparents that paid for holidays and Christmas. There was a joint savings account, which contained more than his inherited £25,000. And there were a number of insurance policies, into which they had been drip-feeding their salaries for more years than he could cheerfully think about.

His family would never need what remained of his inheritance. They'd probably never want to touch it, in the hope or fear that he might some day *come back*, shambling, seaweed-shrouded. But he left them the money anyway.

He redrafted his will one Thursday lunchtime, employing a south Bristol solicitor who expressly was not a family friend.

He was of sound mind.

With the £9,000, he opened three bank accounts under his own name, depositing £3,000 in each.

During the weeks of preparation, he regularly transferred portions of this money from account to account. Because this deceptive flow of capital gave each bank the impression that his financial affairs were fluid and sound, he was able to arrange three substantial overdrafts.

He withdrew the money in instalments. This procedure was time-consuming and repetitive, and it helped that he'd been on sick leave since the previous school year. Each day for several weeks he withdrew from automatic teller machines on Whiteladies Road slightly less than each account allowed him. Computer automation ensured that human attention was not brought to this possibly dubious conduct.

He left early in April. The morning had about it a crisp Englishness that filled him with vague happiness, a pre-emptive nostalgia. He remembered the life he had been living as if it were already a faded photograph. He found himself moving about his house, picking up and minutely examining innocuous objects – a television remote control, a golf ball, a bread knife.

He dressed in his best suit, as if going to work, and took with him a small leather suitcase in which he had packed £47,000: his original investment plus £38,000 from the overdrafts. He felt the thrill of a new life about to begin. Walking for the last time from bank to bank, folding cash into wallet and wallet into breast pocket (he could feel the blank, whirring eyes of disinterested security cameras), he was possessed of a peculiar consciousness, as if viewing himself from a precipitous new perspective.

He left before the kids got home.

II

Andrew and his family lived in a Georgian house in central Bristol. Many properties on their winding, tree-lined street had been converted into flats for young professional couples who wished to live near Clifton without paying Clifton premiums. There were also family houses – university lecturers, bankers moved from London with Lloyds, media types.

What was to become chronic insomnia first made itself known in his late thirties. Sanguine, he imagined it would be a passing problem and, that first summer, he functioned well enough on three or four hours' sleep a night.

The early mornings were quiet, leaf-dappled with shadow, and stone-cool. Fully awake in time for *Farming Today*, he would stretch with great contentment (gently, so as not to wake Rachel), then take the portable radio from the bedside cabinet and wander downstairs, barefoot in pyjamas, to the ground-floor extension he'd built for visitors. His mother-in-law called it the Granny Flat, and the name had stuck.

Although it overlooked the rear garden, the Granny Flat had the familiar but exotic air of a holiday home. It didn't quite feel like his property, from which he extracted a delicate pleasure. There was a single bed, kept made in anticipation of a visit (he never minded); floral print duvets and feather pillows; Rachel's watercolours – Devon seascapes. There was a bookshelf he'd fitted into an alcove, not without complication or a concurrent sense of satisfaction. The lower shelves were lined with art and cookery books and paperback thrillers. On the top shelf was a creased, stained, dog-eared paperback copy of *Captain Corelli's Mandolin* that had been passed from hand to hand on one family holiday.

Every year, they rented a house in a harbour town on the coast of Devon. In the garden was a brick barbecue at which stood Rachel's father and brother. They were oiling trout with a pastry brush, wrapping the fish in Bacofoil and placing the parcels on the grill, where already sausages were blackening on one spatula-flattened side. Because it was an unspoken rule that such jobs as barbecuing meat should be the responsibility of his father- and brother-in-law, Andrew and Rachel prepared the salad.

Rachel found this hilarious. Despite Andrew's protestations to the contrary, she told him (as he shelled hard-boiled eggs and wrestled the tops from bottles of salad dressing) that his voice had temporarily dropped an octave to reassert his compromised masculinity. Then she stood on tiptoe and kissed him just behind the ear.

Rachel's grandmother sat happily enough in a deck chair, reading *Hello!* and *OK!*. The children busied themselves variously with Gameboys, the lower limbs of blameless trees, tepid cans of Diet Pepsi and *J17*.

Andrew's mother-in-law did not arrive at the alfresco wooden table until her husband was almost wretched with worry that her trout would be overcooked. She emerged with red eyes. She had just finished *Captain Corelli's Mandolin*.

That evening, while Rachel's grandmother babysat, they went to the local pub. There was a car park at front, wooden benches set on the grass, each sheltered by an umbrella advertising Holsten Pils. At one side of the pub stood a pebble-dashed extension that housed the family games room. This in turn housed its own bar, which was staffed by an elderly woman who apparently had yet to tire of the borderline atavism of children on holiday, up past their bedtime after too long in the July sun.

Andrew drank pints of lager and lime, his holiday drink. His sunglasses were upended on the table before him. He was a big man with a rugby player's shoulders and neck: his black Adidas polo shirt – All Blacks, a present from New

Zealand – was taut at belly and shoulders. His hair was packed into tight Semitic curls, thinning at the crown and his experimental goatee beard was flecked with silver. He wore cargo shorts and old tennis shoes, ripped at the seams. He'd begun to acquire a belly in the third year of marriage, when a recurrent cartilage injury barred him even from Sunday soccer.

He drove a ten-year-old Volvo. He believed cricket to be a deep communion with the English subconscious and his voice had the appropriate, gentle behest of a commentator, accentuated by his rising West Country inflection. He remained passionate about rugby. His computer password was *jonalomu*. He would not subscribe to Sky Sports.

Lower-middle-class Bristol boy, temperamentally left-wing. He did not smoke, except sometimes at Christmas and parties. He had never been unfaithful to his wife and had in his married life never been impotent, excepting a single, half-drunken escapade with a recalcitrant condom that closely followed Rachel's decision to come off the Pill. He read the *Observer* on Sunday. Sometimes he bought the *Sunday Mirror* to read on the toilet.

Andrew moved with the gentle assurance acquired at cost by any person who since childhood has been one size too big for the world.

Before ten, it clouded over and began to drizzle and they went inside. The main bar was dark with wood and brass. Within ten minutes, heavy rain came in off the Channel and began to beat a tattoo against the leaded windows. They fell into conversation with another group of holidaymakers, three married couples from Yorkshire, two generations. Rachel began to massage the inside of his calf with her insole, having slipped off a yellow, rope-soled espadrille bought the first day from a seafront shop perfumed with heat, inflatable rubber rings and suntan lotion.

The rain did not let up. At 11.30, he and his family walked the short, steep route to the rented house, which overlooked the harbour. His wife (his Rachel) borrowed his denim jacket because the rain made her sun dress clinging and transparent. The jacket made her child-sized and her hair hung in wet tousles across her brow and shoulders. She smelled of rain.

When they entered the holiday-musty cottage, only their eldest, Annie, was awake, watching *Curse of the Werewolf,* starring the young Oliver Reed.

III

While much of his world was asleep, he enjoyed the holiday feeling of agreeably alienated familiarity. He showered, shaved and wrapped himself in a dark-blue towelling robe.

Sometimes he whiled away an hour reading yesterday's newspaper. Then he prepared breakfast for those members of his family currently willing to eat it.

Periodically, Rachel was on a diet: in the bedroom she adopted an expression of glum concentration and squeezed and prodded and examined in full-length mirrors her breasts and thighs and buttocks. At the age of twelve, Annie announced that she was a vegetarian. Andrew and Rachel decided to encourage her in this. They were proud of their daughter and hoped she'd grow out of it soon.

Adam and Steven, the twins, would eat anything, so long as it was not or did not contain fruit. Sometimes on Sunday, Andrew would cook a full fried breakfast for himself and his sons. Cracking eggs into a hot pan sizzling with bacon fat, he never felt closer to them. He didn't fully understand this. He suspected that something primeval lurked at its source, but it pleased him nonetheless.

On the night of Saturday, 31 August or the early hours of Sunday, 1 September 1997, he lurched into wakefulness like a braking truck. He had vividly dreamed the death of a female celebrity and lay awake for many minutes.

In the early hours, he sneaked from the bedroom and padded downstairs to the Granny Flat. In the washed-out pastels of a Bristolian autumn morning (the smell of fresh, laundered cotton), even showering and shaving, the dream-sadness lingered.

He wondered if he should discuss the dream with Rachel. He towelled himself dry and looked for his bathrobe. He padded round the Granny Flat in befuddled circles, like a sleepy cat. The robe hung where it always did, on a hook behind the bathroom door.

He decided not to say anything. He had been disconcerted by the death of his father two months previously. Rachel's strained patience had been tested further by his sudden insistence, against her appeals, on keeping a photograph of him in the sitting room. It stood next to their wedding photograph on the fireplace.

'Fine,' she said. 'Whatever you want,' and they hadn't spoken for two days.

Their relationship had not yet fully normalized. She was still being tautly polite and he quietly amiable.

Downstairs, Andrew turned on the television. Something important seemed to have happened: there was live news on every channel. His first thought, the legacy of a cold-war childhood, was of nuclear war.

He watched BBC1 for a few incredulous minutes. Then he went and woke Rachel, taking the portable radio with him.

Much as families had during the coronation of Queen Elizabeth II, they gathered round the television. On every channel haggard newsreaders, broadcasting live, explained again and again what had happened in Paris during the early hours of the morning. Even the coiffured anchormen seemed unable to believe it.

Andrew and his family were strangely enraptured, brought into silent fraternity by the woman's death. It seemed to intimate something of great significance, something at the insubstantial edges of which the mind could only grasp. Andrew felt close to them, all at once. They did not dress or properly eat until late in the afternoon. Rachel wept and comforted Annie. The twins were silent. The unspoken dream-sadness settled heavily on Andrew's shoulders and entangled him like a musty robe.

He didn't know what time he'd woken up. Nor could he eliminate the possibility that he'd heard wayward news broadcasts during his sleep and retained their content – what televisions and minicab radios had been mainlined into his receptive mind in the late night stillness? What Saturday night revellers returning along empty streets drunkenly pondered aloud the breaking news, echoing faint but distinct in the marital bedroom? It was therefore not possible to say with certainty that the dream had been precognitive.

But he knew it had been.

A woman he'd never met — to whose image he had been exposed for nearly twenty years but to whom he nevertheless had paid little conscious attention — met her fierce consequence in downtown Paris; her limited intellect extinguished, her body rendered askew and crooked by impact.

An oceanic swell of sorrow washed over England. There was a spasm of grief. The morbid incense of flowers piled high, corrupting in the late summer heat. The beloved countenance glimpsed in gently shifting cloud formation.

During those strange days the country could hardly believe it might recover, but it did. It was gently chagrined, as at the memory of a small indiscretion. The shared sense of something numinous and ineffable receded. Britain realigned. It clicked firmly home into the mounting from which it had been shaken.

Andrew Taylor, however, did not. Try as he might, he could not get realigned. He did not click home.

The woman's destruction had shattered something in him like the windscreen of her Mercedes: she had ruptured a psychic membrane and the dream of her death was only the first. Into Andrew's head there surged a geyser of terrible images. Nightmares clamoured and shrieked behind his eyes. The nocturnal world became a feast: the constant eruption of orgasm. He pitched and warped on the mattress, turned in a knot of sweat and bedclothes.

His head swelled with madness, threatened to split like fruit. Kosovo refugees, gaunt and black-eyed on the Macedonian border. A burning man at the wheel of a bombarded truck, lips bubbling and peeling from teeth. He was sealed shut and bound in the dark. He crossed borders on bare and bleeding feet. He wept in helplessness and fear. Taste and smell of black, vegetal soil. He looked down on a pale body, not his own. Defiled and passing away. Blue flesh and ligotage.

He dreamed of rape and cancer. He dreamed of vandalism and mutilation, of soft bodies and impact. He dreamed of penetration. He dreamed of fierce contortion and violent impairment.

He dreamed of murder.

The dreams diminished him. He became hunched, red-eyed, timorous. The malice behind the twist of every smile bared itself to him. He saw knots of vein straining at neck and jaw. Bone superstructure on which living meat was hung. He heard screams of pain in laughter. He saw age slinking behind youth: death behind age. He saw compost and animal flesh. Worms rolled in loops and knots.

The pattern of job and friendships shifted around him, modulated into the choreography of an unknown dance. Schoolchildren sensed that something was amiss with their deputy head teacher who – if not loved – had at least gone essentially underided. But now Mr Taylor wandered the corridors befuddled, like an untimely spectre. They sensed that his purpose was lost. When they addressed him – even his favourites, the sixth-formers, the athletic and the academically talented – he didn't seem at first to recognize them. A spasm of panic would twitch across his features.

Even those admired sixth-formers were still children and

there was little pity among them for a man so evidently teetering on the headland. Jokes were told about him and names were invented. Some of the jokes and nicknames found their way to the staffroom. There was more pity there, not much, and guilty laughter.

Time passed. The laughter did not subside, but it took on a disconcerted undertone, an acknowledgement that something alien walked among them.

Three times a week for fourteen months, he saw a therapist.

For displaced anxiety and depression triggered by the death of his father, he was prescribed Prozac.

One night he freed himself from tangled bedsheets and hurried downstairs. On the back on an unopened gas bill he wrote:

> *have what? three seven zero of what?*
> *we are going to invert.*

Later, fully awake, he saw this message and did not understand it. Along with his family, friends, colleagues and pupils, he began to fear for his sanity.

In the morning, Rachel found him quite still in an armchair. He was pretending to read a thriller. She knew he had lifted the book from the carpet beside him the moment he heard her stir, in order that she would not find him staring blankly at nothing.

One night he said, 'I don't need a doctor, I need an exorcist,' and Rachel looked up from her novel. She laughed and hoped this was the first sign of the Prozac making things better.

But Andrew was not joking.

He saw many doctors, in private clinics paid for by insurance policies he had opposed taking out on political grounds. It was Dr Scobie, Presbyterian and arrogant, who first spoke to him of temporal lobe epilepsy.

It was a mysterious madness. Its locus, the source of his misery, was perhaps a tiny lesion on his brain. He imagined a pullulating knot over his ear, into which surged occult patterns and energies.

Andrew said: 'But what if it's real?'

'What if *what*'s real?'

'The dreams.'

'Real in what sense?'

'You know in what sense.'

Scobie clasped his smooth hands before him on the desk. He twinkled with medical irony.

'Don't you think it would be best to eliminate alternative possibilities before we discuss – alternative possibilities?'

'I'm not imagining it.'

'I'm not suggesting you are. The phenomenon is quite real. It's the *cause* of the phenomenon we're here to ascertain.'

'But what if the lesion is an effect? What if the dreams caused it?'

Minutely, Scobie shrugged his bony shoulders. Glint of sunlight on watchstrap.

'I'm afraid that's not a question I'm trained to answer.'

In the early hours of the morning of 17 December 1999, he dreamed about Kelly Brookmyre.

Kelly was fifteen. She lived in a small village in south Wales. She had disappeared. Nobody knew where Kelly might be.

Andrew woke unable to move. Rachel woke alongside him, bewildered by his mewling. On her knees, her nightdress hiked and one unprotected breast lined with the pattern of rucked bedlinen, she attempted to calm him while he mooed like a cow.

The house came awake. Lights. The children crying. Rachel ushered them back to bed. Sound of doors slamming. She dragged hands through sleep-knotted hair.

The days leading to Christmas were full of distance and awkwardness. Christmas Day: a silent lunch, lips taut and white, cutlery clattering too loud. *Top of the Pops*.

Andrew on the edge of the bed in his new shirt and trousers, sobbing into his palms.

It's a Wonderful Life.

The television news showed that ranks of police and local volunteers spent Christmas Day beating down grass in frosted fields, searching for Kelly Brookmyre's mortal remains.

Her parents, colourless, flanked by senior officers in laundered uniforms, petitioned for her safe return. Bulbs flashed. The shifting of shoulder-mounted cameras.

Few doubted that Kelly was dead.

Except Andrew.

At 2.49 on the morning of 28 December 1999, he awoke and screamed, *Oh Jesus Christ, I'm on fire*.

He was not on fire.

Kelly Brookmyre was an above-average pupil. She was attractive and vivacious and because of this some did not love her.

One female classmate especially had taken against Kelly. This classmate resolved to exact revenge for whatever wrong had been done to her. We can speculate upon exactly the nature of this impropriety (and chances are, we wouldn't be far from the truth), but the particulars need not be recorded.

Somehow (and again, it's perhaps better that we don't seek to understand quite how), this aggrieved girl procured the assistance of her family in pursuit of her teenage revenge. She was assisted by two males, one seventeen, the other nineteen: her brothers. A 51-year-old woman provided further assistance. Her mother.

Either these four or an unknown combination of two or three of them successfully contrived to kidnap Kelly. She was taken against her will to their grey, terraced house where they burned the tips of her fingers on the ring of an electric cooker. They cut her hair with scissors, then shaved it with a Bic razor. They stripped her nude and carved the word *slag* on her belly with the tip of a knitting needle. Foreign objects were inserted into her vagina. A television remote control. A golf ball. The handle of a bread knife.

Kelly was fastened to a single bed with parcel tape and injected with amphetamines. She was blindfolded and the headphones of a Sony Walkman were taped to her ears.

On the morning of Christmas Day, the brothers joined in the search for Kelly. They enjoyed the sense of community spirit her disappearance had engendered in the small town. It felt Christmassy. Were one to examine the relevant video-tape, they can quite easily be identified over the shoulder of a grim police spokesman, beating aside grass frozen white like icing sugar.

At approximately 2.40 on the morning of 28 December, they transferred Kelly to the boot of the family car. They drove her to what the press concurred was 'a nearby beauty spot', where they tipped her into a little-used picnic area that borders one of the main roads leading to town. They poured petrol over her and one of them set her alight.

It did not emerge in court which of them had done so.

Kelly was alive when she was found. She lived for twenty-one hours.

IV

Three months later, in March 2000, Andrew closed the door on his house and double-locked it. He caught a taxi to Temple Meads and a train to the south coast. At the coast, he caught another train to a small coastal town, where he wandered about until he found a quiet pub that took his fancy. Inside, he propped himself at the bar. He drank three pints of Guinness. The pub was quiet and the landlord engaged him in pleasant, inconsequential chat for much of his stay.

He left the pub and took a walk along a coastal path, pausing first to post his suicide note.

My Dearest Rachel. By the time you read this.

It was very dark. There were no stars. The breeze was warm and smelled of nocturnal pollen, of sand and salt-wet pebbles and sea.

He removed his shoes and socks and walked down to the pebbled beach, across the threshold of black seaweed at the edge of the sea, bordered by a luminous tier of foam. It began to rain great warm gobbets. He squatted, heel to haunch, and unclasped the suitcase. He removed a change of clothes and a flattened Adidas sportsbag, into which he transferred £47,000 in cash.

He undressed. Naked in the rain and pale in the starless darkness, he felt pagan and unfamiliar. The pebbles were cold and bruised his tender English soles.

He dressed in the clothes he'd bought for cash that morning. Heavy-weave cotton trousers, khaki, with deep pockets; a warm, hooded sweater. A pair of Adidas trainers.

He took a moment to imagine the police photograph that would be taken: a brown leather and brass suitcase alone on a grey pebble beach, set against a looming grey sky. The thought was dense with the future of those he loved.

By the time he reached the bus stop it was raining heavily. He got soaked through. He waited, hood pulled all but use-lessly over his bowed, dripping head, until an asthmatic single-decker shuddered to a halt alongside the country road.

He rode to the next town, where he registered in a bed-and-breakfast hotel under his new name, Jack Shepherd. He had practised the signature many hundreds of times.

That night he dreamed of his sons and he dreamed of his daughter and he dreamed of his wife. He dreamed of his house. He sat gently on the edge of their beds, while they slept and did not know he had returned. He blew the fringe from their brows and smiled tenderly with love for them.

2

The day William Holloway knocked on her door again, Rachel was alone. Her children were at her mother's, and the house felt far too big and too quiet for one person.

From the shadowed, stone-cool hallway she opened the door to him. He stood there, framed. Forty-three years old. Slender, narrow-shouldered and five feet, eight inches in his socks. Celtic-pale, freckled, gaunt. Small, uneven teeth but fine features; an excellent wide forehead. Strawberry-blond hair. Strands of it lit by sunshine. He was tolerably well dressed, in a black suit, three-button, off the peg. It was clean but rumpled at the back, as if he'd taken a nap in the car. His tie was loose at the throat. He had a prominent Adam's apple, around which nestled patches of raw red shaving rash that looked aggravated by the heat.

The sight of him made Rachel anxious. He'd first questioned

her two weeks before. She'd thought him distant and officious, less interested in Andrew than the money he'd stolen.

But now he inclined his head, a discrete footman's nod. He was hesitant and apologetic.

She wondered if he'd come to tell her they'd found Andrew's body.

He ducked his head unnecessarily as he entered the hallway, an action that seemed to acknowledge her grief. She led him to the sitting room. It ran the length of the house, west to east. At the far end, the east, stood a long wooden dining table. In the centre was placed a blue-and-white ceramic fruit bowl: blackening bananas and drying oranges. The coral skeleton of recently eaten grapes. French windows overlooked the seventy-foot garden, gently inclined, bordered at the far end by apple trees. From the branch of one of these hung a hazardous looking swing.

Facing west, under the bay windows, were arranged two sofas, a television, and a stereo. Separates. Mission, Boss, Marantz. Good enough: not ostentatious. Andrew's.

Holloway inventoried the ranks of CDs, stacked in Ikea towers, in piles on the bookcase, on top of the video recorder. The collection was impressively haphazard. A jewel case lay open on the stripped wooden floor. *What's Going On*. Gaye's face obscured by a red Nice Price sticker.

The room was scented virtuously. It was fragrant with happy family and English summer. Except, of course, Andrew Winston Taylor was presumed to have extinguished himself near Abbotsbury, on the south coast, three months ago.

Andrew was barely absent from the house. There was no want of his imprint. As he sat, Holloway's glance took in the long sitting room: family photographs on bookshelves, on the black leaded fireplace. Vases with flowers, lilies, beginning to dry and wilt. Muslin curtains. No children's noise. The house felt at worst temporarily vacated. It was as if Andrew Winston Taylor, a hefty, robust, pacific man, was merely late bringing the children home from a trip to the zoo.

Holloway perched on the edge of the sofa and leaned forward, feet planted square. Elbows on knees, chin on knitted palms.

Rachel returned from the kitchen carrying a tray on which balanced two long glasses of iced water, a slice of lime in each. Holloway took the glass, drank eagerly. She watched the violent bobbing of his Adam's apple.

He set the empty glass in a ceramic coaster placed near his ankle. Sucked air through cold-tenderized teeth.

Rachel sat facing him, curled on an armchair. She wore faded 501s, a white blouse. Black loafers on bare feet.

'I'm sorry to bother you again,' he said. 'I'm just mopping up. If you see what I mean.'

He blotted his brow with the edge of a cotton handkerchief.

Rachel smiled readily enough and dismissed his apology. Holloway wouldn't have guessed her age with any accuracy. He knew she belonged to a gymnasium. Drove a black Volkswagen Polo. She had about her a considered poise.

Twenty-odd years of quiet, lovable Andrew, bemused by the mystery of his contentment.

He wondered what had driven him to walk into the sea.

He'd read the diary Rachel discovered stuffed beneath the seat of an armchair in the extension. It was a school jotter that Andrew had crammed with obsessive handwriting. Reading this diary, it was not necessary to be a policeman or a psychiatrist or a wife to know that Andrew Winston Taylor had descended into insanity, the nature of which it had been an act of quiet heroism to keep from his family.

Andrew underwent a nervous breakdown (an inaccurate term, essentially meaningless. One Holloway nevertheless understood), or had suffered late-onset temporal lobe epilepsy, or a psychotic episode, after or during which he walked into the sea and took the cold, polluted ocean deep into his lungs. And now he was dead and eyeless, face down and ragged with nibbling. Possibly the tides would wash him up somewhere or other, and some dog out for an early morning walk would stumble across a jellified mass shrouded in kelp.

Holloway had encountered such things before, and worse. But he didn't think he would encounter it this time. He could not imagine why Andrew Taylor should take those 38,000 fraudulently acquired pounds into the great darkness with him.

Perhaps it was merely testament to his peculiar madness, to his unique system of portents and symbols. Perhaps the money meant something. But Holloway didn't believe that either.

Ten thousand people went missing in Britain every year. Some were dead. Most were not. Most could be found, if there was a good enough reason to look.

Rachel leaned towards him, passed a sheaf of photographs.

He thanked her, shuffled through the prints. He looked at Andrew Winston Taylor and wondered at the madness that had driven him to walk from this house, these children, this wife.

'Kelly Brookmyre,' said Rachel.

Kelly's name had passed her lips innumerable times. Its use

was tired with past exasperation. 'In Wales. The Christmas just gone.'

'I remember,' he said, and he did. He had heard this from Rachel, and he had read it in Andrew's diary and he had heard it from Llewellyn, who ran a pub in Cardiff now and was privvy to the stuff that didn't make the papers. Coppers' talk.

Rachel ran a hand through her hair. The glint of June light on wedding ring. Tucked a lock behind her ear.

'It just seemed to push him over the edge,' she said. 'I don't know why, particularly.'

'But you mentioned that he seemed to improve after the Brookmyre murder.'

'He seemed to,' she said. 'But he didn't. Not really.'

'But you had no idea that . . .'

'That he would catch a train to the seaside and drown himself?'

'No.' He looked down at the pad. Scratched out a spiral with blue nib. 'Of course not. I'm sorry. But he seemed in control? He wasn't short-tempered? Or violent?'

'He never even raised his voice,' she said. 'To me or the children. Not once.'

She twirled a stray lock of hair about her index finger. She'd told him all this before. This time he seemed to accept that she was telling the truth.

Each of them seemed dislocated from the facts. She wondered why he was here. Doing his job, she supposed, even though it no longer seemed to interest him.

Holloway glanced at his notes. Hanging men etched in margins. Clockwise spirals. A stick figure with a zigzag mouth lay in a hospital bed.

'But he knew he had problems? He was still in treatment?'

'You know that. You've probably met his doctor.' (He did, and he had.) 'He saw a psychologist for about a year, give or take. God knows it was a struggle to make him go in the first place. He didn't think it would do any good.'

'And?'

She shrugged, once.

'They were talking about temporal lobe epilepsy,' she said. 'But by then they were at a loss, pretty much. It's quite rare, and Andrew wasn't even a classic case.' She sighed. 'It's just neurology,' she said, with a tired emphasis. 'A functional thing. Bad wiring.'

She tapped the side of her head twice. Cuck-oo.

He smiled, tapped his front teeth with the end of a biro.

'I heard once,' he said, 'from a doctor – my wife's friend was a doctor – that if they sever certain nerves, and join them to certain other nerves, you taste vinegar as a loud noise in your ears. Synaesthesia. LSD can do it to you. Well, the good stuff can.'

She laughed, obligingly. She said: 'How long have you been married?'

He tugged at an earlobe. 'Well now. Nineteen years? Twenty? Twenty in July.'

'You get less for murder.'

'Ha. Yes.'

'I can't believe he's gone. Not really.'

Now the creature that had possessed her husband's body was no longer around, she found herself rediscovering Andrew, reassembling a sense of his nearness. Having him dead was like having him back.

It was better.

She encountered an occasional guilt at her want of anger at him, that she didn't feel worse. This feeling would sneak up behind her at odd times, wrap its arms around her breasts, nuzzle its face into her shoulders and rock her gently side to side. She would weep into her fist until it passed. Eventually, it always did.

Holloway pocketed his notes.

'That's enough for now,' he said. 'I'll be in touch. Meanwhile, there's nothing you can do. Take a holiday. Don't wait by the telephone. Take the kids to . . .' (not the seaside) '—Alton Towers. Thorpe Park.'

She laughed because he seemed well meaning. Then she closed her eyes, lifted her chin, nodded.

Holloway was bored by the meagreness of his thoughts. He stood, straightened his jacket a little.

'I can't say I know Andrew,' he said. 'I never met him. But I don't think he meant all this. He wouldn't hurt you like this. Not if he was in control.'

'No,' she said. ' Well. One would hope not.'

She looked up at him from beneath her brow.

He smiled, snaggle-toothed on one side. He had long canines, one of which was chipped by a wedding ring worn round a finger curled into a fist thrown with malice smack into his mouth, ten years before. Longer. The jagged end sometimes caught his lower lip and he looked wasted and undomesticated. This with a delicate, boyish jaw and his freckled skin, still troubled by shaving.

He was scented with something she recognized: Wrights Coal Tar Soap. When she was about to leave for Bristol

University, her father had described its smell as the last pious thing in England. He still made the same joke every Christmas.

Holloway shut the door behind him and stood for a long second in the front garden, squinting. He patted his pockets, checking the whereabouts of wallet and keys.

He wondered what Rachel Taylor thought of his visit. What use in looking again at photographs of a dead man?

Drowned men did not return from the sea.

He patted his breast pocket, removed his sunglasses, slipped them on. Checked his watch. He thought about the £38,000. He had a sense of something loosening in his chest. It was almost relief. In the fatiguing heat of the late afternoon, he began to walk.

He walked towards Whiteladies Road, then turned left and downhill for a few minutes, in the direction of the city centre. He quickly became overheated. Not far from the children's hospital, he turned on to another quiet, tree-lined road. He followed the street as it hooked back uphill, and stopped at a once-grand, detached Victorian house that stood behind a low wall with black metal gates. He closed the gate behind him. He walked to the tall, blue door and rang the bell.

He waited half a minute before a short West Indian woman of prodigious girth answered the door. She was middle-aged and wore a white uniform.

Her name was Hetty and it had occurred to Holloway more than once that this woman was probably the best friend he had left in the world.

'Hello love,' she said, Caribbean West Country.

'Hello sweetheart,' he said. 'How you keeping?'

'Oh,' she said. 'Not so bad.'

Holloway leaned forward to kiss her cheek.

'How are those legs?'

'Oh. Mustn't complain.'

Still, she liked to be asked. She smiled, good and broad. A proper smile. He saw so few.

'And the Tiller girl in there?' He nodded over Hetty's shoulder.

'Not so bad,' she said. 'Not so bad.'

Hetty turned and led him into the coolness of the home's hallway.

Inside, it was cool. The original floor, tiled, decorative, cracking here and there at the edge. A reception desk. NHS posters, bleached pale and brittle with age. Purple shadow and the faint smell of institution, a sweet undercurrent.

He followed Hetty to the television room. Three of the four walls were lined with chairs and wheelchairs. This is where those residents who were able spent their days. Those who sat before the large, double bay windows had turned their backs to summer outside.

He felt the sweat cool on him.

He saw Grace in the far corner. She was etiolated and delicate, graceful in indignity, white-haired and swan-necked, heavily liver-spotted. She sat primly in a wheelchair, a tartan blanket across her lap. She wore a knitted white cardigan and sheepskin slippers. Sometimes her hands made feeble motions, as if knitting.

As ever, she seemed galvanized by his approach. Something pale ignited in her eyes. She reached out a palsied hand and greeted him, beckoned him to sit by patting her lap twice.

Pulling up a chair and excusing himself to the old man on her left, he enjoyed or endured another moment in which it occurred to him that today, for a moment or two, she might know who he was.

Gentle, he touched the back of her hand with two fingers, patted it. He could roll her cool skin between his fingers like kid leather. He was aware of her faint palsy.

'Hello, sweetness,' he said. 'How's my glamour girl?'

She smiled. Her eyes widened in delight.

'Are you Mary's lad?'

'I'm your Lizzie's boy,' he corrected her again. 'Billy.'

She looked him up and down. '*Our* little Billy? Apple cake Billy?'

He patted his belly, rubbed it, smiled.

'That's right,' he said.

'You're a little devil with that apple cake,' she said, and her face softened.

They sat alongside one another, watching *Countdown*. Every now and again she spoke an irrelevancy and he hummed his agreement and patted her hand. At 5 p.m., Hetty brought him tea and biscuits on a plate. He invited her to join him, as ever, and for ten minutes they chatted, each with one eye on *Ricki Lake: Shape up or Ship Out!*

At 5.30, he kissed his aunt goodbye, told Hetty he'd see her soon and left the home. He hurried towards the city centre.

The Watershed was an arts centre. Its bar and restaurant, on the first floor, overlooked Bristol's redeveloped docks. Holloway bounded up the stairs, past Spanish movie posters.

Inside the bar were eleven or twelve people: a disproportionate number of goatee beards and unflattering, narrow spectacles.

Kate waited for him at a table. Chrome and glass.

For three years, Kate had lived with a man called Adrian in a Clifton mansion flat that overlooked the suspension bridge. Adrian had not reported Holloway or pressed charges for assaulting him the previous New Year's Eve.

'Kate,' he said. 'Sorry.' He was breathless.

She had ordered drinks. A bottle of Chablis, a large bottle of mineral water. A half-drunk glass of each on the table before her. He sat, poured a tumbler of water, drained it. Then poured a glass of wine. Drained half of it. Looked up.

'Oops,' he said, and set the glass on the table.

She raised an eyebrow.

'So,' she said. 'Why the delay? Armed siege?'

He wiped his mouth with the back of a hand. Taste of salt.

'Ha. No. No: I popped in on Grace. I hadn't been for a while. Sorry.'

Like his great-aunt's, his wife's face softened.

She said: 'It doesn't matter. She doesn't remember, anyway.'

He shrugged.

'Oh, the women in your life,' she said.

He smiled, trying to be good-natured.

'Have you been waiting long?'

'Five minutes? I knew you'd be late.'

Seeing her smile for knowing him well made his stomach tumble. The previous weekend he'd bought a new suit and tie from Next. He'd worn it for the first time this morning. He hoped he looked OK.

Kate was tanned. She wore a summer dress and flat, strappy sandals. Her hair was dark, cut short: a blunt fringe, feathered across her ears. To him she looked very beautiful.

He remembered similar summer days, similar bars. Since the final dissolution of their marriage, she had acquired a certain serenity, a contentment the profundity of which hurt him.

'So,' she said. 'How are you keeping?'

He leaned his forearms on the table, knitted his fingers.

'So-so. You know. Broken heart. Not sleeping.'

She sipped chilled wine.

'No, really.'

'*Really* really?'

'Really really really.'

He smiled. Deep, fond lines at the corners of his eyes, radiating. 'I'm not sleeping too badly. Considering. Still seeing the hippie counsellor.'

'You're still *going*?'

It was nice to surprise rather than disappoint her.

'Still going. Once a week. Twice, if I experience an urge to take a brick to someone's head.'

'That's really *good*.'

'That's really *embarrassing*.'

She laughed, and he laughed and for two or three seconds they were husband and wife.

He wiped the corner of an eye with a knuckle.

'You'll tell him that?'

That Holloway see a counsellor was Adrian's condition for not pressing charges and losing Holloway his job.

Adrian was a barrister.

She shook her head.

'He still has nightmares. He wakes up at night. He thinks you're in the flat.'

He laughed, and his snaggle tooth caught briefly on his lower lip.

'Come *on*. He's six feet fucking two inches tall and he bench-presses Volkswagens.'

She smiled.

You're smiling because I was able to hurt him, he thought.

'You know what it's like.' The smile fell and weather passed behind her eyes. 'Imagine how he'd feel. Me here, drinking with you.'

A pleasant, sinuous twist of vitriol inside him.

'He doesn't know you're here?'

'He doesn't want me anywhere *near* you. He thinks you're deranged.'

The pleasure modulated in less than a second to something like agony.

'For Christ's sake.'

He read her face, closed his eyes.

'Sorry. Forget the Wurzel.'

'He's not a Wurzel. He's from Bath. He went to Cambridge.'

With that, he laughed. Later he would sob into his knees, as he did every time he saw or spoke to or sometimes thought about her.

She said: 'I don't know why I bother,' and slapped the back of his hand, gently enough. 'You arsehole.'

He drained the wine, poured a second. He lifted the glass and examined the light through it. 'Beautiful,' he said.

'See?' she said. 'You're learning to enjoy it.'

'Hm,' he said. 'I'm thinking of taking a class. In the evenings.'

She said: 'How are you doing? In yourself?'

I am coming apart at the seams.

'Not so bad.'

'Work?'

He shrugged.

'What can I say?'

They had met to discuss the twenty-first birthday of their daughter. Caroline Holloway was in the second year of a media studies degree at Leeds Metropolitan University. She was at an age, he knew, by which she she'd have taken many legally proscribed drugs: cannabis certainly, probably ecstasy or a derivative. Amphetamines, some cheap cocaine, maybe ketamine. Possibly LSD. Not heroin.

She was doing well. She'd met a boy.

He pinched his nostrils. Took a long breath. 'She didn't tell me.'

Kate shrugged. 'She probably didn't think to. It's probably nothing.'

'It's probably nothing, nothing. She doesn't want the third degree about the long-haired lover from fucking Liverpool.'

At the corner of his wife's mouth and eyes were lines that were new to him, who mentally had mapped, and physically had kissed every line, every crease and fold of her body.

He filled her glass. She had to leave in half an hour. Meeting Adrian. They were going on to the theatre.

That evening, Jack Shepherd arrived in north London.

For three months, he'd worked his way along the south coast of England. He stopped in Brighton for three days.

That week there were thunderstorms across Britain. Shepherd sat on the sea wall between the two piers, watching the rain drive into the sea. While traffic hissed behind him, he planned his future.

He walked to the station, head bowed, and caught the next train to London Victoria. He was still damp when he arrived. The Adidas bag slung over his shoulder, he walked along the dirty, wet station concourse, past the diminutive Our Price and large W.H. Smith, to the tube station.

On the Victoria line northbound, he chose Finsbury Park at random and stepped off into the London night. Finsbury Park did not smell like Bristol. It smelled rich with warm rain and exhaust fumes and half-rotten fruit.

Within the first two or three minutes, he believed himself to have seen at least one representative of each ethnic group and major religion represented in Britain. This made him smile as at a grand adventure.

He passed a Kwik Save, no less than three Sunrise Food Stops, the Happening Bagel Bakery, a dilapidated post office, a KFC Express, a Shell garage. It seemed perfect. On Seven Sisters Road, alongside a tower block called Park House, he found a small bed-and-breakfast hotel.

He stopped here and booked himself in. Paid cash. One week in advance.

Bone tired, he fell asleep, fully clothed and steaming gently, on the candlewick bedspread.

He awoke, refreshed, at 8 a.m. and did not remember that he had dreamed.

He set about finding a place to live.

3

Apparently, Rex Dryden wasn't Rex Dryden's real name, but that didn't much bother anybody, least of all Rex Dryden himself. Still less did it vex those five, seven or nine hundred individuals (exactly how many varies according to which newspaper you read) who joined him in the Temple of Light, *Illuminus, in Excelsis.*

'All good churches need at least two names,' said Rex Dryden.

Nor was the question uppermost in the mind of the one, three or five hundred (again, reports vary) who, beguiled by his recognition of their spiritual awareness, took into their mouths and swallowed the soft drink laced with lethal poison he supplied them with shortly before Christmas 1999 in order to speed them into the emancipation of bodily death.

Rex Dryden was built like a bouncer; not tall, all shoulder

and chest and forearm. His legs had bowed beneath the prodigious heft of torso. Yet his movements had about them an unhurried grace whose quality belied the brute fact of his construction. His head was meatily spherical as a watermelon: balding, shaved to stubble. His beard was coarse and close-cropped, silver and black. It extended towards his eyes and into the vigorous snarl of grey hair that sprouted within the fecund hollow between his clavicles.

He wore Savile Row suits and rimless spectacles which lent him the air of a dubious small businessman grown respectable; the kind of man, rude-born, who finds himself, silvermane and bald, clasping spatulate finger and thumb about bone-china handle, taking tea with the Queen.

In life, as on his many television appearances, Rex Dryden displayed both a refined intelligence and a phlegmy, lascivious, east London cackle. He would throw his neckless head far back on expansive shoulders, bark once, broadly and appreciatively. *Hah!* Then he would lower his head and delicately knuckle the moist corner of one eye, and his outsized body would convulse spasmodically for seconds or minutes. His humour was vast. Rex Dryden found almost everything funny. Even himself. Even the end of the world.

When he was done laughing, he might lean towards you and fix you with his eyes, which were quite beautiful, luminous blue and artful, and he might tell you that the world was going to end, and now the laughter in Rex Dryden's eyes was for you, and the guileless simplicity of your disbelief: there would be savagery and disorder, he might tell you, and discord and slaughter and suffering and death, and global destruction and dismay – and for an unguarded, mesmerized moment you might find yourself not quite believing, but trusting in the magnitude of his conviction. Just for a moment. And you might find yourself, like many before you, unable to rid yourself of the thought of him.

Many of those who determined to leave their lives behind and join Rex Dryden (one did not follow him) in illumination were not the kind of people who had imagined they might be capable of such feats. But follow him they did, in their dozens and hundreds. (Quite how many hundreds, of course, is open to speculation. If records were kept, none were discovered.)

Dryden did not ask for their money (although the money came from somewhere). He did not demand that his acolytes abstain from sex, either within or without marriage, nor that they marry strangers in mass ceremonies. Nor was he a predatory sexual libertine who availed himself of the conjugal expedience of his converts. All he demanded, at first, was that they listen to him and seek to understand. He told them that life was wonderful.

He talked of Shiva and Kali; of Orpheus, Prometheus; of Christ and the Buddha and Mohammed; of Knights Templar and Rosicrucians; of Heisenberg and Bohr and Leonardo; of Jack Kennedy and Neil Armstrong; of the Priory de Sion and the Freemasons; of the Apocryphal Gospels and the Revelations of Fatima; of Nicaea and Ephesus; of anti-popes; of pyramids; of Akhenaten and Moses; of the Lost Treasure of the First Temple; the cabbala; of Atlantis; the earth and the sky and a land beyond but within; of Jimmy Stewart and Frank Capra and Bedford Falls; he would talk about history, and Mystery, and what great men had always known: there are those who are greater, and, come the end, the illuminated shall join them.

He did not claim to be a great man; he was a follower of great men: he was Saul of Tarsus, he was John the Baptist, he was Dr Watson. He was Clarence the wingless angel. He was Sweeney among the Nightingales. Broadbacked, hirsute and human, all too human.

He was by no means the first to bring the world this news.

'But I am the last,' he said.

4

I

Jack Shepherd, who once had been Andrew Winston Taylor, was resident in the bed-and-breakfast hotel for two weeks that coincided with the beginning of an uncommonly hot summer.

On his second day in London, an Armenian barber shaved his head. He kept the black, grey-tangled beard he'd been growing for several weeks. From a dusty local optician, where a small bell rang when he opened the door, Shepherd bought a pair of oval, wire-framed spectacles. They balanced like pince-nez on his big face. He looked like a pioneer; a proud, tall man posing in golden-brown daguerreotype. Something was still not right, but it wasn't the hair or the beard, which had at last stopped itching, or the spectacles.

It was the address.

After ten days, he noticed a second load of Japanese tourists being herded on to a Gatwick-bound coach. He suspected they'd been misled about the location and calibre of the hotel.

He realized he was becoming a fixture. Short- and long-term hotel residence was a relative concept.

He remembered seeing a documentary or reading an article featuring a man who (for what reason he could not recall) was resident for a decade or more in the airside departure lounge of Charles de Gaulle airport. The man was a stowaway of some kind, a political prisoner or refugee who didn't qualify for entry into France but who couldn't be returned to his country of origin. So he remained trapped in the interzone of the departure lounge; his belongings on a luggage trolley, his meals provided by sympathetic airport staff and airline crew.

Escaping one life was not enough.

While resident in the hotel, Shepherd avoided social intercourse as far as he was able. He didn't want to speak to anybody. He feared that conversation might press him into shape like a thumb printing its whorls into a ball of clay.

He spent his days repetitiously: breakfast in the Moonshine café on Blackstock Road (two scrambled eggs, beans, sausages, grilled tomatoes, two fried slice and three mugs of bracingly strong tea), while reading the classified advertisements in the local papers and *Loot*. He propped the papers awkwardly against tomato-red ketchup bottles with red coagulate spouts as he shovelled food into his craw. Then he would pick a direction and wander. He noted launderettes, pubs, cafeterias, DIY stores, betting shops, pizza shops, North African patisseries. He walked streets he had no wish to walk again, although he was not assaulted, and streets that reminded him of the life

he'd left, which he also never wished to walk again, for an altogether different reason. He walked streets where loud music
pumping through upper-storey windows inexplicably filled him
with profound contentment. He walked council estates whose
architecture made him dejected and whose tenants he feared.
He stumbled upon peaceful, tree-lined roads whose quiet, suburban peculiarity, adjacent to such deprivation, seemed
grotesque. He imagined that such proximities could prevail only
in London. Sprawling and unplanned. Impartially ravenous.

Wandering, he stopped and read advertisements in
newsagent windows, looking for a room to rent. He needed a
landlord willing to disregard his want of references. This
proved more difficult than he'd anticipated. He was angry with
himself. He could at least have rented a Bristol bedsit for three,
four or six months prior to his departure, leaving it exactly as
he'd found it (perhaps even have had it professionally cleaned!),
and thus picked up a good referee. But it had never occurred to
him to do so and the books from the classified pages of the
Fortean Times had not so advised him.

He didn't have a devious or even a calculating mind, and he
required guidance in such matters.

He'd assumed that landlords, being landlords, would happily
compromise references for rent in advance, cash in hand, plus a
cash deposit against damage. Somewhat surprisingly, this seemed
to have an effect quite contrary to that intended: over the telephone, the proposal made him sound forlorn and suspicious.
Soon he came to hate London landlords, distended parasites on
the hunched, scabrous back of their bountiful mother.

The hotel didn't qualify as a previous address. His previous address didn't count as a previous address, since it belonged to the person he'd previously been. His entire existence lacked corroboration. He felt spectral and temporary.

On the Saturday at the end of his third week, he jotted down the number listed on a room-to-let card posted in a newsagent window on Holloway Road, found a telephone kiosk and dialled the number. After four rings, a woman lifted the receiver. The voice was clipped and very English. She seemed to be addressing someone else. Shepherd heard: '—fucking *message*, you arsehole.' Then, harassed: 'Hello.'

'Hello,' he said. 'I'm calling about the room. Is this an inconvenient time?'

'No,' she said, 'not at all.'

This did not sound altogether true and a short silence followed. He said: 'Is it still free?'

'Yes. Two rooms. Doubles. Listen, there's no point us talking about this over the phone. Would you like to come round for a cup of tea?'

It had just passed 11 a.m. They made an appointment for 12.45. Shepherd stopped off at Woolworth's and bought a digital watch. He didn't want to be late.

After consulting the mini *A–Z*, he decided there was enough time to walk to the address he'd been given, stopping off on the way for a cold drink. In shirtsleeves and sunglasses, a black nylon briefcase from Next slung over his shoulder, he defied the rabble and the heat and exhaust fumes that pooled like industrial soup in the windless heat. He turned from Holloway Road on to Seven Sisters Road and headed into the shimmering distortion.

On the way, he stopped off for a cold drink, but still arrived ten minutes early. He killed time by leaning on a lamp-post and pretending to consult the *A–Z*. The house was a dilapidated Victorian structure; three story and an attic conversion, set on the corner with Stroud Green Road, within sight of a Tesco *Metro*. Behind a low wall, the concrete front garden was cracked and overgrown with etiolated weeds. Behind open windows, undrawn curtains hung inert in the heat.

At 12.45 according to his new watch, he collected himself and marched to the front door. He was hot and damp. Even minor exertion on such a day was fatiguing. Beneath the beard, his skin itched like prickly heat rash.

He rang the bell. Waiting, he adjusted his shirt tails.

The door opened. Behind it stood a woman. She was pale, perhaps in her early thirties. She wore a blunt bob, dyed black, with a severe fringe. It iridesced in the sunlight like a magpie. Her eyes were big and her mouth was small. She wore 501s, faded almost to white and holed at the knees; a black shirt, open at the throat, cuffs unbuttoned. She clutched the door at head height and set her weight on one hip. The shirtsleeve fell back. Her inner arm was blue-white, like fresh milk. Her feet were bare and summer-dirty. On each foot, the second toe was longest by a knuckle.

She came up to Shepherd's chest.

The hallway in which she stood was scented in ways he could not yet specify: the antique pungency of incense and cannabis. Petuli oil. Cigarettes. Some old cooking. The musk of cats.

She smiled, perhaps with some irony, and extended a hand. With her left hand, she shielded her eyes. Wedding band on the third finger.

'You must be Jack.'

At once, he recognized the woman on the phone. Her accent belonged to another era. He imagined her in a flapper dress and low-heeled pumps.

'I must be,' he said, and shook her hand.

She retreated half a step. People often did this, unconsciously calibrating his dimensions.

She said: 'God, you look really hot.'

She stepped aside to admit him. He followed her down a long hallway with worn floorboards. To his left, the hall opened on to a sitting room. Immediately to his right was a stairway with a peeling white banister and uncarpeted stairs. At the far end, the hallway opened on to the kitchen.

It was a layout he recognized.

Islamic rugs were laid upon the floorboards. Heavy with dust and worn threadbare, they curled dangerously skywards at the corners. Bulbs hung on bare cords. Various framed prints were hung on the walls: a Dalí that Shepherd recognized; a melancholy Rembrandt self-portrait; Elvis Presley as the risen Christ; Leonardo's androgynous Baptist with his *Giaconda* smile and obscurely eerie raised finger; Hitler as Grail Knight. Three separate prints depicting Arcadian, pastoral shepherds leaning over and variously gesturing towards a rock set heavy in the earth.

She followed his gaze and arched a slow eyebrow.

He smiled and tried to indicate that he understood although he did not.

Instead, he told her it was a nice place.

At the foot of the stairs she explained that two rooms were available to let: one on the second floor, on the half-landing, next to the bathroom, at £320 a month. Bills included, except telephone. There was also an attic room. More expensive, but with a bit of a view. £440 a month, payable on the first. You could see Canary Wharf from it. The bomb that exploded there on 9 February 1996 had rattled their windows.

He liked the sound of the attic. Apex of the triangle. Point of the pyramid. He was becoming increasingly sensitized to incidental symbolism.

She said he might want to glance at it before he decided. He had already decided, but didn't say so.

Would he like a cup of tea first?

'It'll cool you down,' she said.

He followed her to the kitchen. It was long, high-ceilinged and church-cool. Mauve shadows and cobwebs in high corners. Compared at least to Shepherd's experience of domestic kitchens, it was seriously disordered. There was a white stoneware sink filled with battered pots and pans, cutlery and mismatched, chipped mugs. A half-glazed wooden door with a cat-flap and near it a litter tray set on a brittle yellow newspaper. There were two litter-dried turds in one corner. The floor tiles were cracked, with a motif faded past legibility: original Victorian, protected for many years by linoleum and vinyl. The grouting was crumbling and one or two see-sawed under his weight. There was a geriatric gas cooker with eye-level grill.

At the scarred oak table sat a gaunt, skinny man with unkempt hair. He wore a ragged pair of army-surplus trousers, a ripped pair of skateboard shoes with no socks, a faded T-shirt. Two plaited leather bands hung about one knobby, thick-veined and hairy wrist. He looked like a once-boyish pop star who, through unusual circumstances, had spent ten years as a prisoner of the Viet Cong.

He was reading a back issue of the *New Statesman*. On the table before him was a blue pub ashtray full of crippled, extinguished rollups, a pack of Old Holborn, some Rizla cigarette papers, several lighters and a scattering of magazines: *New Scientist*. *Nature*. The *Fortean Times*. The *Herald Tribune*. *OK! Hello!* There was also an incongruously sleek Apple PowerBook laptop computer, closed down.

From a transistor radio set on the table, Shepherd heard the infinitely consoling intonation of *Just a Minute*. In another life, Andrew Winston Taylor was washing his car or driving to Sainsbury's, or Ikea. Briefly, he mourned himself: a wave of sadness, rising in the small of his back and breaking just behind his eyes.

The woman said: 'Lenny, this is Jack. He's here to see about a room.'

The man glanced up.

Shepherd had the impression they had already met.

Without getting up, the man smiled and offered his hand.

He said: 'How do you do?'

His voice was a surprising baritone, inflected cockney.

The woman said: 'I'm Eloise. This is Lenny.'

She went to the cooker, picked up the kettle, went to the sink and manoeuvred the washing-up such that she was able to direct the flow of water into its spout. Then she put the kettle on to boil. She explained that she owned the house, but didn't say how she'd come to own it: Shepherd understood that such property, even in a relatively insalubrious area of central London, would cost considerably more than the family home he'd left behind in Bristol.

Rather than convert the house into flats, she and Lenny had decided to let out two rooms to lodgers. Shepherd suspected this had something to do with the avoidance of tax. He approved, although Andrew Taylor would not have.

The attic room was approached via some tremendously rickety stairs rendered life-threatening by darkened, curling carpets that dated to the late 1960s.

Three stairs behind Lenny, Shepherd observed the gnarls of his spine, an ambulatory diagram beneath the washed-out fabric of his T-shirt.

Lenny ducked through the doorway, more through impulse than necessity. Shepherd bent almost double. Inside, he straightened. It smelled, mysteriously, exactly as an attic room should. Shepherd took this as an omen. The centre of the room was high-ceilinged, descending into the eaves, much of which had been converted into crawl-space storage.

Shepherd looked through the window. On the horizon he could see Canary Wharf tower, glittering silver through a white haze of pollution like the distant object of a knightly quest.

He offered six months' rent in advance, cash, with an additional month's deposit. He was not invited to sign a tenancy agreement. He checked out of the hotel the same day, transporting what few belongings he had accumulated in two cardboard boxes that fitted easily into a black cab.

Lenny helped him upstairs with one of the boxes, gave him

a set of keys. Then he went back to his reading, leaving Shepherd alone to unpack and settle in.

Shepherd set a box on the bed and wrestled open a sash window. It squeaked. He looked out. Breathed in.

Held.

Breathed out.

II

He spent a few weeks consolidating his new identity, then making it permanent and semi-official. The brochures from the classified advertisements in the *Fortean Times* had advised him to start at the bottom and work up, and this is exactly what he did.

He had not chosen the name Jack Oliver Shepherd at random. Andrew Winston Taylor had been surprised to read in one pamphlet that a legerdemain he'd learned of many years before (in *The Day of the Jackal*) was still available to him.

Long before he vanished, he made a single research trip to the Bristol Central Library, off College Green. A quick scroll through microfiche allowed him to find a child with the same approximate birth date as his own, who had died before its first birthday. There followed a trip to Bristol Register Office, where – because it was merely lawful proof that a birth has taken place, not that it was his own – he was legally able to obtain a copy of the baby Shepherd's birth certificate. In the name of caution he claimed genealogical research, and paid the required fee in cash.

Thus, many months later, Shepherd now had both a

permanent residence and a birth certificate. With this he applied for a provisional driver's licence. He then arranged to take an intensive course of driving lessons over ten days at a local driving school.

He passed the second time (too many ingrained bad habits). Although Shepherd waited a long time before asking him, Lenny proved happy to endorse his driving licence fraudulently, effortlessly faking the signatures of his GP and Eloise's father. One name he signed in ballpoint, the other with a Mont Blanc ink pen he retrieved from his office.

While he awaited dispatch of the licence, Shepherd also applied for membership to as many institutions as he was able: the local library, the video shop, the sports club. He arranged it so that each of these had a reason to write to him.

Soon, with a driver's licence, a birth certificate and other sundry proofs of identity, he was able to open a bank account in his new name. He did so with a deposit of £1,000 in cash.

Ten working days later a cash-point card and chequebook arrived in the post.

For several weeks, he was out of the house most of the day. But he spent the evenings with Lenny and Eloise.

Often they shared takeaways and watched a video. Sometimes they played Trivial Pursuit around the kitchen table. Usually, Shepherd and Eloise shared a bottle of wine, taking it in turns to pay. Now and again, she rolled a joint. Lenny drank draught Guinness from a can with a widget.

Eloise's parents were old money, but they disapproved of her lifestyle (by which he assumed they meant Lenny) and she had little contact with them. She was employed by Hackney council as a music therapist, working with disabled children and adults with learning difficulties. She also composed music, and belonged to various art collectives, of whose shifting, interconnected memberships and political infighting Shepherd could not keep track. But he enjoyed her exasperated gossip.

Other than Eloise, Lenny had no visible means of support. When Shepherd ventured to ask, he licked the gummed strip of a cigarette paper and claimed to buy and sell shares online.

In addition to being a financial genius, Lenny had at least one opinion about everything. He was immersed in a personal project, the precise nature of which was enigmatic, but which he pursued with alchemical, evangelical zeal. Everything was part of this exertion; every book he read (and he sometimes read two a day); every magazine; every print he hung in the hallway and contemplated through narrowed eyes. Everything he said, however mundane or gnomic, skirted an immense, unspoken significance. Lenny had discovered something, some deep structure, proof of which he sought to verify by linking into a coherent pattern clues whose very ubiquity (once one knew where to look) served to confirm his thesis: it was in Hollywood movies, in pop videos, in architecture. It was encoded in the flag of the European Union and the fall of the Berlin Wall; it was encrypted in advertisements carried by cereal packets and the movements of the international stock market. It underlay the structure of the language itself. Beethoven had encoded it in symphonies. It was in the structural correspondence of the DNA spiral to the shape of galaxies.

The single bedroom on the first floor was Lenny's office, to which nobody but Eloise was permitted entry. He spent hours in there, buying and selling stocks and shares online, and following diverse lines of inquiry, each of which (as far as Shepherd could ascertain) unlocked a dizzying infinity of further lines of inquiry.

Tired, Lenny rolled a cigarette and dragged his fingers through hair that stood up and out in every direction. He described the problem as fractal.

Lenny's theories interested Shepherd and they became friends. Shepherd learned that, in order to escape the indeterminate enigma that was the pursuit of fractal ontology (or fractal semiotics, depending on his mood), Lenny liked to walk. Together they began to map out their physical and psychological territory. Lenny had steeped himself in the lore of the East End. He was versed in an interlocking narrative of questionable histories: Nicholas Hawksmoor, Jack the Ripper.

Wrapped in several layers of ragged clothing, Lenny took Shepherd on a three-day pilgrimage. They walked the streets and arteries of the East End and the lines of energy between the Hawksmoor churches. Shepherd experienced the peculiar, pervasive aroma of Smithfields meat market: years of slaughter somehow insinuated into granite. On to the numinous glower of Christ Church. The streets Jack had walked.

This pilgrimage did not allow for a return to one's bed, or indeed any bed. They spent two strange nights huddled on the street with the homeless, two nights in which Shepherd saw and heard and experienced things he would rather have not, and was glad that Lenny carried a knife and a can of mace.

Returning home to a hot bath and clean clothes and daytime television, he felt himself changed.

*

Falls

In the early hours of 29 July 2000, the dreams located him.

He awoke sodden. Tangled in bedclothes.

Lenny ran up the rickety stairs two at a time. He charged into Shepherd's room like a milky-grey whippet in Y-fronts and unlaced Adidas.

'Fuck's *sake*,' he said. His deep voice cracked on a high note. 'Are you all right?'

Shepherd was rigidly upright on the bed.

'Something terrible has happened in America,' he said

Downstairs, Shepherd hunched in a towelling dressing gown while Lenny made him a cup of sugary tea.

A bulletin on Radio 4 broke the story.

In Atlanta, a man called Howard Newton had bludgeoned his family to death before walking into the offices of the North Atlantic Tech Investment Group, where recently he had blown a $400,000 insurance pay-off on bad investments.

Inside, he opened fire with a 9-mm semi-automatic pistol. He killed nine staff and badly wounded another twelve. Cornered, he sucked on his own pistol and blew off the top of his head.

The $400,000 insurance money had been a contested pay-out: life insurance due subsequent to the death of Newton's first wife, whom both the police and the insurance company strongly suspected Newton to have murdered, but which neither were ever able to prove.

Shepherd did not remember dreaming about Howard Newton. He had an afterimage of the dream that did not seem to fit. Two vast, shattered teeth, their stumps still lodged in a lower jaw.

This way, it began again.

5

By the end of 1998, Rex Dryden's Temple of Light had attracted followers and financial backing sufficient to allow him to move his headquarters to a privately purchased ex-public-school building set in a generous estate near the coast of East Sussex. Permanent inhabitants of the Cult Headquarters (as the press would have it) were estimated to have numbered between as few as two hundred and as many as a thousand.

In September 1999, shortly after questions were asked in the Commons, Dryden called the first of what he announced would be three press conferences. It was here that he publicly detailed much of what he knew about the imminent end of the world.

First (and most importantly) it would be very soon.

Uncharacteristically reading from a prepared statement, he said that every historical cycle known to humanity was coming to a close or entering a new phase: we were living in the dying days of the Kali Yuga, the period of 6,480 years which Hindus believe to be the last and most degenerate stage of a recurring cycle in which humankind slowly descends from light into darkness. We were in the twilight of the Greek Age of Iron; a new Age of Gold beckoned. The calendar of the mysterious, ancient Maya, which extended millions of years into the past, came to a sudden end on 22 December 2012. The Age of Pisces, dictating two thousand years of violence, segued violently into the Age of Aquarius, the millennium of wisdom and light, shortly after the year 2000.

The warning signs had been there for all to see: upheavals, wars, volcanic eruptions and the cult of personality. Gaia, the living earth, would take revenge on those who had raped her; ancient prophecies of the annihilation of the species would be brought about by the species itself: there would be plagues of drugs, crime. What Christians called the Antichrist would reign supreme. (Some of those present may have noticed in passing that the digits of the year 1999 signalled both the upended number of the beast, and a one – for the Only One?) However, the Elohim, a race of space angels, were returning to earth. Their aim was to teach us to become not *Homo sapiens* but *Homo spiritualis*. Through them we could become living vibrations in a fourth dimensional plane which some knew as Heaven.

The success of this mission was hindered by the dark forces of the New World Order, and the media were mouthpiece of one of its many heads.

*

Not every journalist present believed everything Dryden had to say. Dryden welcomed their questions. When asked if Elvis Presley was returning to earth with the Elohim, he threw back his melon head and barked an appreciative laugh at the ceiling. After knuckling at the moist corner of an eye, he replaced his spectacles and fixed the gathered reporters with his gaze.

'I'll tell you what,' he said. 'If he is, do you know what I'll ask him?'

He paused, swept the room with his eyes. 'I'll say: "Elvis, how could a higher being make *Fun in Acapulco*?"'

Many in the room laughed with him. The line went unreported everywhere but the *Guardian* and the *Fortean Times*.

There were a few beats of prosaic silence before he continued: 'There hasn't been a single human being put on this earth,' he said, 'in whatever time frame, during whatever historical period, under the auspices of whatever god or empire, who doesn't know, deep down inside themselves, that the universe is a struggle between good and evil.

'I don't know about you, but I believe in what you'd call God. I also believe that the Devil is abroad. And I don't mean he's in France. He's out there right now. And he's in here, in this room, with us. He's King of the World. He's Prince of the Air. We all know that, whether we allow it or not. Deep down. We all know that someone like Hitler wasn't a *man*. Not in any sense we recognize. He was a devil, a demon, a dybukk, and for a while he possessed Germany and foamed and raved and threatened dominion over all the princes of the earth. Look in the history books, the newsreel archives. Turn on your televisions, read your own newspapers, and tell me these aren't the last days. Tell me the Devil isn't unleashed upon the face of the Earth. Show me a man who says otherwise and I'll show you a fool. Now tell me: is it better to curse this darkness, or to light a candle? Next question.'

The next question was the first to be put by a female journalist. Young (young enough to be polite). Prada suit, Jimmy Choo shoes. Hair in a complex topknot.

'What about the rest of us?' she said: 'Those of us who aren't saved. Where are we?'

Dryden rested his chin on a knotty fist. Was silent for a moment. When he spoke, it was with quiet acquiescence. He shrugged.

'What do you want me to say?' he said. 'You're nowhere. Forever. Simple as that.'

On 22 December 1999, Rex Dryden arranged to have one dimpled 250 ml bottle of orange Lucozade distributed to each of those hundreds of men, women and children who had gathered about him in the grounds of the ex-public school in East Sussex. To each of these bottles had been added an odourless, flavourless ingredient which would hasten whoever drank it towards the Elohim and the eternal presence of God.

Of those hundreds who had gathered, an estimated 50 per cent refused to ingest the poison.

Although Dryden was indulgent to their schismatism, he nevertheless requested them to leave the grounds within the hour. All of them did so. Later, media psychologists would try to analyse why not one of them called the police. But not one of them did.

Those faithful who imbibed the poison were instructed to return to their beds, where they would fall into a dreamless sleep from which their bodies would never wake.

When the two or five or seven hundred cult suicides had done as instructed, closing the doors of their dormitories behind them, Dryden waited alone in the study until the sun had gone down, reading Erasmus.

In the morning, the suicides woke as normal. There was much confusion.

Nobody had died.

Upon investigation, all that proved otherwise unusual about the day was that Rex Dryden had disappeared from the compound.

Among a small but significant proportion of the elect, there arose an initially tentative belief that their survival in some way constituted a miracle.

Perhaps Dryden had been assumed directly into the arms of God.

The most vocal proponent of this amended belief system was a sales representative called Henry Lincoln. Henry Lincoln was a deputy of Dryden's. He had personally been responsible for regulating distribution of the poisoned Lucozade. He now claimed to have been visited by Dryden as he slept. The ascended dream-Dryden told Henry that he was risen into the arms of the blessed Elohim. There he would prepare the way for his disciples.

However, the new gospel as espoused by Henry Lincoln was constructed in circumstances that were not ideal, and Mr Lincoln did not convince all the survivors of its veracity.

Instead, many of them decided to leave the extensive grounds of the old public school and return to their previous lives.

With varying degrees of success, most of them managed to do so. Even before the humiliations still to come, there was much anger to learn how to manage and to this end some sought professional therapy.

Most of those who had chosen to remain in the compound eventually left when, on 2 January in the year 2000, the world inexplicably failed to end.

The departure of the final few dozen acolytes made the final item on that evening's news.

The scattering of the faithful left the grounds accompanied by the clicking of cameras and the flashing of bulbs and the bellowed questions of jubilant reporters.

Henry Lincoln, humiliated, wore a knitted ski mask over his face to hide his shame from the congregated lenses.

At the end of January 2000, a BBC television news reporter received in the post what claimed to be a letter from Rex Dryden, of whom there had been no trace since he vanished at Christmas.

In the interim, Dryden had become a byword for the comical medievalism which was discerned to have infected the popular mind in the run-up to what proved to be a rather unexceptional New Year's Eve and the beginning of a third millennium which so far was largely indistinguishable from the second. This was exactly as those who were in a position to know assured us they had always known it would be.

Since the note was handwritten, its authenticity was easily

corroborated. It requested that on 24 February a specific BBC Television news reporter, accompanied by two cameramen and a single sound technician, should set up their equipment in a suite in the Edinburgh Waverly hotel. The suite had been booked in the name of Singh and their arrival was expected.

When the news crew had done as requested, there was a twenty-minute wait before Dryden entered the room. He was accompanied by a handsome, aquiline Sikh in grey three-piece and good brogues.

As they prepared him for interview, clipping a small microphone to his lapel and feeding the cable under his jacket, Dryden appeared sprightly and undiminished. He addressed the representatives of the BBC as 'gentlemen'.

He became serious only when the cameras were running, adopting a severe facial cast. He and Singh sat alongside one another in formal chairs, against a neutral screen that had been brought along for the occasion by the BBC.

Off camera, the reporter's voice: 'Mr Dryden, I believe you wish to make a statement.'

'I do.' Looking briefly to his companion: 'The gentleman to my left is Ranbir Singh. Mr Singh has been my friend and solicitor for nearly twenty years. Mr Singh will read my statement.'

Singh removed from his pocket and unfolded what appeared to be a legal document on creamy yellow A4. His voice was clipped and somewhat officious.

'I read from a statement dictated and signed in the presence of witnesses by Rex Dryden on 25 February 1994. The statement reads as follows:

"I, Rex Dryden, previously known as David Kubler, wish to make the following statement.

"Two days ago, on 23 February 1994, I witnessed on the BBC Television news the conflagration at the Branch Davidian compound in Waco, Texas, which killed David Koresh and an as yet unconfirmed number of his disciples.

"As an artist, I am outraged and inspired by these events and hereby announce my intention to use them as the framework on which I will create the greatest conceptual artwork of the late twentieth century.

"The piece will be called *Illumination*. It will consist of my appropriation of a messianic identity. The work will commence without financial capital or a cohesive, original theology. Using only borrowed materials, the work will culminate on or around Christmas Day, 1999, when I will encourage what followers I have gathered voluntarily to kill themselves in the name of the lies I have told them.

"Assuming the brand continues to exist on the date specified, the mechanism of mass suicide will be the glucose drink Lucozade.

"Because of the longitudinal and experimental nature of this artwork, the location of this mass suicide cannot yet be specified.

"Whatever the degree of its success, I will make the nature of this conceptual experiment known to the BBC on or around 23 February 2000. For the reasons mentioned above, the location of this conference cannot yet be specified.'"

Singh folded the statement and replaced it in his pocket.

'The affidavit of which this is a copy is co-signed and

witnessed by myself and my partner, Richard Joseph Parsons. The original may be viewed by appointment at the London office of Parsons Singh Associates.'

On a quiet news day, the report was fourth lead on that evening's six o'clock news on the BBC. The BBC agreed to share the footage with all other terrestrial and satellite networks in time for their evening broadcasts.

Editorially, the decision was taken to leave uncut the five seconds of silence which followed Singh's completion of Dryden's statement, indicating the interview might now proceed.

When the reporter speaks, off camera, it is in an excited half-whisper.

'Mr Dryden,' he says, 'are we to understand that your so-called Temple of Light was a *practical joke*?'

Dryden cannot quite maintain his calm. Momentarily, he seems agitated with the triumphant hilarity of it. He shifts in his seat and looks to the floor. When he looks at the camera, his face splits into a half-melon grin, cropped out with teeth for seeds.

'A work of *art*, Martin,' he corrects the reporter. 'But (and let me quote Horace): "what is to stop us telling the truth with a smile?"'

The next day, for the first time, the *Sun* chose to repeat one of its own front-page headlines.

Over a slightly pixilated, over-colourized close-up of Dryden's grin, lifted straight from videotape of the previous evening's news, it printed in eighty-point type a single word:

Gotcha!

Falls

6

I

Holloway dreamed he was a tattered crow at the window of Andrew Winston Taylor's house.

He flapped his blue-black wings and became a tendril of ectoplasm that rippled through tiny cracks in damp limestone.

He was a flickering, a dry rustle in the corners of that gloomy building. He was the tick of capillary on optic nerve. He was a discarnate longing that lurked over that deserted and fatherless family, a sentinel to watch over them until the sorrow slipped away and he woke to discover he had been weeping.

That day, Joanne Grayling disappeared.

II

Holloway was the son of Charles and Elizabeth. Charles spent his life in the British army. Elizabeth Fowler, a Halifax tobacconist's daughter, was a Catholic twenty years his junior. Their first child, Sarah, was born with a hole in her heart and did not live. William was conceived unexpectedly several years later. His first sense memories were of military bases in hot territories.

His mother died when he was four, of anaphylactic shock brought on by a wasp sting. His maternal great-aunt acceded to his guardianship. William was shipped off to live with her in Halifax. Perhaps because Grace was old before William was of school age, they formed a strange and tender friendship of abandoned equals.

He never saw his father again.

When he was seventeen, Will joined the Royal Engineers, which took him away from England. He was tattooed in Berlin and Singapore. He left the army at twenty-one to live in Leeds, part of an England whose name he had tattooed above his heart but hardly knew.

Now that tattoo had bled out to an indistinct, blue scroll. A new century was beginning and he lived alone in another city: Bristol, built on the traffic of slaves. His new life seemed in every way disconnected from what had gone before. This was another England, a place where he flicked through discoloured snapshots, his heart hollow for their fading. His mental depth of field had shifted. Leeds, that boy, that decade seemed to have telescoped into history.

Although the present generation's taste for kitsch and nostalgia sought to deny it, there had been little of worth in that half-lit, cheerless decade. There lurked at its axis a recondite absence. For every pair of loon flares, for every Stylophone, for every platform boot, for every Bay City Roller, for every *Saturday Night Fever* or *Dancing Queen*, he remembered a Bobby Sands, an emasculated government, a three-day week: power strikes, postal strikes. He remembered refuse rotting in streets and cadavers left unburied. He remembered National Front marches in English cities and Armalites and petrol bombs in Belfast. And at the decade's dreary fag end, he remembered that hectoring voice; the vulture beak and cartoon stalk from a child's nightmare. Margaret Hilda. In his mind she was married forever with Peter, her fervent Other: dark Peter, a shadow invoked by druidic energy, by the tidal surge of past against future. On street corners, under lampposts, in Bradford, in Leeds transported Dianic priestesses were unzipped, spilling out the future again and again for those who had eyes to see.

The bleak occult seeped into the moors: crooning its song to quiet, mad Peter, in his donkey jacket, his jeans and his clay-clegged boots. His breath steaming, horselike, in cloudless cold. Grave-digging spade in one raw, red hand. Arcane and horrible knowledge coiling and spitting behind his blank eyes. Blooding the decade, the century to come, with a ball-headed hammer raised like a dagger above him.

The Ripper lurked deep in the shadows cast by Holloway's memory. The Ripper was present in his photographs. He was the pyramid of black cast across concrete by an oblique sun hammering on red brick tenements, outside which he and half-forgotten friends stood, smiling, squinting, their eyes lost in shadow. Their pasty skin, the low Yorkshire skies at the end of England. It was an England in which he was twenty-one, and in which he met Kate, who would be his wife.

After leaving the army, he found a job training to repair lifts. He took a room in the Harold's, a Headingley estate of back-to-back tenements. Laundry dried on lines strung across narrow streets.

Late November 1978. Beans on toast on his lap, watching *The Two Ronnies* with Ted and Dot, the couple with whom he lodged. Ted was off on the sick: emphysema. He wore Brylcreem and a grey cardigan with brown leather buttons. Dot's hair was dyed black and lacquered into a beehive. As far as Will could tell, she was almost perfectly spherical. Will's own crew cut had yet to grow out and, too short to style, it sprouted ragged and uneven at his nape and round the ears.

After tea, he stepped outside into the cold wind, turned up the fleecy collar and set off like Shackleton, hands buried in pockets, to meet his mates in the Faversham.

He stepped through the door into a burst of pub noise, blue smoke and moist body heat. The Faversham was crowded with university and polytechnic students. Greasy hair, National Health spectacles, military greatcoats. Hippies in tatty crushed velvet and greasy denim. Punks. It didn't take much to qualify as a punk in 1978; short hair and drainpipes were enough to do it. But there was a preponderance of black, too. The occasional safety pin, a mohair sweater or two. One or two daring mohicans.

Tony was there, and Ian, and whoever else. (His memory was full of half-remembered Tonys and Ians.) They'd be moving to town later, where they would sit round the edge of a discothèque dance floor, supping pints and watching girls.

He'd been there perhaps half an hour when Kate arrived. She was in a group that gathered noisily at the bar, counting out change in their palms and yelling and laughing and pushing. Her hair was short and shone blue-black (she would cringe now, to think of it). She wore a black mohair sweater that slipped alternately from each shoulder.

Looking at her made Will hurt. He told the story often, in later, happier years: at Christmas and birthdays and on holidays. *Honest to God. It was like being punched*.

He snatched glimpses of her during breaks in the conversation. He followed her progress to the lavatory.

He resolved to follow her to the bar and stood, too abruptly, shaking the table. Not unkindly, he was told: fucking watch it, that was a full pint. And he was called a twat. But he didn't hear. He clapped his hands and said: 'Right.'

The bar was four deep and he had Bambi legs. It took some time to push in alongside her.

He said: 'Can I get this one for you?'

She turned and considered him through narrowed eyes. 'I beg your pardon?'

'I said: "I'll buy the next one."'

'No thank you.'

She turned away. He didn't move.

She clicked her tongue against her pallet, turned again. 'Can I help you?'

'Yes.'

(*Chemistry*, she would say, later. *Pure pheromones. Two dogs in the street*.)

'With?'

'Your name.'

She laughed. Her eyes crinkled. She told him.

'And your phone number.'

'I have a boyfriend.'

'One day you might not.'

'Well. If that day comes, you'll have to ask me again.'

'If that day comes I might.'

'Don't hold your breath.'

'I won't. What are you studying?'

'Law.'

'I'll remember that.'

'Why?'

'So we'll have something to talk about.'

He excused himself, bid her goodnight and walked away. It was the bravest thing he had ever done.

It was necessary to force his friends (swearing quietly through gritted teeth: *Lads, just fuck off out of it. Please. Fucking hell*) through the pub doors. He exited only after shoving the last of them into the cold night. They went to a disco and, unlikely as he knew it to be, he kept an eye on the door all night, in case she walked in.

He suggested with great frequency that they drink in student pubs. His mates didn't mind. They professed to hate students, but didn't tire of student parties where they might be offered a joint by some undergraduate terrified of their petulant class antagonism.

Will was able to bump into Kate twice, sometimes three times a week. She wasn't lying about the boyfriend. His name was Sam. He looked like Bryan Ferry's rebellious younger brother and had what Will imagined to be the bearing of a radical poet.

Will found some classmates of Kate who, in exchange for a couple of pints of Tetley with a whiskey chaser, were happy to acquaint him with her timetable. They outlined campus geography for him and he waited for her after class one crisp morning in February. She saw him there, paused long enough to disengage from her companions, then hugged books to her breast and walked on.

He jogged a step or two in her wake, stopped. Called out to her.

She stopped, without turning.

He said: 'Well?'

'Well, what?'

'Are you still going out with him?'

'Oh yes.'

'*Still?*'

'Still.'

'Shame.'

Now she turned.

'Why a *shame*?'

'You're too good for him.'

She laughed.

'What do you mean by that?'

'What I said. You're too good for him.'

'But you'd like me to go out with you instead?'

'Yes.'

'So I'm not too good for you?'

He thrust his shaking hands in the tight denim pockets and set his weight on one leg.

'Oh, you're too good for *me*,' he said. 'You're *far* too good for me. That's the point. Why would I go to all this effort if you weren't too good for me?'

'Oh,' she said. 'Very smooth.'

'I'm not being smooth. Look at me. Do I look smooth?'

He took his hands from his pockets.

'See. I'm shaking.'

'It's cold.'

'Not that cold. And my mouth is dry.'

'You're probably hungover.'

'That too.'

She put her head to one side and regarded him from an oblique angle. By spring they were together.

Kate fell pregnant early the next year, 1980. They argued and separated. Several weeks later, Will turned up at her door bearing daffodils. He asked her to dinner. She refused.

In the hallway, the front door open to the weather, he pleaded with her to keep the child.

He told her he'd applied to join the police force: it was a steady job and it would compliment Kate's chosen career to the best of his limited ability. That morning he had been accepted as a trainee.

She held him. She stroked his hair, whispered in his ear that he was a strange one, a strange one.

Kate was heavily pregnant when they married at Leeds Register Office. With the exception of Kate's Auntie Linda, her family didn't attend. Will asked an old army friend called Geordie to be his best man. His aunt Grace lent him money for the rings and a honeymoon weekend in the Lake District. All together, nine people came.

They held an informal reception in a room above the Cricketer's Arms in Headingley. Will's speech was courteous and heartfelt. Kate wished her parents were there to hear it. When the speech was over, Auntie Linda hugged Will to her chest and told him Kate was a lucky girl. Then she offered a toast to the future, in which all present at that moment ardently believed.

Caroline was born late in September. During the birth, Will held Kate's hand and stroked her sweat-sodden hair, struck dumb with mortal terror at the enormity of what was happening in that shabby cubicle. Later, he cradled the unwashed child, still slick with blood and mucus.

He knew that his love was more powerful, more ferocious, than God.

III

On the day that Joanne was taken, he returned late to his Bedminster flat: rented, one-bedroom, second-floor.

He showered, wrapped himself in a bathrobe and made a

mug of tea before booting up his computer, an iMac that he and Caroline had chosen together and bought from John Lewis. The iMac sat before the sitting room window on an Ikea dining table.

Holloway and his daughter exchanged emails twice daily. It was Caroline's way of maintaining a presence in his life. She sent jokes, apocrypha, urban myths and jPegs that had made her laugh: dancing babies, singing penises. She wrote about books she was reading and places she had been and things she wanted to do. He pecked out lower-case replies with an index finger.

He set the mug on the pine table, pushed aside a sheaf of bills awaiting payment and clicked on the Mail icon.

Caroline hadn't written yet but logged in his inbox were two messages from an unfamiliar address: bedford.falls@virgin.net.

He took a sip of tea and double clicked on the first of the messages. It contained just a brief video clip. There was no text.

The clip was perhaps twenty seconds long. He played it twice. Although the sight and intonation of his wife's passion was familiar to him, and precious and fearful, he had not heard or seen it for a long time.

The film was shot from a high angle: perhaps through an upper bedroom window. Kate laughed throatily and called out to God. She brushed the sweaty hair from her brow. The young man she was fucking reached up a lazy hand and squeezed her breast. She slapped the hand away. He muttered a glottal response. She ground her hips. The young man scowled as if in pain, clutched her thighs.

Holloway sat without moving until the tea went cold. Then he opened the second file. It contained a jPeg attachment, a single photograph. No text.

A naked woman lay bound on a dirty timber floor.

Because she was blindfold and not wearing the dark wig he paid her to wear, it took Holloway some time to recognize Joanne Grayling. Her real hair was blonde and cropped boyishly short. Something had been written on her body: one word. The lettering ran from her pubic bush to her breasts but her position made the word hard to decipher. Holloway saw an A and a T, distorted by the soft fold of her belly.

He closed the file. Opened it again.

He cupped his mouth.

The clip could only have been sent by the man who filmed it.

His name was Derek Bliss.

He was a private detective whose services Holloway had contracted following the breakdown of his marriage. His office was located on a Bradford backstreet, above a launderette whose own sign seemed faded by one wash too many. They met in a workman's café next door, huddled in fixed plastic chairs over a Formica table.

Bliss was a neat, rotund and discretely salacious man with a sparrow's quizzical, orbicular head. He was perhaps five feet four inches in his stockinged feet. He was charming, deferential, effeminate. Clipped, militaristic diction.

Holloway poured sugar into strong tea. For a long time he stirred it, using a brown-stained teaspoon.

He explained what he wanted.

Bliss was to follow Kate and report back to him every week, advising him of where she had been and who she had seen.

By which he meant who she had slept with.

Two weeks later they met again. Bliss stood in Holloway's doorway. He wore Farrah slacks and a police-style sweater over a checked shirt. He handed Holloway a video cassette.

Holloway's stomach went cold and his bowels loosened.

He asked Bliss inside.

He sat and put his head in his hands. He said: 'Oh God.'

Tenderly, Bliss put the tape in the VCR and turned on the television. His shallow breathing accelerated until it synchronized with the muttered profanities of Kate's approaching orgasm. She ground her pubis against the boy in a slow sickle motion, moaned as if in pain. The boy muttered something. Slapped her thigh. The tinny impact registered shockingly clearly. Kate hung her head and brushed the wet fringe from her eyes.

In the grey half-light, the boy's exposed cock shone like Vaseline. Kate lay on her back. Muttered something humourless when the boy slid inside her. His response was too low for the microphone to register. He buried his face in the crook of her neck. He arched his spine and the cheeks of his ass tightened like a fist. Kate's eyes rolled white, like a predating shark.

Holloway asked who the boy was. It took him three attempts to get the words out.

Bliss smiled with fraternal sadness.

'He's a student. David Bishop. University of Leeds. First year, engineering.'

Bliss said he must go. He excused himself to go to the

lavatory. Then, in the hallway, Holloway counted cash into his smooth palm, fragrant with soap.

Bliss left him a business card. He shook Holloway's hand, wished him luck for the future, and left.

Holloway closed the door. He wiped the palm of his hand on the wall, screwed up the business card in his fist, and dropped it into the kitchen bin.

Later, he found beads of semen on the toilet seat.

Some months later, Holloway had occasion to go looking for Derek Bliss. He found that he lived alone in a pretty, stone-built cottage on the edge of Harrogate. Holloway arrived at his bedroom window under cover of darkness. Up the sleeve of his jacket was concealed a tyre-iron.

Shortly after he broke in, it became apparent that Derek Bliss was gone.

The wardrobes were full. There was milk in the fridge, dating to the previous week. Last Monday's *Telegraph*. Junk mail had massed like a snow drift on the coarse mat beneath the letterbox.

Perhaps Bliss had intuited that Holloway would not tolerate having him around, knowing what he knew. Perhaps not. For whatever reason, he'd gone and he never came back.

A full winter passed before somebody, a neighbour, grew curious about some unattended snow damage to the cottage and called the police.

Through the cold, dark months, Holloway's necessarily tentative efforts to locate Bliss had failed. It was summer before he learned via some offhand copper's comment, that Bliss had died shortly before Christmas. He had been several weeks into an extended Australian vacation.

Holloway never learned the full story. Soon, he relocated to Bristol. Since then, he'd thought about Bliss at most infrequently. Sometimes, not often, he truly believed him to be dead. Other times, he imagined him, leering and reddened and glazed like a suckling pig, smirking at girls on Bondi beach.

But Derek Bliss was not dead. And Derek Bliss was not in Australia.

Derek Bliss was back to get him.

His mind was blank. He sat there, clicking the file open, clicking it closed.

Eventually, he hit REPLY.

derek, he tapped, **is that you?**

He listened to the squeal and pop of the modem.

But although he checked his inbox every few minutes for several hours, there was no further communication.

7

On the morning of the massacre in America, Shepherd confessed his precognitive nature to Lenny.

In the early light, with the news reports still coming in, Lenny didn't laugh. He'd pulled on a pair of tracksuit trousers, and padded blearily about the kitchen, making tea. His torso was naked and it was cold. From the laundry basket under the stairs he removed a dirty bath towel and wrapped himself in it like a cloak. He hugged his knees to his chest. His naked feet were pallid and hairy. He was gaunt and unshaved, and his eyes were circled deep blue, as if bruised. His hair stuck up and out in all directions.

Like Dr Scobie before him, he had to accept the facts. Something terrible *had* happened in America.

Shepherd obviously wasn't a deliberate fraud. Lenny had seen the state he was in. It had been a pretty Linda Blair moment.

But was Shepherd an *unknowing* charlatan? Lenny had studied this stuff. Most apparently psychic phenomena, he said,
were connected to the normal function of human memory.
Memory contextualized experience, framing it within a
person's understanding and expectation. Psychics tended to
play down errors in their predictions and greatly to amplify
small accuracies. They probably didn't even know they were
doing it. You remember the times you just missed the bus, but
not the times you just caught it. Chronic gamblers remembered the long-odds winner and forgot the many sure-fire
failures. That was just the way the mind worked. Stuff happened: the mind filled in the gaps and inconsistencies. People
who believed in ghosts saw ghosts. The rest saw shadow and
reflection.

He set his feet on the cold, grubby tiled floor and began to
roll a cigarette. He looked like a refugee.

When we lifted the receiver before the phone rang, he said,
it was because our responsive, animal brain acted more quickly
to a stimulus than our conscious mind. We only became *aware*
of hearing the phone after we'd picked it up. But it did ring
first, and at some level we did hear it. Dream states, migraine or
epilepsy could lead to visionary experience. The presence of
God (or the Devil) could be invoked in a laboratory with a
couple of grand's worth of electrical equipment.

Just because you were really seeing weird stuff, it didn't
mean you were seeing weird stuff that was real.

Coincidence was another possibility. Statistical laws could
be wildly counter-intuitive. What looked extremely unlikely
might in fact be mathematical certainty. It was staggeringly

improbable that a randomly selected individual would win the Lottery that week — but it was a practical certainty that *somebody* would win it. All Shepherd remembered was waking and saying: 'Something terrible has happened in America.' At any given time, there were millions — maybe billions — of people asleep all over the world. Enough bad things happened in America for *somebody's* dream, somewhere, to correspond to one occurrence of it — just as somebody had to be dreaming of Diana the night her car slammed into a tunnel wall like a meteorite. (Lenny put the unlit cigarette in the corner of his mouth and clapped his hands, to illustrate the impact.) Perhaps Shepherd had merely framed a conventional nightmare within his expectation of precognition.

Or perhaps Shepherd was a precognitive psychic.

Lenny wanted to know why that prospect should be discounted. Because there was no such thing? Who was to say?

Unrepeatability didn't equal impossibility. And absence of evidence was not evidence of absence.

Solidity was a functional illusion. It was a perceptual deceit. It was wired into hominid brains produced by random mutation, and it favoured survival on African savannahs an evolutionary instant ago. Those who characterized the pursuing cheetah as separate from its surroundings had a far better chance of escaping its teeth and going on to produce the maximum number of offspring.

Solidity was an interpretation of reality. Every second, they were bombarded with invisible waves of information. They didn't regard as miraculous the broadcast of complex data to distant radios, televisions or mobile telephones. Then why discount the possibility that such waves of information could be generated and received by biological machinery?

Lenny's eyes burned with zeal.

Precognitive psychic experience made impeccable evolutionary sense. It had nothing to do with voodoo or spirit guides or whatever the fuck else. He urged Shepherd to *think about it*. What a superb adaptation it would be for a creature to detect its offspring's distress when that animal was out of sight and earshot! What was supernatural about that? Couldn't Shepherd see from a distance, and hear from a distance, and smell from a distance?

The arrow of time was an illusion. Time present existed in time past, and time past in time present. Matter was mostly space. Every psychic experience Shepherd described had involved the extrasensory perception of human pain and fear and violence. Pain and fear and violence were the Darwinian crucible: that was where the senses were forged.

The eye had evolved seven times in seven different evolutionary tributaries. Given enough time, something as awesome as the eye was biologically inevitable.

Was what happened to Shepherd more miraculous than that?

8

Joanne Grayling had not been heard from since going on a date five days earlier. She always took the time to call home and her flatmates were worried. Joanne's car, a black Volkswagen Golf cabriolet, was found later that day, double-parked and clamped near the Quadrant pub in Clifton. Her handbag was still in the glove compartment. It contained her purse, credit cards, mobile phone and housekeys. A small spray of blood was found on the dashboard.

Had she been a street-corner prostitute, the police investigation might have quietly wound down when she wasn't found after a few days. It was seldom easy to track the pattern of movement and stasis in a prostitute's life, let alone her disappearance and death. Such murders were not easy to solve and there were questions of budget. Nobody cared much, even about butchered whores dumped by roadsides.

But Joanne was attractive, Joanne was intelligent and Joanne was middle-class. She was easy for an ABC1 target audience to identify with and made for good copy. The *Bristol Evening Post* splashed the story on the front page. *Where is our Joanne?* Dolorous grandparents were pictured in the kitchen of their Cheltenham home, the grandfather clutching Joanne's graduation photograph.

The local television news made the missing girl their lead item the same evening. The next day, she made the nationals. No mention was made of how she was paying her way through university. She was just a brilliant, beautiful, missing graduate student.

The Avon and Somerset Constabulary admitted they were 'very concerned' for Joanne's wellbeing; Jim Ireland, the senior investigating officer, made a televised appeal for information relating to her disappearance. In the hope that a student might provide crucial information, an incident room was set up on the university campus. A dedicated hotline number was publicized on radio and television and in the newspapers. Student volunteers distributed leaflets bearing Joanne's photograph, the hotline number and a plea for information.

Many called the number – senior citizens who had seen a girl who looked like Joanne boarding a coach to Glasgow, a train to Wales, or shopping in Top Shop. A minicab driver remembered dropping her in Shakespeare Avenue, Horfield. Calls were logged from violent sexual fantasists; heavy breathing in damp bedsitter silence. There were hoaxers and religious bigots. Three different calls identified Joanne as a millennial sacrifice to the Annunaki, the reptilian masters of the world, whose numbers included Queen Elizabeth II, the Rothschild family, Bob Hope, Rex Dryden, George Bush and Kris Kristofferson.

I will, they were assured. *I will personally ensure the matter is looked into*.

All potential leads, however tentative, would be followed up. The violent fantasists and the hoax callers were reported and logged. They too would be followed up and one or two would successfully be prosecuted for wasting police time.

The campus incident room was the focus of a psychic maelstrom. Around it seethed misplaced love and ancient hatreds. The television had shown a brief clip of videotape; Joanne as bridesmaid at a friend's wedding. She passed briefly before the lens; threw back her head and laughed. The media settled on this image as the abstract of Joanne Grayling. A young woman: blurred, smiling. The quickly established familiarity of the clip led strangers to believe themselves connected with her. She was a blank that crackled with the projection of wayward daughters; of successful children who didn't call or write; of careless, beloved grandchildren; of unattainable women whose very existence seemed to spurn angry, lonely men.

II

The Joanne Grayling investigation was big news: there would be cancelled leave and a great deal of compulsory overtime. But Holloway was not chosen to be part of the investigating team.

For the first two days he stayed calm.

There was nothing else he could do. No course of action was available to him.

Instead, he brooded on the possibility that Joanne was Bliss's accomplice, rather than his victim. Holloway was aware that his powerful abhorrence for the idea, his reluctance to accept it, was rooted in vanity. He'd seen it a thousand times in other men. It was an act of discipline to acknowledge it in himself.

This is what Joanne did. She fucked people for money.

He wondered where Bliss had been and what had brought him back. He invented means by which he and Joanne had come to meet.

He thought of them. Sitting down somewhere. Planning this. Laughing at him. Bliss's eager, probing little cock in her painted mouth, his ejaculate mixing there with the ghost of Holloway's.

He searched the internet for any reference to Bliss. Found nothing.

He wondered how many people were out there, trying to get him.

As best he could, he avoided the newly jammed and overrun corridors. It was easy to evade notice while a high-profile, highly mediagenic investigation was under way.

He caught up on paperwork and other administration. He collated the documentation that detailed the disappearance of Andrew Winston Taylor. He set it alongside other casework.

Forthcoming inquests and court appearances blurred and merged.

He strained to catch passing snippets of conversation.

For lunch he ate egg mayonnaise sandwiches from the

newsagent on the corner, washed down with Coca-Cola from a two-litre bottle.

Returning home on the evening of the second day, he found a new message waiting in his inbox.

It was a photograph of a screwdriver.

Later, he went for a walk. Stopping off in a number of pubs on the way, he passed through Redland and Horfield, down Gloucester Road and into Broadmead, the ugly concrete shopping centre. Broadmead had been caused to rise from the ruins left by the Luftwaffe. On a single night in November 1940, most of Bristol's town centre and ten thousand houses were obliterated. Hitler spoke of the city's eradication, and had not been far wrong.

Holloway hailed a taxi. It took him back up Park Street, along Whiteladies Road and into Clifton.

The Parragon was a monumental crescent of Bath-stone mansion blocks. Palest yellow in the darkness, their front aspect reared high over Bristol. Gardens went down in tiers towards Avon Gorge. The last house on the crescent belonged to Adrian, Kate's partner. They shared a penthouse, whose long balcony overlooked the suspension bridge. Adrian's income as landlord of the remaining properties greatly surpassed Holloway's full-time salary.

Holloway wore a butterscotch mac from Marks & Spencer and a navy-blue suit from Next. Copper's shoes with Dr Marten soles. The stripy purple and blue socks Caroline gave him one Christmas. She'd bought him underwear too: Homer Simpson bellowing 'D'oh'.

Caroline had been in the first year of her degree. She was excited by ideas and philosophies she soon would forget, or which would come to bore her. She told him: 'D'oh is the *cogito ergo sum* of the postmodern era.'

He didn't understand what she meant and didn't feel qualified to ask.

The door was glossy black, like Downing Street. Alongside it was set an eight-button intercom and grille. He pushed the top button.

Dot dot dot. Dash dash dash. Dot dot dot.

There was a long wait, broken by a tinny crackle and a familiar man's voice, bleary with sleep.

'Hello?'

'Adrian. It's Will.'

A longer pause.

'Will, it's gone midnight. It's ten to one. What do you want?'

'To see Kate.'

'Kate's asleep.'

'Please.'

'Call her tomorrow.'

'Adrian. Please. Come on.'

'You're pissed.'

'I'm not.'

'You sound it.'

'I'm not. Listen. Really.'

'Jesus, Will. Is this about Caroline? She's not here.'

'I know she's not fucking there.' He calmed himself. 'Five minutes,' he said. 'Come on. Five minutes.'

'Go home, Will.'

There was a faint clunk as, gently enough, Adrian replaced the handset.

Holloway pulled back a foot to kick the door, thought better of it. He took a mobile phone from his pocket and dialled their number from memory. Twice he heard out the answerphone message. The third time, Kate lifted the receiver. He pictured her running a tired hand through her hair. He could smell the sleep in the crook of her neck, the musky warmth behind her ear.

She said: 'Give us a moment.'

He sat on the cold stone step until the latch buzzed behind him. He pushed aside the door and stepped into the hallway, where he passed a communal cheeseplant and a wooden bureau upon which was spread what remained of the day's post, before taking the carpeted stairs two at a time, his coat billowing behind him. On the landing of the fourth floor, he paused to catch his breath. He was breathing heavily when Adrian opened the door.

Adrian was a big man, blond and burly. Wavy hair receding from the temples. He was barefoot in untucked white shirt over faded 501s.

'Adrian,' said Holloway.

Adrian barred the doorway. 'This is my house,' he said.

'I want to talk to her,' said Holloway. 'That's all. Just for one minute.'

Adrian waited for a moment, sighed, removed his arm. Holloway passed through.

It had high ceilings for a penthouse apartment. The master bedroom, Holloway knew, was about the size of his entire flat.

One bedroom was known as 'Caroline's room', although she stayed there only rarely. Adrian, divorced, had no children of his own. The third bedroom they used as an office and gymnasium. Adrian lifted free weights and ran half-marathons. He played squash and the occasional game of rugby. Kate practised pilates.

The sitting room was palatial. Recessed lighting. Wooden flooring, elegantly aged. Enormous sash windows with peeling sills. Three sofas. A rustic oak dinner table. There were no curtains. The room reflected back on itself. There were framed photographs on a lead fireplace: Kate. Kate and Adrian. Kate, Adrian and Caroline: arms round each other's shoulders, leaning forward, smiling and squinting in the sun.

Cuba. Adrian had taken them to Cuba.

Something classical and soothing was playing at low volume. He didn't know what.

Kate stood in the centre of the room. A worm shifted within him. She too was barefoot in jeans and a clean blue shirt a size too big for her. Her arms were crossed. He imagined a giant hand lifting her by the hair like a bath plug: the room turning liquid, spiralling away.

'Well?' she said.

He cupped an elbow and pinched the bridge of his nose. Reflected in a mirror above the fireplace, Adrian shrugged and jutted his lower lip.

Holloway said: 'Can we talk? In private. Just for a minute.'

She said: 'You reek of booze.'

Adrian went to a cabinet, removed a whisky bottle and heavy tumbler and poured himself a large measure of Laphroaig.

It seemed to Holloway that the house might collapse under its own weight and bury them all. And that would be that.

Kate said, 'Come on,' and Holloway followed her into a kitchen that looked like a spread from a mid-market Sunday supplement. He ran fingertips along the cool black granite of its work surface.

He remembered the first time they made love. Leeds, 1979.

This woman shared not a single cell with that lost girl. Each of her constituent cells had divided and died, divided and died. She was a different person, an incremental and deteriorating copy of who she once had been. Knowing this, he didn't understand what he felt, although he knew it to be love.

She put the kettle on to boil.

'Whatever happened to Sam?' he said.

'Sam who?'

'*Sam* Sam. Boyfriend Sam.'

She looked confounded.

'God knows,' she said, eventually.

He took the steaming mug of black coffee from her hands.

'Careful,' she said. 'It's hot.'

'Did you ever see him again?'

'Who?'

'Sam.'

'What? No. I just *said*. Not for years. Is that what this is about?'

'Never?'

'For God's sake. Never.'

She tore Kleenex from a roll and uselessly rubbed her hands dry. He knew her anger as intimately as her passion. Perhaps better.

'But you thought about him?'

'What do you mean, thought about him?'

'Nothing. You thought about him. He crossed your mind.'

'Of course he crossed my mind. Of course I *thought* about him.'

'Whatever happened to him?'

'Who? Sam?'

'Yeah. Sam.'

She shrugged. 'How should I know?'

He sipped, scalded the tip of his tongue and the roof of his mouth. 'What about Dan Weatherell?'

She fixed him with a stare and her voice took on a warning note.

'What about him?'

'Are you two still in —,' he set down the mug '— contact?'

She pursed her mouth. 'Fuck you, Will,' she said.

He falsified it slightly, monitored her reaction.

'Somebody sent me photographs,' he said. 'Of you having sex with a man. In Leeds, by the look of it. In the flat you shared with Penny. Well, I say man. Boy. He looks about twenty.'

The moment froze, setting them in a stark tableau. Kate facing away from him, squashing Kleenex into a ball. Holloway looking at the floor. A helix of steam rising from the surface of the coffee.

Kate turned to him.

'I beg your pardon?'

'Somebody sent me photographs,' he said. 'Of you having sex with a man. In Leeds.'

'What man?'

'I don't know. How many were there?'

A gleam of contempt flickered across her eyes.

'What man?'

'I don't know,' he said. 'I told you, I don't know what man. That's the point. I don't know what man.'

'Who sent it to you?'

'I don't know that either.'

'What did he look like?'

'Who?'

'Who do you *think*?'

Acid raged in his stomach.

'He was very young.'

She put a hand to her mouth.

'I don't believe this,' she said. 'I don't understand. How can this have happened?'

He said: 'That's what I came here to ask.'

She looked at him. 'What do you mean?'

'I thought you might know something.'

'Like what?'

'Like who sent them.'

'Of course I don't fucking know who sent them.'

He trembled with the effort of staying calm. He said: 'It didn't seem an unfair thing to ask. In the circumstances.'

She lifted the kettle. It was half full of recently boiled water.

Holloway held a warding hand before him and retreated a step or two.

Behind him, Adrian wrenched open the kitchen door.

He said: 'Please leave. Right now.'

Holloway glanced over his shoulder.

'You heard me,' said Adrian. 'Right now.'

Holloway turned. Adrian glowered monolithically down on him. He interpreted Holloway's grinning entreaty as malice and raised his fist.

It was like being hit by a car.

Outside, Holloway sat on the kerb and hawked blood into the gutter until the rain grew too cold and he decided to walk home.

In the early dawn, he let himself in, hanging the sodden mac over the bathroom door. He rinsed his mouth with saltwater until it ran bloodless.

He left a tub of Ben & Jerries to defrost while he took a shower. These preparations had all the cadence of ritual.

He remembered Joanne Grayling in the same early morning light: bending, nude, to peer in the fridge. Her breasts and belly lit green. Her toes bunched on the cold linoleum. The wig she wore for him perched atop the iMac.

He remembered sitting, detumescent and self-conscious, at the Ikea kitchen table, making a note of how in future he would be able to transfer money directly into her bank account. He joked about establishing a direct debit and she glanced briefly, luminously, over her shoulder and laughed. His own abstract of Joanne Grayling. That single moment of intimacy.

He padded barefoot now to that same desk.

The video clip attached to the latest message from bedford.falls@virgin.net was perhaps two minutes long. Its high quality and flat colours suggested it had been taken with a digital camera secreted somewhere in his own sitting room, probably close to the iMac or the low bookshelf alongside it. It would not be difficult for someone who knew what they were doing to enter and leave his flat. The necessary surveillance equipment could be purchased easily and inexpensively.

In the clip, Holloway leads Joanne Grayling into the sitting room. She wears an evening gown and a sleek, dark wig. She stands before him. Holloway reaches out. He takes her shoulders in his hands. He kisses her neck, her throat. His palm traces the curve of her hip and thigh. She doesn't look at the concealed camera lens.

Holloway repeats a single word.

Kate, he says.

He watched the clip several times, then mechanically spooned ice cream into his mouth until his teeth ached. When the tub was finished, he went to bed. He stared at the ceiling while the watery sunrise bled colour into the room.

He didn't sleep that he remembered, and rose before the alarm. He showered again and dressed in a shirt and suit which still hung in dry-cleaners' polythene. The rain had passed.

To gain entry to the station, he had to walk a gauntlet of a news crews, journalists and curious civilians. He passed before ranks of recording lenses.

He'd been at his desk for perhaps half an hour when the Joanne Grayling case blew wide open. There was a flurry of activity throughout the station. It was several hours before Holloway could establish what had happened. The reports conflicted slightly, but he ascertained that an audio tape had arrived, addressed to James Ireland. It was postmarked Cardiff. On the tape a girl claiming to be Joanne (later identified as such by her grandparents) read from what was assumed to be a statement prepared by her kidnapper.

'The friends of George Bailey want you to know that I am alive and well. I have food and water and am warm. They will not hurt me unless they have to.'

Then she read out the headline from the previous day's *Bristol Evening Post*.

III

Holloway absented himself from the station, marching as if with purpose past the assembled lenses, the compound eye of the ravenous media. He walked to the nearest McDonald's and ate a Big Mac and an apple pie whose contents bore a close functional similarity to napalm.

He was at a loss what to do. He feared returning to the station and he feared going home to see what waited in his inbox.

Alternately, he hoped that Joanne was working with Bliss and that she was not.

He stuffed Big Mac detritus into the bin provided, and went to see Grace.

Hetty opened the door to him.

'You look like death,' she said. 'Whatever can be the matter?'

'Sinus,' he said, and waved his hand close to his temple. Hetty pursed her lips and shooed him inside. He allowed himself to be shooed. He was comforted by the weight of her palm in the small of his back.

Grace was in the television and games room. A knitted white

shawl was draped round her dainty shoulders. He kissed her on each cheek. Her sweet, powdery scent carried the elusive trace of his childhood.

He kneeled alongside the wheelchair. Perhaps by accident, Grace lay a hand along the tense line of his jaw. He took the hand and kissed it.

When he was a child, she had bathed him and towelled him dry and dressed him in soft cotton pyjamas.

Today she was bewildered by his presence. She would not meet his eye. She strained her neck to turn from him.

He looked over his shoulder at Hetty.

Hetty said: 'It's not so good a day.'

He patted Grace's wrist. It felt like kindling. He let it go and stood beside her. He rested his hand lightly on her shoulder.

'It'll be that little terror from up the hill,' said Grace.

He said: 'Is that who it'll be?'

'He's got a look about him,' she said. 'I'd watch that one.'

'I'll do that. I'll watch that one.'

'Have you seen my watch?'

'No. Where is it?'

'It's gold.'

'Is it? Is it a gold watch?'

'From the Queen.'

'Oh, lovely.'

'She brought it here.'

'Who? The Queen?'

'In a helicopter.'

'Goodness me,' he said. 'How special. A gold watch from the Queen.'

'And our George was there. He wanted a watch. But he weren't allowed.'

'Did he? He wanted a watch, did he, our George? Our Uncle George.'

'Bloody bugger.'

'Who? Uncle George?'

'Bugger and arsehole. Bugger and bloody arsehole.'

She set her mouth as if in resolve. Then, in a tremulous and croaking voice, she began to sing. He didn't recognize the song. Its lyrics urged him to accentuate the positive. She accompanied herself with her hands, making small flowing movements, as if she were conducting.

Hetty smiled for his bewilderment. Will followed her to the narrow staff kitchen. She leaned against the sink unit while he made them a cup of tea. He made himself busy, cleaning teaspoons, boiling the kettle.

Hetty said, 'Come now. No tears.'

'I'll be all right. Biscuits?'

'Top right-hand cupboard. Rich Tea. Come now.'

He clattered through the cupboards, removed the tube of biscuits.

'It's just —' he said.

'I know, love.'

He took five biscuits from the pack and arranged them on a saucer like the face of a die.

'Do you think she's in there?'

Hetty took the tea. She stirred it, twenty times clockwise, twenty anticlockwise. Then she set it down on the work surface and dunked a biscuit.

'Who can say?'

'You can,' he said. 'Of all people. You're a world-renowned expert.'

'Hush now with your nonsense,' she said, and batted his upper arm. She folded the soggy biscuit into her mouth. Then she said: 'Who knows where we go?'

He held her gaze.

'Sometimes I think she's there,' Hetty conceded. 'But it's like she's visiting. You know. It's like her spirit has come down just to visit. It's like that with all of them. Suddenly they shine, just for a short while. Then they're gone again and there's no telling when they'll be back. The rest,' she said, gesturing around her. 'All this. I don't know. Maybe it's like a dream her soul has, when it's in heaven.'

He laughed and sniffed back snot. 'Bollocks,' he said.

She laughed, outraged, and slapped his elbow.

'Well, I don't know,' she said. 'How the hell am I supposed to know?'

When he returned to his desk late that afternoon, nobody commented on his absence. Nevertheless, he ostentatiously set a box of flu-strength Lemsip on his desk and sniffed miserably and repetitively.

At 7 p.m. his phone rang. He lifted the receiver and spoke his surname.

The man on the wire held his breath for a moment.

'Are you the police officer with red hair?'

The voice was a murmur, catarrhal with intimacy.

Holloway took the handset from his ear and squinted

quizzically down the receiver as if he might see something there.

'I beg your pardon?'

'Are you the police officer with the red hair?'

'Bear with me for one moment,' he said, and cupped his hand over the receiver. 'What the fuck is this?' he said, over his shoulder. 'Does anyone know about this?'

Tony Roberts furnished him with a gappy grin from beneath his grey copper's moustache. His drinker's gnarl of nose wrinkled.

'He asked for you.'

'Fuck he asked for me.'

'He did! He said, quote, is there an officer present with red hair?, unquote.'

Holloway grinned. 'Fucking ha ha,' he said. 'What's his name? Do we know him?'

Roberts shrugged and jutted his lower lip, tired of the game now. Holloway flipped him a middle finger and returned to the call.

'How can I help?'

'Is this the officer with red hair?'

'This is Detective Sergeant William Holloway.'

'Please. Do you have red hair?'

Holloway cradled the receiver between neck and shoulder, wheeled himself closer to the desk and scrabbled round for a pen. He extended an arm to its limit and snagged a red biro.

'Well,' he said. 'Auburn, possibly.'

Tony Roberts roared and Holloway grinned over at him.

Waiting, he drew clockwise spirals on blank note paper. He

sighed. Cross-hatched the descending spirals. Drew wavy lines like steam rising from water. 'Sir, I am about to replace the handset.'

'Please. Don't.'

Holloway drew a circular, smiley face.

'Joanne is alive.'

His arm jerked. He dropped the biro and knocked an empty mug, which rotated on its base like a settling puck.

'Who is this?'

'Please listen. I know how this sounds.'

'Sir,' said Holloway, 'do you have information pertaining to the whereabouts of Joanne Grayling?'

'Oh, dearie me,' said Tony Roberts.

Holloway ignored him.

'She's alive,' said the caller. 'She's . . . in a shed or a hut. It's dark and she's afraid. But he hasn't hurt her.'

'I see,' said Holloway. He thought he might pass out. He pinched the tender skin inside his wrist until his mind cleared.

'Please,' said the man. 'I know how this must sound. But please listen to me. There is something to do with trains. There is something to do with trains and water.'

'I see,' said Holloway. 'How did you come about this information?'

The man took a ragged intake of breath.

'I dreamed it.'

Holloway surged with relief.

'I see,' he said.

He wanted to punch the air.

'Please,' said the man. 'Don't hang up.'

'I'm not hanging up, sir. Please continue.'

'Just give me one moment. I know how this sounds.'

'I'm sure you do.'

'Are you able to act on this information?'

'We are doing everything in our power.'

'That's not an answer.'

'But it is an assurance.'

There was a long pause during which Holloway sought to control his breathing.

'Wait,' said the man.

'I am waiting, sir. Do you have any more information?'

'I don't know.'

'I see.'

'Please.'

'Please what?'

'Please listen.'

'I'm listening,' said Holloway. He recited from his notes. 'She is in a shed or a hut. There is something to do with trains.'

'And water.'

'Of course. There is something to do with trains and water.'

As Holloway knew he eventually would, the man replaced the receiver. He listened to the dial tone for a long time.

He would log and report the call. Along with all the others, it would be followed through to source, if possible.

Tony Roberts was just about pissing himself.

'Care in the fucking community,' he said, and shook his head wisely.

Holloway smiled and replied. But his hands were clamped to the desk, anchoring him to the world.

He was cursorily debriefed about the call. Nobody was much concerned by it. It would not be the only crank call taken that day. There would be more tomorrow, and the day after that.

He drove home. The dust in the flat seemed to have settled, as if he were returning from a fortnight's holiday. He touched the walls in the hallway with strange nostalgia and closed the door softly behind him.

He hung his jacket on the bedroom door and ran his head under the cold tap in the bathroom. He looked at himself, pale and mottled, in the bathroom mirror. He put the kettle on and opened a packet of chocolate and hazelnut Boasters. Then he went and logged on.

There was a message from bedford.falls.

He recalled the temptation to throw oneself from a high place, simply because it is high.

Dear Detective Holloway
An unstable man with a history of mental illness is
obsessed by his ex-wife. Consumed by morbid jealousy,
he murders her lover.
Later, he enacts bizarre revenge on the wife by
murdering a whore he has dressed to resemble her.
It doesn't look good, does it?
The materials in our possession will be passed on to your
colleagues in the Avon and Somerset Constabulary if
you dont do exactly as instructed, when instructed.
With all kind regards,
The Friends of George Bailey

Cut and pasted beneath the message text was a scanned newspaper clipping, dated August 1998.

It reported the apparently motiveless murder in Aberdeen of a young man called David Bishop.

He clicked on FILE, then SAVE AS.

The iMac's monitor froze. The desktop image contracted to the screen's centre. The computer seemed about to crash. There was some prolonged internal whirring, after which the computer righted itself with a loud crack. But the message from bedford.falls was no longer there.

Holloway tried not to panic. He did some exploratory clicking round the screen. He explored directory after directory. He performed keyword searches. Nothing worked. The message had gone. All the messages had gone. Nothing he did brought them back.

IV

He phoned Kate. He begged her to see him. Eventually, she named a chrome and blond-wood bar in Clifton and agreed to meet him at 10 p.m.

He was early. He ordered two long gin and tonics and took a freshly vacated table in the far corner, from which position he was able to watch her enter. She passed through the patchy, mid-week crowd with studied elegance and hung her jacket on the back of the chair opposite him.

She said: 'Christ. You look awful.'

'Thanks,' he said. 'How are you?'

She busied herself, rummaging in her handbag and removing a fresh pack of Silk Cut ultra mild.

He said: 'You stopped.'

'I started again.'

Their eyes met. The silence between them was punctuated by the arrival of the drinks. Each took a sip. Then each said the other's name at the same time and laughed.

Each invited the other to speak first.

She said: 'How's your face?'

Holloway rubbed his jaw with the heel of his hand. 'I think he loosened a tooth,' he said. 'One of the big ones. Right at the back.' He gurned and waggled a molar with the tip of his tongue. 'That one,' he said. 'Right at the back.'

She leaned forward and narrowed her gaze. 'Right,' she said, as if she could see. She tutted.

Holloway said: 'Sorry.'

She hooded her eyes.

'What for?' she said. 'Exactly?'

Her manner made him grin and he lifted his eyes.

'Oh,' he said. 'Everything.'

She broke the seal and lit a cigarette.

He said: 'You never told me about the boy.'

She searched his expression for provocation, found only neutrality.

'How could I have?'

He tugged once at the hair on his nape. 'I would have understood,' he said. But his expression admitted the lie. He acknowledged her disbelief with half a wave.

Her face softened. 'Will,' she said. 'It was such a long time ago.'

He knew what she meant. Their marriage was reduced to a sequence of abstract psychological textures and sense impressions. Events had merged and faded. An old argument might be invoked by the scent of his aftershave: the day of his daughter's birth by the sun-baked interior of an empty car. Of the millions of words he and Kate had spoken, he fully recalled not a single sentence.

'Why would he do this?' she said. 'After all this time? How did he even find your address?'

Nevertheless, her betrayal ached like an ancient insult.

'It wasn't him.'

He audited her expression.

'How could you know that?'

It was a question to be evaded.

'Have you seen him?'

'Who? David?'

'Yes. David.'

'What, recently? God no.' She looked at the table. 'Not after that night. That was the last I saw of him. He called a few times. But it was a one-off. It was a bit of a joke, really. Penny thought it was hilarious.'

She smiled, sadly.

Holloway bowed his head. 'It was a bad time,' he said. Kate didn't respond. This was a habitual recital, a euphemism dressed as an acknowledgement.

He lifted the gin, knocked it back, raised his hand to order another.

The hand still raised at shoulder height, he said: 'Was there anyone else I don't know about?'

She clicked her tongue. 'No. There was not.'

He said: 'It's important that you tell me the truth.'

She warned him with her eyes.

There was silence until his drink arrived. He took a big sip. Then he said: 'Is there anything you haven't told me? About that time.'

'Nothing,' she said. 'Why would there be?' She sighed. 'Will, I don't want to go over this and over it. Not again. I can't bear it.'

'What about Adrian?'

'What about him?'

'What does he know?'

'About what?'

'This.'

She said: 'Fuck you,' under her breath and made as if to leave. He reached out a restraining hand.

He said: 'Please. This is important.'

She sat, coat in hand. 'This is *surreal*. I don't believe you're doing this.'

'Doing what?'

'This. Again. We're separated. Get over it.'

'It's not that,' he said. 'Believe me.'

She folded the coat into a bundle on her lap.

'Well. Good.'

'Has he filmed you?'

She recovered the cigarettes from her bag. Her hands shook and it took a while.

'Kate,' he said. 'I need you to be honest.'

She leaned close enough to spray him with spittle. '*No he has not.*'

He had barely slept for thirty-six hours.

'You haven't kept any home movies,' he said '— secretly or otherwise, that Adrian might've found and decided to pop in the post to me?'

'Oh, Christ,' she said. 'Jesus Christ.'

He grabbed her wrist. 'Somebody is trying to get me, Kate. Blackmail me. Or something. Somebody is setting me up for something.'

She squirmed from his grasp.

'This is mad,' she said. 'It's not happening.'

He wanted to punish her. *The boy you fucked is dead*.

There was something in her eyes he had not seen for many years. Fear of him, perhaps. So he calmed down and they talked for a while and he told her not to worry. Then he watched her stand and leave and go home to Adrian.

At home, he thought for a long time about killing himself.

He never fully understood why he chose not to. He just stood there, in the electric light, wondering what he was going to do.

9

The day Shepherd was rejected for a job as a minicab driver, they saw the news about Joanne Grayling.

Shepherd was morose and disheartened. Although Eloise and Lenny privately agreed that his ineptitude must have been truly wondrous, they tried to cheer him up. They ordered a takeaway.

Shepherd turned on the TV. He forked greasy chow mein into his mouth.

They saw the report and others like it four times that evening: twice on the BBC, once on ITV and again on Channel 4.

External shot of a low-rise, red-brick police station. An austere reporter, behind whom various personnel can be seen entering and leaving the building.

Joanne Grayling was last seen driving a black Volkswagen Golf.

She had arranged to meet friends in Bristol's fashionable Clifton
area. Police are very worried for her safety and have appealed for
any member of the public who might have information to come
forward —

A photograph of Joanne. Close-up. Head thrown back.
Laughing. Blurred.

The following morning they watched similar reports on
GMTV and BBC *Breakfast News*.

Absently, Eloise folded a triangle of white toast and Marmite
into her mouth. She wore a long T-shirt and thick woolly socks,
and her sleek, blunt bob was sleep-disordered.

'Jesus,' she said. 'That poor girl.'

Shepherd was on the sofa in his stripy pyjamas. An uneaten
bowl of Cornflakes was warming in his lap. He looked car-
toonish and unkempt. His toenails were horny and
nicotine-yellow.

He looked at Eloise.

'She's alive,' he said.

Eloise wanted nothing to do with it.

'This isn't *research*,' she said, with a twist of real contempt.
She and Lenny were upstairs in the bedroom. 'It's not an *experiment*. It's just another Lenny mind-fuck.'

Lenny laughed.

'Then what harm can it do?'

Late for work, she was hunting for her shoes.

'If he'd dreamed an *address*,' she said. 'Or even a *name*, for
God's sake, I might think differently.'

She looked beneath the bed.

Lenny said: 'But what if it helps the girl?'

'What girl?' said Eloise. She retrieved an alternative pair of shoes from the wardrobe, hastily polished the toes with a cuff. 'She's not a *girl* to you. She's an *objective*. She's just a piece of true crime.'

Lenny looked hurt. He made his most endearing monkey face.

'Come on,' he said. 'That's not fair.'

Eloise balanced on one leg, tugging on a shoe.

She said: 'You know more about dead girls than live ones.'

But when she had gone, Lenny and Shepherd decided to make the call anyway.

Because Lenny assumed that most domestic telephone conversations were recorded, they chose to make the call from a phone box at the top of Holloway Road. Close to a tube station and several main bus routes, it offered various means of escape.

They wore beanie hats and sunglasses. Shepherd towered over Lenny like a toothless fighting bear on a length of chain. Lenny loped along the pavement in Travis Bickle chic: olive drab and faded denim and RayBan Aviators. Not without difficulty, they squeezed into the booth together.

'There is something to do with trains and water,' Shepherd muttered down the line. Clutching the receiver, his knuckles glowed orchid-white through the hairy skin.

At length, he replaced the handset in its cradle. He looked blank.

'Fuck,' he said.

Fearful of passing police cars, they hurried across the road towards Highbury Fields. Here they removed the beanie hats.

They walked to Blackstock road, where they ate a morose, wordless lunch at the Moonshine café.

10

In the early morning, Holloway drew aside the blind.

The world was crisp under a blue sky, like an impossibly accurate scale model. He glanced up and down the street. Other than the sinuous flicker of a startled tomcat, he saw no movement.

He dressed in his best, Italian-cut Marks & Spencer's suit. Blue shirt, iridescent green tie. Suede shoes with rubber soles. Into his jacket pocket he slipped a lock-knife.

Settling behind the wheel of the new, tomato-red Nissan Micra, he popped the ring-pull on a can of Coke and drank it in a single draft. He belched fruitily and started the car, pausing on the corner to turn the radio on. The *Today* programme was just beginning.

It was about to end, handing over to *Midweek*, when he crossed the knotted spine of the Pennines into Yorkshire. It was a melancholy thought that the landscape he considered to be his heartland did not reflect his long absence or mark his return.

He parked at a roadside picnic area and sat on a wooden table close to the lay-by. The wind ballooned his jacket and threw his tie over a shoulder. He scanned the moors.

He did not doubt this land contained a power.

Lesley Anne Downey in the ground.

Peter Sutcliffe.

He remembered cars and vans racing to Manchester, full of young men in Leeds United colours. The exhilaration at the tribalism of it. The blood on the land.

Barry Prudom is our friend.

History telescoped away from him. Chamberlain clasping Victorian lapels. Churchill a mythical animus, soul of the moors, the Sussex downs; the Fens. Hitler a Grail Knight astride a steaming war-horse. The winter sun reflects on silver armour. The horse stamps, impatient, at bloody soil. The old Gods at his shoulder.

As a young constable, Holloway looked out of depth in his uniform, as if it were half a size too large. He took hurt offence at copper's talk. He was faded and weakened after working door-to-door on the Yorkshire Ripper case, and fearful at Elland Road, where thousands of drunken men hated him and chanted:

Barry Prudom is our friend, is our friend
Barry Prudom is our friend,
He kills coppers

Shoots the bastards one by one, one by one
Shoots the bastards one by one
Barry Prudom

Caroline's birth obliged Kate to take a year away from her degree. The three of them lived in a one-bedroom flat above a bakery in Headingley. Kate's university friends didn't come round.

As time passed, the university found ways to accommodate Kate's requirements; certain grants and subsidized childcare facilities were made available to her. She made new friends who did come round.

One day in 1983, Will came home to find Kate's sister cuddling a sticky-faced and noisily protesting Caroline. The next week, Kate's mother and father paid a visit. There were tears of reconciliation and some formal introductions. Kate's father approved of Will, of his determination to do his best by his small family. That Sunday Will and his father-in-law went to the cricket, and the Sunday after that. The following week, her brother came along.

They spent that Christmas at the family house in Manchester. The following year, Kate passed her degree with a good first. Her father offered her a £20,000 loan to subsidize her postgraduate study.

In 1984, busloads of Essex policeman were shipped in to break Yorkshire picket lines. They beat accompaniment on their riot shields and rode superb, chestnut horses as if into battle: brutal mercenaries wielding blood-clotted batons. Legally picketing miners in jeans and T-shirts scattered before their onslaught. Will's tattoos became objects of shame.

He drove on and into Leeds.

The city centre was like a bereaved old friend, returned from abroad with new clothes. A Leeds more familiar to him pulsed beneath the façade of the new, as if it were a projection on a flimsy curtain. He passed the Wool Exchange, turned along the Headrow, the chalky white university clocktower.

In Headingley, at the junction of Hyde Park and Victoria Road, he pulled up outside a detached, stone-built Victorian house. Perhaps formerly impressive, it had crumpled and settled like an old hat. There was a catastrophically overgrown front garden, in the centre of which four stone steps led to the front door.

Self-consciously lackadaisical, listening to music on a portable stereo and smoking Marlboro Lights, four young women and a young man were arranged on the steps. One of the young women was his daughter.

Like the city to which she had elected to return and see out her youth, Caroline was a flickering sequence of superimpositions. Everything she had ever been gleamed faintly round her edges like a corona.

She wore three-quarter-length cargo trousers and rectangular, gold-rimmed sunglasses with green lenses. Nike walking sandals and a plain white cotton vest top. There were no more piercings that he could see, but her hair was even shorter and hennaed into spikes – the kind of haircut students who called themselves punks wore in 1978.

He slammed the Micra's door behind him.

She sauntered over to him, smiling and squinting in the sun. She put her weight on one hip and said: 'Hello, dad.'

He saw himself in her, and Kate: her mother's hips, his colouring, pale skin, heavily freckled. Green eyes, but her mother's nonetheless, that animated her face, even in repose.

It was not possible for a young woman even of Caroline's age to greet a parent without some awkwardness, an imperative to which he capitulated by nodding once, somewhat vaguely, and scowling like James Dean.

'Nice day.'

She stood before him and gently tugged on his lapels. Then she stood back and half turned:

'Have you met everyone? Steve, Becky, Camilla, Lucy?'

He nodded to each in turn, categorizing them half consciously and without guilt. The girls: two white, middle-class. Girls' school, followed by a mixed-sex private sixth form college. The third black, third-generation North African, cropped, bleached hair and the clothes of an androgyne. The boy was slim and louche, in clubber's clothes. Long hair in an elastic band, sideburns. A day's stubble round his chin only and sub-hippie paraphernalia round his neck and wrists. Sinister Oakley sunglasses. A pouch of Golden Virginia and a ripped pack of green Rizlas on the ground next to him.

Holloway glanced briefly over the rim of his sunglasses and said hello. Then Caroline linked her arm through his and led him up the cracked, weedy stone steps, her fellows shifting this way and that to accommodate their passage, into the damp coolness of the hallway. It stank of cat piss.

The old house had been converted into six flats on three floors, including the attic. The cats who pissed in the hallway seemed to be nobody's in particular.

Caroline led him into the first flat on the left, which presumably she shared with one of the girls on the steps outside. It was full of mess, which he automatically assessed and concluded to be exclusively feminine. In the sitting room, an iMac computer sat on a rickety wooden table. Its monitor showed dust and fingerprints. The computer had been a joint gift from Holloway, Kate and Adrian. (Adrian had insisted Holloway be permitted to contribute.) Over it was thrown a pair of blue jeans, turned inside out. Caroline had a thing for Apple Macintosh.

He stood in the centre of the room, watching the traffic of people outside, while Caroline went to the kitchen, from which she returned balancing two mugs and half a pack of chocolate Hob Nobs on a book called *The Gulf War Did Not Take Place*.

She said: 'For God's sake, take off your jacket. You must be boiling.'

He compromised by removing his tie. The air was cool at his throat.

The sofa was orange and swampy. He sank into it, first gingerly, then rather further than he had expected. Hastily, he corrected the balance of the mug. Then he set the tea on the floor and dabbed at his scalded inner thigh with the cuff of his jacket.

He said: 'How are things?'

'Good,' she said. 'My Post Feminism and Popular Culture dissertation is nearly finished.'

He raised his eyebrows. 'Finished?' he said. 'That's amazing. How long did you say it had to be?'

'Fifteen thousand words.'

He looked blank.

'What's that in pages?'

'Oh. I don't know. Loads. Millions.'

'It sounds like it. What's it called now?'

'*Flicking the On Switch*.'

He laughed approvingly and she beamed in response.

'Cheeky monkey,' he said.

She took a half-empty pack of ten Marlboro Lights from the hip pocket of her cargo pants and offered him one. He declined (he had not smoked since New Year's Eve, 1989), but watched her as she lit a battered, bent cigarette with a disposable lighter.

She sat back, exhaling. She crossed her legs and tapped her foot. Her mother's action, recreated precisely and entirely unconsciously.

He felt himself to be in two places, two times, simultaneously.

He said: 'Did you manage to get that address for me?'

He had called her two days before, from a public telephone.

From the same hip pocket she removed a much folded sheet of A4 paper which he took with steady hands.

'Good work,' he said. 'Well done.'

Shortly before he disappeared in 1995, Derek Bliss sold his share of Executive Solutions to his junior partner, Henry Lincoln. In 1997, Henry Lincoln sold Executive Solutions to another detective agency, William Gull Investigations, Ltd, which was based in York.

'Good work,' he said again. 'Clever girl.'

The paper clasped in his fist, he began violently to vibrate.

Caroline said: 'Jesus, dad.'

He looked at his hands. Muscles twitched beneath the skin.

'I haven't slept,' he said.

'You look terrible.'

He asked for sugar and she dashed to the kitchen, returning with a jar of Gale's and a stained teaspoon. Holloway shovelled honey into his mouth. When the jar was empty, he sat back and closed his eyes while Caroline made another cup of tea.

'Dad,' she said. 'You really need to see a doctor.'

'I will,' he said. 'As soon as I get the chance.'

She watched him sip. 'You always say that. Mum thinks it's diabetes.'

'It's not diabetes.'

'Who says?'

'I say.'

'And you're a doctor, are you?'

'Is your mother?'

'At least she knows how to take care of herself.'

Holloway let it drop.

He said: 'I need you to drive me to York.'

She'd been clubbing the night before and didn't feel able to drive. Fiercely protective and full of imagined horrors, he had taught her well. But, after lack of sleep, the drive to Leeds and what he thought of as a hypoglycaemic episode, was in no fit state himself.

She suggested her boyfriend drive them.

Listening to her quiet pleading over the phone, Holloway slipped into a doze from which he woke with a start. Before him stood Caroline and an unshaven, handsome young man in jeans and a hooded sweater. The young man introduced himself as Robert. His hair was short and dark, tightly curled and prematurely thinning at the crown. Holloway liked him. He regretted the manner of their meeting.

In the back seat of Robert's rattletrap Ford Escort, Holloway slept again. Intermittently, he was woken by the sweet sound of his tone-deaf daughter humming along to the radio. It was summer and it was hot, and the songs on the radio sounded old and familiar to him, although they were not.

Even looking back, even knowing he was wrong, Holloway remembered about his marriage only a solar happiness, a ceremonial intensity that lay beneath the surface of the everyday.

His wife and his daughter.

Kate worked long hours. En route to various promotions, she endured the protracted, circular exasperations and temporary setbacks of office politics. Holloway submitted to his own professional incentives: he wanted to get out of uniform, to bring home a detective's salary. During her first two years at secondary comprehensive Caroline had problems which nearly broke his heart. But they solved the problems by moving her to an all-girl's school, where she was happy. There was the death of Kate's father. He remembered Kate sobbing into her fist at the kitchen sink. There was the fond chaos of the family bathroom, his razors blunted on her legs, her roll-on and his aerosol, the tights and socks and knickers and bras spilling from the laundry basket.

But he knew he didn't remember correctly. An absence had gone undetected. Because one day, fourteen years after they married, she told him she was leaving him for Dan Weatherell, a married man, and he punched her face and fractured the orbit of her eye. Then he took a breadknife and sliced open his forearms.

Kate moved Caroline into a house that belonged to Penny, a close friend, herself newly divorced.

Upon being discharged from Leeds General Infirmary, Holloway made a legal undertaking not to contact or come within a fixed distance of her. In exchange, she agreed not to press a charge of GBH with intent.

In the end, Kate didn't go to New Zealand with Dan Weatherell.

She understood the relationship to have reached a natural and amicable end. She never learned that Holloway had driven Weatherell round the back of a darkened trading estate, that he punched Weatherell in the throat and beat him across the head and shoulders and ribs and kidneys with a rubber cosh; that he put a knife to Weatherell's throat until he wept and begged to live.

Weatherell went back to his wife. But there remained no question of Kate's returning to Will.

Holloway grew familiar with the geography of the bedroom ceiling, with each of its minor whoops and undulations. After six weeks, then two months, then three, the Prozac had yet to take effect, had not even diminished his sex drive, for which he secretly had prayed. He was exhausted by the daily exertion of rising from bed and washing and shaving. Paperwork shimmied like heat haze before his eyes. His short-term memory faltered and he had blackouts. He would start and look about himself, and for a moment he would not recall where he was, or to whom he had spoken, or why.

He continued to be tormented by images of Kate's nudity and passion. Jealousy and longing had long ago merged until one could not be distinguished from the other. He fetishized the memory of her body, as he had fetishized the fact of it. He could not become aroused except by the thought of her. He pictured her fucking and being fucked.

Falls

It was for this reason that he contracted Derek Bliss.

It was Bliss who tenderly put the tape in the VCR and turned on the television, it was Bliss who showed him the film. The boy's exposed cock, shining like Vaseline. Kate on her back, muttering something as the boy arches his spine and the cheeks of his ass tighten like a fist.

And Bliss knew what Holloway had done.

Shortly after completing a brief treatment in a psychiatric hospital, Holloway drove to Aberdeen and broke into David Bishop's flat. Bishop and his flatmates were at work, so Holloway spent much of the day watching television: *This Morning* with Richard and Judy, *Countdown*, *15 to 1*. At 5 p.m., before the first of the housemates returned home from work, he concealed himself in David Bishop's wardrobe. He waited there until everyone had come back, eaten, watched TV and eventually gone to sleep. Then he crept from the wardrobe and, in the half-light, he crawled on his hands and knees along the grubby carpet to the edge of Bishop's bed. He pressed a hand down on Bishop's mouth and kneeled on his chest. He rammed a screwdriver through each of Bishop's eyes. Then he wiped his hands on a corner of bedding, let himself out and drove home.

II

Robert pulled up outside the address Holloway had given him: a recessed doorway abutted by souvenir shops.

Holloway kneaded his eyes. He felt shabby and damp.

'Right,' he said.

He slid from the rear driver's side door and stood in cloudless sunlight. Shoals of pensioners parted for him on the narrow pavement. He clapped his hands twice.

'Right,' he said. Once for each clap.

He brushed at the crumpled suit, tucked in the tail of his shirt and straightened the knot of his tie in the wing mirror. He kneeled at the window and told Robert to park the car and wait for him on the corner. Robert pulled away.

The firm announced itself with a modest brass plaque. William Gull Associates Ltd. Private Investigations. Holloway pressed the button on the faux-brass intercom. Waiting for an answer, he checked over the high nooks and corners for CCTV or digital security cameras. Locating none, he wondered if he had looked well enough.

He was admitted by an irritated buzz. The hallway smelled of dust and paint.

He paused at the foot of the stairwell to collect his thoughts. 'Right,' he said, before turning the corner of the first landing. Before him was a door with the company name etched on glass in italic.

Holloway was composed and ready.

He stepped into a reception about the size of a double bedroom. The sash windows, which overlooked the slowly milling street, admitted two diffuse beams of light. A row of modular chairs faced a reception desk, upon which were arranged a telephone and answerphone, a desk diary and a beige PC. Behind the desk sat a neatly comported receptionist in ladies' golf wear, large spectacles on a chain and a fearsome permanent wave.

He asked if Mr Gull was available for immediate consultation. She invited him to wait for one moment, put her head round the corner of an office door, and returned to inform Holloway that Mr Gull would see him shortly.

He supposed the ten minutes he waited symbolized the passive aggression of the struggling small businessman.

When eventually he was invited to go through, he found that Gull's office was bedecked like a psychiatrist's: dark wood panelling, worn leather upholstery. An antique desk, varnish worn pale on the edges and corners. At the windows hung white venetian blinds, edged with dust, through which the light shone opalescent. Three walls furnished with books. It was an interior conceived to promote confidence in a certain clientele.

Gull sat at the desk, his outline softened by the scattered light. On first estimation, with the window behind him, he seemed younger than his sixty-odd years. His hair seemed blond and discrepantly abundant. On second glance, it resolved into a nicotine-yellow thatch, heavily shot with grey. Beneath it, Gull's face had collapsed into gloomy repose. Loose wattles and a drinker's nose. Ex-copper. Broad in the beam. Twenty-five years' service. Pensioned off for some misdemeanour, probably borderline criminal.

He half stood and shook Holloway's hand, invited him to sit. His suit was good enough but greasy at cuff and seat.

'Mr Holloway.' He wrote the name.

'Two l's.'

'Of course.' He laced his hands and said: 'What can I do for you?' But before Holloway could reply, Gull interjected: 'Have we met?'

Holloway lied. 'I don't think so.' He couldn't remember the occasion, but had a brief sense memory of a long-distant summer and cricket whites. The taste of warm Tetley in a plastic glass. A different life.

Gull rolled his tongue along the crenelated roof of his mouth.

'Cricket?' he said. 'Do you play?'

'No,' said Holloway.

Gull was solemn with disbelief. Then, with a papal gesture, he invited confession.

Holloway leaned forward and lifted a spherical glass paperweight from the desk. It was a York Minster snow scene. He sat back and crossed his legs, tossing the paperweight in his palm like a cricket ball. It was about the same weight.

After a measured pause, he said: 'I'm looking for Derek Bliss.'

He indexed the parameters of Gull's hesitation.

'Could you spell that?'

'You know how it's spelled.'

Gull took the nib from the paper and regarded Holloway from beneath a heavily ridged brow.

'I'm sorry?' he said.

'I don't have time for this,' said Holloway.

Gull's eyes were level and did not leave Holloway's.

'Perhaps we should start again. I'm afraid the conversation's gone over my head so far.'

'Five grand,' said Holloway. 'Cash. In your hand. As soon as you tell me where I can find him.'

'So it's a missing person,' said Gull, and pretended to make a note on his pad.

Holloway grinned. 'That's not what I meant.'

Gull sat back in the leather chair. 'Then I'm not sure I can help you.'

'I see,' said Holloway. He stood and said, 'I'm sorry.'

Gull shrugged, amicably.

Holloway put his balance on his back foot, drew back his hand and bowled the paperweight into Gull's head. There was a wet crack. The impact smashed Gull from the chair.

Holloway slid across the desk, reaching into his pocket.

Robert had parked outside a nearby newsagent. At Holloway's approach, Caroline unwound the passenger window.

'What's that?'

'What's what?'

'In the bags.'

'Papers.'

'And what's that?'

'What's what?'

'The wet stuff on your shirt.'

'Nothing,' he said, and got into the car.

As they drove back to Leeds, Holloway flicked through the paperwork Gull had eventually surrendered into his custody. Invoices, receipts, expenses claim forms, affidavits. Photocopied sheets of A4 lifted from hanging files. He scanned pages of text quickly and mechanically, hoping his eyes might settle on a name, an address, anything he recognized. But there was nothing; just the looped reiteration of Gull's too elaborate signature. None of the files predated the sale of Executive Solutions to Gull's firm.

Back at Caroline's house, he made a game of it. He handed a

sheaf of paper to Caroline, Robert, Steve and Camilla and instructed them to look for certain key words and addresses. His name, his wife's. Dan Weatherell's. Joanne Grayling.

Given the official-looking but salacious content of the documents, it proved easy to convince everyone that they were about covert police business. Holloway rather implied he was the kind of maverick copper they all liked to watch on television, which seemed explanation enough. But after several hours they had come across nothing.

Holloway could believe that Derek Bliss had come back to get him. But he couldn't believe that he'd come alone. Bliss was a parading little bantam. (He recalled with horror the contemptuous beads of semen left on the toilet seat.) But nevertheless, Holloway thought of him as an effect. Behind him there was a cause, some grave corruption: somebody who wished to punish and humiliate both Kate and Holloway. It seemed clear to him who that must be.

Bliss had run to Australia. Dan Weatherell lived in Wellington, New Zealand.

It was close enough. Somehow, the two of them had met.

It was not impossible. It wasn't even unlikely. Bliss was an experienced private investigator. The most cursory investigation into Holloway's private life would unearth Weatherell's name. Tracking him down would be elementary.

He imagined them. Hating him. Planning. Concocting.

Close to midnight, he strode wordlessly from the house.

The night was pleasantly warm. He walked towards a phone box he had noticed outside a pizza takeaway on Hyde Park

Corner. He pumped a series of pound coins into the slot and from memory dialled a New Zealand number.

It rang for perhaps half a minute. It was answered by a man with a slow voice.

'Hello.'

Holloway bit down on his lower lip.

'Who is this?'

'You know who this is.'

The line crackled.

'I'm sorry?'

Holloway waited.

'It's Will,' he said.

'Will. Is that you? Will Holloway? Will, Jesus Christ almighty. What's up?'

Holloway sniffed back a tear.

'Why are you doing this to me?'

'Hold on. One moment please.' There followed a series of thumps and crackles. Perhaps the speaker had moved to another room. 'Run that by me again.'

'Why are you doing this to me?'

Pause. 'Will? Is that Will? You're going to have to help me out here, mate.'

'Don't *mate* me, you fucker. You know what I'm talking about. You fucking *know*. You fucker. You unbelievable fucker.'

'Now. Slow down. You're raving. You sound like a *madman*. Slow down. What are you talking about?'

'You know what I'm fucking talking about. Was it Bliss?'

'Was it *what*?'

'Bliss.'

'Was what bliss? Jesus God, what are we talking about here?'

'Was it his idea? Or was it yours?'

'Slow down, mate. Slow down. I'm lost. You lost me way back.'

'I won't go down,' said Holloway. 'No matter what you do to me. I won't go down.'

'Will, has something *happened*? Has something happened I should know about?'

'You're not that clever. You're not that fucking clever. You think you know about cutting people open? I'll tell you what – before I let them send me down, I'll come and find you, you fucking *cunt*, and I'll show you all about cutting someone open. I'll show you what cutting someone open is all about.'

He slammed the receiver down, then lifted it again and smashed the handpiece to pieces against the body of the telephone. He walked back to Caroline's house the long way, his head down.

Back at the flat, he seemed calm.

He was too tired to drive, but he had to be back in Bristol that night. He'd taken a risk by calling in sick.

He'd worry about the car another day. He said: 'What time is the last train?'

She looked at her watch and told him it had probably left an hour before.

Diffidently, Robert offered to drive him overnight and Holloway gladly accepted. Robert and Caroline sat up front in the Micra, listening to muted late-night radio. Holloway wrapped himself in a musty blanket and closed his eyes to the soporific hiss of tyres on empty motorway. His head nodded on his chest. Something wise rested peacefully on his heart and lungs.

Half asleep, he saw his life as a sequence of nodes, moments that broke the mirror pool of memory. Viewed suddenly from a new perspective, they linked in an unexpected sequence and revealed a new pattern.

The pattern was projected inside his daisy-pale lids. Its peripheral codes were expressed by the ebb and flow of traffic, the alternating bands of yellow light that passed over him. As they entered the city limits, its chaotic, non-repeating sequence was expressed in random knots of people and aimless henges of refuse. It was in neon signs that flashed in takeaway windows and in the dispersal pattern of the half-seen homeless.

He understood that he was an agent of this pattern although he could not guess at its meaning or intent.

Waking, he saw the present bend back and pleat around the past.

They pulled up to his door shortly before dawn. Hollow-eyed, he led them inside. Cool dusty smell of rented hallways. The dawn chorus.

Robert moaned, sat in the armchair and put his head in his hands. Caroline put the kettle on. Holloway went to the bathroom and ran cold water over his neck and head. He emerged with a towel wrapped round his shoulders like a boxer. Robert was asleep in the armchair. His head lolled back on his shoulders and he snored softly.

Holloway nodded at him.

'Nice lad.'

Caroline knuckled her eyes. She had stayed awake to keep Robert company.

She said: 'How long since you slept properly?'

He shrugged. 'I don't know. Two days? I slept in the car.'

'I'm worried about you.'

'I'm fine.'

'You're not fine. Have you spoken to mum?'

He nodded.

'And what does she say?'

'About what?'

'About the state you're in.'

'I'm fine.'

She lifted the receiver.

'I'm calling her.'

'What – now?'

'Right now.'

'It's quarter to five.'

She glanced at her watch.

'Then tell me what's happening.'

'Nothing.'

'We've been through this,' she said.

'Through what?'

'You know through what.'

'You don't understand.'

'I'm calling her right now. Look at me. I'm calling.'

'Caroline,' he said. 'Look. I'm under a lot of pressure.'

'I can see that. What pressure?'

'Just pressure.'

'I'll stay,' she said.

'You can't. You've got exams.'
'Not for months. It's the vacation.'
'Caroline,' he said. 'Please.'
But she would have none of it.

He kicked off his shoes and lay otherwise fully clothed on the bed. Caroline woke him at 8.45. He had been dreaming about Derek Bliss. He sat up with a start. It took some time to work out where he was and how Caroline came to be there. He thought he might have dreamed Leeds until he saw the dry brown splatter pattern on his blue shirt.

The station had called. 'You have to go in right now,' she said. 'It's urgent.'

Before he had time to clean his teeth, a police car was waiting outside, its blue light silently spinning. He made them wait until he was at least presentable and kissed Caroline goodbye. He knew the driver well and bid a grim hello. They stopped off on the way to the station and he bought breakfast, American Hard Gums, a KitKat and two cans of Coke.

11

That morning the station had received a ransom demand, a laser-printed sheet of A5, postmarked Cardiff and addressed to James Ireland, the chief investigating officer. Among other things, the letter specified that Detective Sergeant William Holloway should deliver the ransom.

The criminal psychologist assigned to the abduction did not consider this demand exceptional. In fact, such an injunction accorded with the psychological profile she had compiled of the suspect. Despite the use of the first person plural in all communications received thus far, she believed him to be a white male in his mid-forties or early fifties, working alone. He would be of high intelligence but largely self-taught and without advanced formal qualifications. He was likely to be a working-class grammar-school boy. He lived alone – plenty of time to deliberate and plan – but had at least one failed marriage behind him, possibly two or more. He was prone to brooding, did not relate well to women and had few close friends. There was a high probability of previous convictions, although he had not gone so far as kidnapping. Possibly he had tried to blackmail an employer or corporation that had provoked his wrath. Perhaps he had threatened to tamper with baby food, or off-the-shelf medications. He had some knowledge of police procedure and may have applied to join the force and been rejected. There might be a physical disability or – given his probable age – perhaps he hadn't met previous height restrictions.

The suspect believed the world to have done him a great and sustained wrong, for which he in some way held the constabulary responsible. Why else demand ransom from the police, if not to humiliate and taunt them with his intellectual superiority? A more uncomplicated kidnapper would seek to avoid the authorities altogether. A great deal of thought had gone into formulating and executing this plan, which must have altered from revenge fantasy to workable reality in tiny increments over many years. The crime was not sexually motivated: at its heart lay his drive to personal vindication. He saw the kidnapping of Joanne as a matter of logistics. He would prefer to release her alive because he believed the public would then admire him as a latterday Robin Hood. But he would kill her if he felt he had to.

Possibly Holloway had arrested him in the past (this was already being looked into). But it was equally possible the two had struck up a conversation in a pub or on a train or in a café.

Either way, he wanted Holloway to be the bagman.

*

Jim Ireland was long, dolorous and hunched. He told Holloway that the ransom demand had only been received following an interminable season of taunts and threats.

The amount requested, £185,000, was uncommonly specific and relatively low considering the effort entered into. It was likely to have a specific, highly symbolic significance. It might relate to money the suspect believed was owed to him. He had also demanded that £25,000 be paid into two bank accounts, for which two cash cards and a PIN would be provided. Since cash withdrawals could easily be traced, this was probably the kidnapper again asserting the superiority of his cunning. Acting on the psychologist's advice, the police had decided to meet these demands.

Then Ireland showed Holloway the letter that had arrived that morning:

The monies will be delivered by Detective Sergeant William Holloway.

From 7 p.m. tonight, W. H. will drive clockwise round the one-way system in Bristol city centre. He must have petrol sufficient for at least 200 miles. He should carry a pen, paper, and a pocket A–Z of Bristol and the West Country, but no radio or other transmitter.

We will send a message to him via the POLICE STATION. It will not be possible to trace this message. The message will be relayed to W. H. on a mobile phone provided for this purpose. W. H. will be instructed to proceed to a certain telephone box at a certain time, where he will receive further instruction. The mobile

phone must then be discarded from the driver's side
window. We will be observing to ensure this happens. If
it does not happen you will not see Joanne again.

All messages will be prerecorded. No further
communication will be entered into. The monies
should be in equal quantities of £50, £20 and £10 notes,
wrapped with the cashcards in polythene of at least 120
microns, then taped with parcel tape. The package will
then be wrapped in a double layer of brown paper and
tied by a nylon cord with a looped handle. The
package is to measure no more than 400 mm x 400 mm
x 100 mm.

Detective W. H. must keep this package visible at all
times, under his right arm. He will be directed to a
series of different telephone boxes. In one he will find a
plastic box about the size of a paperback book, on top
of which will be two LED bulbs: one red, one green.
The red light is an ANTI-TAMPER device. Any
attempt to interfere with the box will cause this light to
illuminate. The green light is a TRANSMITTER-
DETECTOR.

If either of these lights illuminate no further
communication will be entered into and Joanne will
remain nowhere, forever. In addition, within seven days,
we will derail a passenger train using two rigid steel
joists. This will result in multiple fatalities.

Any attempt to use road blocks, bugging devices,
helicopters, satellite observation, marker dye or hidden
transmitters will be detected and will result in the death

of Joanne and the derailing of a passenger train with
massive loss of life.

No attempt should be made to follow Detective W. H.
He will be followed over quiet roads that can easily be
checked and any pursuing aircraft will be heard.

If these instructions are carried out to the letter and
the monies found to be in a fit state, the location of
Joanne will be made known to you and you will never
hear from us again.

The Friends of George Bailey

Holloway read the letter three or four times. He asked if the
stuff about anti-tamper devices and transmitter detectors could
be true.

'Who knows?' said Ireland. 'Who wants to take the risk?'

Ireland talked him through options that had already been
discussed at great length: if they ignored his threats and tried to
negotiate, there was a good chance the kidnapper would act on
them. A dead girl would be bad enough, a derailed passenger
train quite another. Two rigid steel joists hammered upright
between rail tracks would project an express train off the rails
like a missile.

They could disseminate a false profile to the media, calling
the kidnapper sexually immature, homosexual and education-
ally subnormal, hoping to provoke him into unplanned action
that revealed his whereabouts. But Ireland called this 'pretty
dangerous stuff'. If the kidnapper hated the police now, how
would he feel then? He might derail a train just to punish
them.

The only option available was to concede to the kidnapper's demands: pay the ransom and trust the psychologist that he was likely to give the girl back. Then they could concentrate on catching him. Such men always slipped up eventually. It was a question of patience.

It was not thought necessary or desirable that Holloway learn the mechanics of the investigation, so for an hour or two he was left to his own devices. He went to his desk and waited. All incoming calls were diverted and monitored. He stared at some paperwork. Then he picked up a copy of the psychological profile and read it through again.

Aspects of it described Bliss as far as Holloway knew him. But it also described Holloway to an acceptable degree of accuracy. The resentment for the police force could be recalibrated as the repressed fury of a man passed over for promotion once too often.

He switched on his mobile and called Caroline. 'I'll be home late,' he said. 'Look. I'll leave my keys behind the desk. Why don't you and Robert pop round and get a copy cut? I'll leave you a few quid to spend. Go for a drink. See the sights of Bristol.'

Arranging this killed a few minutes: putting keys in the envelope, looking for a marker pen, writing her name carefully in block capitals, walking to the desk, leaving the envelope and instructions with the desk sergeant.

When he got back, the criminal psychologist was waiting for him. In kitten heels, she topped six feet and, ample as she was, moved with expansive theatricality. She wore a rather glamorous trouser suit.

'Jenny Lowe.'

Holloway shook her hand.

'Right,' she said, and indicated that he should follow her into Ireland's purloined office. 'We don't have much time.'

Holloway and Dr Lowe spent several hours role-playing future scenarios. Lowe played the kidnapper, extrapolating from her profile how he might behave under stress.

This involved the psychologist bellowing at and insulting Holloway like an enraged sergeant major until her throat hurt and his head rang. She made him flustered and confused. He wondered how much worse the day could get.

Because there was no way to know if the kidnapper was bluffing about his technical expertise, wiring the car was not deemed worth the risk. Nor was concealing an armed officer in the boot or attempting to follow Holloway by car or helicopter.

At 5.30, he climbed behind the wheel of the tomato-red Micra. His peculiar apathy was exaggerated by the seven or eight trips he took clockwise round Bristol's central one-way system. He found himself stopping at the same lights, reading and rereading the same billboard posters; overtaking and being trapped behind the same buses.

The mobile phone they'd given him rang at 7.40 p.m. Somebody had programmed it to play (Everybody Was) Kung Fu Fighting.

Ireland directed him to a phone box outside a Thresher's off-licence on the Wells Road, not far from the Three Lamps. He reminded him to discard the mobile: Holloway tossed it mock-ostentatiously from the window. Then he nudged the accelerator.

He was outside the off-licence by 7.50. He parked, walked to the phone box: ran back to the car, picked up the package, jammed it under his right arm and walked to the phone again. It rang on the stroke of 8 p.m. and he lifted the receiver.

The recorded voice on the line belonged to Joanne Grayling. She read haltingly, like someone struggling to decipher bad handwriting.

There was a noise in his head like a television tuned to static.

She directed him to a telephone box in Dutton Road, Stockwood, BS14. He would receive further instructions at 8.20. He should remember he was being watched.

Returning to the car, he paused to dry-heave into his fist. Behind the wheel, he consulted the *A–Z*. Dutton Road was a long, crosier-shaped street that ran off Sturminster Road, which was the main conduit to Stockwood, a council estate on the south-east edge of town. He drove there at speed.

It was a narrow street, lined by identical council houses. Cars had parked on either kerb and it took him some time to negotiate the main length of the road and find the telephone box. The phone had been ringing for perhaps thirty seconds when he lifted the receiver.

In the same monotone Joanne told him to run his hand over the base of the telephone unit, where he found taped a set of car keys. They belonged to a patched and dented Ford Capri parked opposite the booth. This was to be his vehicle for the rest of the journey.

He looked left and right. A mixed group of adolescents passed by and a local hard man with a mullet walked a Staffordshire bull terrier to the fields. On the corner, two young women in short skirts were deep in conference over a pushchair. Nobody seemed interested in him.

Briefly, he familiarized himself with the dashboard of the Capri. Then he drove through a low-rise shopping centre and along a road lined by matching houses. The late summer sun was setting and clouds were beginning to gather. Soon a fat droplet of rain exploded on his windscreen. Stockwood faded away behind him and he found himself in the countryside. He experienced some difficulty negotiating Bristol Hill, a steep, twisting lane leading into Keynsham. Here he took another set of instructions in a public payphone outside the Methodist church.

He was directed to Stanton Drew. It would have been a long drive even had he not been in an unfamiliar car that did not handle well, and had there not been heavy rain, and had he not taken one wrong turn after another, reversing from roads that revealed themselves to be treacherous muddy lanes, back on to directionless B roads, and into shifting curtains of rain.

Eventually he found it: a small village that spiralled from the hub of an ancient pub, whitewashed and thatched. In its grounds stood the remains of a druidic stone circle.

A red phone box stood on a small green outside the pub, next to a rotting park bench. Holloway was ten minutes late. The journey from car to phone left him sodden; he stood in the phone box jogging from foot to foot, pleading under his breath for it to ring. When at last it did, he snatched it up and barked: 'Hello.'

Joanne's recorded voice did not mention his tardiness. As he listened, a bead of water vibrated on the tip of his nose.

On the way back to the car, he slipped into the pub. Inside was polished mahogany and winking horsebrass. The rain drummed insistently on the walls and windows. He ordered a pint of Coca-Cola, no ice, and drank it in a single draft. He belched off the excess gas outside, as thunder cracked and rolled above him. The rain turned to hail.

He rested his forehead on the wheel until the spasm of hail had passed, then drove on.

At a phone box on the junction of two B roads near Somerton, he was given a long set of instructions that he hurried to get on paper, balancing the package on one raised knee and using it as a writing surface. He was told to search the long grass behind the phone box. Outside, on his hands and knees (the package still tucked under his right arm and his spiral-bound notebook stuffed in his inside jacket pocket) he found what one might expect to find in the long grass outside a rural call box. He also found a Huntley and Palmer biscuit tin that had been sealed with waterproof tape.

In the humid interior of the Capri, his wet hair in spikes, he picked and bit at the end of the tape as the rain drummed on the roof. Inside the tin he found a plastic package about the size of a paperback book. On its upper surface were two LEDs. After testing its convincing weight in the palm of his hand, Holloway set the box on the dashboard, as instructed. There was also a Motorola consumer walkie-talkie handset in there. He'd seen them in Dixons. He lay it on the passenger seat, face up.

His scribbled notes led him in a roundabout way to Glastonbury; then back along the A361, past the tor, which stood vertical against the darkening sky like a broken finger. On towards Frome.

By now the rain had eased off and it was darkening. Cloud cover like dirty pewter. There was no moon. He raced along B roads: stopped alongside dripping hedgerows and hunched beneath the car's interior light, cross-referencing the *A–Z* with his notes.

On B roads and half-forgotten tracks, he bypassed Shepton Mallet, then Frome (via Lower Whatley and Great Elm). At 10.45 he arrived in Saltford, a commuter town outside Bristol fading into slow decline. So far, the intricate directions had taken him in a rough circle. They led him now in a decreasing spiral through Saltford itself, its quiet streets and shopping centre, and on to the south-eastern edge of town. Finally, he pulled off the A4 and on to a muddy side track. He killed the engine.

Outside, the night was cool. The clouds were beginning to thin. He caught a passing glimpse of stars.

He had parked on the periphery of a deteriorating suburban golf course. Its chainlink boundary fence hung loose on crooked posts. Several hundred metres to his right, a long row of council houses backed on to a few acres of allotment.

The night was still and damp. His clothing rustled loudly when he moved. Ahead of him, at the edge of the muddy and rutted track, a road cone had been placed beneath the shadow of a stunted tree. He tipped it. Underneath was a white-painted brick, attached to which was a laminated piece of A5 paper. It read:

GO TO THE RIVER → → → → → →

Behind him, a tangled hedgerow bordered a steep embankment. He beat his way through the chest-high bushes. The foliage whipped at his eyes. Coming to the edge, he saw the embankment plunge abruptly to a footpath, directly alongside which surged the river Avon. Gripping the parcel between right arm and ribcage, Holloway clambered down to the path. Although he took a shallow descent, he lost his balance and slithered the final few metres on hands and knees. The parcel came to rest in a shallow puddle, one corner overhanging the river.

He regained his feet and made a brief effort to wipe mud from his knees. He stood in darkness. Beside him, the river slapped quietly at grassy banks. The embankment obscured the few lights of Saltford that might have provided some comfort. The narrow, muddy footpath extended into the darkness before and behind him. On the opposite bank was a railway track.

As he spotted another white brick a dozen metres ahead, a passenger train hurtled past on the far bank; a headlong explosion of noise and light.

Its passing seemed to compound his loneliness. He was keenly aware that nobody in the world knew where he was, except the man who wanted him to be here.

There is something to do with trains and water.

The thought brought him up short.

He almost stumbled over the white brick. The attached laminate message read:

NOW GO TO THE BRIDGE → → → → → →

The going was difficult; several times he nearly slipped into the river. Several times he was tempted to let himself. He imagined his floating head, driven downstream by the irresistible current. He knew how cold the water would be just a metre below the surface, and how deceptively powerful. Death by drowning. Andrew Winston Taylor. William Holloway.

After half a kilometre of precarious slipping and sliding, a railway bridge began to resolve from the darkness before him.

She is in a shed or a hut.

He paused, then steeled himself and passed under the bridge. For a few seconds the darkness was perfect. He held a hand before him like a blind man. Fingertips brushed slimy brickwork: he heard the furtive activity of rats. On the far side, he paused to recover the breath he'd held.

The walkie-talkie handset beeped. It took a few moments, first to identify the source of the sound, then find the receiver. It beeped again, twice. He lifted the handset to his ear, pressed SPEAK and uttered one, quiet word:

'Hello?'

The handset crackled.

'Attach the parcel to the rope.'

He did not recognize the voice.

He looked round, then up. A rope was uncoiling in loops from the bridge above him. Its end dangled at face height. It looked like a climbing rope. Difficult to trace, of course; paid for in cash at Millet's. To the end was attached a climber's D clip: the kind of fastener a mountaineer or an abseiler might secure himself to.

There is something to do with trains and water. She is in a shed or a hut.

The handset crackled again.

'Attach the loop at the top of the parcel to the D clip and secure it.'

Holloway stuck the handset in his pocket and set the parcel on the footpath. He took hold of the rope –

She is in a shed or a hut.

– and began to unscrew the restraining arm of the D clip.

The rope hung like a plumb line. It ascended into darkness. He could not imagine who stood at its end.

He yearned for the security of the Capri, to which he had developed a fond attachment. He longed for it, abandoned and unlocked near the allotments.

She is in a shed or a hut.

'Attach the loop at the top of the parcel to the D clip and secure it.'

The sheds on the allotment overlooked the steep embankment. From one of their small windows, it might be possible to see the embankment, the river, even the railway line on the far bank.

There is something to do with trains and water. She is in a shed or a hut.

'Attach the loop at the top of the parcel to the D clip and secure it.'

He pressed the TALK button.

He whispered: 'Derek? Derek, is that you? Is that who this is?'

'Attach the fucking loop at the top of the parcel to the D clip and secure it.'

Although the embankment was muddy and steep, Holloway thought he could get to the allotments quicker than whoever stood in the darkness above him.

'Is that you, Derek?' he said. 'Are you up there?'

'I'll ask once more. Remember your warnings. Attach the loop at the top of the parcel to the D clip and secure it.'

Holloway cupped the D clip in his hand and held it there, feeling its weight, the slack loop of rope.

Stranger things had happened. You couldn't spend twenty years as a copper and not hear stories.

There is something to do with trains and water. She is in a shed or a hut.

Men he respected, thoughtful, hunched over pints, sharing strange anecdotes about people who knew things they could not have. Cases solved. Bodies located.

People saved.

If he could recover Joanne, he could make everything all right. At worst, he could buy her silence with his own.

She is in a shed. She is alive.

He closed the D ring in his fist and jerked down. He was rewarded with a surprised grunt and the sound of feet scrabbling for purchase on gravel above him.

'Fuck you, Derek,' he said. He picked up the parcel and ran.

The embankment was no easier to climb than it had been to descend, but at least he was able to use both hands, slipping his wrist through the loop at the top of the parcel. Tufts of grass and scrub bore his weight: his feet slipped this way and that.

His breath wheezed and rattled. He saw erupting spirals of colour.

He heard a small engine being kicked into life on the railway bridge, probably a motor scooter. But by then he stood on the crest of the embankment. Briefly, he became snared and disorientated in a bramble bush, on the other side of which he found a muddy path leading back to the road. Once there, he took another a few seconds to orientate himself. Then he ran at speed to the allotments.

He clambered over a collapsed chainlink fence. There were eighteen plots, two rows of nine. Each terminated in a decrepit hut big enough to keep a few tools in, some packet seeds, perhaps a kettle and a mug or two. Peas climbed bamboo poles. There were neat rows of cabbages and potatoes, plants he could not identify. Wet soil clegged up the soles of his shoes as he ran to the door of the first shed, calling her name. The rotten door ripped easily from its hinges. The shed smelled pleasantly of soil, dampness, old wood and paraffin. But there was nobody inside.

He swore, ran to the next shed, wrenched its flimsy door aside. Then a third. A fourth.

The Motorola handset buzzed. A stitch pierced Holloway's ribs. He bent double, one hand resting on his knee, and put the handset to his ear.

Holloway could hear the moped's engine, idling in the background.

The man on the line said: 'I hope you know you've killed her.'

He wanted to answer, to say something, but his breath was too laboured.

'I'm going to rip out her windpipe with my fingers.'

Holloway looked at the sky. Through a clearing in the clouds he saw the glinting of an aeroplane's lights. He wondered where it was headed. Gravity seemed to have weakened around him.

He pressed the SPEAK button.

'Please, Derek,' he said. But there was no reply.

He heard the moped's engine straining as it droned away.

Holloway watched the movement of clouds across the moon.

He wondered if it might be possible to explain what he had done.

Some part of the kidnapper's purpose – Derek Bliss's purpose – had been to enact a contest. To taunt and humiliate. The police. Holloway.

Perhaps the psychic who called him had been an accomplice. Perhaps this is simply what Bliss sought to prove: that a desperate man will believe anything.

Holloway took a last look round. He thought about what Bliss knew.

Then he began to run.

Part Two

The Road to Ruin

At core, men are afraid women will laugh at them.
At core, women are afraid men will kill them.
Gavin De Becker, 'The Gift of Fear'

12

Not long after James Ireland picked up the phone and told his superiors that DS William Holloway might not be coming back, an anonymous tip-off to the *Evening Post* led the police to Joanne Grayling's body. She was in a hut alongside a disused railway siding just outside Keynsham, a small town between Bristol and Bath.

Joanne's naked cadaver was propped against the wall in a sitting position. Her arms had been hacked off at the elbows and placed upright in two mock-crystal vases that had been placed on a low table in the far corner. She had been decapitated and her head placed in her lap. The officer who found her screeched like a child when his torch beam passed across her eyes.

In lipstick, the word KATE had been written on her body in words that ran from pubis to breastbone.

*

In the weeks that followed, Shepherd barely left his attic room. In his stripy cotton pyjamas, he looked like a cartoon hippopotamus.

Every morning Lenny brought him a pile of newspapers. It was the *Sun* which first named the police officer assigned to deliver the ransom as the prime suspect. A predictable and ferocious uproar followed. James Ireland's judgement was called publicly into question. Questions were asked in the Commons. The home secretary and the chief constable reiterated their absolute support.

With the newspapers Lenny brought a pack of Rich Tea biscuits and a chipped, bone-china mug of tea on a stained tray commemorating the wedding of Prince Charles and Lady Diana Spencer.

Shepherd scanned the headlines.

The Avon and Somerset Constabulary commenced a damage-limitation exercise whose effect was limited by the collective furore. The public was reminded that nobody had yet been charged with the murder of Joanne Grayling, and that several lines of investigation were currently being pursued. But the assembled media were not in the mood to doubt. When a costly manhunt failed to locate Holloway (leading to the widely-voiced accusation that it had been organized solely for its public relations value), the media's carnivorous attentions turned to his estranged wife and daughter, who moved first into protective custody, then hiding.

Since Holloway continued to be nowhere, the police announced their wish to interview two members of the public who might have information helpful to the inquiry. They were particularly keen to speak to the caller who tipped them off to Joanne's whereabouts. Additionally, they wanted to speak to the clairvoyant who had called Holloway at the station. This anonymous caller had described Joanne's location in some detail. It was intimated that the two might be the same man — perhaps somebody who knew something about the killing, but was afraid to come forward. Possibly the calls were made by an innocent witness, or witnesses. Either way, the police wanted to speak to the man, or men in question. He was assured repeatedly, in the press and on television, that he was in no legal trouble and his anonymity was guaranteed. But in the hope that somebody might recognize and identify his voice, a recording of the clairvoyant's call was to be played on that month's BBC *Crimewatch*.

The programme went out the following Thursday.

Rachel Taylor settled down on the sofa and prepared to watch. She'd taken an interest in the case when first she realized that, not long ago, the prime suspect had sat on that very sofa, sipping a glass of water. It seemed absurd that William Holloway, whom she had taken to be a temperate man, had done something so bestial.

At night she dreamed of testifying on his behalf.

That Holloway had disappeared with a bag of money connected him to Andrew. In the moments before going to sleep, or mesmerized at her computer, she sometimes wondered if there might not be some deeper interdependence, something that rippled through time and linked their two souls. Perhaps Holloway had looked too hard for Andrew, had shuffled through those photographs too often; had tapped Andrew's mind and understood too readily whatever it was he found there. Andrew's suicide and the murder of Joanne Grayling resonated with a muttered implication, a tremor like the drowsy shudder of the earth beneath her feet. At night the house seemed to rustle with the movement of spirits. For the first time in many years, she slept with the light on.

Alone of her three children, Steven joined her to watch the programme. He was so unlike his more robust, non-identical twin: to his brother Adam the notion that something might be wrong with mum was inconceivable and not to be borne. Annie was sleeping over at a friend's. She saw her father's death as a kind of mendacity. She had not yet acknowledged that Andrew's suicide cast complex new shadows in their family history. Because there was nobody else to blame for this sudden, unlatched vertigo, she blamed her mother. Rachel was baffled by the ill-tempered reticence of her daughter's grief, which was complicated further by the hormonal *el Niño* her adolescence was turning into.

So Rachel and Steven Taylor watched *Crimewatch* curled up alone together on the big, red sofa. They had Coke and wine and Doritos with guacamole dip.

The presenter reminded them that they were to hear the tape of a phone call made by a self-professed psychic to DS William Holloway, shortly before the murder of Joanne Grayling. Anyone who recognized the voice could phone *Crimewatch* free of charge.

Against the visual clue of rotating tape spool in close-up, Holloway said his name against the background hiss.

('Is that him, mum?'

'Yes,' she said. 'Shhh,' and nudged him in the ribs with her
elbow.)

How can I help?

Is this the officer with red hair?

This is Detective Sergeant William Holloway.

Please. Do you have red hair?

Well. Auburn, possibly.

[Laughter in the background]

Sir, I am about to replace the handset.

Please. Don't . . . Joanne is alive.

Who is this?

Please listen. I know how this sounds.

*Sir. Do you have information pertaining to the whereabouts of
Joanne Grayling?*

*She's alive. She's . . . in a shed or a hut. It's dark and she's afraid.
But he hasn't hurt her.*

I see.

*Please. I know how this must sound. But please listen to me.
There is something to do with trains. There is something to do with
trains and water.*

Rachel leaned towards the television. She watched through
narrowed eyes. She indicated with her hand that Steven should
keep quiet. He lay an uncrunched Dorito silently on the arm of
the sofa.

She is in a shed or a hut. She is alive.

'That's Andrew's voice,' she said. 'That's your dad.'

Steven reached out and touched her shoulder.

'It just *sounds* like him, mum,' he said.

Suddenly, savagely, her eyes welled. She hugged her boy

fiercely. But she looked over his shoulder all the same, committing to memory the number on the bottom right-hand corner of the screen.

Shepherd, Lenny and Eloise watched the programme in a shared state of disbelief.

Eloise heard out the tape of her tenant's voice and stood.

'Well, that's just great,' she said. 'Thank you both, very much.'

Lenny said: 'If it's all just coincidence, what are you so bothered about?'

'Because you've made me feel involved,' she said. 'And I'm not.' She paused in the doorway. 'Jack,' she said. 'Go to the police.'

She left the room.

Lenny had no answer. He rolled a cigarette and looked at Shepherd, who sat with rigid spine, hands splayed on knees, staring at the muted television. He could not fully appreciate that the police were actually looking for him. The absurdity and the humiliation were more than he was able to reconcile. Something under the surface of things had spun wildly out of control, something whose shape seemed to change each time he caught a glimpse of it in the corner of his eye.

He said: 'Do I really sound like that?'

'Sorry?' said Lenny.

'My accent. Is it that strong?'

Lenny looked at him strangely.

'Yes,' he said, and left the room.

Lenny followed Eloise to the kitchen. She was uncorking a

bottle of wine. She poured a glass and drained it; refilled the glass and drained it again. Then she drew the back of a hand across her upper lip.

'It's just so stupid,' she said.

She set the glass on the scarred kitchen table.

'Anyway,' she said with obscure bitterness. 'Fuck it. What does it really matter? What's one more dead girl, in the grand scheme of things?'

Joanne Grayling was buried in a small Church of England cemetery in Cheltenham. The funeral was attended by her extended family, university friends, school teachers and neighbours. After consultation with the chief constable, it was decided that no representative of the Avon and Somerset Constabulary would attend.

The churchyard was girdled by an eagerly sombre throng of onlookers, news reporters and local police. Her interment was the third lead story on the television news.

Along with many hundreds of others, Jack Shepherd sent flowers. He looked for them on TV, stacked against the low wall of the graveyard, close to the metal railings. But he didn't see them.

13

The following Monday, Shepherd caught an early train to Bristol.

It squatted on the skyline, lowering at its returning son. As the train bisected its raggedy suburban edges, it opened its maw to receive him.

He stepped from the train. Temple Meades reared above him. Its interior was like an industrial tabernacle. He imagined it filled with steam and smoke. Men and women in Victorian dress.

Hiking the Adidas bag over his shoulder, he saw himself in the window of W.H. Smith. The image was transparent. He looked prophetic and spectral, towering over passers-by. His eyes were piggy and squinting behind the wire-framed granny glasses. Head shaved bald and wild beard shot through with grey.

The bitter, powdered old women in the taxi rank kept a twisted eye on him. The accent had become foreign.

He caught a taxi to the police station. He watched Bristol go past. The Hippodrome. College Green. Park Street. The banks on Whiteladies Road.

The taxi dropped him outside the station. He waited before going in. The televised news broadcasts had made the building familiar, but its proximity had no effect on him. It was too studiously neutral, like a municipal library. The news crews had long departed.

Inside, it smelled like school. The desk sergeant hunched over a mug of milky tea and a tabloid newspaper. Shepherd approached the desk. The officer obscured the newspaper with a meaty forearm.

He greeted Shepherd with the irked cordiality of all men who wore epaulets.

Shepherd set the Adidas bag on the floor. He said: 'I'm here to see Detective Inspector Ireland.'

DI Ireland was not available. The desk sergeant offered to find someone else.

Shepherd told the desk sergeant why he was there. The officer didn't change his expression or miss a beat. 'One moment,' he said, and lifted the receiver on his desk phone. As he spoke, he glanced from Shepherd to the phone, from the phone to Shepherd.

Shepherd retreated. He planted himself in a moulded plastic chair too small to properly accommodate his bulk. While he waited, he tried to read the *Guardian*. His teeth hurt.

A middle-aged officer with cropped, thinning hair had

emerged from behind the reinforced doorway before Shepherd had unfolded the sports section. The officer introduced himself as Sergeant Graham Newell.

Newell led Shepherd to a stale and windowless interview room. He invited him to sit at a cigarette-burned Formica table. They were joined by a young WPC.

Newell asked if he would like a drink. He said no.

Newell broke the seal on a new cassette and loaded the tape deck. He pressed RECORD. Then he introduced himself again. He named the WPC as Constable Hadley.

He read out Shepherd's name and the date and time. Shepherd was given a full caution, then reminded that he had not been arrested. Actually, he'd begun to wonder. He was free to leave the station at any time. He was entitled to free and independent legal advice. If he wished, he could speak to a solicitor, on the telephone if he preferred. Newell asked if he understood. Shepherd nodded. Newell asked him to speak aloud for the tape. Shepherd said: 'Yes.'

Newell referred to a sheaf of documents. He cleared his throat.

He said: 'So. Mr Shepherd. According to what you've told me here, it was you who phoned DS William Holloway at this station at 3.37 p.m. on —' he referred to his notes, and read the date. 'At this time you attempted to communicate certain information concerning the whereabouts of Joanne Grayling, who at that time was considered to be a missing person.'

'That's correct.'

'Can you tell me why you did that?'

'Yes. I had a dream.'

'You had a dream.'

'Yes.'

'Could you give me a bit more detail?'

'That's all there is.'

'Well now. Let's see if it is. What did you dream *about*, exactly?'

'Joanne Grayling.'

'I see. And did you know Joanne Grayling?'

'No.'

'Had you ever met Joanne Grayling?'

'No.'

'To your knowledge, had you ever seen Joanne Grayling?'

'No. Never.'

'I see. And DS William Holloway?'

'No.'

'Well, you *phoned* him. You asked to speak to him.'

'I did not.'

'Then why are you here, Mr Shepherd?'

'Not by name, I mean. Not specifically.'

There was a great deal more. Eventually Newell stopped. He composed himself and drew in a long breath. He tugged at an earlobe.

He asked if Shepherd wanted to clarify anything. Then he looked at his watch. He said: 'Interview concludes,' and recited the time. He removed the tape and sealed it with a label he took from his breast pocket. He asked Shepherd to counter-sign. Then he handed him a piece of paper that documented the purposes to which the tape could be put and the conditions in which it would be kept.

Newell excused himself. He left WPC Hadley in the corner.

Shepherd tried to read the handout. It was dull. He flattened it on the burned table. A headache pressed down on his eyes.

At length the door opened again. A gangling, funereal man in a suit and loosened tie entered the room.

'Mr Shepherd?'

'Yes.'

'My name is James Ireland. Please come with me.'

He followed Ireland up a resounding flight of stairs into a small office cluttered with filing cabinets and paperwork in various degrees of disarray. Ireland sat behind the desk and invited Shepherd to sit. They were joined by a large woman in a carmine trouser suit and a fringed pashmina. She introduced herself to Shepherd as Dr Jenny Lowe and sat alongside him, just within his peripheral vision.

Ireland assured him again that he had not been charged with anything. He was not a suspect, but they were very keen to eliminate him from the inquiry. He had not been charged with anything. He could speak quite openly without fear of ridicule or censure.

He played a tape of Shepherd's conversation with Holloway.

Sir, I am about to replace the handset.

Please. Don't . . . Joanne is alive.

Who is this?

Please listen. I know how this sounds.

Ireland stopped the tape.

'Is that your voice?'

'Yes.'

Ireland massaged his temple with a thumb. He rested his eyes for a moment.

'And you live in . . .'

'North London,' said Shepherd. 'Near Highbury.'

'Near the Arsenal?'

'Quite.'

'I've been there,' said Ireland, 'once or twice. When I was younger. To see Liverpool away. Couldn't face it now. London's a bit much for me.'

'I know what you mean.'

'I'll bet. You don't sound like a Londoner.'

'No. I'm from Bristol.'

Something in the room tightened.

'Oh, I see. Where in Bristol?'

'Well, I was born in Frenchay. Then I lived in Redland.'

'It's nice, Redland. Nice area. When did you leave?'

'Ooh.' Shepherd pretended to count back. 'Years ago. I don't know. Five years. Six? Six years.'

'And there's no family?'

'None.'

'I see.'

'My wife left me.'

'I see. I'm sorry. So – actually – you have nobody to corroborate your claim to be the man who called Detective Sergeant Holloway.'

'Do I need corroboration? You've got the tape. You can hear it's me.'

'We'll have the tape properly analysed,' said Ireland, cordially enough, 'if I deem it necessary. But I'm hoping it won't be. Can't you think of anybody?'

'Well. There's my landlord. He was with me when I made the call.'

'Your landlord?'

'Yes.'

'His name?'

'Lenny.'

'Lenny —?'

'Kilminster.'

'Lenny Kilminster. And Mr Kilminster's address?'

'The same. I lodge.'

Ireland sat back. He let Dr Lowe interrupt.

She said: 'Can you tell us exactly *why* you made the call, Mr Shepherd?'

'I wanted to help.'

'And how did you think it would help?'

'I don't know.'

She looked at him for a long second. Then she deferred back to Ireland.

Ireland had exhausted his cultivated patience. He warned Shepherd that he could be charged with wasting police time, not to mention a number of more serious offences. He took some time about it, and went into some detail. Shepherd knitted his hands in his lap. Then Ireland excused himself and stomped from the office. The door rattled in its frame.

Lowe ignored Ireland's exit. She sat on the edge of the desk and made a call. A couple of minutes passed while she rifled around in a capacious bag. Eventually she produced a video cassette. At the same time, a young officer appeared in the doorway, pushing before him a television and VCR on a wheeled, tubular metal trolley. The young officer plugged everything in, handed the remote control to Lowe and excused himself.

She pointed the remote at the video and, with a non-essential flick of the wrist, pressed PLAY. They watched the early evening BBC news report that broke the Joanne Grayling story. A reporter declaimed grimly in the Bristol sunshine. The low-rise, red-brick police station was behind her back.

Lowe pressed PAUSE.

'Is this the report you saw?'

Shepherd said it was.

She fast-forwarded the tape.

'And this?'

She showed him the ITN broadcast that went out the same day.

She stopped the tape, rewound it.

She said: 'Now, can you tell me if these two reports have anything in common? Besides the obvious.'

He said: 'Not that I can see.'

She asked him to look once more. They watched the tapes again. Shepherd leaned forward. He parted his beard like Victorian skirts and rested his jaw on his cupped hands. But he saw nothing.

'No detail?' she said. 'Nothing strikes you as being at all strange?'

A band across his eyes was slowly tightening.

'No,' he said.

'Look again,' she said.

She read his expression. 'Just once more.'

Rewind, fast-forward, pause. The reporter's image froze and flickered laterally behind fuzzy stripes of poor tracking. Lowe approached the TV. She tapped the screen with her pen. Just behind the reporter's shoulder, a man was moving into shot.

'Watch him,' she said.

She pressed PLAY. The man walked fully into frame. He walked to the door of the police station. He stopped and looked over his shoulder. The morning sun shone in his red hair.

She said: 'That man is Detective Holloway.'

When Shepherd had been escorted back to the interview room Lowe lifted the phone and called Ireland back to his office.

She said: 'He saw Holloway on TV. He's in the background, walking into the station. ITN shows him leaving again, a bit later on. Who knows why he picked up on it? Perhaps it was just the red hair. Perhaps he entered the shot at a significant moment. Whatever: who knows? So, Shepherd goes to bed and has a nightmare about Joanne. And in the nightmare, his unconscious dredges up the image of the red-headed policeman he'd seen on TV twice that day.'

Ireland searched in his top drawer.

'And by coincidence it was Holloway?'

'Oh,' she said, 'there's no real coincidence about it. He *worked* here, for God's sake, and there were a thousand cameras stationed outside.'

Ireland slammed the drawer.

He glanced over the surface of his desk. He picked up a

sheaf of paper, squinted at it, put it down again. He removed his glasses and lay them, upended, on the desk.

Distracted, he said: 'It's one more embarrassment I can do without.'

'Jim,' she said. 'You saw him, for God's sake. He's like a penitent schoolboy.'

He patted the desk until he found his glasses again. Then he put them on.

'But not a guilty one,' she said. 'He's no more guilty than the poor woman who called to tell us she'd heard her dead husband's voice on *Crimewatch*.'

She leaned forward and moved a greasy-cornered pile of A4 from a collapsing in-tray. She pointed. Ireland said 'Ah', and picked up a bottle of Pepto Bismol. He began to struggle with the childproof lid.

He said: 'But some of the details were spot on —'

'Oh,' she said. 'Rubbish. Look.'

From the mess on his desk she lifted a spiral-bound map of Bristol and the West Country.

'Name a page,' she said.

'Twenty-four.'

He dropped the lid on the table and swallowed glutinous, bright pink liquid.

She flicked through the book. Then she lay it flat on the desk. Her finger hovered over page 24. 'Right,' she said. 'Give me a grid reference.'

'3C.'

She stabbed her finger down on the page.

'Right,' she said. She rotated the book so Ireland could see it.

'Look. To the right of my finger, about an inch: there's the river Avon. If you look closely, you'll see that my finger is actually *resting* on a railway line.'

His lips glistened pink, as if with cheap lipstick. He wiped them with the back of his hand.

She said: 'Pick an urban environment and, almost by definition, you're close to water and railways – depending on how you define "close". And, one way or another, where there's a railway there's a shed.'

He took the map, examined it, put it down again. He belched and pressed the tips of his long fingers to his sternum.

'That's all very well and good,' he said. 'But it's another coincidence and I'm not happy with it.'

'Oh, it's not coincidence at *all*,' she said. 'It's just psychology. A lifetime of television murder mysteries are jumbled in his head. One night he's disturbed by a news report about a missing girl. Who can say why? That night, his subconscious throws up a few of those images. He thinks, suddenly, he's got the Shining. But he hasn't. All he's got is a low-grade mental health problem.'

He was nothing more than one of the nutters who dogged such investigations – who, indeed, had already dogged this one. The law of averages demanded that one of them would be right about something, one day. Clearly Shepherd was disturbed, but she didn't think he was dangerous. And he had nothing to do with the death of Joanne Grayling.

Ireland gave the order to check Shepherd out and let him go. A couple of hours later, Newell returned to the holding cell. He showed Shepherd the door.

Neither Ireland nor Lowe returned to thank him for his co-operation.

Outside the station, Shepherd found a rotting wooden bench. He sat and collected his thoughts. It was nearly 4 p.m. He wanted to take a walk to get the smell of the station off him.

He slung the bag over his shoulder and headed to where he used to live.

It wasn't far. He walked for perhaps twenty minutes. Then he set the bag down on the corner of Chandos Road, in sight of the newsagent where he used to buy the Sunday papers and sweets for the kids; the organic butcher where Rachel liked to buy their meat; the Italian restaurant where they sometimes ate a groggy Saturday brunch.

He knew by looking at the house that nobody was home.

A passing Jeep Cherokee slowed to look at him. He supposed he didn't look much like a Redland house-owner any more. And the sportsbag on the pavement beside him was about the right size to stuff in a VCR.

He imagined Andrew Taylor glancing from the bedroom window and seeing Jack Shepherd, staring at the house from the corner. Andrew would have the cordless digital telephone in one hand, ready to call the police. He would be making notes: time, place, date and description. The man was six foot two or three, he would write. Middle-aged, white male. Big build. Shaved head, heavily bearded. Mid-to-late forties. Small, wire-framed spectacles. Olive drab army jacket with many pockets. Worn blue jeans, battered running shoes.

Shepherd smiled. He removed his spectacles and wiped his

eyes. The house maintained an impassive countenance. It was moved in neither one way nor the other.

Strange, how he knew by the simple fact of proximity that it was empty. He wondered where the children were. Rachel.

He crossed the road. The cool, familiar shadow of the hedge passed across his shoulders.

At the side of the house, just beneath the kitchen window, they kept a spare key beneath a concrete plant pot. He didn't know what kind of plant it contained, but it didn't look well. The key was kept there for the children, at his suggestion. It was still there, in a zip-lock plastic freezer bag. Indeed, it might not have been moved since he put it there. He'd given the kids dire warning not to tell anybody. If somebody found the key and burgled them, he said, the insurance company would not replace the TV or the video or the Playstation. They rolled their eyes, all three of them, and elbowed and pinched and jostled one another. But they listened and they did as they were told.

He removed the key from the freezer bag and let himself in through the kitchen door. He walked into the musk of them, their compound smell. Four of them, who had been five. And the cat. It infused the walls, the floor, the air.

Issey Miyake, Natrel Plus.

The morning's washing-up was piled in the sink: a few breakfast bowls, teaspoons, mugs, a buttery knife, a fork whose tines were sticky with seedless raspberry jam. A pot rimmed out with soggy egg. There was a scattering of damp crumbs beneath the toaster, a spillage of tea, milk. Cereal cartons had been left unclosed. He took the Crunchy Nut Cornflakes from the shelf, closed the inner bag and replaced the box in its proper slot on the shelf, between the Weetabix and the Special K.

He touched the wall.

The cat glared at him from the hallway door.

'Hello, Hungry Joe,' said Shepherd, quietly.

The cat swiped its tail once, then showed him its arse and undulated prissily away.

On the table next to the telephone in the hallway was a photograph of him. Andrew and Rachel, Dorset, 1992. It was taken by her father. Shepherd lifted the frame. As he adjusted its angle, the reflected light obscured first his face, then Rachel's. He rubbed dust between thumb and forefinger. He put the photo back on the table.

He climbed the stairs. They creaked beneath his weight. He recalled sneaking up these stairs, late, after a work Christmas party.

When he saw the chaos in the bathroom, he laughed once, out loud. The boys' deodorant and shaving foam. He wondered when they started using it. Inside-out tights, an empty Tampax box, toothbrushes in a water-stained, chromium holder. Their bristles leaned as if shaped by a prevailing wind. Dove soap, Gillette shower gel. The portable radio on the window sill hadn't been properly turned off. He could hear the low murmur of Radio 4. A small pair of boxer shorts had been trampled underfoot into the sodden bathmat. Somebody had left a Swatch on the shelf, next to a new but lidless tube of toothpaste that had been squeezed from the middle.

He sat on the edge of the bath. He watched a beam of sunlight move through twenty degrees.

Falls

In the twins' disordered bedroom (DO NOT ENTER!!!, read the sign he had allowed them to Blu-tac to the door) he breathed the fungal air of male adolescence: the cheesy feet, the unwashed armpits, the sweaty bedding, the sharper top-notes of deodorant and aftershave. He ran his hand along the frame of the bunkbeds. There were new posters on the wall: Manchester United, Tupac Shakur, the Phantom Menace. Pamela Anderson in a red swimsuit. There was a new PC on a rickety workstation. On the chest of drawers, the portable TV and Playstation were veiled in dust. He drew his finger down the screen. With the darting tip of his tongue, he touched the dust that clung to his fingertip.

Next door, Annie's room was pastel and neat, fragrant with perfume and soap. On her dressing table a collection of coffee mugs bloomed with grey mould. He picked up a mug, examined it, made a repulsed face, smiled. Her PC table was crowded with books and sheets of photocopied A4. He ran his palm along the crisp duvet cover. It released a burst of her scent, and for a moment he imagined she was behind him, over his shoulder.

'Dad,' she would say (he knew her so well), 'you grew a *beard*.'

He entered the marital bedroom with some reluctance. Something had changed. The wardrobes were the same. The curtains. The dressing table with her perfumes and her make-up: a grubby white bowl of foundation, a tube of mascara clogged black round the rim. He pulled open a drawer, slowly closed it again. Her underwear, laundered and folded. Photographs had been jammed in the mirror's frame. Rachel, the kids, her family. None of him.

He realized what had changed.

There was a new bed.

The cat sashayed in there after him. It leaped upon the new bed and curled on the pillow. It stared at him with eyes like headlamps.

He looked at himself in the full-length mirror.

He wanted to come home.

But there could be no coming home. The people who lived in this house had marked his death, and had been sad. But that sadness had been accommodated within their lives. The farther he receded in time – as his children became adults, as his wife bought a new bed, as the cat grew older and more cantankerous, as the apple tree in the garden added another inch, as new school years were started and completed, and office politics ran their circular and repeating course, as Christmas came, and Easter, and summer holidays and bonfire night, and exams, and university, and promotion, as friends divorced and remarried, as new lovers enticed – the fainter grew the mark he had left here, the impermanent stamp of who he had been. He was fading like the Polaroid of a good moment; like something broken and left outside, blanched now with sun and swollen with rain.

The cat followed him to the kitchen door and into the garden. It watched him replace the key in the bag under the potted plant under the kitchen window. He was tempted to say goodbye to it, to stoop and caress it under the wishbone of its jaw, to feel the muscular squirm of its skull in his palm.

But the cat wanted no part of him. When it was convinced he was not coming back, it returned to the house via the cat-flap he had fitted when it was a kitten, while the children played badminton in the garden behind him and Rachel spoke to her mother on the telephone about who would be coming to who next Christmas, fully five months early.

Shepherd was back in London in time for *EastEnders*. Eloise had cooked him a fish pie.

The police had already spoken to Lenny. He felt grieved and betrayed. For two or three days he didn't speak to Shepherd, and for a week after that he was curt and rather clipped. But soon enough he got over it.

14

Somehow, a researcher for a satellite television station tracked Shepherd down. He never learned exactly how. He supposed a police officer somewhere had benefited financially from the transaction.

All he knew was this: one day he picked up the phone to a delighted young woman called Chloe, who, when he dolefully expressed his unwillingness to appear on camera, responded: 'Oh, *absolutely*,' and proceeded to bully him into doing exactly that.

His identity would not be revealed. He would appear on screen in silhouette and his voice would be electronically altered. He would be paid £500. Cash.

He asked what the programme was about.

She told him: 'The supernatural.'

A new Rover 200 arrived for him at 11 a.m. on the day of

recording. Through the curtains, Eloise and Lenny watched him leave. They looked like proud parents. Eloise gave him an abashed, supportive little thumbs up.

He didn't say much to the driver, who listened to Capital FM all the way. The television studio was located in a low-rise industrial complex on the extreme north edge of London. It was as if commuter-belt suburbia segued into an internment camp, upon which shone a triumphant imperialist sun.

He stepped from the car and thanked the driver. Clearly, the driver didn't give a shit either way. Shepherd brushed himself down and walked into Reception. He smiled at the receptionist. After a very few minutes, during which he sipped delicately at a cup of tea, he was introduced to Chloe. She was surely no older than twenty-one or twenty-two, perhaps five foot two. She wore a spiky, pixie haircut, heavy-rimmed spectacles and very baggy clothes in shiny modern fabrics. Shepherd felt old. He cast an obelisk shadow over her.

She led him like a trained elephant through the natty reception area into the working corridors of the building. Young people in various states of high anxiety bustled this way and that. Chloe showed him the Green Room. He had always associated the name with the glamour of television. Sean Connery sat in the Green Room and told golfing stories with Jimmy Tarbuck before appearing on *Parkinson*.

He was disappointed. The Green Room was about the size of a double bedroom. There were threadbare carpet tiles on the floor. Pressed against the walls were the kind of chairs that might be found in a dentist's waiting room. In one corner, on a wheeled stand, stood a large, rather ancient television. Its screen showed an empty row of superior chairs in a darkened, empty studio. Some black loops of cable were in shot. Along the lower edge of the screen he saw the brief, lateral movement of a camera dolly.

On a coffee table next to the television was a tinfoil tray of sandwiches and some flasks of the kind that might be found at a sales conference in a Midlands hotel.

'Tea's on the right,' she said. 'Coffee on the left. It's no smoking but you can ignore that if you must. We all do.'

He looked at her meaningfully.

'Don't worry,' said Chloe. 'We don't bite!'

He said: 'What do I have to do, exactly?'

She put her hands on her hips and made a face that told him he was very naughty.

She said: 'When the times comes —'

'It's not live or anything?'

'Oh no. It goes out on Thursday night. In the eleven o'clock slot. When the times comes, we'll lead you to the studio and sit you down. You'll be miked up and Geoff will ask you some questions —'

'There's no audience?'

'No. Don't worry. The discussion will be edited and shown to a studio audience tomorrow. The panel on tomorrow's programme will debate what you've said.'

'Who else is coming?'

'They'll be here in a minute,' she said.

Next door, in an even smaller room, he was invited to perch on a revolving stool before a big mirror. A pleasant Glaswegian woman with a face the colour of a satsuma smeared make-up on that bit of his face still visible above the beard. She dabbed it with a triangle of sponge on his bristly scalp. Then she offered to neaten his beard and moustache. He thanked her. Her scissors clicked hypnotically.

In a matter of minutes he looked like a scholarly lumberjack.

When she was finished, he experienced a brief moment of panic.

He went next door to the Green Room. He was still wearing the hairdressing gown. Chloe was deep in conversation with a young man in a Gap T-shirt.

He interrupted them. He said: 'Why do I need make-up if I'm going to appear in silhouette?'

'Oh,' she said. She made a concerned moue. 'Did nobody speak to you? Did nobody call? It's OK,' she assured him, 'we changed the format. Don't worry. You would've been in silhouette if we were going live with an audience. As it is, it'll be edited so that only your eyes or your mouth or whatever are on screen at one time.'

His legs were numb.

'You absolutely promise?'

'Oh, absolutely.'

'Do I sign something to that effect?'

'If you like,' she said. 'Absolutely. I can sort that out with Colin in ten minutes. Don't move!'

He never saw her again.

He poured himself a cup of tea. He spilled UHT milk on his shoes. The little drops looked like sperm.

One by one, three more guests arrived. Each was accompanied

by a Chloe clone. One of them was a slim young Brazilian man with long legs, who suggested they call him Tony.

The first guest was a stout, somewhat tweedy woman. She introduced herself with the kind of abrupt civility that suggests a Tory bigot. He made her a cup of tea. She thanked him distractedly, as if a hot beverage was her ancestral due.

She and Shepherd watched the silent screen, upon which technicians dragged cables and huddled in urgent-looking conversations.

Next to arrive was a popular scientist called Julian. Shepherd recognized him from the television. Lenny had angrily dismissed him as a professional sceptic. Julian's clothes were slightly donnish, but his accent had a touch of Estuary round the edges and his hair was luxuriant and dandified.

He said, 'Hello again!' to the woman. Hearty and cordial adversaries, they shook hands.

They heard the fourth guest arriving at Reception. He announced himself with a series of raucous cackles. The loud presence was followed into the room by the man who projected it. He was squat and powerful. He moved like a bouncer. He wore a grey suit and purple silk tie. He had a shaved, bowling-ball head and a grey beard that bristled like a boar.

He marched up to Julian and pumped his hand.

'Nice to see you again, mate,' he said. Then he moved to the old woman, whose powdered cheek he kissed with exaggerated delicacy, like a thuggish fop in a powdered wig.

'And how are you, doll?'

He squared up to Shepherd. He rubbed his hands like a barrow boy.

'I don't think we've met,' he said. 'Have we?'

Shepherd wiped a palm on his thigh and extended his hand. 'Jack,' he said.

'Well, I hope you're all right, Jack,' said Rex Dryden. 'I'm Rex.'

They shook hands. Then Dryden said: 'Let me get at those sandwiches.'

He peeled back the Clingfilm like the skin from a rabbit.

Shepherd felt vaguely affronted and proprietorial, as if sole rights to the sandwiches were his.

Dryden scanned them with an index finger.

'The trick,' he said, 'is to find something without avo-fuck-ing-cado in it. That's why they call them green rooms.'

He picked up a sandwich and shoved it into his maw. He champed on it in a way that aroused in Shepherd a protective feeling towards his distant children. He watched a sliver of chicken riding those cheerful lips like a dingy in rough weather.

Before Shepherd could subtly push himself past Dryden and get to the sandwiches, they were joined by the presenter. His name was Geoff. Shepherd had never heard of him. Geoff's hair was bouffant in a way that marked him out as second-rate. His eyes had the ingratiating slipperiness of one who glances over shoulders at parties.

When Geoff had introduced himself and appealed to them to be at their ease, Dryden, Julian and Patricia visited Make-up. Each returned the colour of a different citrus fruit.

Shepherd was prepared for the studio to be surprisingly small. Famously, everything and everyone involved with television was surprisingly small.

Nevertheless, its smallness surprised him.

One by one, except Dryden, they were guided into swivel-ling, leatherette chairs. Impassive and wordless young people urged them to pass microphone cables through their clothing.

Shepherd was seated in a chair slightly to the left of the main group.

Geoff walked off to consult with some clipboard-holding young men and women in the corner. He sipped professionally from a waxed cardboard cup of coffee.

There were five cameras: four pointed at the leatherette chairs, another at a wooden lectern that had been erected in one corner. Each camera was operated by a man in his early forties. Not one of them gave any sign that he gave the least proportion of a flying fuck about what was going on. Their assurance, like that of mechanics in a backstreet garage, was subtly emasculating.

The guests took their seats and each was asked to speak into their microphone. Each pushed their chin into their throat and said: *Hello. One-two. One-two,* before a bored floor manager told them to try again, pretending the microphones weren't there. They were told to speak to Tony on camera 2.

While attendants fiddled with his microphone Geoff the presenter ran through his introduction. In repose, his face looked older.

Dryden took his place behind the wooden rostrum, and then, with less perturbation than Shepherd thought possible, the taping began.

The studio went dark. Camera dollies moved like daleks across the polished floor. Stooping young runners moved trailing cables out of the way of their casters. A single light fell on Geoff the presenter. He fixed the camera with his serious gaze, behind which there twinkled what he thought of as his trademark ironic sauciness.

'Hello and welcome to the programme,' he said. 'Well: after all the doomsaying and the soothsaying, life as we know it did not come to an end. Planes didn't fall from the sky. The microwave ovens didn't stand up in open revolt. The River of Fire turned out to be – well, a river of water. It's the year 2000. Summer's here. Suddenly, we've got new concerns: our decaying transport infrastructure, *Big Brother*. But cast your minds back, just a few short months, to the turn of the twenty-first century. What happened to all the prophets of doom? All the millennium buggers? All the scientists and the New Age gurus who stood in line to say our time was up? Do they *still* insist there are more things in heaven and earth than are dreamed of in our philosophy? Or have they packed up and gone home? Has the New Age gone to ground?

'Our guest speaker requires little introduction. Nowadays, Rex Dryden describes himself as a transcendental comedian. But it wasn't so very long ago that he was responsible for duping several hundred perfectly ordinary people into believing some outrageous claims he made on behalf of his so-called religion, the Temple of Light. To kick us off this week, we asked Rex Dryden why there are so many people who will believe in anything – except, that is, a future.'

The light dimmed over Geoff's head. A second picked out Dryden. He clutched the sides of the lectern and leaned forward slightly.

'It's a well-known fact,' he began, 'that, when members of

the public recognize celebrities in the street, they've usually got one thing to say. John Cleese was driven mad by people reminding him not to mention the war. Now, I'm not what you'd call a celebrity, but occasionally, people do recognize me. And they always ask the same question. "Rex," they say. "Whatever happened to the end of the world?"'

Dryden bared his teeth in a smile.

'I always give them the same answer,' he said. 'The end of the world hasn't gone anywhere. It's just round the corner. It always has been.

'A few months back, several hundred people drank poison, just because I asked them to. Or at least they thought they did. Actually, they were drinking Lucozade.

'Who would do that? Who would kill themselves, just because somebody asked them to? Were these people mad? Most people would probably say yes. But I'm not sure I agree.

'A few years back, I saw the movie *Braveheart*. At the film's climax, Mel Gibson is being tortured to death at the order of the English monarchy. They're cutting off his arms and legs and slicing him open and rooting around in his guts with hot tongs. And while this is happening, he's shouting one word at the sky. He's shouting the word *Freedom*.

'Now, if I was in Mel's position, I'd be making a lot of noise as well. But it wouldn't be freedom I'd shout about.

'The first time I saw *Braveheart*, I thought it was a comedy. I thought it was *Monty Python*. I thought Mel was going to jump up off the torture table and hop around on one leg, telling everyone it didn't hurt, that it was only a flesh wound, that the English were all cowards, that he would take them all on.

'I remember thinking: I wouldn't let a kid watch *this*. Not in a million years. That's not heroism, that's *idiocy*. It's one thing truly to die in the name of freedom. It's another thing to be killed for your country. Too often, we assume the two are equivalent. But they're not. Quite the contrary. After all, what *is* a country? It's an abstract. It's an idea sometimes (but not always) expressed by geography. Countries expand, countries contract. A country is legislation, specifically designed to restrict your freedom, intellectual and physical. A country exists to make you a productive unit. A *consumer*. You're fuel to your country's economy. And all over the world, and all through history, people have been happy to kill, and to die for exactly that idea. For this *Monty Python* idea of what freedom is.

'A government provides one freedom. It frees us from the tyranny of true choice. Modern democracy dazzles us with ephemera and calls it liberty. Meanwhile, the important decisions are made on our behalf. Partly, that's because we long to be told what to do.

'Stanley Milgram proved that to us. His experiment proved that perfectly decent, upstanding American men in short sleeves and flat-top haircuts would electrocute an innocent man to death for no other reason than that a stranger in a lab coat told them to. And this, remember, was not in pursuit of national and racial ideology. The subjects were told they were taking part in an experiment about *learning*. For that, they were literally willing to kill: just as long as the man in the white coat agreed to accept legal responsibility for any consequences arising from their actions.

'We shouldn't kid ourselves. We *love* to obey orders, to

disavow ourselves of responsibility. We abhor what happened in Europe during the 1930s and 1940s. We comfort ourselves that we would have sheltered Jewish families in our garden sheds, in our attics, our cellars. Our cupboards would be bursting with grateful little Jewish children. It's a comforting idea. But it's an illusion. We're lying to ourselves. We would've done exactly what *was* done. Because we'd've been too scared to do otherwise.

'We could save lives every day – just as we dream we would've done back then. Every 3.6 seconds, somebody in the world dies of hunger. That's 24,000 people a day. But don't listen to me. Read the newspapers. Do the sums yourself.

'Every ounce of excess fat we carry on our bodies, all this lard we hike around and get depressed about on the beach: every surplus ounce of it could've been used to keep alive one of those starving human beings. Every CD we buy, every nice new tie, every tank full of super unleaded, every pint of Stella Artois: everything we consume, we consume at the cost of human life – because every penny we spend on our whims and desires, every time we act as a consumer, we contribute to the grand sum of human misery. Every single night, we could go to bed knowing that somebody, somewhere, is alive because of our direct action. But we don't do it. We don't want to, because we don't think it's worth it. A Paul Smith suit, a holiday in Greece, a pair of Nike shoes is worth more to us than human life.

'That's what the anxiety at the end of the century was actually about. We were scared to confront the truth about ourselves.

'Of course, we've buried that fear. We inhumed it within a series of secondary concerns to make us feel good about ourselves – not least of them our sudden concern for what we call the environment.

'Environmentalism is the referred guilt of serial murderers. Conservationism is a deliberate misconception of nature. It's an attempt to redraft the planet the way we wish it was: an idyllic, paradise garden. But natural selection does *not* conserve. It changes and modifies with absolute, unceasing savagery; with utter disregard for suffering and pain. Earth isn't a paradise garden. It isn't *fixed*. There's nothing to conserve. Continents collide, mountains are rammed into the sky, are scoured flat over millions of years. It gets hot, it freezes for millennia. In some form, Earth will endure until the sun goes cold: no matter what we do to it, or to each other. If you want to know about climate change, talk to a dendrochronologist. They'll tell you that there's been climate change and catastrophe the like of which we can't begin to imagine. And life always bounces back.

'We come, we go. We don't mean a thing. But we're all we've got. Each other and this little bit of time.

'And we don't care!

'The millennial year was arbitrary. It was utterly without meaning. Think for a moment about the sheer scale of that hubris: imagining that God might work according to a faulty, unhistorical, human calendar. How typical of us.

'So, what was our millennial anxiety about?

'I'll tell you.

'What if, by some small chance, God *did* come back? What if there *was* a hell? Well, then: it wouldn't be the hungry people, and it wouldn't be the dispossessed, and it wouldn't be the tortured, the forfeited and the ruined who were burning. It would be us.

'We are the greatest evil at large in the world today. And, secretly, we know it.'

The single light over the podium dimmed. In the half-light, Dryden took his place with the other guests in the semi-circle of chairs.

When the lights came back up, Geoff was still referring to the sheaf of notes he had been struggling to read during Dryden's speech. He looked up, shuffling the papers like a newsreader. The small error of timing would be edited to make him appear icy and professional.

He leaned forward. He rested his chin on his fist.

'Rex Dryden,' he said. He sounded concerned. 'That's a very disturbing world-view.'

'Well, that's sort of the point,' said Dryden. 'That's the point I was trying to make with *Illumination*.'

'*Illumination* being what you called,' Geoff referred to his notes, 'your epistemological installation.'

'Yes.'

Geoff looked challenging.

'But it's a point you could only make with – if you'll excuse me – a bunch of fruitcakes in a big house on the Sussex Downs?'

Dryden smiled at him.

'The best art leads to what you already know,' he said. 'So does a good joke.'

'But isn't it rather a *bleak* joke?'

'Perhaps humankind really can't bear very much reality.'

'Aha,' said Geoff, as if he had spotted a hole in the argument.

He lifted his chin from his fist. 'Sylvia Plath.'

'T. S. Eliot,' said Dryden.

Geoff smiled indulgently and nodded as if, being wrong, he was making a subtle point of his own. He turned to Julian.

'Julian Grammaticus,' he said. 'You're familiar to many of our viewers as a very public face of modern science. How do you respond to Rex Dryden's point?'

'Well,' said Julian. He seemed to be exaggerating his Estuary twang for the benefit of the cameras. 'I have to say, I don't *entirely* agree with Rex's analysis.'

There was polite laughter among the group, including from Dryden.

'My *own* deductions wouldn't be nearly so bleak,' said Julian. 'Perhaps that's just because I'm an optimist. But I tend to believe it's actually because I'm a scientist, rather than an artist.'

'Or indeed a transcendental comedian,' said Geoff.

'Quite,' said Julian. 'Now, it might sound trite, but to science knowledge is more relevant than Truth—'

'Oh, come on,' said Dryden, as if Grammaticus were delivering a blow lower than was worthy of him.

Geoff furrowed his brow.

'Please,' he said to Dryden. 'Let him finish.'

Dryden sat back in his chair. He knotted his hands in his lap and grinned that Julian should continue.

'— but that doesn't *necessarily* make a scientific position any more comfortable than Rex's,' said Julian. 'A lot of what we've learned about ourselves in recent years has confirmed what many had long suspected to be true. We're driven by urges similar to those of other animals – territoriality, status, sex. But it's important to remember that *urges* is all they are. We're *not* slaves to these drives, or to our genes. Or to anything else. We're conscious beings, and it's in the conscious control of these unconscious drives that we best exhibit that humanity —'

Dryden interrupted with an index finger. He sat forward.

'The Milgram experiment was set up,' he said, 'in such a way that the subject could hear what he believed were the dying screams of the so-called learner, the man whose learning ability he thought was being tested. Sixty-five per cent of the subjects *still* pressed the switch marked DANGER: SEVERE SHOCK. Even though they could hear the hysterical pleading of inno- cent men. A lot of them carried on pressing the switch, even when they believed the learner was dead.'

'Well,' said Julian. 'Quite. But I have to say, the Milgram experiment is no longer thought to be quite as absolute as we once imagined. It's not certain that Milgram's subjects actually believed they were delivering electric shocks to innocent people. It's possible they'd intuited the nature of the experiment, and didn't want to ruin it. They were still playing to expectation, but to an altogether different set of expectations than people imagine. But that's beside the point. What I was going to say is that, actually, we learn more every day about the evolutionary mechanisms that underlie altruism and selfless behaviour patterns.'

'That altruism is based on reciprocation?' said Dryden. 'That I can get what I want by being nice to people who have it?'

'It's a bit more complex than that.'

'It always is. But isn't that what it boils down to?'

'Not exactly, no. That's rather a tabloid exposition.'

'It's not exactly one in the eye for Nietzsche, though, is it?'

'Well, actually, I'm not sure,' said Julian. 'It's a scientific means to clarify and justify the mystery of human goodness; it tells us definitively that goodness is a kind of strength. That seems like a worthwhile endeavour to me. And one in the eye for Nietzsche, incidentally.'

'*It's a Wonderful Life*,' said Dryden.

'Well, yes,' said Julian, warily. 'It certainly *can* be —'

'No. The movie. Have you seen it?'

'That's the one with Jimmy Stewart,' said Geoff.

'That's right,' said Dryden. 'Jimmy Stewart wishes he was never born, and an angel called Clarence grants his wish. He gets to see what the world would've been like without him in it. It's my favourite film of all time. My absolute desert island movie.'

Geoff nodded. He said: 'Are you going somewhere with this?'

'Absolutely,' said Dryden. 'Listen. Jimmy Stewart plays George Bailey. He lives in Bedford Falls, the archetype of small-town America. Or the Hollywood dream of it. George Bailey dreams about getting out of Bedford Falls and seeing the world. But George Bailey runs the Building and Loan. He's the only man who stands between the poor people of Bedford Falls and the evil Mr Potter. So he stays, and he watches his life pass him by. One Christmas Eve, disaster strikes: some money goes missing. The authorities think George Bailey's to blame. For George, with all his crushed dreams, in his draughty old house with his adoring wife and his beautiful children, it's all too much. So he decides to kill himself.'

Julian's smile had stiffened somewhat. He said: 'I don't see where this is leading us.'

'Bear with me, ' said Dryden. 'Now, Clarence the angel rescues George Bailey from suicide and shows him what life in Bedford Falls would've been like, if he'd never been born. And it's *terrible*. Bedford Falls is called Pottersville because of course, without George to stop him, evil old Mr Potter is the most powerful man in town. Pottersville is like Sodom and Gomorrah, except nobody's having a good time. Everyone George knows and loves is unhappy. All his friends are broken people. Because George wasn't around to help them, you see? George's goodness has touched so many lives. And if he'd never been born . . .

'Well, George decides to face his problems. He begs Clarence to be allowed to live again, and he runs home through snowy old Bedford Falls, to face the music. Except there's no music to face. His friends – the entire town, all the people he's been good to, all the people whose lives he's changed – have turned up at midnight on Christmas Eve. They've all brought all the money they can afford to bring, to get George out of trouble.

'I love that film. I cry every time I see it. Every single time, without fail. It makes me weepy just to think about it, the way George kisses his wife and hugs her like she'll burst and wishes her a merry Christmas, and her eyes glisten with adoration, and the bell rings on the Christmas tree and we know Clarence got his wings, and George's brother the war hero turns up after being given a medal by the president, and the whole town sings "Auld Lang Syne".

'But I cry because it's not *true*, Julian. If it was true, we'd see the friends of George Bailey crossing the road to avoid him. George Bailey *has* no friends. We'd hear them gossiping about the trouble he'd got himself into. We'd hear them saying they'd always thought he was too good to be true. We'd see them turning their backs on him when he needed them most.'

Julian smiled with one side of his mouth.

'You see,' he said. 'I'm not sure that's *true*, Rex.'

'Of *course* it's true,' said Dryden. 'If a little goodness goes such a long way, if it touches so many lives, then why is there so little of it?'

Geoff interrupted.

'At this point,' he said, 'I'd like to bring in another guest.' He turned to face the camera. 'Earlier this year, John Smith (as we'll call him) woke from a nightmare. That evening, he'd seen a news bulletin reporting the disappearance of Joanne Grayling, a young Bristol student he'd never met.

'John Smith was an ordinary man: hard-working, law-abiding. Yet that night he believed that, somehow, he had learned *psychically* of Joanne's whereabouts. So, the next day, he did what he believed was the right thing: he called the Bristol police and told them what he knew.

'In fact, despite John Smith's best efforts, Joanne Grayling was tragically killed. Although it is a matter of public record that detective William Holloway is wanted for questioning in connection with her death, this terrible case remains unsolved. So: John Smith, in your own words, tell us what happened the day William Holloway lifted the receiver and took your call.'

Shepherd tried his best. By now he had recounted the incident a dozen times. On each occasion, it sounded progressively more absurd.

While he spoke, the others leaned forward in their chairs. They watched from under raised eyebrows. Geoff furrowed his brow with cultured gravitas, resting his chin on a fist. Despite the heat of his mortification, Shepherd's voice broke when he described watching the news the day Joanne's body was discovered.

Patricia interjected.

She leaned over and squeezed his knee. The snout of a camera lens swivelled to follow the movement.

'I can see a young woman,' she told him. 'She's standing at your shoulder. She's smiling. It's a very beautiful, very peaceful smile. She's happy. She wants – yes, she wants to thank you. She wants to thank you for everything you tried to do.' Patricia smiled. Eccentric English teeth: yellow, crooked and tea-stained. The colour of old, brittle sellotape. 'This is not our home,' she assured him. 'This world is an illusion. Our true selves are vibrations in the astral plane. We are creatures of light, creatures of God.'

'But Satan was the bringer of light,' said Dryden.

'Satan was an angel, too,' she told him, with a smile.

Geoff and the others listened to her benevolently.

Geoff said: 'So, in a sense, we're all angels?'

'Exactly!' said Patricia.

By then Shepherd knew he was lost.

Back in the Green Room, Brazilian Tony handed them each a glass of tepid Chardonnay. Geoff thanked them in turn, but his on-screen lustre had faded. He seemed smaller, hunched and rumpled and weary. Rather than wine, he took a small glass of whiskey and water.

Patricia was brusquely coquettish with Dryden. Julian was peppery for being upstaged. They huddled in an awkward group. Nobody spoke to Shepherd until the first glass of Chardonnay was finished.

Then Dryden turned to him. Shepherd's skin burst into gooseflesh. He felt the bumps race up his spine. His scalp went tight, as if sunburned. The hair on his forearms stood on end.

'You all right?' said Dryden.

'Yes,' said Shepherd. 'Someone just walked on my grave.'

Dryden clapped his shoulder companionably. He was half Shepherd's height and twice his width. Shepherd sensed tremendous physical strength.

'Don't worry about it,' Dryden said. 'People *dance* on mine. And I'm not even in it yet.' He cackled, his frog-wide mouth set with too many milky little teeth. Dryden knit his brow and examined Shepherd's expression. He put his pumpkin head on one side. Then he jabbed Shepherd playfully in the sternum.

His voice had darkened, but he didn't lower the volume. The others turned to look at them. Brazilian Tony put his hand on one hip and pouted.

'Don't worry,' said Dryden. 'About what anybody says. Don't give it a thought. You were wrong. So what? At least you were trying to do a good thing.'

Shepherd didn't answer.

Dryden said: 'Are you worried about the programme?'

Shepherd hung his head. It didn't seem possible to tell Dryden a lie.

'Yes,' he said. 'I am, a bit.'

'Well, don't,' said Dryden. 'Don't worry. It'll be watched by a few thousand people who don't give a toss about what's being said, and who won't remember it in ten minutes.'

Shepherd wanted to believe that.

'Then why are you here?'

'Because I'm *selling* something,' Dryden said. 'I've got a book coming out and I'm going on tour in a month or two.'

'I don't even know why I came,' said Shepherd. 'I didn't want to.'

Dryden winked. He chortled. He clapped Shepherd's shoulder and let his hand rest there.

'Maybe something *told* you to come,' he said. 'Maybe some power brought you here, for some higher purpose.'

He fixed Shepherd with his laser eyes.

Shepherd was possessed of the odd sensation that his feet had unlatched from the floor. He imagined he was floating to the ceiling like a helium balloon.

A girl who looked like Chloe but who was not Chloe put her head round the door. She announced that Dryden's car had arrived. He thanked her and tossed the remains of his wine down his craw.

'Don't you worry,' he told Shepherd. 'It doesn't matter how you handled yourself or what you said: they'll edit the programme the way they want to, anyway. That's the name of the game. And then it's broadcast —' he rippled his fingers like seaweed. 'And for a few minutes, it's on a few screens in a few corners, in a few houses in a few cities in a small country nobody gives a toss about any more, and a few people might pay some passing attention to it. And then it's gone, and, once it's gone, it's nowhere, forever.' He looked at Shepherd with his head tilted to one side.

'Anyway,' he said. He offered his spadelike hand. 'Nice to meet you. Keep in touch.'

Shepherd shook the hand, once. His skin crawled. He wiped his palm on his thigh. Dryden seemed not to notice. He kissed Patricia, shook Julian's hand and left. Brazilian Tony showed him the way.

Like an afterimage of the sun, the sense of his presence lingered. It rendered them silent. When it had faded, they were left embarrassed in each other's company. The light seemed to have dimmed. Their muttered voices echoed as if from hospital walls.

Shepherd waited until he was confident that Dryden's car had safely departed, then he sloped over to Brazilian Tony like a head-hung yeti and pleaded quietly to be allowed home. Brazilian Tony seemed to think this was an exceptional idea and gambolled down the corridor, his clipboard clutched tight to his bony chest.

15

Shepherd was glad to get home. This time he didn't bother to thank the driver, who still didn't seem to give much of a shit either way.

Shepherd slammed the front door behind him and stomped upstairs, to the lodgers' bathroom next to the unlet room on the third floor. The experience had been worse than he'd expected; worse than handing himself in at the police station. Hardly worth the £500.

He stepped into the bathtub and ran the shower hot. He shampooed his rasping head and sweaty beard with menthol Head & Shoulders. Then he washed his hairy body with Dove Cleansing Lotion. He turned off the shower and ran the bath, getting out to clip his finger- and toenails while the tub filled. He polished a squeaky portal in the steam on the bathroom cabinet mirror; trimmed the hairs in his nostrils and ears with a pair of scissors going rusty at the hinge. He stepped gingerly into the hot bath and, as far as he could, stretched out. His knees stuck out like pale, conical islands. He listened to the portable radio.

Later, with a stripy beach towel wrapped round his hairy belly, he padded up to the attic room and deodorized his armpits. He lay some freshly laundered clothes out on the bed and steamed dry.

He was trying not to think what he was thinking. His head swirled and eddied with complex connections.

He dressed in clean cargo trousers and a short-sleeved, checked shirt. He opened the creaking sash window. A cloud of the city filled the room. Late afternoon, late summer air; exhaust fumes and uncollected rubbish gone sweet with decay.

Downstairs, Lenny and Eloise were waiting for him. Lenny brought in a pot of tea and some Hob Nobs.

Eloise said: 'How did it go?'

Shepherd sat. The sofa creaked like a sea-going galleon.

'Oh,' he said. 'I don't know.'

She sat facing him, in an armchair whose covers had been repaired with duck-tape.

'Was it that bad?'

He knuckled the tip of his nose.

'It was awful.'

Stupidly, he thought for a moment that he might cry.

He told them about it. Eloise thought it was comical, in a pitiable way. But she was good enough to suppress her smile and nod and make supportive noises. Lenny was outraged. He stomped up and down the room, cursing. He punched his hand like Burt Ward playing Robin.

'It's disinformation,' he yelled, with passion. 'It's fucking disinformation.'

Shepherd protested.

'Oh no,' he said. 'It was all quite genuine.'

'You were *set up* —' Lenny brought himself to a standstill. He was breathing heavily with the exertion. Beads of sweat on his upper lip. His hair stuck up. He cupped an elbow and pinched the bridge of his nose. 'That bloke,' he said, 'that presenter. I know him. He's a known sceptic. Well known. Well, I say sceptic. *So-called* sceptic. I wonder whose pockets he's in.'

Eloise laughed. 'He's not in *anybody's* pocket,' she said. 'For God's sake, Lenny. It's a fucking late-night talk show on digital TV!'

Lenny pitied her naivety.

'No,' he said. 'Oh, no, no, no.'

Eloise laughed.

She said: 'Haven't you had *enough*?'

Lenny said: 'So, you think it's coincidence that it was on Sky? Of all channels? You think that's accidental? Grow *up*, Eloise.'

She held up her hands in disbelief. 'Jesus,' she said. 'Whatever.'

She shook her head.

'I don't believe this,' she said. 'You're just *losing* it, Lenny.'

'Losing it, bollocks,' he said. 'This is an *injustice*. It's a set-up. Putting Jack on screen with Rex Dryden is an attempt to discredit him . . .'

'How can you *discredit* him any further?' She caught Shepherd's eye. 'Sorry, Jack.'

('That's all right,' said Shepherd, but nobody was listening.)

'Because Jack's the real thing,' said Lenny. 'And Dryden's a self-professed fraud. He's a fucking spiv. He's a wideboy. He's wider than the sky. Having them on together is guilt by association.'

'And why would they do that? Why would they bother?'

'Because Jack was close to the *truth*. Jack was *on* to something.'

'On to *what*?' said Eloise. Her voice had ascended an octave. She turned to Shepherd and said: 'I'm sorry, Jack, but I have to say this. He was *wrong*, Lenny. He didn't get anything right.'

'But he was *nearly* right.'

'There's *no such thing* as nearly right!'

Lenny munched malevolently on a Hob Nob.

Eloise stood. She forced a smile that quivered unsteadily.

'Can't we let this drop now?' she said. 'And get on with our lives? Can't we just, you know, *move on*? I can't remember a time when this wasn't happening.'

'Oh God,' said Shepherd, who also wished it would stop. 'Please yes.'

'There,' said Eloise. She pointed at Shepherd as if Lenny might not know where he sat. 'There you go. Let's call it a day, right here and now. Let's not even watch the stupid programme.'

Lenny fell into an armchair and muttered something about Wittgenstein.

Eloise's shoulders sagged. In her normal register, she said: 'I fancy a drink. Does anybody fancy a drink?'

Sulkily, Lenny wiped crumbs from the corner of his mouth.

'Go on then,' he said. 'I'll have a Guinness.'

'I meant,' said Eloise. ''Let's go the pub.'

They agreed it was a good idea.

The Cricketer's Arms was on the next corner, and it was early enough to get a table – although the only one available was placed in the corner, beneath the large, wall-mounted television. The sound was on mute, but the bar staff kept glancing towards the screen. The All-Blacks were playing.

Shepherd put £50 behind the bar. Eloise objected politely.

He said: 'It's my birthday.'

She said: 'Is it really?'

He shrugged. 'Why not? It might as well be.'

She squinted at him. Then she reached over the table and pinched his upper arm.

She said: 'You're really weird, sometimes.'

He rubbed at the pinch. Then he tugged at his earlobe.

'Well,' he said. 'So would *you* be.'

'Well, yes,' she said. 'I expect I would be.'

Deftly, he thought, Shepherd changed the subject. He asked after Eloise's working day. Much of her attention recently had been given to a young autistic girl who possessed an unusual musical proficiency. After hearing a piece of music once, Mary could play it by ear, no matter how intricate the melody. Yet she was without interactive skills. She suffered brain blindness, an inability to conceive what someone might be thinking, or indeed that it might be possible for another to think. Her playing was without nuance; a clattering blitz of melody. Already the local television news had been in to film her. At her parents' suggestion, she played the Rachmaninov Piano Concerto that had featured in *Shine*. There had been articles in the *Evening Standard* and the *Sunday Telegraph*. A BBC documentary crew were interested in following her progress for a year.

Falls

Eloise was unhappy about Mary becoming a minor local celebrity, made worse by her parents' willingness to financially exploit her. Lenny didn't think they could be blamed. He agreed it was distasteful – but it wouldn't harm the girl. She was beyond humiliation. She was an android.

(This irritated Shepherd, who wondered why Lenny couldn't just shut up for once and agree with Eloise.)

Eloise balked. She and Lenny quarrelled in a baiting, animated fashion that only a friend could know was amicable. Shepherd was largely excluded, but at least they weren't talking about Joanne Grayling or William Holloway. Then Lenny went to the bar to refresh their drinks.

Eloise nodded in the direction of his knotty spine.

She said: 'He cares more than he lets on.'

Shepherd looked into his empty glass.

'Some men are like that,' he said, draining a dreg that was not there.

'He's a bit of a puritan,' she said. 'Deep down. He has these very high moral standards. He expects too much of people. So he pretends to expect nothing.'

'I hadn't thought of it like that,' said Shepherd.

Lenny squeezed through the pub crowd clutching their drinks and four packets of crisps to his chest. A man with long, thinning hair and a leather jacket began to pump money into the CD jukebox. They were forced to endure 'Stairway to Heaven' at ear-bleeding volume.

Lenny bellowed: 'Have you been talking about me again?'

Eloise took her drink. She shouted at him: 'There *are* other topics of conversation.'

He kissed her forehead.

'Of course there are,' he shouted back.

She reached up to slap the crown of his head. He slumped heavily on the greasy circular stool.

Shepherd spoke loudly into his ear: 'Eloise was telling me what a caring person you are,' he said. 'Deep down.'

'Was she now?' Lenny yelled. 'Well, it's pretty deep down, then.' He looked at his sternum. 'Deeper than I can see.'

Eloise said: 'You're an arsehole, Kilminster. You *X-Files* geek.'

He smiled, a bit sadly, and opened a packet of crisps. He shouted into Shepherd's ear, spitting moist cheese-and-onion crumbs.

He said: 'A million times nothing is still nothing, you know?'

Shepherd wanted to laugh, but then he saw that Lenny was quite serious and he felt lonely and foolish. He remembered with photographic clarity his visit to Andrew Taylor's house.

The pattern, the old pattern, was hissing and spitting behind his eyes. It would not go away. He was weary with the unending bleakness of it.

He said: 'Let's drink to that,' and went to the bar. He returned with a bottle of champagne and three slightly grubby tulip glasses.

Eloise said: 'What's all this about?'

'Oh, I don't know. Let's raise a toast.'

'To what?'

'To Joanne Grayling.'

Shepherd poured. The glasses swelled with mousse.

They clinked glasses.

'To Joanne,' said Eloise.

Falls

With the evocation of her name, the atmosphere contracted. Shepherd topped up their drinks.

He said: 'I have a confession to make.'

He saw that Eloise had anticipated him.

He turned away from her desperately entreating gaze. He looked at Lenny instead.

'William Holloway,' he said.

'What about him?'

Shepherd sighed. For a moment he considered the wisdom of speaking.

Then he said: 'He didn't do it.'

Lenny set down his glass.

'What makes you say that?'

'Stairway to Heaven' came to a merciful conclusion. Their ears rang with tinnitus.

Shepherd leaned over the table.

'*It's a Wonderful Life*,' he said.

Eloise rolled her eyes. She downed her champagne and slammed the glass down hard on the table. Another song came on the jukebox. 'Losing My Religion'.

'Right,' she said. 'If you're going to start this bollocks *all over again*, I'm off.'

She searched their expressions for any sign of hope. Then she swore under her breath and hastily gathered up her bag and jacket from the empty stool. She stormed from the pub. They watched her leave.

Then Shepherd told Lenny all about it.

16

I

The next morning, they bought and watched a DVD copy of
It's a Wonderful Life. They agreed it was essential to find
William Holloway.

To Shepherd it seemed impossible. Lenny conceded it would
be difficult. He suggested it would be better to concentrate
instead on finding Holloway's wife and daughter.

People behaved oddly when a loved one had committed a
crime. The more terrible the crime, the less accountable their
reaction to it. Nobody wanted their husband or their father to
be a butcher of young women. Holloway's arrest and incarcer-
ation would prove beyond legal doubt that he was just that. So
Lenny believed the women might have an idea of Holloway's
whereabouts, even if they hadn't told the police about it. Or
even each other.

But Holloway's wife and daughter were themselves in hiding. It seemed to Shepherd that, if the super-evolved predatory instinct of the assembled tabloid press had not located them, their own chances were vanishingly slight.

Lenny scolded him.

'Remember,' he said. 'An assumption is a thing you don't know you're making.'

They didn't *know* the tabloids hadn't found the Holloway women. It was just as likely that the papers were temporarily co-operating with the police, withholding certain information and deferring certain stories, perhaps in exchange for 'leaked' exclusives when the case finally broke. The papers' very silence on the subject since the initial flurry of reportage might be a part of the police's overall strategy.

'But if they're not hiding from the press,' said Shepherd, 'who are they hiding from?'

'*Everyone*,' said Lenny. 'Would you want *your* friends calling, in the circumstances?'

Shepherd thought about Rachel.

'*No*,' he said.

Although Lenny had decided the problem was surmountable, the problem of how to go about actually surmounting it vexed him for several days. He rejected Shepherd's suggestion that they simply hire a private detective. He held such men and their abilities in low esteem.

For the rest of the week, Lenny drank many cups of strong, white tea with one sugar and smoked himself to tension headaches, which he dispelled by watching *15 to 1*, *Countdown*, *Watercolour Challenge* and *Ricki Lake*. He ran his hands through his hair. He read and reread old newspapers that reported on the Temple of Light, the killing of Joanne Grayling, the events that followed. He plugged in the Playstation and sat crosslegged before the television screen, playing *Driver* for hours at a sitting. The tip of his thumb blistered and bled. He nibbled at the swollen balloon of skin. He popped Nurofen Plus into his mouth like chocolate raisins and muttered and cursed to himself as though Shepherd was not there.

Eventually, he had formulated his plan. He asked Shepherd to buy them two return train tickets to Leeds.

They travelled up on the Monday morning, first class. On the train, they swapped sections of the *Guardian*, spreading them noisily flat on the table. They took it in turns to make frequent visits to the buffet car and returned with super-heated hamburgers in Styrofoam clams, or cheesy corn puffs that took skin from the roof of the mouth. The people in business suits cast them sidelong glances. At some point, each of the business men and women yapped garbage into a mobile telephone. They spoke a form of English Shepherd barely recognized, full of puffed-up, bellicose instruction and military metaphor.

Lenny revelled in the incongruity. He wiggled his little finger at his ear, symbolizing the small, flaccid penises of everyone around them. When he'd finished the newspaper, he ostentatiously produced a tatty Penguin copy of *Crime and Punishment* from his overnight bag and settled back into his seat.

The train pulled in to Leeds station at lunchtime. They slung their overnight bags over their shoulders and walked though the city centre. Shepherd didn't mind spending money on first-class travel, but he resented overpaying for a hotel room they would barely see, except to sleep in. So they booked in to a bed-and-breakfast on Upper Briggate, close to the Odeon. The obese proprietor wore a T-shirt several sizes too small; from its lower hem there emerged a great swell of purple striated, hairy flesh. He wheezed as if sexually exerted and gave every impression that renting rooms to strangers was a hazardous business and more trouble than it was worth.

They asked for adjoining single rooms. The proprietor rolled his eyes and exhaled. He apprised them curtly – as if suspecting it might be their fault – that the lift was out of order. Cowed by his wrath, they crept shamefully up three flights of narrows stairs.

Shepherd's room was laid out like a bedsitter and smelled faintly of seared cotton. It was clean enough. The remote control to the ancient portable television was held together with cracked, yellowing sellotape. He dumped his bag on the single bed and joined Lenny in a similar room next door.

Lenny had done the research. Most of the city's student population lived in the Leeds 6 postal district, just north of the city centre. The newspapers had reported that Caroline Holloway lived in the Hyde Park area, so they hailed a taxi outside the Odeon, huddled in their coats because it was beginning to rain, and asked the driver to take them to the biggest student pub in Hyde Park. It was a short journey. The taxi turned off the Headrow, past the Merrion centre and the bone-white university clocktower, the Parkinson building. Hyde Park itself, tree-bordered, flashed by on their left.

The pub was named for the park. It was a hangar of a place

that stood across the road from a kebab shop, a Blues Brothers themed pizza takeaway, a boarded-up second-hand bookshop and a shop that sold vegetarian footwear. Inside, six pool tables and a bar that ran the length of two walls seemed hardly to take up space. Patrons roamed the worn carpets as if in an east European airport terminal. Knots of students played pool, hunched over tables, gaped at televisions mounted in high corners.

Lenny insisted that his plan was glorious in its artlessness: it relied for success on human weakness, and therefore couldn't disappoint. Because Caroline Holloway was connected with a celebrated murder (albeit indirectly), she had become a campus celebrity. Celebrity was social currency. Even those who could not claim to have met her would exaggerate their connection to and relationship with people who did.

There were limited degrees of separation within such an interconnected community: the network of people who claimed to know Caroline would have spread exponentially, like mould on a slice of bread. People who knew her vaguely would claim to be among her closest friends. People who knew and didn't like her would claim she was a wonderful person, a good friend. It would be socially stigmatic to admit, even to a stranger, that one was not in some way acquainted with her.

So Lenny's plan consisted of buying drinks for students and engaging them in conversation, into which he would introduce the topic of Caroline Holloway. Eventually, he believed, they would track this intricate grid of hearsay and gossip back to someone who actually knew her. Thus they might eventually come to learn where she was.

Shepherd doubted it would work.

Lenny insisted he have some confidence in him.

'And lack confidence in the probity of others,' said Shepherd.

'Come on,' said Lenny. 'We're talking about *students*.'

Inside the Hyde Park, Shepherd got them drinks while Lenny set them up at a pool table. Lenny suggested they order drinks they didn't like, thus regulating their intake. So Shepherd ordered himself a Bacardi and Coke and got Lenny an American Budweiser, a beer to which he was ideologically opposed.

Lenny gripped the bottle by the neck and said: 'Ha ha.'

They set a proprietorial pile of £1 coins on the edge of a pool table. The blue baize was pilled like an old sweater. As the afternoon passed, the pub began to fill. Young men and women took their places at the other pool tables. Lenny offered a game of doubles to anyone who hung round, watching, or who looked on resentfully at the pile of cash that secured the table for many games to come. Some joined them, others chose not to. Either way, Lenny made little overt effort to ingratiate himself. He had a faintly menacing presence and was edgy and irritable while playing; but he played impressively. He ran jerky, quickfire rings round the more ponderous and less skilled Shepherd.

Judging the moment, Lenny would line up a shot and ask his opponent if they knew Caroline Holloway. Most simply said no, supped from their pints and played on. One or two leaned on their cue and told him to fuck off. Lenny never pressed the issue, and he never lost a game.

Although they continued to nurse their drinks, Lenny

moved on to Guinness and Shepherd whiskey at about 7 p.m. Thus, when they left the Hyde Park some time after 10 p.m., they were tottering and befuddled. They queued in the take-away, then found a bench on the underlit fringes of the park, sat down and ate their doner kebabs. Shepherd got chilli sauce and shreds of lettuce in his beard. To shake off the pub fug, they agreed to walk back to the hotel. Rain was intermittent and the streets of Leeds 6 were quiet. Buses passed them. Fiercely illuminated from within, they carried no passengers.

Shepherd, who was not much of a drinker, woke late with a hangover. He rolled around the narrow bed for a while, not long enough, then crawled to the bathroom and hunkered under the wretched, rusty discharge from the showerhead. He sat in the tub, hugging his knees and let tepid water trickle intermittently over his scalp and down his spine. His beard was odorous with lamb fat, stale cigarette smoke and chilli sauce. He could smell his own breath. He soaped his beard with complimentary shampoo that had the look and consistency of semen.

He dressed and banged on Lenny's door. They went to find a café. Lenny was trembling. He had puffy, violet rings round his eyes.

In the café, Lenny broke the snotty meniscus of egg yolk with a triangle of fried, white bread. 'Fuck,' he said, and put his head in his hands. He removed a strip of Nurofen Plus from his jacket pocket and popped six pills into his mouth. He dry-swallowed and offered the strip to Shepherd, who chastely declined, sipping from his orange juice.

By the time they got to the Hyde Park, their heads were clearing and they were resolved, if not actually ready, to start again. This time they took a break early in the evening, eating pizza from the box on the park bench they'd occupied the previous night.

Towards closing time, Lenny asked a hulking rugby boy who'd just lost four frames if he knew Caroline. The boy was built to Shepherd's approximate dimensions, with a quiff of curly blond hair. He wore chinos and a checked shirt. His face was flushed cherry-red. He set his pint glass on the baize and took a lowering step towards Lenny.

Lenny leaned on his cue. From his pocket he took a small aerosol of mace. He showed it to the boy, who examined it minutely. He called Lenny a cunt and blundered off to join his exclusively male companions in the farthest corner of the pub, where he began publicly to exaggerate what had just happened. Within a week or two, it would become a gun that Lenny showed him.

Someone tapped Lenny on the shoulder.

He turned. A casually dressed, elegantly balding young man squared up to him. The young man asked Lenny who the fuck he was.

Lenny collected what dignity he was able.

'My name is Lenny,' he said.

'Why are you looking for Caroline Holloway?'

'Do you know her?'

'Nobody here has a story to sell.'

'Oh, mate,' said Lenny. 'I'm not a journalist. Do I *look* like a journalist?'

'What does a journalist look like?'

'Fair point. Well, I'm not.'

'Whatever. Fuck off.'

'Look —' said Lenny.

The boy punched him.

Lenny fell over.

Silence descended upon a section of the crowd.

Lenny got to his feet. He rubbed at his jaw.

'What the fuck was that for?'

The young man punched him again.

He didn't fall over this time, but he stumbled back several steps, spilling the head from a number of pints. A circle of onlookers formed.

'Fucking *stop that*,' said Lenny. His shoulder and thigh were wet with spilled lager.

The young man raised his fist.

Shepherd was aware of the disturbance. Long familiar with the dynamics of playground fights, he pressed through the cluster of onlookers and put himself between Lenny and the young man. He asked what was going on.

The young man craned his neck to look Shepherd in the eye. Some of his righteous defiance melted away. His fist fell to his side. He gauged Shepherd's dimensions: the fierce-looking beard, the shaved head; the wire-rimmed spectacles.

'Fucking hell,' he said.

Lenny pointed at the young man.

'He hit me.'

'What did you say to him?'

'Nothing!'

'You must have said *something*.' Shepherd looked at the young man. 'What did he say?'

The young man took a step back.

'Nothing,' he said.

'Well, OK,' said Shepherd. 'If you say so.'

'I think he broke my nose,' said Lenny.

'No he didn't.'

Shepherd didn't take his eyes off the boy.

The boy jammed his hands in the pockets of his windcheater. He looked downcast and apprehensive.

Lenny let go his nose and glowered at Shepherd.

'Jesus,' he said. 'You sound like my headmaster.'

'Oh, sod this,' said the young man. 'I've had enough of this. I'm off.'

As a final gesture, he pointed a theatrically indignant finger at Shepherd's nose.

'Just stop it. Go away and leave us alone.'

Shepherd took the risk.

'I'm the man who phoned Caroline's dad,' he said.

The boy stopped. Before he could formulate an answer – Shepherd could almost see his mind working – the landlord arrived. Bow-legged and fruitily enraged, he threw them out.

Outside, the boy made no attempt to disengage from them. They huddled under a streetlamp. Lenny sniffed back blood and scuffed his feet on the pavement.

Shepherd gave the boy a version of why they were in Leeds. He told him what happened at the police station in Bristol. He told him what kind of idiot he felt like.

The boy cupped his mouth and listened with his head hung low. When Shepherd was finished, the boy hugged himself and turned to face the park. Cars passed; a bus. People entered the pub; people left. Currents of takeaway scent eddied on the cold night air.

The boy looked at the sky. The city was encased in a bubble of water vapour and electric light pollution. Rucked, low clouds like dirty bedlinen.

He said: 'I don't know what to say.'

'I don't know what to say either,' said Shepherd.

He extended a hesitant hand and left it hanging in the damp air. He introduced himself again.

The boy searched his expression, shrugged. They shook hands. The boy's name was Robert.

Robert turned to Lenny. He buried his hands deep in his pockets and kicked a crippled can of Coke along the pavement.

'Sorry,' he said.

Lenny threw Shepherd a look; a twist of the upper lip and a glimmer of derision.

'Don't worry about it,' he said.

They followed Robert to a balti house a short way down the hill. It stood at the corner of a long, red-brick terrace whose end walls were plastered with faded and ripped flyposters advertising night clubs and gigs by exotically named student bands. They were the only patrons; the restaurant wouldn't begin to fill until closing time. They were attended by two Indian waiters in white shirts and embroidered waistcoats. Each of them was handed a large, laminated menu and they were seated at a corner table wrapped in a floral, plastic covering.

They ordered three steins of cold Tiger beer. Despite the earlier pizza, the booze had made Shepherd and Lenny hungry. They dipped shards of poppadom into mango pickle while Robert talked.

Robert was a close friend of Caroline. They assumed this to be contemporary student-speak for boyfriend. By midnight the previous evening, news had reached him that two more journalists were in the Hyde Park, asking about her. Within moments of his entrance this evening, someone had pointed Lenny out to him.

Lenny smiled at Shepherd. 'Told you,' he said. There was a chitinous black crust of blood rimming one nostril.

'What?' said Robert.

'It doesn't matter,' said Shepherd. He asked about Caroline.

Robert shook his head. He jutted out his lower lip and shrugged expansively.

'What can I say? She's having a nervous breakdown, practically.'

'Have you talked about it?'

'What do you *think* we've talked about? Everyone thinks her dad cut off a girl's head. What do you think we talked about? It's all there is to talk about. It's all *anyone* wants to talk about.'

Shepherd put his elbows on the table. He balanced his spectacles on his brow and massaged his eyes.

'She doesn't think he did it?'

'Of course she doesn't think he did it. He's her dad.'

Shepherd looked left and right.

'We don't think he did it, either,' he said.

Robert snapped a poppadom and dipped it in mango pickle. He mumbled something.

They stayed for nearly three hours. By the time Robert stood to leave, the restaurant had filled, become raucous, then emptied again and fallen silent. They had shouted themselves hoarse; now they murmured conspiratorially. The waiters hung about impatiently at the bar.

Robert told them about Holloway's trip to Leeds. How Caroline had told him that Derek Bliss's company had been bought out by William Gull Associates Ltd, whose principal offices were in York. How, exhausted, Holloway had asked Robert to drive him there. Holloway was inside Gull's office for less than twenty minutes, and emerged with blood on his shirt and reams of old paperwork stuffed into several distended carrier bags. How that night, he asked Caroline and Robert and two of their friends to examine this paperwork, searching out references to himself or his wife. How they had found nothing. How Robert had driven him back to Bristol the same night, because he was off work on the sick, claiming to have the flu.

'He *looked* like he had the flu,' said Robert. 'That's the thing.'

The next day, Joanne Grayling was murdered and Holloway disappeared with the ransom money.

Caroline and Robert gave full statements, after which two detectives from the Avon and Somerset Constabulary visited the York offices of William Gull Associates, Ltd. Gull told them that a complete stranger arrived one afternoon and started talking about someone called Bliss, of whom Gull had no knowledge. He seemed genuinely surprised when the detective informed him that Derek Bliss had been a partner in Executive Solutions, the company Gull acquired from Henry Lincoln.

Gull stated that Holloway assaulted and threatened to kill him, and removed a great deal of important paperwork from the premises. When asked why he hadn't reported the assault or the theft, Gull laughed and told the officer: 'Come off it. I was a copper, too, lad. Once upon a time.'

Gull's story was verified when the stolen files were identified among the belongings in Holloway's bedroom. They were kept back as evidence. The police searched the rest of Holloway's flat; they went through the hard drive of his computer, looking for deleted files and emails. Nothing was found that pertained in any way to the murder of Joanne Grayling.

They discovered that Derek Bliss had died several years previously, apparently of a fatal cardio-vascular accident while vacationing in Australia. His ex-business partner, Henry Lincoln, was now a travelling representative for a trade book publisher. He had a substantial mortgage on a mock-Tudor house outside Basingstoke, a company Ford Mondeo and two Representative of the Year awards framed in his hallway. He was mystified by the police's visit. Lincoln had been a sleeping partner of Bliss. He knew nothing about the mechanics of running such an operation. The police thanked him. That line of investigation was suspended. At best, it would probably prove to be only peripherally connected to the Chapman murder. Perhaps Holloway had panicked, had second thoughts. Tried to call in some old debts.

Under further questioning, Caroline claimed no knowledge of Gull, or Derek Bliss; nor had Holloway's ex-wife, Kate. Neither was able to suggest what Holloway's connection to them might be.

'I don't know what he was doing up here,' said Lenny. 'But *something's* not right with that picture, is it?'

Robert said he would try to arrange a meeting with Caroline.

The next evening, he met them in the narrow lobby of their bed-and-breakfast hotel. He told them that Caroline did not wish to be contacted. He would not tell them where she was or give them her phone number. But he promised to ask her one more time. He would contact Shepherd in a few days. Shepherd wrote down their home number for him. He and Lenny checked out of the hotel and caught a night train home. They watched their hollow-eyed reflections in the windows of the empty carriage as the train clattered and swayed towards London.

Three days later, Robert called.

Finally, she had agreed to meet them, on the condition that Robert take them to her. That way, they wouldn't know her location until they arrived. They were to bring no cameras or other recording equipment. They might be gone for some days and would need several hundred pounds per head to cover expenses. Shepherd agreed to cover the costs – including Robert's – and the two hung up cordially enough. Then Shepherd went to the box in the bottom of the wardrobe and counted his money again.

II

The evening prior to their agreed meeting at King's Cross station, Robert knocked on the door.

He told Eloise from the doorstep that he wanted to verify everything Shepherd and Lenny had told him about themselves. He set his jaw firm and said he was sorry if it seemed rude, but that included where they lived.

Eloise nodded heartily.

'Very wise,' she said.

Robert was handsome. His olive skin was unblemished and though his woolly hair was thinning he looked small and young and vulnerable out there on the doorstep with his big brown eyes and shabby undergraduate chic. Eloise asked him inside. Entering, he ducked his head unnecessarily. He paused to investigate the framed prints in the hallway. Hitler as Grail Knight. Poussin's strange pastoral *Et in Arcadia Ego*. Leonardo's John the Baptist, with his cryptically elevated index finger and artful smile.

In the lounge, she invited him to sit. Shepherd was watching the news. A big toe protruded from a hole in his sock. She told him to make Robert a cup of tea. He got to his feet and hurried off to join Lenny, who was cooking.

Eloise yelled out to Lenny that one more would be joining them for supper.

Lenny's voice reverberated down the hall. 'I hope he's not a fucking vegetarian.'

'Are you?' said Eloise.

'No.'

Eloise cupped a hand to her mouth. 'He's *not*.'

'Well,' Lenny yelled. 'Good,' and made angry cluttering and crashing noises.

Eloise insisted that Robert sleep in the spare room. When finally he agreed, she went to the downstairs airing cupboard and gathered an armful of clean white bedding.

'So,' she said. 'You're the one who punched Lenny.'

Robert shifted in his seat.

'Yes,' he said, eventually.

'Nice one,' said Eloise. 'I expect he deserved it.'

Before breakfast the next morning, Shepherd went out to pick up the hired MPV.

Lenny waited outside, hugging himself on the pavement, especially so he could laugh at Shepherd when he put the cumbersome vehicle to the kerb. Then he slapped his upper arms, opened the boot and began to throw in the luggage.

'We look like people with special needs,' he said. 'On a fucking day trip.'

For reasons she had not chosen to disclose, Eloise went with them. Shepherd suspected she wanted to keep a tempering eye on Lenny. She wore an old, three-quarter-length leather coat that smelled like an Oxfam shop, and tatty Dr Martens with mismatched laces.

She closed the door of the house, double-locked it, and joined them in the back of the MPV. At first, the three of them sat in a line, but Shepherd was too big. He shifted up a row and spread himself out. Robert took the wheel and Lenny closed the sliding door.

While Lenny, Eloise and Shepherd bickered about what radio station to listen to, then what CD, Robert drove them to the south coast. He drove without speaking, his little bald spot turning left and right as he read the road. His eyes flitted occasionally to the rear-view mirror.

They reached Folkestone. On the Eurostar, they crossed to France beneath the cold, brown Channel. Turning on to French roads, Robert spread a map across his lap. Flattening the map in order to refer to it, he several times swerved into oncoming traffic.

Fearing for their continued existence, Eloise rested her chin on the driver's headrest, close to Robert's ear, and suggested to him that she navigate.

Robert said: 'I can't let you do that.'

'Why ever not?'

'I'd have to tell you where we were going.'

'Oh,' said Eloise. 'For goodness sake.'

She turned to the rear and rolled her eyes. But she found no succour there. Lenny's expression implied that Robert's objection was quite sensible.

'But we're going to die,' she said.

She suggested to Robert that he divide the journey into stages: then she could navigate, leg by leg, without needing to know their eventual destination. Robert said he would think about it. While he was thinking about it, he almost ploughed headlong into an oncoming Honda Civic.

Later, when he felt able to meet her gaze, he glanced in the rear-view and said: 'OK. Good idea.'

With the vehicle still in motion, Eloise grabbed her bag and scrambled over to the front seats. She spread the map on the dashboard. Driver and navigator shared a family pack of lemon bon-bons. By virtue of her position, she had authority over the stereo. She put on some Mozart. Lenny hated Mozart. He was a Wagner man, if anything.

Late in the afternoon, they arrived at Chinon, a medieval village set beneath the ruins of a long-destroyed chateau, through which tourists now roamed. Robert had reserved big, noisy rooms in the Hotel du Point du Jour, on the quai Jeanne d'Arc. Shepherd opened his window and stared at the street below. He remembered taking school coach trips to France. The unique disquietude of attempting to exert command over forty adolescents on foreign soil.

In the morning, he rose early and took a walk. He was the last of them to arrive at breakfast: Lenny was folding and stuffing whole buttered croissants into his mouth and Eloise was sipping bitter coffee while reading about the town in a tourist pamphlet, copies of which were scattered liberally over the hotel. Robert had arrived shortly before Shepherd. He was untucked and downcast. The previous day had taken its toll on him.

Lenny passed him a basket of warm rolls, complete with little packets of butter and jam.

'Eat,' he said.

Robert rubbed his belly and swallowed a belch.

'I don't eat breakfast.'

Lenny waggled the bowl. 'No,' he said. 'Eat.'

'He won't shut up until you do,' Eloise told him, so Robert gave up and sat down to join them. They made further room for Shepherd at the small table: they squeezed elbow to elbow, ripping rolls and spreading butter with blunt knives; slurping and spilling orange juice and coffee.

Shepherd was happy.

The autumn made the countryside mournful and strange, but Robert seemed more relaxed at the wheel, and (having survived the previous day) his passengers were more at ease about being driven on the wrong side of foreign country roads by someone who had not been eligible to vote at the last general election. Robert described a slow, circuitous route, descending on their unknown objective in a loose spiral. More than once, Shepherd noticed minor landmarks – certain signposts and crossroads – they had already passed, coming in a different direction.

Nobody else commented on this. He didn't mention it to Lenny who, despite his supposed internationalism, was not overjoyed to be in France anyway. It was too full of the French, whose proximity made him nervous. The deeper they got into the country, the more sullenly he crouched on the back seat.

About midday, they ate lunch at a Chinese restaurant tucked away on a small-town backstreet. Lenny found a tobacconist and bought the *International Guardian*. They didn't stock his brand of rolling tobacco, so he folded himself up on the rearmost corner seat and blew Marlboro Light smoke out of the window, into the vehicle's slipstream.

Their destination proved to be Bourges, in the centre of the country.

Robert took a while finding a place to park the van: when he had, Shepherd fretted about leaving the luggage so they spent another twenty-five minutes finding and then parking outside the hotel. Robert checked in on their behalf, leaving their baggage piled alongside the concierge's desk. Then they followed him on foot into the town's medieval *vieille ville,* where half-timbered houses and gothic turrets crowded the winding cobbled roads like a mouthful of bad teeth.

Shepherd wanted a sense of history. Such places never felt haunted to him. He couldn't feel the taint and discoloration of hundreds of years. The Bourges *vieille ville* might have been constructed from fibreglass ten years previously. Yet still the sight of a Bakelite telephone or a ration book under a glass case in a provincial museum could stupefy him with the awareness of unspooling time.

Robert took them to a café on the rue des Beaux Arts. The afternoon shadows were long and there was a bite in the air, but they took an outside table nevertheless, in view of the cathedral of Saint-Etienne. Out of earshot, Robert wandered up and down the pavement, nodding and talking into a mobile phone. Then he replaced the mobile in his pocket and joined them at the table.

Lenny ordered a Pernod, the others beer. They sat and waited. There seemed little to say.

They were on their second drink and beginning to warm up, when a shadow fell across the table. Shepherd looked up.

The girl might have been a phantom in indigo denim and suede Converse.

Robert jumped to his feet. He and the thin young woman hugged for a long time. Then he introduced Caroline Holloway to Eloise, Lenny and Shepherd in turn. She moved to set her small rucksack on the table: Robert pushed aside empty beer glasses and Lenny's ashtray, making room to accommodate it. Then he found her a chair. Caroline sat and removed her sunglasses. Her eyes looked bruised.

She asked if anyone minded and lit a Marlboro Light before anyone could say yes.

They waited.

With an edge of impatience, Shepherd said: 'Would you excuse us?'

As one, the others apologized and stood. They tried to gather their things with too much haste, dropping coins and wallets and phones and cigarettes. Shepherd watched the girl from the corner of his eye. She looked at them as if they were a poorly rehearsed, importunate street theatre company.

When they had gone, he said: 'I'm sorry about that.'

She shrugged. She seemed younger than her years, which he knew to be twenty-one. It was as if she had retreated to childhood. She was skinny. He hoped she was eating properly although he suspected she was not.

He asked Caroline if she would like a drink. She ordered a coffee. When it arrived she held the warm cup in her hands like a candle. Shepherd felt he had made no contact with her. He set aside his half-drunk lager and explained at length why he was there.

He said: 'I truly believe him to be innocent.'

She laughed once, bitterly.

'Yeah,' she said. 'Right.'

He disregarded her affected bitterness.

He said: 'The last few months must have been terrible.'

She crossed her legs and jigged her ankle.

'Yes.'

He wanted to place his hand over hers, checked himself. Instead he rested his big palm flat on the table.

He said: 'Now I'm here, I don't know what to say.'

'Are you a reporter?'

'You know I'm not.'

'Then why *are* you here?'

'I told you. To help.'

'How?'

'I want to find him.'

'You can't.'

'Why not?'

'No one can find him. He can't be found.'

'There's nobody who can't be found. But I do need your help to find him.'

'I don't know where he is.'

'I know what it's like,' Shepherd said, 'to be far from home.'

She looked at the table.

'I don't understand what you want.'

'To help your dad.'

'He's gone,' she said.

'I can bring him back.'

'No, you can't. Not if he doesn't want to come home.'

'Of course he wants to come home.'

'You don't even *know* him.'

'True.'

'Then why should you bother?'

He shrugged and could not answer.

Because I want to go home, too.

'Are you really the man on the phone? The psychic?'

'Yes.'

She pressed one nostril closed and sniffed through the other.

'What's *that* all about, then?'

'I wish I knew. I really do.'

He smiled sadly; his beard split along the middle like a coconut.

'Look,' he said. 'I know this must sound mad. It sounds mad to me, when I say it. But look at Robert. He trusts me – and he only wants the best for you.'

She stirred the coffee and poured in some milk. She watched the revolution of a spiral galaxy.

She said: 'Robert just wants to believe you can help. He's desperate to get things back as they were.'

'Is that such a bad thing to want?'

She said: 'I can't believe I'm even having this conversation.'

'Nor can I.'

'Look,' she said. 'I'm sure you mean well.'

She dropped two rough cubes of sugar into the cup; hesitated; added a third.

'One for dad,' she said, just loud enough for him to hear.

Shepherd raised an eyebrow.

'He's got this really sweet tooth,' said Caroline.

Shepherd smiled again, gently, as at a pleasant memory.

'I didn't know that.'

'He used to embarrass me in restaurants,' she said. 'On purpose. When I was younger. You know. He'd skip the main course altogether and just order something from the dessert menu. And for dessert he'd order another dessert. Just to wind me up.'

Shepherd put his head on one side.

'Do you look like him?'

'I don't know. I think I *take* after him. I'm much more like him than mum.'

'How is your mother?'

It was the wrong question and he knew it.

She narrowed her eyes.

'How do you expect?'

He wanted to apologize. He didn't know how, without losing her further.

She took a gulp from the coffee, set down the cup it in its swimming saucer.

He said: 'Please don't go.'

'Really,' she said. 'I shouldn't even be talking to you.'

'I want to help him,' said Shepherd.

'Well,' she said. 'You can't.'

She slipped a few francs under her saucer, slung the small rucksack over her shoulder and walked away. It would have been easy for him to follow her, but he chose not to. She walked slowly, as if cradling something broken, and she turned the corner like a wandering ghost and was gone.

Shepherd got the bill, left a few coins in a saucer, then went for a walk. Their cash was running low, so he found an ATM and withdrew 3,000 francs. He found a small bookshop and browsed for a few minutes. His French was not good, and the English Language section was restricted to best-selling titles he was already familiar with: *A Year in Provence*, *Bridget Jones's Diary*, *Chocolat*, *Captain Corelli's Mandolin*. He flicked through a couple without interest. Then he broke the spine and bent the covers of some Jeffrey Archer paperbacks.

He ambled back to the café. The others were waiting for him inside. He grabbed a chair and sat by Eloise.

'No go,' he said.

'Well,' she said. 'Never mind.'

'I did warn you,' said Robert.

Lenny made a dismissive hand gesture and lit a cigarette.

'I don't know what I was thinking,' said Shepherd.

Robert peeled off early, but the rest of them stayed in the café until late. They emerged into the night drunk and morose, their thoughts full of solitude and murder. Lenny had spent a good deal of the evening trying to convince Shepherd to take a detour on the way home. He wanted to visit Rennes Le Chateau in the Languedoc. He told Shepherd about a mysterious priest called Saunière, and a fabulous buried treasure. And the tomb of Jesus Christ.

Shepherd agreed it would be interesting to find the tomb of Jesus Christ, but he was currently too tired. He suggested they come back in the spring, which seemed to keep Lenny happy enough.

The hotel reception was oak-panelled and lit with electric candles. A vested concierge stood behind a long wooden counter. There were numbered pigeon holes where he kept messages and room keys on big plastic fobs.

Lenny and Eloise planned to visit the bar and then perhaps a club. Shepherd couldn't face the prospect and rode the clanking old lift to the third floor. His luggage was waiting at the foot of his bed.

He went through the usual hotel ritual: checking the bathroom, the wardrobes, the bedsprings. He took the remote control from on top of the TV and found BBC World, alternating it with CNN, MTV and a frenetic Spanish gameshow in which contestants and presenter were permanently, and fascinatingly, on the edge of outright panic.

He called room service and ordered an omelette and a bottle of Burgundy. He dined and drank alone. Then, without unpacking or undressing, he fell asleep on the bed.

He woke with the rising sun. He had a crick in his neck and a foul, gummy mouth. Experience suggested he had been snoring. He knew he snored like a buffalo.

His overnight bag contained a ripped Sainsbury's carrier bag into which he had forced his dirty laundry. He had one clean shirt left and a single change of underwear. He showered with a hungover sense of shame.

He was dressed and ready for breakfast by 7 a.m. He took the lift to reception and went for a walk. The town was coming to life. He bought a French newspaper and a litre of mineral water, which he had drained and discarded within a minute or two. The air smelled different. It was the smallest indices of cultural difference, the familiar and half familiar, that most accentuated his sense of foreignness.

He returned to the hotel at 7.30. He was the first guest in the small, rather baroque restaurant. He folded the newspaper in half, laid it on the white linen and tried to decipher the text while shovelling food into his mouth with his left hand. He paused only to dab at the corner of his mouth with a crisp napkin. (Morsels of food often became entangled in his facial hair, something about which he was becoming somewhat neurotic: eating, he was forever dabbing and rubbing at his mouth in a manner that may itself have been distasteful to some.) Slowly, the restaurant filled with other guests. He was joined by a German family, a pair of elderly Americans and a couple of solitary diners who kept their eyes lowered to minimize unwanted social contact.

Just before 8, Robert walked into the restaurant and pulled up a chair.

Shepherd looked at him.

He said: 'What happened to you?'

Robert was unshaved. It was not so much that that he had not showered, although clearly he had not. He smelled like somebody who (like Shepherd) had slept in their clothes, but who (unlike Shepherd) hadn't changed them when he woke up.

Robert ran his palm over his bristly jaw.

He said: 'I was with Caroline.'

Shepherd nodded.

'I thought so.'

He poured Robert a coffee.

'She gave me something.'

'Milk?'

'No. She told me not to show it to you under any circumstances.'

Shepherd brushed crumbs from the table and closed the newspaper.

'Then why are you telling me?'

'Because I think she wants you to see it – but she didn't want to say so.'

Shepherd pressed his palms together.

He chose not to deliberate on the ethics of encouraging Robert directly to contravene an unambiguous request from a young, vulnerable woman who trusted him alone of all people left in the world.

'What makes you say that?'

'Just – you know. The way she acted and that.'

'And how did she act?'

'Like she *wanted* to believe you could help, but she couldn't bring herself to. She kept asking all these questions about you —'

'Like what?'

'Like, did I think you were just —'

'What? A loony?'

'Well, yeah. Pretty much. And what did you really want with her dad?'

'And what did you say?'

'That I didn't know.'

'Didn't know what? That I wasn't a loony, or what I really wanted with her dad?'

'Well. Both, really.'

Shepherd scratched his jaw and twirled a curl of beard round his index finger.

'And what do you think?'

Robert picked up a knife. He held it close to his eye, examined each of its planes, exploring his distorted reflection. Then he lay the knife on the table again, adjusting its position until it aligned at ninety degrees to the table's edge.

'I just want things back as they were,' he said. He reached into his back pocket and handed Shepherd a much creased sheet of A4 paper. The lines along which it had been folded into eighths were almost translucent.

Shepherd forced himself to hesitate, then took the paper from Robert's hand. It was the printout of an email.

> dear caroline
> i did not do this terribl thing i did not kill that girl or hurt her
> i am all right please put this behind you if you can
> you can do anything you want dont let this stupid
> mess stop you. do your college work it will all be ok
> in the end im sure
> please look after your nonny grace she always loved
> you more than anyone when you were young you
> played in her fur coat you thought it was an island do
> you remember
> Dad xxxxxx

Shepherd read it three times.

Without looking up, he said: 'May I keep this?'

'What if she asks for it back?'

'Will she do that?'

'Who knows?'

Shepherd read the email twice more. He wondered if it might have helped his children, had he written something similar, had he explained to each how he loved them. Or would it have been worse than wordless abandonment and suicide?

He folded the printout into quarters along the translucent creases and handed it back to Robert. He tried to betray no exhilaration at the first psychic scent of William Holloway.

He considered waking Lenny and asking about the technicalities of tracing emails. Then he thought that, wherever Holloway had been when he wrote the email, he'd be there no longer.

But it didn't matter. William Holloway was abroad. Perhaps he was awake and alert at this very moment. Active in the world.

Shepherd said: 'I need to see her, Robert. I need to see her again.'

Robert shook his head.

'She's not in a good way. It wouldn't be good for her.'

'I think she knows where he is.'

'No can do. Sorry.'

'Then her mother. Is she with her mother?'

'I don't think Kate wants to see you. She warned Caroline not to.'

'Please,' said Shepherd.

'I don't know.'

'You said yourself that Caroline wanted me to see the letter —'

'But she can't know that I showed it to you. I promised her.'

Shepherd balled his fist.

'Then what good will it do?'

Robert ripped open a bread roll. He began to spread a triangle of soft cheese.

'I can't.'

'Bloody hell, though, Robert,' Shepherd hissed between his teeth. 'We're so close.'

Robert ate his roll with cheese, clod by clod.

'I could try speaking to Kate,' he said, when the roll was finished. He began to prepare a second. 'But I'm not promising anything.'

Shepherd reached over and grabbed his shoulders.

'Please,' he said.

'She won't want to know.'

'But you'll try?'

'I'll try,' he said. 'Once more.'

III

Eloise and Lenny were still not up and about when, early that afternoon, Robert drove Shepherd to a village twenty kilometres out of town. He parked the MPV in a small tourists' parking lot and pointed out the sole café. Robert waited while Shepherd went and got himself a coffee.

Shepherd tried again to read the newspaper. The meaning and context of the printed words shifted. Every few minutes, he glanced at his watch. Kate Holloway was twenty-five minutes late.

He heard the café door open, looked up and knew it was her. She was shorter and perhaps older than he'd imagined.

'Mr Shepherd?'

He pushed back the chair and stood. She displayed not a flicker of anxiety at his size or his appearance.

'Please sit,' he said. 'Can I get you a drink?'

'Mineral water.'

Neither seemed able to break the silence and they listened to the ticking of the clock until the bottle of Evian arrived on a small tray, with a straight glass containing ice and a slice of lemon.

'It's a pleasure to meet you,' he said.

Before she could answer he gave her a pained smile.

He said: 'That's not quite what I meant to say.'

If he'd hoped for an encouraging grin for this nervous ineptitude, none was forthcoming.

'Let's be clear about this from the outset,' said Kate Holloway. 'I'm here because Robert practically begged me to see you. That's the only reason. He's been good to my daughter. He's taken a lot of this mess on his shoulders. It hasn't been easy for him. He's still a boy, for goodness sake. It's cost him at least a year of study, but he's stuck by her. There's not many that would. But I wish to God he'd chosen to have nothing to do with you – because God alone knows why he did. But Robert asked me to see you, and out of respect for him, here I am.

'I'm here to tell you that I'm not interested in your crackpot theories about who killed that poor girl. Because my ex-husband killed her. Is that clear?'

Shepherd couldn't meet her eyes. He looked intently at the back of his hand and scratched an itch that was not there.

He said: 'I don't think he did.'

'Well,' she said. 'Good for you. I'm sure that helps you sleep at night. So: I've heard what you've got to say, and I'm not interested. Now stop bothering me, and stop bothering my daughter. Or I'll call the police and I'll prosecute you for stalking us. Do you understand me? I'll have you sent to prison, Mr Shepherd. Don't think that I won't.'

'But he needs help.'

'Of *course* he needs help,' she said. 'Of course he needs *help*, for Christ's sake. But he doesn't need *your* help.'

'Mrs Holloway —'

'Ms Summerland. I haven't been Mrs Holloway for a long time.'

'Of course. Ms Summerland, I can't explain how, or why, but I feel a strong connection to your husband —'

'I'll *bet* you do.'

He wanted to continue but the look in her eyes warned him to stop. Her irises raged like hot metal.

'Look,' she said. 'Robert assures me you mean well. But I have no idea who you are, and I have no idea where you come from. So please let me say this once: none of this has anything to do with you. You have nothing to do with me, or with my daughter. You have nothing to do with Will, or with what he did. You have nothing to do with anything. You have no business here, of any kind. Can you understand that? However much you imagine it to be otherwise, there is no special connection whatever between you and my ex-husband. If I can do anything for you, it's this: I can suggest that you go home and *think* about your reasons for coming here – really *think* about why you've gone to all this time and effort, and come all this way just to harass me and my daughter —'

He bristled like a hedgehog.

He said: 'Harass is rather a strong word.'

'Is there another? Clearly we didn't want to be found. Clearly we don't want anything to do with you. But that didn't stop you. That sounds very much like harassment to me. So, please: go home, back to wherever you're from and—'

'And what?'

'See a doctor,' she said.

It felt like a kick in the stomach.

She remained rigid in her seat, elbows on the table, fingers locked. Eyes incandescent and unblinking.

'I dream about it,' he said. 'Every night.'

'So do I. So do we all.'

'I dream that I killed her.'

The rage dimmed and modulated and became fear. Kate glanced over her shoulder. She seemed to seek the eyes of the watchful patron.

Suddenly, it became clear to Shepherd that Kate had phoned ahead. She'd told the patron she was coming along to confront an obsessive stalker. She would appreciate it if he were to remain close at all times. Shepherd noticed that the patron's hand hovered over the telephone. Kate shook her head minutely. He took the hand away.

Her fear waned. The contempt shone brighter.

'You're not a psychic,' she said. 'You're a fantasist. You have a mental illness. There's no connection: not to Will, not to me, or to Caroline and I hope to God not to poor Joanne Grayling. You *want* there to be a connection, I'm sure you even *see* a connection. But it's entirely delusional.'

He tried not to sound sullen and angry. His voice came out flat and uninflected.

'You think he did it.'

'Of course I think he did it. *Because he did it*.'

He watched her read his face. He saw her frustration and irritation that he presumed to feel wounded on Holloway's behalf.

She said: 'Listen. I'll tell you something. He'd already had one nervous breakdown. Seven, eight years ago. Around the time we separated. First he became obsessed with a murderer, a man called Bennet. My God. How I remember the name. At the same time, he found out I'd been having an affair. He smashed up my house and he slashed his wrists and forearms with a breadknife. And he punched me in the face and fractured my cheekbone and the orbit of my eye. He might've killed me if the police hadn't arrived. There was so much blood around, they thought he already had.

'We'd already separated when that happened. Much later, I allowed him to move in with me and Caroline in Bristol. I nursed him back to health. It took a long time. He'd beaten me up, remember. He'd put me in hospital; he'd traumatized my daughter, but I still took him in, and I nursed him until he was well. Are you listening to me?'

He was still examining the back of his hand.

'Yes.'

'Good. We separated because I had an affair with a man called Dan Weatherell. This was seven or eight years ago, you understand?'

He nodded.

'The night before they say Joanne Grayling was killed, Will phoned Dan Weatherell in New Zealand and threatened to kill him. *The night before.* He was ranting and raving and threatening to cut him open. To cut him open. I know that because Dan phoned to ask what on earth was going on. Let me tell you, he was really scared. As well he might be. When Joanne is found, she's got *my name* written on her body in red lipstick. Does that sound like an innocent man to you? Does it sound like a man who is reconciled to the past? Does it sound like a man who's grateful that the woman he assaulted loved him enough to take him in and make him better? Does it sound like a *sane* man?'

She waited.

Shepherd didn't know how to respond.

'No,' she said. 'It doesn't sound like that, because it *wasn't*. It was the act of a *dangerous* man. An obsessed man. A *sick* man. Don't tell me what William Holloway is or is not capable of, Mr Shepherd, because there's only one person in the world who knows that better than me. And she's dead.'

She stood. The water remained untouched in its bottle on the table, the ice slowly melting in the sweating glass.

'I want this all to go away,' she said. 'I don't want to have these thoughts in my head. I was getting married this year, for God's sake. Imagine that. I was going to get married. My daughter was going to be my bridesmaid. You know the one; the sick, pale girl you spoke to yesterday. The girl who's trying to come to terms with what her father did to another girl, who wasn't much older than her. He cut Joanne Grayling's arms off while she was still *alive*. So I want you to go away, Mr Shepherd. I want you to go away and leave us alone. And if you don't go away and leave us alone, I will do everything in my power to ensure that you're punished as severely as the law will allow. Do you understand me?'

He burned with shame and injustice. But he kept his gaze low and nodded.

He didn't watch her leave, but he heard the slamming of the café door, the rattle of the glass in the old wooden frame.

He couldn't bear the continued, silent scrutiny of the patron and took a franc note from his wallet without checking the denomination. He left it under a saucer and trudged outside.

He found a low wall and rested until some of his strength had returned. Then he went and found Robert in the MPV. Robert was listening to David Bowie.

Robert drove Shepherd back to the hotel, but only in order to check out and pick up his luggage. He had decided to spend a week or two with Caroline and Kate. He still had not told Shepherd where they were actually staying, and he never did.

Shepherd shook Robert's hand and thanked him. Robert said he wished he could have been more help. Shepherd said he had been a great help, and insisted on taking his bags and loading them into the taxi.

He stood on the pavement, waving awkwardly as the taxi pulled away. The sight of Robert's bald spot filled him with paternal tenderness. He went to the hotel bar and ordered a scotch, which he nursed in silence until Lenny and Eloise returned at six. They were laden down with shopping bags.

Shepherd smiled. It was good to see them.

Eloise said: 'We bought you a jumper.'

He wore it the next day, behind the wheel of the people-carrier. As they headed towards England, Lenny suggested they take a detour to Normandy. He wanted to see the site of the D-Day landings. This time they indulged him. On a blustery, squally day they walked the length of Utah beach and back again, while Lenny rhapsodized about the incomprehensible scale and import of what had transpired there: about the violent murder of all those thousands of young, frightened men. He wondered aloud how it could be that such a place was not haunted.

Neither Eloise nor Shepherd, tramping arm in arm through the damp sand behind him, could answer him why. But it was true. The beach was a strip of brown, edged with black oil and shiny kelp. The grey sky bulged low above their heads. White gulls, points of light, flitted in shifting currents of air.

There were no ghosts.

17

I

Six days after the death of Joanne Grayling, William Holloway boarded the Eurostar at Waterloo station. He wore a week's stubble, aviator sunglasses and a baseball cap with the peak shadowing his face. The casual clothes of a much younger man.

His commitment to escape had been immediate and total. Within a very few minutes of ripping the last door from the last potting shed, he stole a cancerously rusty Vauxhall Astra. Observing the speed limit, he drove the Astra to Bath and dumped it. In Bath he stole a Honda Civic, which he swapped in Swindon for a Volkswagen Polo. He discarded the Polo on a residential street in Ealing. He left all three vehicles unlocked with the driver's side window rolled down.

By the time he arrived in Ealing, the sun was rising. He walked a couple of miles and caught the tube at Ealing Broadway. The carriage was nearly empty and the train's rhythm was soporific. His head lolled on his chest. When he woke, the carriage was full of pale, hazy London commuters and a ragged east European beggar. He changed at Holborn.

Outside King's Cross station, he stepped into the shimmering, profaned London daylight.

The journey to the capital afforded him time to meditate on the immediate future. He was determined that escape should be his sole consideration. It was an intricate discipline to reflect on nothing else.

He knew it would be many hours, possibly days, even weeks before Avon and Somerset began to piece together what had happened. Nobody had the least idea where he might be or what had happened to him. His own car had been abandoned outside the phone box in Stockwood. Nobody but the kidnapper knew that that he'd driven to the drop-off in a Capri, let alone where the drop-off point might have been. He'd done all he could to ensure the cars he stole were stolen again.

Nevertheless, he imagined helicopters clamouring in the Bristol darkness, ensnared in pillars of bright, white light. In his mind they buzzed and probed fields and gardens. He imagined all the cars he had driven that day being immediately recovered, identified and fingerprinted. He imagined an email from the Friends of George Bailey arriving on James Ireland's desktop: the scanned newspaper articles that would be attached; the video clip of Kate brushing the sweaty hair from her brow, laughing throatily, grinding down on David Bishop. Poor David Bishop, who they found dead long ago, lying in his bed with screwdrivers pushed through his eyes.

The low-resolution video clips: William Holloway and Joanne Grayling in a black cocktail dress.

He weeps.

Kate, he says.

Sometimes he was able to re-absorb the swell of panic, to drive it back inside himself like a prolapsed organ. And sometimes it almost pleased him to think of the chaos he'd left behind, the utter confusion.

Either way, he knew that in due time the police would arrive at the conclusion nobody wanted to arrive at.

But by then he would be long gone.

He spent the first night in a corroding backpackers' hotel off the Edgware Road. The mattress was mildewed and damp and skittered with parasites.

He rose early. He knew what to do, but first he had to find out where to go.

It was easy.

Thirty-six hours after his arrival in London, the full repercussions of the story had not fully broken. News reports were fragmentary, confused and contradictory. Jim Ireland had yet to make a clarifying statement. There was limited consolation to derive from this. Ireland would presume Holloway to be monitoring the investigation. Such was the proclivity of the personality type that committed crimes of this nature. Ireland would not suffer the investigation's progress to be jeopardized by releasing potentially compromising details to the media.

Probably, when the time came to make a full statement, a senior officer would subtly insult him, perhaps implying he was sexually impotent and of below average intelligence. This would be contrived to provoke and offend what they assumed to be his maniacal hunger for status and peer recognition.

He wondered what his former colleagues thought of him. He knew well that coppers distanced themselves from the varieties of carnage they commonly encountered. The more brutal the death, the blacker the humour of those who attended it. Emergency ambulance crews awarded style points to the bodies and bits of bodies strewn over motorway sliproads and suburban pavements.

So he wondered what Avon and Somerset were saying about him, privately. Probably they loathed him: not for murdering Joanne Grayling, about whom they would care little, but because he had caused them great embarrassment and compulsory overtime.

He wondered about his daughter.

He made himself stop.

After one more night in a soiled hotel, Holloway took possession of two fake passports of acceptable quality in the back room of a three-storey, terraced house close to Highbury stadium. He also bought £3,000 in clean money at 40p to the pound. The passports and the cash were brought to him by a bulky spud of a man in Arsenal colours. He heard the sounds upstairs of a game of poker under way.

Earlier, Holloway had bought a leatherette suitcase from a

dusty-windowed, discount luggage store outside Finsbury Park tube station. Into this he transferred the bulk of the cash, clean and otherwise. He caught a minicab to Waterloo. The driver stank like a wet dog. At Waterloo, Holloway bought a better suitcase, the upright kind with wheels. In the lavatory, he transferred the cash into it. There was a utility cupboard close to the wash basins. He hid the cheap suitcase in there.

From W.H. Smith he bought a novel, a newspaper and a bag of Werther's Originals. Then he joined the fluid crowd fusing with the body of the train. He was travelling first-class. As he boarded, he noted with satisfaction that many of his fellow passengers were Japanese and American tourists, few of whom would be on the alert for a wanted English policeman. The remainder were English and French businesspeople. They could be expected to take less notice of their fellows than their laptop computers and mobile telephones.

The train appeared to progress with teeth-grinding deliberation. Holloway imagined that a police car was shadowing it: if he only turned his head, he would see its flickering white form through the midsummer hedgerows. He imagined plainclothed and uniformed policemen walking the length of the train, checking passports and tickets. But no policeman came and when the train entered the Channel Tunnel and picked up speed, he swelled with gratitude and relief. He made his precarious way to the lavatory, where he suffered a short, fierce burst of diarrhoea. He checked his forehead. He was clammy and feverish. He sat on the lavatory until the train erupted into the brittle French daylight.

*

On arrival at the Gare du Nord, he purchased American Express traveller's cheques to the value of £2,000. The desk clerk expressed no surprise or concern at the number of high-denomination notes Holloway handed over. Emboldened, he spent much of the morning exchanging ever-larger amounts of cash for traveller's cheques at various banks and American Express offices. Some of these cheques he cashed immediately at other nearby banks. With this cash he bought yet more traveller's cheques.

That afternoon he sat in a café on the Left Bank and ordered a series of large espressos, into each of which he dropped three or four cubes of sugar. He allowed his mind to clear. He watched Parisians and tourists come and go, because that's what you did in Paris. When some of the exhaustion had lifted, he ordered a toasted ham and cheese sandwich. Concerned that he might be dehydrating, he followed the coffees with a large bottle of mineral water.

He made his way to the crowded Champs-Elysées, where he found a white and chrome boutique that was air-conditioned to a fridgelike chill. He paid cash for two summer suits, four shirts, underwear and socks. He left the goods for collection later. A few doors down, he bought a pair of shoes. From a pharmacist he bought a toothbrush, deodorant, shaving equipment and some plasters to prevent the new shoes blistering his heels. From a tourist information booth, he bought a city map cum guidebook. He picked up his clothes and hailed a taxi. He showed the driver a mid-range hotel listed in the guidebook.

The room was clean but shabby round the edges, in brown and cream. It had the faint odours of damp and antiquation.

He sat on the spongy bed and closed his eyes and slept. When he woke it was dark and he was sure the lobby was full of English policemen. He went to the bathroom and stroked his throat ruminatively in the black-spotted mirror. It rasped beneath his fingers. He made the shower short: a ten-second, high-pressure burst of cold water, followed by a ten-second burst of hot. Another ten cold, ten hot. Then he quickly soaped himself, shaved and towelled himself dry. He dressed in a new suit.

A scruffy, unshaven young man in a baseball cap had rented the room. A smart, red-headed middle-aged man in a light grey summerweight suit and black shoes left it.

The clerk with whom he settled the bill was not the clerk from whom he'd taken the room. Despite his early departure, he paid in full. Another cab took him through the white and gold centre of Paris and on to the airport.

He caught a late business flight to Berlin. Disembarking, he was beyond tired. He took a room at a generic airport hotel. Everyone spoke English with no discernible accent. He ran the shower, but had to lie down before the exertion of undressing. He fell asleep to the sound of CNN. He woke at 6 a.m. and lay awake in the darkness, staring at the ceiling and listening to the white noise coming from the bathroom.

If he spent enough nights in such rooms, he might simply fade away. The maids would find his bed rucked and empty and untainted by human odour.

He sat up. Acid sputtered in his gut.

It came to him that he had been murdered. He had been taken forever from the world, stolen from his daughter. This understanding brought him closer to Joanne. He understood now how their lives had tessellated. The convergence reached back through time. He had been there during her childhood, a dark orb behind the childish light in her eyes. He had been the shadow of a face cast on the wall during her first kiss. And in her turn, she had always been with him. She was the discarnate sigh at his shoulder when he married, the knowledge in the black, new-born eyes of his daughter. She was the objectless sadness in hotel rooms.

He spent the day in Berlin, buying and changing more traveller's cheques. Soon the dirty money would be dilute, like a carcinogenic trace element in purified water.

That evening, he left for Hamburg.

He completed the ad hoc money laundering in Frankfurt. To his knowledge, the money was not marked and the used notes were non-sequential. But he thought it possible the cash could be marked in a way he didn't know about and couldn't identify. He'd paid out a good proportion of it in commission, but at least he was now confident that he would not be discovered by carelessly spending the wrong note on the wrong day, at the wrong establishment.

There was plenty left. He wasn't sure exactly how much, but enough to last for quite some time; especially if he began to exercise some frugality.

The time had come to slow down.

Tired of Germany, he flew to Prague. He spent a week there and flew on to Rome. From Rome he travelled to Greece. Piraeus was ozone and diesel smells, the calling of gulls. He bought a four-week ferry pass. In Paroikia on the island of

Samos, he took a room in a whitewashed pension. He stayed there for some weeks.

The cranked-up torque of his musculature loosened. He spent long, shaded days under a beach umbrella. Behind the sunglasses, his eyes were blank. A dust sheet had been thrown over his thoughts. Under it there lurked unspecified contours. He dined alone in the evening, and set his head early on the pillow. His skin smelled of sun and salt and Ambre Solaire.

He didn't remember deciding to move on: he seemed to snap into consciousness as the plane descended upon Barcelona. Another taxi. He took a room in the Hotel Habbanna. He set his luggage down. In the granite, deco room there was an enormous bed. He sprawled on it like a starfish.

In the morning, he happened upon a crumbling, secluded square just off the tourist bustle and pickpocket press of the Ramblas. The square was bordered by cafeterias and restaurants. He spent a slow morning breakfasting on tapas, English tea and mineral water. He consulted a city guidebook and in the afternoon paid a visit to the *Sagrada Familia*, Gaudí's twisting, hallucinatory anemone of a cathedral. He paid the fee and ascended its high spires. He peered vertiginously over the city. Barcelona winked beneath the diaphanous haze of pollution. The moment fluoresced in him.

As an adolescent, he had secretly cut himself on the arms and ribs and chest with razorblades or shards of broken glass. Slow, deliberate bisections. Between the carving of flesh and the ebony weal of blood, he ceased to exist.

He watched the sun set from the tower of the *Sagrada Familia*. Then he went to a bar and thought about it.

Back in his room, he flicked through the erotic pay-per-view cable television channels. He saw a thirty-second clip of this and a ten-second burst of that. The outcome was a shifting, nullifying collage of satyriasis. With the volume muted, the images were ridiculous. The postures were silly, the facial expressions burlesque. The European films were underlit and heroin-blank. The bodies on which they centred were pale and veined and mottled and hairy-moled, so that Holloway felt a tug of affection for their owners, even the scrawny man wielding a raw club of penis that shone like a healing burn. Other scenes he recognized at once as American: inhumanly solid breasts that swelled fungally above pinched waists. Neurotically shaved and depilated adult pudenda. All sanitary and barren. Lust without passion. American pornography was overlit and without shadow. Intersecting planes of pink and white and brown. Abrupt badger stripes of hair: gleam of mucus. Hot stink of shit and spermicide.

It seemed a joyless and comical prank that this act, rendered here in its various but essentially unchanging inanity, could so blight the brief passage of human life on earth.

He wondered if pornography might function as a cure for sex. Perhaps young men consumed it so eagerly because it disengaged them from the profundity of their own fear: their most primal dread was rendered farcical. Not even bestial. Lobotomized.

Watch enough and you might never want to have sex again.

The idea made him sad, like old photographs did, and he smiled to himself, watching an American-Asian girl pretend to enjoy being anally skewered on a three-foot dildo.

The next morning he bought a ticket to Wellington, New Zealand.

II

Despite spending two nights in Hong Kong en route, he arrived at Auckland bleary and crumpled. His consciousness felt negligently tethered to his body. It bobbed in his zombie wake like a party balloon. His feet were swollen.

Once it had been established that he did not intend to bring any dangerous fruit into the country, Auckland proved to be the most accommodating of airports. The corridors and walkways were ornamented with potted, indigenous plant species. Native birdsong had been piped in. Smoked glass windows overlooked gigantic docked 747s.

He went to the Air New Zealand desk and confirmed his connecting flight to Wellington. It left in two hours, so he found a luggage trolley and walked to the domestic terminal. In a moulded plastic seat, he punched and bundled his hand luggage into a pillow. He fell asleep at once. When he jerked awake and looked at his watch, he couldn't work out where the time had gone. He went to the lavatory and passed a thick, odorous stream of dark urine. He examined his tongue in the mirror. The sight was alarming. He went to Whitcoulls and bought a litre of Evian and five Cherry Ripes, bars of cherry coconut in plain chocolate. The mixed strangeness and familiarity of the horizontally ranked confectionery reminded him how far he was from home. By the time he had washed down this meal (he could not work out which meal it had been), the time had come to board his flight.

It was a small plane and he was a nervous flier, but nevertheless he fell asleep before take-off.

He awoke as the aircraft tipped into a vertical dive. He bloomed with hysteria. It was a long minute before he convinced himself they were not about to slam into the heavy earth.

The air crew remained nonchalant (Holloway was well-practised at assessing when they were not) and continued to go about their business. The plane swept low over the water. Too rigid with dread to enquire otherwise, he took it on faith that the pilot was not about to ditch in the Pacific. In fact, Wellington's approach runway jutted into the bay like an uncompleted motorway bridge. When the aircraft's landing gear first brushed the tarmac and squealed, so nearly did Holloway.

Outside the airport terminal, he rested his weight on a low wall that bordered the short-stay car park. He squinted in the oblique white slant of Wellington light. Everything was altered. The sunlight came from strange angles. Distant lettering on road signs and advertisements was abnormally distinct. He could see tiny bumps and depressions in the tarmac. The details of his own rumpled clothing and soiled skin. Sweat and sebum were a sheen on his forearms. Crystals of salt at the root of tiny hairs.

The sky rang crystal blue above him. White concrete shone like a temple. Parked and passing cars were bursting nodes of primary colour. The white and silver of skyborne aircraft.

He moved to the taxi rank in dreamlike weightlessness. He

tried to calculate what time of day it was, then what day. He reached the front of the queue. The taxi driver left his seat and came round the car to collect Holloway's bags. It felt like being rescued.

The driver was broad, with a low centre of gravity. He'd greased his thin grey hair into a DA and his blue shirtsleeves were rolled to the elbow, revealing heavily tattooed forearms. He sat behind the wheel and swivelled to face Holloway. He rested a forearm along the back of the seat.

'Where can I take you, mate?'

Holloway tried to think. After a while, he thought of the word he was looking for.

'A hotel.'

'Do you know which hotel?'

'Oh. Anything half-decent. Whatever.'

'This your first time in Wellington?'

He lacked the strength to lie.

'Yes.'

'That'll be right.' The driver nodded and pursed his lips. Then he said: 'Listen, I'll tell you the truth. This is my second day behind the wheel.'

'Right,' said Holloway.

'It's not that I don't know *Wellington*,' the driver said. 'I know *Wellington* like the back of my hand. But I've been away.'

Holloway trundled along the conversational rut.

'Really? How long?'

The driver was pulling from the airport now, on to the main road.

'Twenty years. Give or take.'

'Long time,' said Holloway.

'Bloody long time.'

'Right.'

'Right.'

They drove for a while, in the easy silence of two men who fully understood one another.

'So the thing is,' said the driver, 'I can tell you what hotels were good twenty years ago —'

'Oh. Right,' said Holloway.

'You get me? Wellington's changed a lot in twenty years. A lot. Now, I don't want to tell you somewhere's great, just because it was great in 1982. Do you get what I'm saying?'

'Look,' Holloway said. 'Anywhere. Anywhere will do.'

'Sure?'

'Sure.'

'Right you are. You got any preferences about the route?'

'No.'

'You ever seen the bay?'

'No.'

'Oh, mate. You have to see the *bay*. You can't come to Wellington and not see the *bay*.'

'Great,' said Holloway. 'OK.'

'Right you are,' said the driver. He threw the cab into a screaming U-turn. A giant hand buried Holloway in the vinyl seat.

'Don't worry, mate,' the driver said. 'She'll be right.'

Holloway was too tired not to take his word for it.

They raced along the coastal road, which ascended into steep green hills. The landscape was exotic and familiar. Gorse clung to the upper hillsides, undulating tree ferns to the lower. The roadside was lined with toetoe. It bowed like pampas grass; from its centre emerged feathery, head-hung pom-poms.

They passed an erratic strip of weather-beaten dwellings. Each was completed to a different design. Some were ramshackle and uncertain; their wooden frames worn smooth by salt wind hitting the Cook Straight off the Tasman Sea. Others were smart family homes in jaunty pastels. New 4 x 4s squatted in their driveways.

To their immediate right, the ocean surged and eddied at the rocky, beachless seashore. The driver stopped to show Holloway a blue penguin. The bird sprang happily from the boiling foam of a breaking wave and planted itself on a wet rock. It hunched its shoulders like a gumshoe in a raincoat. Holloway watched the penguin through the window. The penguin looked back at him through little black eyes. Then it waddled in a half-turn and dumped itself back in the tidal surge. He watched its head bob like a ping-pong ball until it was lost from sight.

They drove on.

Round the camber of headland, Wellington unveiled itself. It was a pearly crescent, set tight to the windy bay; the lunette of a God's nail. Standing on reclaimed land, the city climbed on its outer curve into steep hills. White houses collected in their deep green slopes and gullies.

He had not expected the city to be so abundantly green, nor its once-colonial downtown to be so contemporary and metropolitan. He tipped the taxi-driver and decided to get himself a coffee before looking for a hotel.

He found a café on the edge of Civic Square, which was a pristine fusion of Victorian architecture and late twentieth-century postmodernity. He planted himself on a metal alfresco table and ordered banana cake and cappuccino. He felt misplaced and disconsolate. This was a bright new place. He was old-world, and worn and filthy: a spectral reminder of colonial antiquity.

It had been a long way to come, and to a stranger place than he had imagined, to commit a murder.

18

He was in no rush. For nearly three weeks, while he assimilated and got over the jet lag, he familiarized himself with Wellington. He spent hours strolling downtown. He window-shopped and bought a wardrobe of appropriate clothing. The months spent in Europe and the weeks on a Greek beach had left him tanned and his hair bleached nearly blond. He wore loose khaki trousers and bright short-sleeved shirts. He took day trips to local places of interest. He ate in cafés and browsed the Te Papa museum and the bookshops. He committed to memory the secrets of Wellington's orientation: the linking alleys and the unexpected culs de sac. The dream-city began to solidify. It sent taproots into his mind. The eagerly courteous young waiting staff in the cafés and diners learned to recognize him.

Hiya, Will. Cake and a Coke?

At the end of the second week, he went to an internet café and found the official website of Victoria University, Wellington. He made notes in a spiral-bound reporters' pad, then read and reread some pages of secondary interest.

The next morning, he put on a suit and tie and caught a taxi to the university. The campus was like a small town within the Wellington suburbs. Its faculty buildings were in the various signature styles of the 1970s, the 1950s, the 1940s. The Hunter Building was gothic and ivy-clad. The students differed in no visible way from their British counterparts. They didn't seem conscious of Holloway's existence. The suit rendered him invisible. He thought better of testing this theory by sitting with the undergraduates and buying himself a coffee in the refectory, but he did browse the campus bookstore, his sunglasses tucked safely away in a sober breast pocket.

He explored the campus for hours, taking regular breaks for Coke and Cherry Ripes. He satisfied himself of its layout before finding the faculty of English. It was located on the eight or ninth floor of the 1970s Von Zedlitz building, but alongside it were small Victorian cottages in which lecturers kept their ramshackle offices. His heart beat hard and he sat on a low wall until the giddiness passed. He supposed that if anybody were to notice any incongruity, this would be the moment: a man dressed like an accountant but wearing RayBan Aviators, perched on a wall and eating a Cherry Ripe. He smiled at the thought. It was his first sighting of himself for many weeks.

The moment wavered. The idea grew in him that shortly he would blink and look about him. His head would clear with a pop and he would wonder what he was doing here. Why had he travelled across the world to sit outside a university faculty clutching a briefcase that contained a mace spray, a hunting knife with serrated blade, parcel tape and a length of nylon rope?

Then Dan Weatherell walked past.

Holloway's hand reached down to clasp the edge of the wall, so that in his light-headed shock he did not roll forward, face-first on to the pavement. He felt unprepared and extravagantly prominent, sitting on a wall with broad-leafed, indigenous vegetal matter swaying pleasantly behind him in the New Zealand breeze while the man he had crossed the planet to kill strolled past, deep in conversation with a colleague or perhaps a graduate student.

It did not seem fitting to Holloway that Nemesis should be encountered with a Cherry Ripe in his hand.

But Weatherell didn't see him, and Holloway forced himself not to turn his head and follow his progress. Finally, Weatherell passed the clouded edge of his peripheral vision. Still Holloway did not care to look: he feared that Weatherell had been a hallucination, a psychotic wish-fulfilment.

But Holloway's imagination would not have done to Dan Weatherell what time had.

Holloway thought he might pass out. He stuffed the half-eaten chocolate bar into his pocket and strode from the university campus. He jogged on to the street and tried to hail a taxi. Half a dozen had passed before he recalled that in New Zealand people didn't hail taxis in the European manner. He set off to find a rank, but by then the sense of urgency had evaporated. It wasn't such a long way back to his hotel, so he turned in its direction and began to walk.

He decided to kill Weatherell at home.

There would be fewer potential witnesses and he would be able to take his time. He could ask Weatherell how he'd met Derek Bliss, and how long they'd been planning to do this to him.

Although it would be given under duress (under torture, if necessary) Holloway considered taping Weatherell's confession. Perhaps it could be used to mitigate the case against him, should he be caught.

But he would not get caught. He knew that. When Weatherell was dead, he would simply fly to Brazil, or some other country with no extradition treaty. It would be many months before he even became a suspect – if he ever did. Nobody in this country knew him, or could connect him in any way with Dan Weatherell. He would leave New Zealand using the second passport, which he had not yet used. Even if somebody were to witnesses him leaving the scene, and his description was somehow connected to the man staying in his hotel room, he would have left the country using another name. In order that he become a suspect, it would first require Kate to learn of Weatherell's death (which did not seem likely, if they had not been in contact since the end of their affair) and then to connect that death with her missing ex-husband (which seemed scarcely more probable), and finally for her to relay her suspicions to the Wellington police. The Wellington police would then be required to display an active interest in what she told them, and devote resources to its investigation.

He would not be caught. If for some reason he was identified and located, it wouldn't happen until it was too late to do anything about it. He would invest what was left of the money; perhaps in a beachfront bar or a guest house. If he was careful and exercised some imagination, it might be possible to live in some style.

Or he could take his own life.

He could walk along the stark black beach at Piha and into the ocean. When the crashing ocean reached his narrow throat, he could dip his head into the foreign water, the harsh saline burning his mucus membranes, and he could take the water down and go to sleep.

Either way, he didn't mind. But he would not be caught.

It took him a week to buy a second-hand car. A certain instinct led him to the kind of car-yard he was looking for. It was a battered, silver-grey Subaru hatchback and he paid far too much for it. Had he not suspected as much, the scrupulously blank eyes of the man into whose hands he dealt the money, note by note, would have told him. But Kooznetzoff looked dangerous, and anyway, he didn't mind. He spent the morning giving the Subaru a trial run, adapting himself to the automatic transmission. Then he waited outside the campus car park to follow Weatherell home.

It took him three attempts. The first evening, Weatherell's fat-wheeled Mitsubishi Pajero pulled away too quickly at the lights and Holloway lost him round an unexpected bend. The next night, Holloway was caught at a red light and lost sight of it. On the third attempt, it was easy. He stuck to the white

Pajero like a pilot fish. He followed it up steep, curving roads into Khandalla. The streets were lined with wind-twisted trees. Impressive white houses overlooked the city far below and beyond it the the blue, twinkling bay. Distant, coloured flecks were wind-surfers. Tiny jet skis and motorboats buzzed and scudded the surface.

The Pajero turned into a plant-lined, concrete driveway. Holloway drove on for a few metres, then pulled to the kerb on the opposite side of the road. He twisted the rear-view mirror, noting which house Weatherell went to.

He drove back to his hotel. He sat on the bed and dialled room service. He ordered a vodka, ice, no tonic. But when it arrived, he left it undrunk on the bedside table. He called down for a Coke, instead.

The next afternoon, he broke into Weatherell's house.

It was a large, two-storey structure that backed on to the hillside. At the front it spread on to a broad, flat lawn that overlooked the far-off bay, but the rear garden was dense with plants whose swaying, fleshy leaves overhung the two flights of concrete steps by which one descended to it.

Holloway took the steps briskly but did not run.

Gaining entry to the house was easy. A kitchen window had been left unlatched. He opened it fully and hiked himself on to the windowsill. He used his arms to brace himself in the frame and sprang across a sink full of unwashed plates and mugs. He landed on his feet on the quarry-tiled floor.

He brushed himself down. The house smelled of new carpets and coffee and woodshavings.

The internal kitchen door opened on to the long, narrow sitting room. Large, bright sofas and parquet flooring, with scattered rugs. A second door in the far corner. Maori sculptures with grotesque faces stood in the corners and on the windowsills. Low wooden bookshelves were haphazardly stuffed with hardbacks, paperbacks, framed and unframed photographs, decorative bowls and saucers containing buttons, loose coins, unidentifiable odds and ends of metal and plastic. No TV that he could see, but an impressive stereo. French windows opened on to the garden, which was bordered at the far end with swaying copper beech.

The French windows were open. In the garden there sat a woman in a wheelchair. She was reading a book.

At first, the sight of her puzzled Holloway. He couldn't work out who she might be. He had accepted without question that Weatherell, like himself, had never found a partner to replace Kate and lived alone. But, of course, Dan Weatherell had been married when he and Kate met. His contract at Leeds University had been for a single academic year. His wife had professional commitments of her own and did not join him. Holloway knew – had always known – that Weatherell returned to her when the relationship with Kate ended.

He wondered how different all their lives might have been had this woman only accompanied her husband to England all those years ago.

He stood in the French window and watched her. He wondered if she knew about Kate. He decided that she couldn't. She seemed too content and dozy in the leaf-dappled shadow ever to have been hurt so badly. Her curly hair was cut short

like a choirboy. She was pale, with a touch of ruddiness round
the cheeks. She wore angular tortoiseshell spectacles.

As he watched, she lay the book in her lap and massaged her
neck, rolling her head on her shoulders. She removed the spectacles and rubbed at her eyes. She looked at her watch. Then she
turned the wheelchair abruptly about and rolled back to the
house.

Her speed and dexterity took Holloway by surprise. He
threw himself behind the sofa. He crouched there, believing it
impossible that she had not seen him. He couldn't breathe. He
wanted to piss. He bit down on his fist to stifle a nervous
giggle.

She wheeled past him and into the kitchen. The door swung
closed behind her.

He heard the fridge door open and close. Then something
being laid on the table: the rattle of a cutlery drawer. The tinny
sound of a local radio station news broadcast.

The kitchen overlooked the steps that led back to the road.
While she remained in there, it would not be possible to leave
without being seen.

Holloway guessed that the door at the far corner of the sitting room would take him through to the hallway and the
possibility of exit: if he waited in the hallway, he could escape
through the front door when next she entered the sitting room.
He thought he could do it without her hearing. If not, he would
be gone before she was in a position to see and describe him to
her husband.

In a spidery half-crouch, he scuttled from behind the sofa
and pressed his eye to the crack in the door. She displayed no

inclination to leave. A dog-eared, floury and sauce-stained cook book lay open on the kitchen table, alongside a half-glass of wine, the last from an empty bottle she'd set down on the edge of the sink. As he watched, she lifted herself in the wheelchair to press her full weight on the flat of a large blade, crushing the breastbone of two poussins.

He looked at his watch.

He wondered if the garden might provide an alternative means of escape. But he knew that, if somebody saw him – and if he went leaping over hedges and through people's gardens, somebody surely would – then he could never come back. He scratched an eyebrow and tried to think.

A car pulled in to the driveway.

Holloway punched his forehead with the heel of his hand.

The clunk of a car door opening.

The woman called out through the wide-open kitchen window: 'You're early.'

A car door slamming.

Distantly: 'Yeah.'

'Did you remember to get wine?'

'What do *you* think?'

Weatherell entered the kitchen through the unlocked door. On the table he set down a carrier bag containing three bottles of wine. He shrugged a bag made heavy with books and essays from his shoulder and set it on the floor, near the doorway. He took off his jacket and hung it on a kitchen chair, then removed his tie. He dangled it over the jacket. He kissed his wife on the forehead, then the lips.

'I thought you'd forget.'

'Yeah, right.' He jiggled on the spot. 'I'm bustin',' he said. He made an exaggerated waddle towards the door.

Holloway threw himself behind the sofa again. He heard the swish of Weatherell's trousers and the slight exertion of his breath as he hurried past. There was a toilet in the hallway. Weatherell's grunt of relief was followed by a powerful, extended surge of urine on water. Then there was silence as he shook and zipped. The roar of the flush. Weatherell kicked off his shoes in the hallway and returned to the kitchen in stockinged feet. He left a trail of sweaty footprints on the parquet floor. Holloway watched them evaporate. His skin crawled with shame and disgust.

In the kitchen, Weatherell said: 'How's it been?'

'Bad today. I read.'

'That's good, love. That's really good.'

'Are you even listening to me?'

'Course I am. I mean it's good you got to read.'

'Are you OK?'

'Course. Yeah.'

'Why are you so early?'

He took a corkscrew from the cutlery drawer and opened the wine.

'What's the point of being there at all,' he said, 'if you don't get to leave early, every now and again?'

Weatherell was not the man of Holloway's memory. He remembered Kate's lover, the man for the love of whom she had left him, as a gloomy, Byronic figure, with a dark, heavy fringe and intense, unblinking eyes. This man was shorter, stouter. He shambled as he walked and wore clothes that needed pressing: a pastel-pink shirt with short sleeves and biros in the breast pocket. Grubby khaki chinos. He had sweaty feet and a belly. His socks were worn transparent at the heel. His greasy hair was combed carelessly back from his brow. He wore a goatee beard in need of a trim.

'I got no work done,' she said. 'Not a jot.'

Weatherell opened a low cupboard.

'Take a day out, for God's sake. Any luck with the real estate agents?'

'Not even a call.'

'You leave messages?'

'About a hundred.'

'Jeez. Those guys.'

He took some sweet potatoes from the cupboard and dumped them on a double spread of newspaper. He sat alongside her at the table and began to peel.

'Look,' he said. 'Never mind.' He dumped a potato in an empty pan and pulled a curl of peel from the blade. He picked up another and said: 'I had another phone call today.'

'What sort of phone call?'

'The English guy, asking to come and see me at home.'

'About what, this time?'

'He wouldn't say. Not over the phone. That's why he wants me to see him.'

'Are you going to?'

He took a sip from her glass.

'What? See him? *Fuck* no. I'm worried that he's – you know. A pickle short of the full burger.'

She smiled, set the poussins with some crushed garlic on a

baking tray. Drizzled over some olive oil. She went to the fruit bowl and put three lemons in her lap, returned to the table and cut them in half. One by one, she squeezed the halves over the tiny, hollow chickens. Then she arranged the squeezed halves in the baking tray.

They talked some more about selling the house, independent access to which was becoming more difficult for her. But the house-hunting was not going well.

The discussion disheartened them and for a while they sat in silence at the table, sharing and refilling the same glass of wine. A couple of flies buzzed the crushed poussins, and Weatherell brushed them away with a flick of his wrist.

'I know,' he said. 'Let's go to the beach this weekend.'

A brief silence.

'I don't know, Dan.'

'Christ, Liz. You're talking a couple hundred bucks, max. I'm not talking Fiji here. I'm just saying, let's go up the coast. I'm talking maybe the Road to Ruin.'

At first Holloway was not sure he'd understood Weatherell correctly. But he repeated it three of four times in the next few minutes. *Let's just go relax at the Road to Ruin*.

'Honey,' said Liz. 'Are you OK? You seem a little freaked out.'

Weatherell was slicing some mushrooms. He shrugged.

'It's this house thing,' he said. 'It's getting me down, I guess.'

'Don't worry about the house. We'll be right. There's plenty of time.'

'Yeah,' he said. 'I know. I know that.'

She said: 'There's something else.'

'No, there's not. I'm fine. I'm tired.'

'It's that phone call, isn't it?'

He lay the vegetable knife down and ran a hand through his hair. He left little shreds of mushroom there.

'Dan, what did he actually *say*?'

'Nothing. It's just – stupid.'

'Then tell me.'

'It doesn't matter.' He started chopping again. He gathered himself and said: 'Are we going away or what?'

A lock of hair fell across his brow and he brushed it away.

Liz agreed that they would set out on Friday for the Road to Ruin. Weatherell took the tray of poussins to the oven and slammed it in. A brief burst of heat.

Holloway hid out behind the sofa for perhaps half an hour while they stayed in the kitchen. Then, still in his socks, Weatherell carried two folding tables to the patio. He returned for the bottle and a basket of bread. Liz followed him to the garden.

Holloway peeked over the back of the sofa. He watched and listened for any sign that they might be headed back to the kitchen. But they were talking in a low, summer murmur. Liz reached out and tickled the back of Weatherell's head. He nuzzled closer to her. Holloway wondered how long the small birds would take to roast.

He lurched through to the kitchen and out of the door. His legs were cramped and numb for the crouching. He wondered if he could make it up the two flights of concrete steps. Leaves tickled his face. Burrs caught in his hair.

Later, he picked them out, one by one, in the hotel bathroom mirror.

19

On Friday, he drove the Subaru hatchback through 600 km of landscape that proved to be wholly inconstant.

He took the Gold Coast north from Wellington. The ocean was to his left. The sky was broad and flat and endless. He drove through familiar-looking suburbs, listening to the Best of Fleetwood Mac with the window open. The suburbs began to thin out, giving way to semi-rural towns. These small communities became widely separated, then thinned like vapour and he passed into open countryside.

He took the Foxton Straight through the Wairarapa, crossing into the North Island's agrarian heartland. He thought of Scotland, but the Wairarapa hillsides were young and jagged, as if their brittle rock was newly shattered.

He passed through one-street towns — a general goods store, a petrol station, hardware stores, real estate agents, tearooms — that might have been dumped by a Midwestern twister. He stopped at one such town to lunch in a tearoom. Inside, it glimmered with the dusty ghost of the provincial 1950s.

Back on the road, it was the Subaru's engine that first alerted him to a long, insistent gradient. Gradually, he left sheep-farming country behind him. At its apex, the Desert Road opened on to a vast volcanic plateau. To the west, mountains faded slowly into view. He knew that one of them, Ruapehu, long believed dormant, had erupted two years before. The ferocity of its awakening had darkened the sky and coated the North Island with a thin fur of ash.

He arrived at the shores of lake Taupo, an inland sea whose beaches were pumice. Its depths boiled with geothermal currents. Mountains reflected on its surface like gloomy sentinels.

He pulled up to the scree at the side of the deserted road. He left the car and spread the map on the roof to check his position. He wanted to understand the spectacle. He couldn't. He turned a full circle. A sound like gravel beneath his feet. The landscape rushed away from his mind. Its scale and its emptiness eluded comprehension.

It was like travelling into primal, geological antiquity. A country of ancient ghosts.

He sat down on the harsh soil and watched the lake. Tendrils of haze shifted and evaporated on its surface. Two or three cars passed him. He looked at his watch and decided to drive on.

He descended from the volcanic plain as the sun began to set in the west. At lower altitudes, scrubby native bush gave way to patches of high pine trees. The patches grew: threw out connections to one another. Became clumps of woodland.

As it grew dark, he found himself alone in a forest without limit.

Deep in the dark, luxuriant woods, the land was fiercely steaming. The ground bloomed suddenly with great, white clouds that carried on the breeze and obscured the road and sky before him. The air was thick with sulphur.

After many miles, the trees began to thin. He saw the lights of a city.

He had arrived at the Road to Ruin. It lay before him, surrounded on all sides by the vaporizing earth.

He'd asked a familiar young waiter in one of the cafés off Wellington's Civic Square if there could really be a place in New Zealand called the Road to Ruin. There was a Bay of Plenty and a Poverty Bay. A Road to Ruin would complete the trio, but Holloway couldn't find it on his map or any reference to it in his guidebook.

The waiter swept his blond pony tail off one shoulder and said: 'Mate – you mean *Rotorua*.'

Rotorua was a tourist destination set on the volcanic, new earth. It catered to those who wished to bathe in its hot mineral springs and witness some geothermal violence.

The town had been built to a grid. Its streets were lined with tearooms, hotels, fast food outlets and shops that catered to the wants of its visiting consumers. But there remained something of the frontier about it, as if Rotorua stood on the hinterland between worlds.

After a cursory drive round, Holloway checked in at the Sheraton.

He woke at 5 a.m. When he had showered and dressed, he went to the hotel car park and searched in the early morning light until he found a familiar Pajero. He re-parked the grey Subaru in an empty slot nearby. By now it was approaching six. He went to Reception.

He had dressed in cargo shorts and a blue, Hawaiian shirt, pulled a Gap baseball cap low over his eyes. He took a seat opposite the desk, crossed his legs and pretended to read a newspaper. His own daughter would not have recognized him.

Weatherell and his wife didn't show up until eight. Holloway supposed they'd enjoyed a lie-in. Liz was walking with the aid of a stick. Weatherell followed her, pushing the empty wheelchair. Outside the lift, she stopped and lay a hand on his elbow. He kept pace, funereal step for funereal step. They left the wheelchair with an obliging member of staff at the restaurant door.

Holloway watched them enter, then he folded his newspaper and followed. He took a seat close to the window, a few metres from Weatherell's back.

He watched them eat an unhurried breakfast, interrupted with brief snippets of muttered conversation and a snorted laugh or two. Holloway caught the eye of a mismatched pair of men in the corner and looked away. He wondered if he looked suspicious, if perhaps something in his manner or his gaze hinted at his intent. He forced himself not to stare at the Weatherells, in case the two men were watching him. Instead, he concentrated on a page of the newspaper that already seemed so familiar he might have recited it from memory.

He waited until they had nearly finished breakfast. Then he walked to the car park and sat low in the driver's seat of the

Subaru. It was another half-hour before the Weatherells appeared in his rear-view mirror. He wondered where they'd been for so long. Dan Weatherell had put on a floppy sun hat with his washed-out University of Wellington T-shirt, baggy shorts and flip-flops. His legs looked hairless and nude, like an old man's.

Holloway followed them at a prudent distance. With some judicious light-jumping, he was able to keep three or four vehicles between them. It was to his benefit that the Pajero was the size of a house.

He followed them to Whakawerawera, which his guide-book told him was a thermal park and Maori cultural centre. It was sited on the edge of town. From the car park, outside the wooden boundary fence, he saw the muscular spurt of a hot water geyser and heard the yells of people caught in its spray. Drifting clouds of steam half obscured the park entrance.

Judging by the empty lots in the car park, the thermal park was not yet half full. He waited until the Weatherells had paid and entered before joining the short queue. At the turnstile, he bought a pamphlet that folded out into a simple map of the park.

Through the gates he found a souvenir shop and a cafeteria. He checked to ensure the Weatherells were not inside.

The park was not yet busy. Small groups of visitors maintained a muted, respectful distance from each other. White clouds flowed and eddied like battlefield smoke across the ruined, cratered landscape. Only the most resolute plant life had taken hold here; unearthly species with needle-like leaves.

The path through the fissures and splits in the earth was marked by wooden duckboard walkways. Arrows painted on the walkways corresponded with those marked on his map. Thus he was able to navigate the blighted earth. Keeping close enough to the edge of a German coach party for a casual observer to assume he was part of it, he followed the Weatherells from minor crater to minor crater: cleaves and gashes in the earth, within which smoke billowed and rolled and hot grey mud seethed.

He left the Germans and, separated from the Weatherells only by a ragged haze of vapour, he followed them across a bubbling mud flat. The geyser stood at the mud flat's centre. Its eruption was accompanied by a sudden hot spray of water that dropped vertically from the clear blue sky and soaked his clothing. The brief shower was followed by a dense, warm cloud of vapour that caught on the wind and engulfed him. He became disorientated. He caught shifting glimpses in the fog, forms that might have been the Weatherells, or trees, or his own refracted shadow.

He waited until the smoke had cleared before proceeding.

He caught up with them five minutes later. Liz was standing. She had joined Dan in leaning on a metal railing. They overlooked a crack in the crust of the planet. Coloured mineral deposits encrusted its walls, like a witch's grotto. Its depths ebbed and rushed with super-heated water and boiling mud that exploded forth in a great roar of steam and heat.

Holloway waited under a needle-leafed bush while a crowd of Japanese joined them: took photographs, passed on. The Weatherells showed no inclination to move. He wondered if this was a special place for them.

They kept their silence, contemplating the seismic violence

beneath them. His hand was clasped over hers. Holloway walked to the handrail and grabbed it in both fists. He stood a metre from Weatherell.

He said: 'I've come to get you, Dan.'

There was a moment without sound or motion. Then Weatherell turned his head.

The earth hissed and roared beneath them.

'Will?'

Holloway removed the baseball cap and threw it to the wet ground. Inexplicably, since he had felt no emotion until this second, his eyes welled with tears of self-pity and rage. He removed the sunglasses.

'I told you I'd come for you.'

Liz took a shaky half-step forward. She lay a protective hand on Dan's shoulder. Dan took it in his and squeezed.

'Honey,' he said. 'Why don't you go back to the car?'

'She's not going anywhere,' said Holloway.

She fixed him with frigid contempt. There was no fear there.

'What do you want?'

'He doesn't want anything, love. Just go on back to the car. I'll be there in a minute.'

'Stay where you are.'

'Will,' said Weatherell. 'I don't know what's going on. But, whatever it is, it's got nothing to do with my wife.'

'Not with *your* wife. No.'

'For Christ's *sake*, Will. Let's just you and I can go somewhere and talk. Jesus. You should see yourself.'

Holloway put a hand to his mouth.

'Oh,' he said. 'You're unbelievable.'

Weatherell made a pacifying gesture with his hand. He looked left and right.

'Will,' he said. 'I don't know what's going on here.'

'*You* are what's going on.'

'Listen to me. I don't *understand* that. I don't understand what you're talking about.'

With urgent, furtive movements of his left hand, Weatherell edged Liz behind him.

From the hip pocket of his shorts, Holloway took out the hunting knife.

Liz said: 'Run, Dan.'

He squeezed her hand.

'Will,' he said. 'Please don't do this. You don't know what you're doing.'

'I can't believe what you did to me,' said Holloway.

'I didn't do *anything*,' said Weatherell. 'Come on, this can't be about Kate, can it? This can't be about *Kate*, for Christ's sake? That's a million years ago.'

Holloway blinked rapidly. A passing drift of steam obscured Weatherell, made him a grey shadow on white fog.

He looked at Liz, leaning now on the railings for support. He couldn't meet her eyes.

'Will,' said Weatherell. His tone of voice had changed. He looked left and right. 'I don't want to fight you. But you're scaring me, mate. Now, if you take one step forward with that knife in your hand, you won't leave me with any choice. Do you understand that? I'm warning you, Will. Stand back. Stay away from us.'

Holloway tried to speak. But now he needed them, no words would come.

'I'm not kidding round,' Weatherell said. He looked hurriedly to his left and right, as if preparing to yell for help. 'Take another step and I swear to God I'll fucking kill you, Will. I'm not joking now. Put the knife down.'

Holloway glanced into the pit below him.

He wondered what it would do to a human body.

'Please,' said Weatherell.

Holloway shook his head.

'No,' he said.

Weatherell licked his lips.

'Whatever it is you think I did,' he said. 'I didn't. OK? Whatever it is – it wasn't me.'

Holloway saw himself mirrored on beads of moisture that had condensed on the blade. He saw himself reflected there a dozen times, inverted in miniature.

He took a step.

Two figures emerged from the steam.

The first was a big, shaven-headed man who wore wire-rimmed spectacles and an unruly, tangled beard. He was accompanied by a skinny, scruffy younger man with a grown-out blond crew cut. He wore gold-rimmed aviator sunglasses that had slipped down his nose. Both were breathing heavily.

'Jesus fucking Holy Christ,' said Weatherell. His voice had climbed an octave. 'Where were *you* guys?'

The younger man joined the Weatherells and held up his hands, as if in surrender.

'Sorry,' he said. 'We lost you. All the smoke. The big geyser.'

'The fucking *smoke*? You've got to be joking me, right?' Weatherell pointed at Holloway. 'That bastard's fucking crazy.'

The younger man muttered something. It sounded to Holloway like agreement.

'You fucking *promised*,' said Weatherell. 'You fucking *swore* to me.'

'What can I say? Sorry.'

'He's fucking *sorry*. I guess it's OK, then. Jeez. You fucking *arsehole*.'

The younger man splayed a gently restraining hand on Dan's sternum.

The bearded man took his place between Holloway and Weatherell. Holloway relaxed his grip on the handle of the knife. Measured against the bearded man's girth, it seemed an ineffectual weapon. His hand dropped to his side.

The bearded man and Holloway faced each other.

Something passed between them.

Will said: 'Do I know you?'

He felt empty.

The big man took another step forward.

Holloway could smell him: a sweaty mustiness, like an old book.

'No,' he said. The voice was gentle, without threat or frailty. He spoke with an English accent.

He held out his hand.

For a moment, Holloway nearly obliged: he had to stop himself passing the blade, handle first, into the man's grip.

Then he laughed.

'What's going on?'

Shepherd kept his hand out.

Holloway was nearly overcome with hilarity.

'Who the fuck *are* you?' he said.

'I called you,' said Shepherd. 'The day Joanne died. I called you at the station.'

Holloway laughed.

'Fuck off,' he said.

He looked around, as if cameras might lurk in the bushes.

'That's not true,' he said.

Shepherd lowered his hand. He wiped his palm on the leg of his trousers.

'You're joking,' said Holloway. 'Is that really who you are? What are you *doing* here?'

Shepherd said: 'Caroline sent me.'

The sound of her name was like cool water.

'She told me where to find you.'

Holloway turned and grasped the railings. He stared hard at the fluid earth.

Through the corner of his eye, he saw the younger man leading the Weatherells away. Dan moved with short, stolid, shocked steps, as if ankle-deep in mud. He was gesticulating furiously with his right hand. The frame of Liz's wheelchair was flecked and caked with grey mud. The younger man attended them like a paramedic.

Holloway and Shepherd were joined by a Japanese tour group. Holloway put the knife in his pocket and stooped to pick up his baseball cap. He settled it on his head. Its crown was muddy. He leaned on the railing.

Some of the tension left Shepherd. He sighed and let his shoulders drop. He took the rail in both hands and faced the boiling pool.

He said: 'Have you ever seen *It's a Wonderful Life*?'

Part Three

A Wonderful Life

Hark, hark
The dogs do bark
The beggars are coming to town
Some in Rags
And some in jags
And one in a velvet gown –

'Hark, Hark', from 'Mother Goose'

20

I

It was not until they returned from France that Shepherd told Lenny about his conversation with Kate Holloway.

It was Lenny who suggested they track down Dan Weatherell. He had a strong feeling, he said, that Dan Weatherell was their next logical step.

But the experience in France had left Shepherd despondent. He said he was uncomfortable with the expense a trip for two to New Zealand would involve. He didn't say as much to Lenny, but (one way or another) William Holloway had already cost him too much of the money he'd taken time and care to misappropriate. He'd planned to rely on that cash for three years, four if he was careful.

He had anxiety dreams about destitution.

Lenny, who had never retracted his claim to financial genius, offered to pay the fare. He said they could travel business class if Shepherd preferred. And he would look after any expenses they incurred.

Shepherd said no.

He said: 'I think we should just let it go.'

Lenny said: 'Of course. Right. OK.'

Then he went to the kitchen, made a cup of tea and took it upstairs to his office. And that was that.

Although they lived in the same house, Shepherd and Lenny saw little of each other for several weeks. The decline in their friendship made Shepherd mournfully nostalgic. He, who had forgotten so much, still remembered with remorse boys who were best friends at nine and ten, and nodding acquaintances in school corridors at fourteen. He remembered all their names, these long-ago, lost boys. Colin Fairgreaves. Brian Hunt. Steven Kierney.

To assuage his fears of penury, he took an evening job washing up in a local Italian restaurant. By day he found employment as a cleaner at the University of North London, pushing a whirling, motorized polisher along trainer-smeared corridors. He made plans for the future. He considered applying to the Open University under his new name. If he worked hard, he could have a Bachelor's degree in three years. After that, he could requalify as a teacher. He might have fifteen years as a professional ahead of him, albeit at a comparatively junior level.

Or perhaps it would be easier to go abroad, using the name he was born with and the qualifications he had already been awarded. He could teach English in Japan, perhaps China. Conceivably, he supposed, a charitable organization of some kind might appoint him to a school in central Africa.

This had always been a kind of idle ambition but now the idea took root and became an intention. He began to investigate organizations that might employ him. He appraised the risk of returning to his original name. Surely any charitable database would not be linked to any missing persons register or other police catalogue? He considered asking Lenny. Then he thought better of it. He would need to shave the beard, grow his hair a little. To look like a teacher again. Like Andrew.

He applied for a job as a council refuse collector. Meanwhile, he began weekly to set some money aside towards the deposit on a flat of his own. He wondered how he would break this news to Lenny and Eloise.

When Caroline Holloway phoned him, he told her to hang on and took the cordless handset to his room.

He told Caroline it was nice of her to call.

She told him she'd not stopped thinking about him. She thanked God every day that someone in the world wanted to help her dad.

Shepherd gathered that she and Robert had ended their relationship. Caroline had found a new love: she had been Born Again. She was living in an evangelical Anglican commune in Cornwall.

She made it sound like a pastoral idyll: Shepherd imagined the wide-eyed, damaged young people gathering at breakfast to butter their rolls and offer praise to Jesus for their daily bread. The spirited literalism of the newly fervent.

He took the cordless phone and sat heavily upon the bed. Not for the first time, he considered the monasticism of his own surroundings.

'I'm happy for you,' he told her. 'I'm happy you've found some peace.'

'And what about you? Have you?'

'Me? Goodness no. I'm far too old for that. But I am *reconciled*.'

He heard her smiling down the line.

'You remind me of dad,' she said.

Shepherd was familiar with such projection. Classrooms were full of children who longed for paternal attention and approval. Not just those whose fathers were absent.

'Do I?'

'Yes. He's funny, too. That's the kind of thing he'd say. When he was depressed.'

He smiled for her acuity.

'Has he been in touch?'

'No,' she said.

She hesitated.

'But I think I know where he is.'

He tried not to ask. The silence between them hung heavy on the wire.

Somehow, he knew she had closed her eyes and crossed her fingers, maybe even her legs, like she was desperate to pee. She was offering a silent prayer to her new Lord, Jesus, that Shepherd would put the question to her.

He said: 'Is he in New Zealand?'

The phrasing of the question amazed her and she let loose a kind of scream. Then she cupped the receiver in her hand and said: 'How did you know that?'

He made a Zen face and said: 'Just go on, tell me what you were going to say.'

'That's *amazing*,' she said. 'There's no *way* you could have known that.'

He said: 'Go on.'

In an exultant rush, she said: 'Well – mum spoke to Dan . . .'

'Slow down. Dan?'

'Weatherell. He was mum's boyfriend. He lives in New Zealand. We lived with him for a while, when mum and dad first split up.'

'Oh yes.'

'Did she mention him?'

He waited.

'Not to my recollection,' he said.

'Right. Well, anyway, Dan told her that he's been getting calls —'

'What kind of calls?'

'The kind where someone hangs up when you answer. He's pretty freaked by it. He doesn't know what to do.'

'Has he called the police?'

'Apparently not. What would he say? He called mum, instead.'

'Does he know about —'

'Joanne?'

'Yes.'

'Kind of. Yes. I mean, mum told him and everything. But I don't think it's a big deal in New Zealand.'

He smiled. That William Holloway was not, by default, a big deal somewhere in the world did not seem natural to her.

He said: 'Has your mother called the police?'

'Not yet. She doesn't know what to do. She never told them about the call Dad made to Dan before – he left. She said she didn't think it was important. She said she didn't want more of the past being dragged through the dirt . . .'

He could hear the exact phrasing and intonation of those words on Kate's lips.

'So she hasn't called them?'

'She doesn't know what to say if she did. She told Dan it might well be some call centre stuck on automatic redial. It happens, apparently. All these lonely old people think they're getting anonymous calls, and it turns out to be British Gas, or something. Some call centre in the Midlands stuck on redial. Or whatever. She's worried she's jumping at shadows.'

'And is she?'

'No. I think he's there. He never liked Dan – well, he wouldn't.' She paused again. He heard the bassy rumble as she shifted the phone in her hand. 'He always sort of blamed Dan for —'

'Everything,' said Shepherd.

'Yes,' she said. 'Pretty much.'

'Well,' said Shepherd, 'he would, wouldn't he?'

Two days later, he knocked on the door of Lenny's office. He'd never dared to do so before.

After a brief, almost managerial hesitation, Lenny bid him enter.

The office was small and square and its many shelves were jammed in every plane with hardback and paperback books on demonology, numerology, alternative theology, magic, alternative history, para-politics, para-psychology, SAS evasion and survival techniques and – perhaps strangely – P.G. Wodehouse. Books that could not be shelved teetered and tottered in heaps and piles on the floor. Lenny sat at a second-hand writing desk, tapping with two rigid fingers at the keyboard of his PowerBook. He was online.

He looked up.

'What can I do you for?'

'Can I come in?'

'Make yourself at home.'

He said this in the full knowledge that it was not possible for Shepherd to do so. Shepherd felt like Alice after she had drunk the wrong potion.

Lenny span to face him on the blue Office World swivel chair. His expression suggested this had better be good.

Shepherd was keenly aware that he was intruding. So he reached into his breast pocket and on to the table he slapped two return tickets to Wellington, New Zealand.

Before they left, en route and after their arrival, they differed on how best to proceed. But Lenny's assessment of Weatherell's crisis psychology proved about right.

Dan Weatherell was scared. He thought a bad man was after him and he thought there wasn't much anybody could do about it.

Lacking any evidence to authenticate his anxiety that he was being stalked by an English psychopath, he was embarrassed about calling the police. He hated to think he might be thought neurotic, perhaps worse, a paranoid crazy, one of the loony tunes who called the police every five minutes with crackpot theories about this, that and the other. He could almost hear the gags about the crazy, jealous ex-husband, because – in the end, and stupid as it sounded – wasn't that what it all amounted to?

He longed for a higher power to take the problem out of his hands, to absolve him of his doubt and uncertainty and inability to take definite action.

'He is, after all,' said Lenny, 'an academic.'

After a calculated and allusive introductory phone call ('I'm a friend of Caroline and Kate Holloway'), Lenny went alone to visit Weatherell at the university. He wore the suit he'd found bunched in a sportsbag beneath his bed. He hadn't cleaned it or pressed it. It was rumpled beyond belief and gone in the crotch, in addition to which his hair stuck up like a madman's and he wore skateboarding trainers. But he didn't seem to care and it didn't seem to matter. In the end, he made none of the false claims he had prepared, and he didn't use any of the bogus IDs he'd brought along with him.

He simply said: 'We've come to find William Holloway,' and it was enough, because Weatherell wanted to hear that more than he wanted to hear anything else in the world.

Weatherell and Lenny spoke at least once a day for two weeks. They met several times at the university. On the second occasion, Lenny glimpsed a figure he thought might be Holloway outside the English faculty. Not wishing to startle him, he said nothing until they were out of sight. By the time he was in a position to ask Weatherell, the man had gone. On other visits, Lenny twice noticed a grey Subaru idling on the corner of Kelburn Parade, close to where Weatherell parked his car. He couldn't be certain the driver was the man he had seen outside the Von Zedlitz building because he wore sunglasses and a baseball cap pulled low over his eyes. But he was pretty sure.

When Weatherell suspected burglary, he called Lenny rather than the police. Nothing had been taken, but certain items – books and trinkets, some photographs – had been minutely repositioned. You could tell by the dust on the shelves. And he'd found a crumpled candy wrapper behind the sofa. Neither he nor Liz ate Cherry Ripes.

Lenny counselled him not to worry.

Holloway had not been in his house.

'What makes you say that?' said Dan. 'What would he have done, if he had been?'

Lenny changed the subject. He told him the wrapper had probably blown in from the garden. Wellington was a pretty windy town.

When Weatherell told him they were going away for the weekend, Lenny suggested they drive rather than fly. By now Weatherell seemed willing to do exactly as Lenny told him, so long as it protected him from any possibility of encountering William Holloway.

Lenny told Weatherell he'd know if Holloway tried to follow him over 500 km of open road. He suggested they keep an eye open for a little grey Japanese hatchback. Dan did as instructed and, as Lenny promised, saw nothing unusual. Once they got to Rotorua, he and Liz began to relax. But over breakfast in the Sheraton restaurant, Lenny thought a slight, tanned figure across the room might be Holloway. He wanted to confront the man right there, but Shepherd insisted they consult with Weatherell, who (after all) was the only one present who'd ever actually met him.

In Reception, Lenny and Dan argued about it for half an hour. Weatherell said it could not have been Holloway. Shepherd agreed with him. Shepherd would have known. He would have known by the energies in the air.

Weatherell admitted he'd seen the man for the briefest of seconds, but whoever it was, he was too tanned, too relaxed to be Holloway. He was too casually dressed, for Christ's sake. It just wasn't in William Holloway's nature to go about on serious business dressed like Brian fucking Wilson.

'Will Holloway,' he said. 'He's not what you'd call relaxed. You know what I mean? He's kind of an uptight guy.'

But Weatherell looked scared. He might have been repeating a mantra. The magic words, if repeated often enough, would make the man in the restaurant not be the bad man who wanted to hurt him. The idea that it might have been Holloway was somehow more frightening than waking up to find him at the foot of the bed.

Although he didn't think the man was Holloway, Weatherell was eager to pack up and go home. Lenny promised him again that Holloway had no intention of hurting him. It wasn't in his psychology. Probably all he wanted was to talk. Holloway's rational mind knew that Weatherell was not responsible for the circumstances he found himself in. But he needed something, somebody to hold responsible. If he actually confronted Weatherell, he would also confront his own carefully constructed delusional framework – and he couldn't afford to let that happen.

Eventually, Lenny said, he'd just go away. It was a form of depression, and it would probably lift. And anyway, he and Shepherd would be there. They wouldn't let Weatherell out of their sight for a minute. Not one minute.

'You're going to have to promise me, now,' said Weatherell. 'I don't mind telling you, I'm pretty spooked here.'

Lenny promised. Weatherell deflated. He jammed a floppy sunhat on his head and stomped from the lobby.

Later, while they were illegally parked opposite the hotel, Lenny was convinced of the familiarity of a Subaru hatchback that pulled out of the Sheraton car park.

That was a moment.

He turned to Shepherd.

They looked at each other.

Lenny said: 'Fuck me. I think it's actually him.'

He was so excited he stalled the car three times and pulled into the traffic with a banshee shriek that made it feel like a real pursuit. They caught sight of the Subaru three blocks ahead. As Lenny had predicted, it seemed to be tailing Weatherell's 4 x 4.

Without talking, they followed the Subaru to the edge of town. Under his breath, Lenny sang songs from the Clash's first album. They followed the man who might be William Holloway through the turnstile into Whakawerawera thermal park and Maori cultural centre and Lenny, who was marginally the less conspicuous of the pair, shadowed him through the souvenir shop and cafeteria.

He rejoined Shepherd outside the souvenir shop. Shepherd was pretending to select postcards from a wire spinner that threatened to topple each time he so much as brushed it.

Still they doubted it could actually be him.

In a way, they both hoped it wasn't.

Later, after Lenny had led the Weatherells away, Shepherd leaned on the railing and told Holloway his name. It was a curiously flat moment.

He had not cried for many years, not even when his father died, so he couldn't guess at the source of the sudden, unexpected grief that made him grip the railing as if he were on the deck of a liner. The sadness seemed unconnected to the stranger before him, the little man in the baseball cap to whom he felt no bond or affiliation, no relationship of any kind. He was just a stranger in a Hawaiian shirt, at the first sight of whom the William Holloway in Shepherd's mind tapered and dissolved, like the picture on an old TV screen. It left an absence whose parameters he could not, already, quite recall.

II

On a wet November afternoon, they touched down at Manchester airport.

At the passport control desk, Holloway couldn't feel his legs. He was certain that customs would search him. If they did, they could hardly miss in excess of £100,000, in various currencies, taped up in a bin-liner in his capacious hand luggage. But the passport officer waved him past and he moved unhindered through the Nothing to Declare channel.

Shepherd experienced a similar anxiety. He was travelling on Andrew Taylor's passport. But nobody was interested in him either.

Of the three of them, only Lenny arrived in the UK with a passport that might stand up to full and close scrutiny. But the sight of uniforms made him nervous. He walked past Manchester customs and excise like a man trying hard to look casual and unconcerned. So they singled him out and went through his luggage. Because this always happened to Lenny, he refused to carry the most innocuous contraband through customs. He had incinerated his fake IDs in New Zealand.

About twenty minutes later, he joined Holloway and Shepherd in Arrivals.

Holloway had never thought to see England again. While they waited for Lenny, he went to buy a newspaper. Everything he saw spoke of the whole: the lettering on the W.H. Smith sign: *The Times*, the *Daily Mirror*. Werther's Originals. Mars bars. Walker's cheese-and-onion crisps. The near-identical accent of the staff, despite the variety of their ethnicity. The old couple who stood together in the queue to buy a pack of mints.

When Lenny arrived, glad at least to have been spared what he cheerfully called *the old rubber glove*, they went to the Avis desk and hired a car.

Outside, the air was cold and wet and smelled of aviation fuel. Whining planes broke the low cloud, encased in shafts of light. Holloway shivered in his summer clothing as they struggled to locate and identify the right vehicle in the hire compound. Then he threw his bag into the boot and huddled, quivering, on the back seat. Lenny took his place at the wheel and familiarized himself with the dashboard layout. Shepherd slid back the passenger seat as far as it would go. None of them spoke. They were too tired and it was too cold.

Concerned that her phone or indeed her person might be bugged, Lenny hadn't spoken to Eloise for nearly three weeks. Holloway assured him this probably wasn't necessary, but it didn't seem to matter. Neither did the fact that Holloway was still technically a serving British police officer. You couldn't be too careful where possible surveillance was concerned, Lenny told him. What with one thing and another, Holloway was inclined to agree.

Lenny was not a good driver; he was erratic and impulsive and he weaved between lanes like a speeding bumblebee, but he made good time and he got them there alive. He was eager to get home. He slowed down only when they hit a snarl of traffic on the North Circular.

They unpacked the car. The luggage seemed heavy. The freezing drizzle had soaked to their joints.

Lenny put the key in the door.

He called out: 'Home again, home again, jiggedy-jig. Anybody home?'

Eloise ran barefoot from the sitting room. She threw her arms round Lenny's neck. She planted a kiss on his cheek. She said: 'I missed you, John Dillinger.'

Lenny eased her away.

He said: 'Elly. This is Will.'

She looked at Holloway.

'Oh,' she said.

Holloway could not smile. He shifted his position. Whatever he did, it looked like what a murderer would do. So he just stood there, on the cold doorstep in his summer clothes, while the house's fragrant warmth radiated out to him.

'Oh, God,' said Eloise. 'Right. OK.'

She nodded, vaguely, and stepped aside to let them enter. She pressed herself almost flat to the wall when Holloway passed her. Lenny took him to the sitting room. Shepherd hung back. He scuffed his shoes on the welcome mat, and closed the door behind him.

Eloise had not moved.

Shepherd set his bag down.

Quietly, he said: 'How are you?'

She whispered: 'How do you think I am? I'm like someone whose husband just brought home a murderer.'

'He's not a murderer,' Shepherd hissed back. 'That's the point.'

By now, though, it hardly seemed to matter.

Eloise ran a hand through her hair. A few strands of her blunt fringe stood vertically. She looked at Shepherd as if she had never met him.

She said: 'Right. This has gone too far.'

She ran upstairs. On the first landing, she leaned over the banister and called Lenny. The house froze.

Lenny went stomping upstairs like a loose-limbed teenager about to be berated.

Shepherd and Holloway sat silently in the sitting room while upstairs Lenny and Eloise argued.

After a few minutes, Shepherd said: 'Fancy a cuppa?'

'Yes,' said Holloway. 'Please.'

'Milk?'

'A bit. Just a dash.'

'Sugar?'

'Please. Four.'

'Four?'

'Please.'

Shepherd was gone a long time, far longer than it took to prepare two cups of tea and find some biscuits. But when he returned, Holloway had not changed his position and Eloise and Lenny were still screaming at one another.

Holloway took a chipped mug. He thanked Shepherd.

'He should've called ahead,' he said.

Shepherd dunked a stale digestive, then folded the crumbling, sodden disc into his mouth.

'What can you do?'

'You can't blame her,' said Holloway.

Shepherd agreed.

'No,' he said.

Eloise packed her suitcase and left that evening.

If they expected her departure to make Holloway anxious for his continued safety, it didn't. Lenny insisted with some passion that Eloise would under no circumstances go to the police, or mention Holloway's presence to anybody. He became tearful at the thought of her wounded but absolute loyalty.

Holloway told him he understood, that it was OK, that he appreciated the reassurance.

'She'll be all right,' said Lenny, for his own benefit.

'Of course,' said Shepherd.

'Of course she will,' said Holloway. He might have been injected with Novocain.

'Right,' said Lenny. He clapped his hands and tried to look cheerful.

The room, the house, was suffused with a sense of unreality.

'Anything else, before I get some sleep?'

'There is one thing,' said Holloway. 'I'd like to see my aunt.'

They tried to talk him out of it, but it was no good. The next morning, Lenny drove Holloway to Bristol. Shepherd stayed at home. Holloway was pleased to be free of him, if only for a few hours. Shepherd's dolorous presence made him uncomfortable. That discomfort made him feel grudging and at fault.

Holloway remembered little about his final days in New Zealand. He lay in his hotel bed, watching television and eating sporadically and badly. He rose only to write, then destroy letters of explanation and apology to Dan Weatherell.

Meanwhile, Lenny was co-ordinating a flight home for the three of them. Every three or four hours he checked up on Holloway, by phone or in person. And several times a day, he phoned Dan Weatherell, to assure him that Holloway remained safely locked away in his hotel room.

Shepherd took the opportunity to go and watch the test match.

Holloway didn't see much of him. He thought that Shepherd seemed somewhat depressed. This suggested that he'd come as something of an anticlimax. Perhaps in this was rooted his guilty antipathy.

At the airport, Holloway remembered assuring the clerk that he had packed his own luggage. He remembered the low whine of the engines and the horrid, piss and-shit-stink of the chrome lavatory several hours into the long flight. But most of all, he remembered the way Eloise had thrown herself at Lenny when he arrived home.

He saw in that moment that Eloise would never have left Lenny, had it not been for the arrival at her door of William Holloway, surrounded by the flickering aura of his lost, imagined women.

Yet Lenny accepted her temporary absence with equanimity. He did not doubt her intentions or worry about what she might be doing. He did not construct imaginary betrayals. And so neither did Holloway. It had not occurred to him to examine or question the nature of this confidence in Eloise.

Lenny was as different from Holloway as it was possible for a man to be, who shared a mother culture. Even his unlimited paranoia was the fountainhead of an abnormal joy.

Holloway did not see himself in Lenny. Lenny was a mystery to him. Yet he found his company familiar and comfortable.

When Shepherd told Holloway about Dryden, about *It's a Wonderful Life* and Joanne Grayling and Charles Manson and *Helter Skelter*, it sounded fractured and unconvincing. It left Holloway feeling galled to have been tracked down by an obsessive freak.

But in Lenny's mouth it all made sense. Lenny was sane and articulate and animated and fervently evangelical. He illustrated each of his points by clapping or punching his hand. He gave Holloway pages of research materials. These included a five-page printed document whose first entry was dated 63 BC: 'countless numbers of Jewish citizens deliberately jump to their death when Pompey captures the city'.

But it was the last page Holloway was interested in.

1978: Jonestown, Guyana. Jim Jones leads 913 members of the People's Temple to their deaths, by drinking cyanide-laced Kool-Aid.

1993: Vietnam. Believing they will go straight to Heaven, fifty-three villagers commit mass suicide with primitive weapons

1993: America. Seventy members of the Branch Davidian cult die when fire ends a fifty-one-day siege by police and federal agents of the ATF.

1994: Switzerland. Forty-eight members of the Solar Temple are found burned to death in a farmhouse and three chalets. Five further bodies, including that of an infant, are found in Montreal.

1995: France. Sixteen members of the Solar Temple are found burned to death in a house in the French Alps.

1997: Canada. Five members of the Solar Temple are found burned to death in a house in Saint Casimir, Quebec.

1997: America. On the same day, thirty-nine members of the Heaven's Gate cult are found dead after committing mass suicide in shifts. Previously, many had genitally mutilated themselves.

1999: UK. Rex Dryden cons approximately 400 followers of his fake millennial cult, the Temple of Light, into drinking what he claims to be poisoned Lucozade.

2000: UK. Rex Dryden instructs unknown followers to enact the first of many millennial sacrifices, ordering the murder of prostitute Joanne Grayling. His reasons for choosing Joanne Grayling, if any, are currently unknown.

'Dryden's been dropping hints and clues,' Lenny told him. 'He's been taking every opportunity to go on the record about his obsession with *It's a Wonderful Life*. Obviously he's instructed whoever was sent to kill Joanne to refer to it at every opportunity. Possibly he sees it as an allegory of death and redemption. Or the demise of capitalism. The extinction of global super corporations. Whatever. He's using specific symbolism, but it's peculiar to his own mythos and difficult to interpret. It might not even be consistent. It doesn't need to be. These movements have a certain internal logic, a self-sustaining momentum. Once the adherents have chosen to believe, they believe no matter what.

'Dryden's the first modern celebrity to run a genuine death cult. And it was Dryden, or Dryden's followers, who did this to you.

'He thinks he's a Lord of Misrule,' said Lenny. 'The Old Trickster. King of the World. Prince of the Air. Well, he's not,' he said. 'He's just a cunt.'

Lenny steered with his right hand and evangelized with his left. There was still a lot he wanted to tell Holloway about, not all of it connected with Rex Dryden. Holloway didn't mind, any more than he minded Lenny shifting gears with teeth-grinding inefficiency and appearing to change lanes at random.

His driving was accompanied by a discordant choir of outraged horns.

But Holloway grew tense when they entered Bristol's city limits. He pulled the borrowed beanie hat over his ears and turned up the collar of his jacket. Then Lenny said: 'You look like a car-thief,' and he turned the collar down again.

They parked outside the nursing home. The ticking of the engine accentuated the silence in the car. The home was grey against the milky winter sunshine.

Lenny said: 'Are you sure about this?'

Holloway was eating a king-sized Mars bar.

'I deserted her,' he said.

'It's not like you had a choice.'

Holloway screwed up the wrapper and dropped it on the floor. Lenny's eyes followed it, returned to his passenger.

'I'm scared she's going to die,' said Holloway.

Lenny rested his forehead against the steering wheel.

'It's just such a risk,' he said.

Holloway grinned.

He said: 'Look, if I get arrested, you can dedicate yourself to my release.'

Lenny smiled tightly. 'They will call the police,' he said. 'The minute they see you.'

Holloway's hand rested on the door handle.

'Do you think she knows?'

'About what? Joanne and that?'

'Yeah.'

'Didn't you say it was Alzheimer's?'

'Yeah.'

Lenny leaned over Holloway to retrieve his tobacco tin from the glove compartment. He began to roll a cigarette.

'Then no,' he said. 'She doesn't know.'

Lenny licked the gummed paper, lit the cigarette. The smoke seemed very blue against the colourless winter backdrop.

'But if you have to do it,' he said. 'You have to do it.'

Holloway opened the passenger door and stepped onto the pavement. He took a step or two towards the nursing home. He imagined Hetty opening the door, seeing his face. His aunt Grace, not knowing he'd been away. The sweet, powdery smell of her.

He walked through the gates and up the drive and stood at the bay window. He knew that, behind the yellowing net, Grace remained in her unknowable limbo. He wondered if time moved for her at all. When she knew, however transiently, that apple cake Billy had come for her, did she see a child? Or did she believe herself to be humouring a delusional madman?

He wanted Hetty to know that he didn't kill Joanne. He wanted to make a cup of tea in the kitchen and share a plate of biscuits with her, Jammy Dodgers or Rich Tea, and talk about what had happened, the places he'd been.

But if she opened the door to him, she would only see a murderer. She would say, *Oh my goodness*, and she would slam the door and she would run to the telephone on the desk and she would call the police. Or she would be silent and shocked, one hand at the gold St Christopher round her throat, and she would allow him entry like Eloise had, and hang back, around the telephone, and mutter fearfully into the receiver while he kneeled at Grace's side.

He squinted through the tiny gaps in the net, but inside he could see only gradations of shadow. Any movement might have been the vibration of his own eye. He knew that anybody inside could see him quite clearly, a scruffy man with a woolly cap pulled down over his ears, cupping a hand over his brow and pressing his face to the glass. So he jammed his hands in his pockets and turned away. He half ran, half jogged a step or two and joined Lenny in the hire car.

Lenny had kept the engine running. The moment Holloway was inside, he pulled the car away with a screech. By the time a male nurse came to the door, they were too far away, and too wreathed in smoking rubber, for him to take down the car's registration.

By the time they arrived back in north London, it was dark. Lenny parked outside the house. For a while they sat silently in the car, listening to the engine tick. Through the sitting room window they could see a blue, flickering light. Shepherd, alone on the sofa, watching television.

They stepped from the car, shivering. Condensed breath ascending to the yellow sodium haze. On the pavement, they exchanged a meaningful glance, shut the car doors quietly, and went to the pub.

It was almost empty. A few drinkers, older men, clung to the darker corners and tatty booths. Holloway went to the bar and got two pints of Guinness.

Holloway set the pint on the table before Lenny. 'You were right,' he said. 'We shouldn't have gone.'

'Cheers. It doesn't matter. No harm done.'

'Not for lack of trying. Cheers.'

Lenny lifted his beer and took a small sip. He did not reply.

'Story of my life,' insisted Holloway.

Lenny set the glass back on the table. He sighed.

'Tell me about it,' he said.

He did not mean that Holloway should tell him about it.

Holloway took a long draught from the glass. It left a foamy white moustache.

He said: 'I was married for fourteen years.'

Lenny hummed a long, uninterested affirmative.

But Holloway went on.

He said: 'She was too good for me.'

Lenny nodded. They were quiet for a while. He could feel Holloway looking at him. He gave up. He sagged and nodded again, this time to show that Holloway should continue.

Holloway wiped his upper lip. He said: 'You'll hear men say they never looked at another woman.' He looked sheepish, and for a while he watched people come and go at the bar. 'But in my case, it was true. I never did. Not seriously anyway; not for more than a second. She was absolutely the only woman for me. Do you know what that feels like?'

Lenny shrugged.

'Elly and I are happy,' he said. 'I suppose it could change.'

'I doubt it.'

He laughed.

'You don't even know us.'

'I can tell,' said Holloway.

Lenny was disarmed. He looked at the table.

He said: 'Yeah. Well. You know.'

'The thing is,' said Holloway. 'Despite everything, I never felt at ease. I always thought she'd married beneath her. And over the years, you know, I began to wonder. The first time we —' and again he was overcome by coyness. 'The first time we did it, was back at her student digs. At the time she was going out with this bloke. Sam. And, over the years, I began to think: if she could do that to him, could she do it to me?'

'And did she?'

Holloway laughed.

'No,' he said.

He seemed elated, bitterly delighted by the admission. 'No, she didn't. Not until I left her.'

He chuckled, as if it was too funny for words.

Lenny drew in his jaw. He thought for a bit. Then he said: 'I thought *she* left *you*.'

'That's not how she saw it.'

'What about Dan Weatherell?'

'He came later.' Holloway stared into his pint. 'I used to tease her,' he said. 'About men. Men on TV, actors, men in the street, men she worked with. Trying to work out who she might be attracted to. It was all a big joke. Ha ha. She played along. She was good enough to pretend it was a joke. But over time I suppose I wore her down. I badgered her.'

'It happens,' said Lenny.

'You think so?'

'Of course.'

'I suppose,' said Holloway, doubtfully.

'Did you talk about it? As a problem, I mean.'

'We tried to. *She* tried to. But there were no —' He fought for the right word. Then he said: 'I thought she was humouring me.'

Lenny was confused.

'So in the end, it was *you* who left *her*?'

'In a manner of speaking.'

He enjoyed Lenny's expression.

Shortly before Christmas, Kate told him about Dan Weatherell.

At first Holloway was stupefied. He could only think to ask how long it had been going on.

Six months.

He remembered her looking at him with unendurable pity. And then, gently, she said: 'You left me first.'

He looked at her, bewildered, trying behind his eyes to rewind the last six months.

'What?'

'For your job.'

He snorted derisively through both nostrils.

'What are you talking about?'

She said: 'Will, look at yourself. You're never home.'

He drew a long breath. Pinched the bridge of his nose.

He said: 'I hate my job.'

Something like laughter welled up inside him.

'Jesus,' he said.

The idea seemed pornographic. He looked around himself, as if for something misplaced.

Then he punched his wife in the face.

By the time the police arrived, he had destroyed the contents of the sitting room, the indices of their marriage: the furniture and their photographs, the television and the VCR: he had ripped the curtains from their rails and thrown chairs through windows. He ground shattered glass into the carpet, upended the table at which they ate their Sunday lunch, and ripped the legs from it. He used the legs as clubs. He bellowed terrible words and things that were not words at all. Kate made a ball of herself in the corner, behind an upended bookcase, her knees drawn up to her broken face.

When there was nothing left to smash, he deflated and walked to the kitchen. From the cutlery drawer he removed a serrated breadknife. Three times, he drew the blade across his inner forearm. The flesh snapped back like elastic. The fresh wounds were labial, pink. Then there was a slow, rich gathering of blood. It swelled into a gleaming black meniscus, then spilled into rivulets and dripped and dropped like heavy rain on the tiled floor.

When the police arrived, the knife was at Holloway's throat. He had taken a moment to prepare himself. He remembered becoming aware of a great commotion. Steve Jackson, a beat copper he'd known for seven years, tackled him. The two of them slipped and slid on the tiled floor like new-born giraffes.

Then he was flat on his back. Jackson was pinning him with his knees and babbling into his radio. Holloway relaxed under his weight. He focused on the strip light. It seemed softly to fluoresce.

*

Lenny was silent for several seconds. Then he drained his pint. With an index finger, he scratched at a raised eyebrow. Then he tugged at the skin beneath his jaw. He blew through pursed lips, as if secretly impressed.

'You were ill,' he said, at length. 'People do things.'

Holloway appreciated the effort.

'I was in hospital,' he said. 'Not for long. Not for long enough, as it happens. When I got out, she'd left and taken Caroline with her. Gone to live with a friend. I had too much time on my hands. And I – well, you know. I couldn't get it out of my head.

'Her and Weatherell?'

'Well. Yes and no. Weatherell had gone by then. I don't think I was good for their relationship.'

Lenny scratched at his eyebrow.

'Weatherell went back to New Zealand,' Holloway continued. 'Kate stayed in Leeds. But in a way that was worse. At least I *knew* about her and Weatherell. I began to obsess about other men. I couldn't stop thinking about it. Kate and someone else. Anybody else. In the end, I thought it would drive me insane. One way or another, it seemed better to know. I'm not even sure what I wanted to find out. But I hired a private detective. To follow her.'

Lenny said: 'You're *kidding*.'

'Oh I wish I was.'

'What happened?'

'Not much. Not in the grand scheme of things. She had a one-night thing. She slept with a student.' He swallowed, took a sip from the pint. 'David Bishop.'

'You got this from the private detective?'

'Certainly did. He was very thorough. He *showed* me. He'd filmed it. He'd put a camera in Kate's bedroom.'

Lenny made a face. 'Is that even *legal*?'

Holloway smiled. His snaggle tooth caught on his lower lip. 'Do you think I cared?'

Lenny held up his hands. 'Hold it there,' he said. He pushed back the stool and hurried to the bar. He returned with two more pints. 'Right,' he said, settling himself. 'Go on.'

'Before Joanne disappeared,' said Holloway, 'somebody sent that film to me.'

'Somebody?'

'Well, who else could it be? The man who filmed it. His name was Derek Bliss.'

Lenny slapped his forehead with his fingertips.

'That's why you went to Leeds to look for him.'

Holloway nodded.

'That's why I went to Leeds to look for him,' he said. 'Except Derek Bliss is supposed to be dead.'

Lenny was nodding enthusiastically. The conversation had taken a direction he could identify with. He made an encouraging noise. 'Stroke,' he said. 'Australia. Apparently.'

Holloway continued: 'Right. Because of everything that happened, I thought Weatherell must be behind it all, working with Bliss. I thought they wanted to punish me. But I wasn't thinking straight. She wasn't – Dan didn't love her that way. And I was – you know. I wasn't myself.'

He looked up, checking Lenny's expression.

'It's OK,' said Lenny. 'Go on.'

Holloway drew a long breath. He knit his hands on the table. He spoke with a distracted frown, as if reciting from memory.

'Listen,' he said. 'You're suggesting that Derek Bliss actually is dead. OK. I accept that as a possibility. And I accept that Joanne's murder may be associated with Rex Dryden. But equally, you must accept that we don't know in what way. Or why.'

'We will.'

'I accept that too. But listen. That film – the film of Kate and the boy – dates from a time when Bliss had a business partner, Henry Lincoln. It might have passed into Lincoln's hands any number of ways. Christ, perhaps he and Bliss got their jollies to it on a lonely Saturday night.' He scowled. Remembered those long-ago beads of semen on the toilet seat. 'It's quality material,' he said, and raised the glass to his lips.

Lenny kept his gaze steady.

'So,' said Holloway. 'It makes sense to me that we assume Lincoln to be involved, somehow. Perhaps it was Lincoln who actually sent me the film. Or perhaps he supplied it to the person who did.'

'But it could've been copied a thousand times,' said Lenny. He read Holloway's expression. He said. 'Look, I'm sorry to say it. But it's true.'

'Of course it's true. Christ, it's probably posted on the internet, for all I know. Watch My Lusty Wife Enjoy Horny Student Stud. Or whatever. But that's not the point. Whoever sent me the film knew stuff about me that nobody else knew. I assumed it was Bliss – but only because I'd never met Henry Lincoln. I'd never heard of him. But I know about him now. So he's next in line.'

Lenny nodded.

'OK,' he said. 'That makes sense.'

'Now,' said Holloway. 'I'm not saying there's a direct connection between Lincoln and Joanne. There probably isn't. But there must be a link of some kind between Lincoln and Dryden. Whatever Lincoln's involvement, there's a lot we could learn from him.'

Lenny nodded again.

'Nice one,' he said.

Holloway leaned forward. 'Robert told you about Lincoln,' he said. 'What do you remember? What did he tell you?'

Lenny sat back. He spread a hand on each thigh. He laughed. 'Well,' he said. 'Apparently he lives in Basingstoke'

On the way home, they stopped off for a curry. Having a weak stomach, Holloway ordered a korma. Lenny had a vindaloo. They took back a lamb pasanda for Shepherd.

They found him sulking in front of a video.

Lenny and Holloway didn't mention their conversation in the pub. They ate curry from foil tubs and watched the end of *Tootsie*.

When the food was finished, Holloway sighed and belched and went to the kitchen. He returned with a roll of bin bags, one of which he unrolled with a flourish of the wrist (one of his private rituals). He began to throw away the empty containers and their greasy, orange-smeared lids.

Shepherd watched him.

He said: 'I'd've done that.'

'It's not a problem,' said Holloway.

Shepherd stood. He motioned that Holloway should hand him the bin bag.

'Really,' said Holloway. 'I don't mind.'

'Sit down,' said Shepherd. 'I'll do it. I know where everything goes.'

Holloway smiled.

'I know where to find the bin.'

'I know,' said Shepherd, patiently. 'But really I should double wrap it. Or the foxes will get in.'

Holloway paused for a beat.

He said: 'The foxes like curry, do they?'

Shepherd looked at him.

'Yes,' he said.

'Right,' said Holloway and handed over the bin bag.

Shepherd busied himself. To Holloway he seemed content and effeminate, prissily ursine. He went to the kitchen and returned with some Domestos wipes and cleaned down the coffee table. He tied the bin bag in a double knot, then opened a second with a busy, palm-rubbing action. He manoeuvred the first bin bag into the second. Then, gratified at a job well done, he left the room, clutching the bag by its knotted neck.

'Fee, fi, foe fucking fum,' muttered Holloway.

Lenny snorted guiltily.

The next morning was Saturday. Holloway rose early and went to make some toast. Lenny was at the kitchen table, listening to the *Today* programme and drinking a mug of tea. Shepherd had already left. Lenny didn't know where he'd gone.

They drove to Basingstoke, stopping off on the way to breakfast at a Little Chef. As soon as they got there, they inadvertently left again; catapulted out of the city by an arcane system of roundabouts.

Lenny cursed and swore and thumped the steering wheel and did not see the humour. They pulled up to the side of the road. Lenny got out and smoked two cigarettes before he was able to talk.

Then he and Holloway bickered over the map. A white-lipped silence descended upon the car. But eventually, they found their way to the town centre and located a parking slot.

They ate lunch in McDonald's, then wandered about the shopping centre until they found a bookshop. Inside, an elderly couple in dark overcoats stood gazing down upon the contemporary fiction table as if waiting for something to happen. A pale, fat woman with badly bleached hair squatted at the true crime section, about to burst like a plum from her purple leggings.

Otherwise, Lenny and Holloway were the only customers.

Holloway felt two pairs of cool bookseller's eyes settle on them. He was uncomfortable. But Lenny seemed entirely un-affected and, as they had previously agreed, he wandered away to examine the shelves.

Holloway approached the counter.

'Morning,' he said.

The female bookseller ignored him, preferring to observe the behaviour of the woman in purple, who was now glaring at the true crime section as if it had in some way offended her. The male regarded Holloway from behind the reflective surface of circular spectacles.

'Hi,' he said, as if being compelled to commiserate with Holloway for something. 'Can I help?'

'I hope so.' Holloway smiled. 'I'm trying to find somebody. An old friend.'

The bookseller pressed his lips until they were rimmed white. He crossed his arms and nodded that Holloway should continue.

'He's a publisher's rep, actually. I used to know him.' He waited for a reaction, of which none was forthcoming. 'In Leeds,' he added.

'Right.'

'Henry Lincoln.'

'Right.'

He waited for the bookseller to uncross his arms.

He didn't.

Holloway pressed on. 'I was just wondering. Do you have an address where I might be able to contact him?'

'I can give you the publisher's number, if that'll help.'

He didn't think it would. He imagined the company would be unwilling to give out home addresses based on personal enquiries.

'Just his mobile would be great.'

From across the shop, he caught Lenny's eye.

The bookseller made a pained expression and at last unfolded one of his arms. He rubbed at his unshaven jaw.

'I don't know,' he said.

He squinted into the middle distance, as at the desert sun.

Holloway relented.

'OK,' he said. 'I'll take the number of his company.'

The bookseller looked irritated. Suddenly, he ducked beneath the counter. Holloway thought he might simply be trying to hide.

As Holloway waited, the fat woman in the purple leggings approached the counter, upon which she dumped a pile of paperback books, each on the topic of sexually motivated serial murder.

As far as Holloway could tell, the old couple at the contemporary fiction table had yet to move a centimetre.

Pretending to examine a randomly selected paperback, Lenny had taken to surreptitiously examining the motionless pensioners, as if they might perhaps be some kind of exhibit.

As the second bookseller scanned and bagged her catalogue of genital mutilation, the fat woman in the purple leggings quietly but plainly announced: 'Fucking cunt.' This was followed by something less distinct. It might have been 'Bob Marley'.

Holloway was becoming alarmed.

He jumped when the first bookseller slapped on the counter a publisher's seasonal catalogue.

'The address will be in there. In the back.'

'Cheers,' said Holloway. From his pocket, he removed a pen and a notepad. He licked the tip of his index finger and began to flick through the catalogue.

'At the back,' the bookseller reminded him. He seemed anxious to take the booklet back into his possession, and secrete it safely beneath the counter.

Holloway thanked him. He felt the displacement of energy as the fat woman in the purple leggings waddled from the shop.

The back pages of the glossy catalogue indeed listed the publishing company's head office address. It also listed the contact details of relevant personnel. There was a list of sales directors

and product managers; a marketing director and several managers; a publicity director whose entire department consisted of
women called Sophie and one lonely Camilla. Finally there
was a list of field sales representatives. Beneath each name was
recorded a mobile telephone number.

Beneath each number was listed the representative's home
address.

Before the bookseller could snatch the catalogue away from
him, Holloway rapidly scribbled down Henry Lincoln's details.
Then he closed the catalogue and handed it back to the bookseller, who took it from him with great delicacy, as if it now
concealed used toilet tissue.

Both jubilant and affronted, Holloway went and found
Lenny. He joined him in gazing, enchanted, at the stationary
old couple, who maintained their vigil at the contemporary
fiction table.

With some excitement, Lenny told him: 'I think they might
be dead.'

Holloway faltered.

'Don't be stupid,' he said.

'How can you be sure?'

'They're breathing.'

'They're not.'

'They are.'

Lenny half turned to face him. Through the corner of his
mouth he said: 'Can you look me in the eye and tell me honestly
that you can see them breathing?'

Holloway changed tack.

'Lenny,' he said. 'They're *standing up*.'

'It can happen.'

'No it can't.'

Lenny thought. Then he said: 'Go and prod them with something.'

'*What?*'

'Go on. Go and prod them. See if they fall over.'

Holloway changed tack again. He said: 'For the past ten minutes you've been studying the jacket of *Scruples* by Judith Krantz.'

Lenny looked down in horror. He slotted the book back on to the shelf. He wiped his palms on his chest.

'Let's go,' he said.

Lenny had intended to buy a Basingstoke *A–Z* in the bookshop, but the experience with *Scruples* had embarrassed him. They went to a newsagent instead.

Back in the car, Holloway navigated. Henry Lincoln's house stood on a new estate on the southern edge of town. A pale cul de sac of half-brick, mock-Tudor houses faced a central, communal park. Shining cars parked on driveways.

They drove round the cul de sac twice before they were sure they'd got the right house. Lenny pulled up and yanked the handbrake.

Holloway put the *A–Z* in the glove box, then stood on the pavement. It was newly laid and unbuckled by winter frosts. He audited the house. In every window hung a net curtain. The front lawn was clipped and neat round the edges, as it was in every lawn in the development.

Holloway approached the door and rang the bell. He listened to it ring emptily in the silent hallway.

He said: 'I don't think he's home.'

Lenny stood at his side. He dug in his pockets, looking for his tobacco.

'Maybe he's in the bath.'

'I don't think so. The house sounds empty.'

'What does an empty house sound like?'

'I don't know. Empty. You know what I mean. I can't hear a radio or anything.'

'Try again.'

Holloway shrugged, pressed the bell for fully half a minute. They waited, then stood on the driveway, looking up. Lenny thought he saw movement behind an upstairs net curtain. They craned their necks and squinted, but if there had been any movement, it was not repeated.

'It's no good,' said Holloway.

They waited in the car, listening to the radio. Holloway cranked open the passenger's window a notch to let out Lenny's smoke, which was giving him a headache. Lenny put on a Lenny Bruce CD. Holloway listened without laughing. He had always disliked jazz and anything to do with it.

They took it in turns to get out and stretch their legs, walking desultorily round the little park, whose lawns were dotted with canine faeces of greatly varying size and quantity. It grew dark and cold and they huddled in the car with the heater on. Eventually, a car swept into the cul de sac, following the glare of its headlamps. But it contained a young family, not Henry Lincoln, and they put Holloway and Lenny under suspicious scrutiny as they passed. Holloway sat lower in his seat. In the wing mirror, he watched them disembark – all dressed in Gap

khakis and coloured fleeces – on to their gently inclined driveway.
The mother hustled the gawping children through the door. The
father hesitated for a second or two. He looked in their direction,
swinging his keys round his index finger, then went inside.

Holloway muttered: 'They're going to call the police.'

'You think?'

He nodded and scowled. 'They're just the sort.'

'Fuck it,' said Lenny. 'Let's go then.'

He turned the key in the ignition and they drove home.

Shepherd had woken at 4 a.m. He couldn't get back to sleep.
For a while, he tossed and turned. Distantly, he could hear
Lenny snoring, sprawled alone in his double bed, whose grey-
ing sheets he had not changed since Eloise left.

Eventually Shepherd sat up and turned on the bedside lamp.
He tried to read. But his eyes skipped over the paragraphs like
a stylus on a damaged record. He rose and dressed.

By sunrise, he had set off on a walk.

In the grim winter daylight, he walked through the turnstile
at London zoo. So early on such a cold day, late in the season, it
was almost deserted. Thin mist clung to the ground.

He looked at disconsolate animals huddled in cramped,
Victorian enclosures. Then he sat for an hour in the sweet,
damp warmth of the elephant house, and thought about home.
It seemed a long way away.

On Sunday, Lenny told Shepherd about Henry Lincoln.
Shepherd pretended not to sulk about it. They watched the
EastEnders omnibus in uneasy silence.

On Monday, Lenny phoned Lincoln's workplace. A woman called Miriam answered the phone and told him that Mr Lincoln would not be in for the rest of the week.

So the three of them crammed into the car and drove to Basingstoke. The day was grey and wet, and the journey seemed very long. They waited outside Lincoln's house. The car's confined, humid interior quickly became intolerable.

Lenny ran out of patience. He got out and walked to the boot. He stood in the rain and waved a tyre-iron at Henry's Lincoln's house.

He shouted: 'Hello, Henry!'

Holloway massaged his forehead. He swore, then opened the door and got out. Huddled into his pockets, he joined Lenny at the edge of Henry Lincoln's neat, rain-lashed front garden.

'What the fuck are you doing?'

He was too tired and too cold and too wet to be angry.

'He's in there,' said Lenny.

'No he's not.'

'Yes he is.'

'He's hardly going to come out now, is he?' said Holloway. 'Not while you're waving a tyre-iron like a fucking caveman.'

Lenny's hair was in sleek, sodden spikes, like an otter. Water ran in rivulets down his brow.

'Bollocks,' he said. But he walked back to the car and returned the tyre-iron to the boot. They got back in the car and waited as long as they dared. The house gave no hint of occupation.

On Tuesday the weather was worse. Over breakfast,

Holloway talked Lenny out of going back. Rain drummed on the kitchen windows and wind thumped at the ancient frames.

They could not afford to have somebody to call the police, Holloway said. If they kept going back, it would happen sooner or later. They would think of another way to speak to Henry Lincoln. There was plenty of time.

Holloway had an idea.

He said: 'Give me one of those matchbooks.'

While making arrangements for later that week, Lenny had lifted a generous handful of white matchbooks from a glass crystal ashtray set on the reception desk of the Caliburn Hotel. Now he passed Holloway a half-empty, dog-eared example. Matt black on glossy white, its legend read: The Caliburn Hotel, London.

Inside the lid flap, Holloway scribbled Thursday's date and a time. Then he addressed an envelope to Henry Lincoln and argued with Lenny about who should go out in the rain and post it.

On Thursday they confronted Rex Dryden.

21

There had been many opportunities to do so. Dryden's travelling side show, the *Hot Zombie Revue,* had been touring the country. At the same time he was promoting his autobiography on local television and radio. The book was called *The Nature of My Game,* and he grinned on the dust jacket like the kind of man you wouldn't want near your sister.

The tour ended with three consecutive nights at a north London venue called Papa Doc's. Papa Doc's stood directly opposite the phone box from which Shepherd made his anonymous call to the Avon and Somerset Constabulary. Its address was 128, Holloway Road.

'You just can't argue with symbolism like that,' said Lenny. 'Think of the book rights.'

Lenny had become what he called 'interested' in making money from what he now called *the story*. Candidly, he told

Holloway that, long term, he was thinking of a two-part television drama to be broadcast on BBC1 over the Easter weekend.

'Who would play me?' said Holloway.

'Oh,' said Lenny. 'I don't know. Let's think about that when we've sold the rights.'

'David Caruso,' said Holloway.

'David who? David *Caruso*? He's *American*.'

'He's got the right hair.'

'Duh,' said Lenny. 'They can *dye* hair, Magnus Magnusson.'

'OK,' said Holloway. 'Jude Law.'

Lenny laughed.

Then he saw that Holloway did not seem to be joking.

He scanned a short newspaper paragraph. Thoughtfully, he said: 'Don't you think Jude Law might be a bit – youthful?'

'Duh,' said Holloway. 'Make-up.'

Lenny made a show of turning the newspaper page.

'Well,' he said. 'He's too tall, as a matter of fact.'

'That won't matter,' said Holloway. 'It's not like it'll be a *documentary* or anything.'

Lenny closed the newspaper.

'You are not going to be played by arseing Jude Law,' he said. 'So live with it. Move on.'

'Sorry,' said Holloway. 'I didn't know Jude Law was taken.'

'Well, fuck you – Columbo.'

'*Columbo*?'

'Yeah. Columbo. We'll get Peter Falk to play you. Let's see how you like that.'

'He's too old.'

'Duh. Make-up. And he's about the right height.'

'He's *American*.'

'You need an American,' said Lenny primly, and opened the newspaper again. 'For the international markets. It's a well-known fact.'

'All right,' said Holloway. 'We'll talk about it later. What about Jack?'

'I don't know,' said Lenny. 'I haven't made up my mind. I was thinking Terry Waite.'

'I was thinking Bette Midler,' said Holloway.

'Bette would be better,' said Lenny.

II

Henry Lincoln had told the London office that he was suffering from flu.

They had no reason not to believe him. He was a reliable salesman who often met his monthly targets. His mileage was high, his diary was meticulous, his expenses modest. For all that jokes were told about his habit of retiring early during the annual sales conference (Henry was not what you might call a drinker), he was popular with buyers and colleagues alike.

In the five years since he had first taken the name Henry Lincoln, he had yet to take a single day's sick leave. He had even taken as holiday those far-off, dead days spent waiting for the end of the world at the ex-public-school building in Sussex, when he was a follower of and deputy to Rex Dryden.

Perhaps it was by virtue of some unconscious prudence that Henry didn't inform his boss that he wouldn't be coming back in the new year (because there wasn't going to be one). After all, he'd been let down before. For his part, the sales director dimly understood that behind Henry's request for special leave lay some obscure religious practice. Religion was a tricky area where employee rights were concerned, and there was little for a publisher's sales department to do between Christmas Day and 2 January.

At the time, Henry was the truest of true believers in Rex Dryden's apocalyptic vision. Or so he had long accepted. Of late, that very prudence – taking the end of the world as holiday – had given him cause to question the depth of his erstwhile faith.

For many years, Henry had been seeking a doctrine to adopt and live by. Many times he had been disappointed. If he were to be honest, Rex Dryden was last in a long line of higher beings, religions, political movements, women and public institutions in which he had attempted to make the ultimate spiritual investment.

He had long despaired of finding something to live for. He'd tried the police force, the army, the Catholic Church, the Conservative Party, the Church of Jesus Christ of Latter Day Saints, Buddhism, five wives, the National Front, the Green Party and many others.

Each had rejected him, or had been found wanting. Usually both.

Humiliation was not something that he took to. More than one of those five ex-wives was beneath a patio as a result. And

Rex Dryden had humiliated him when no further humiliation could be endured.

His call to the office was taken by Miriam, the occasionally fearsome departmental office manager. She was sympathetic, and asked if there was anything she could do.

He told her: 'You're very kind. But no thank you, Fiona.'

When the call was finished, he wiped his hands on the fluffy white towel that hung over a rail in the downstairs lavatory. Then he made himself a cup of tea and took a seat at the kitchen table in his mock-Tudor home. He referred to the fat A5 Filofax, which he usually kept in his briefcase. Its edges were dark with grease. Henry's hands were plump and soft, the square fingernails manicured and opalescent, like mother-of-pearl. He used his mobile telephone to cancel his week's appointments.

He spent that week inside his mock-Tudor walls. For many lonely hours he stared at the long strip of his back garden. It was dripping and melancholy against the English winter sky: mulchy greens and leafless twigs against muddy, grey cloud.

Henry didn't forget to eat, or forget to drink or sleep. But to remember was an exercise in discipline.

Once again, it was self-respect that kept him going. Pride had seen him through so many difficult times, even the conflux of marital and other events that had led him to change his identity. For Henry Lincoln was not the name his parents had given him.

That name was Derek Bliss.

Several years before, as Derek Bliss, he had owned a private detective agency in Bradford. Bliss had created Henry Lincoln as an alias, and listed him as sleeping partner. Possibly he had done so with exactly the contingency in mind of fleshing out a fraudulent identity he could adopt at a later date. He no longer remembered.

He did remember that there had come a time (shortly after the death of his fifth, bigamously married wife) when a dangerous man called Holloway finally made it no longer convenient for him to be Derek Bliss. Henry Lincoln's empty skin had been hanging there, waiting for him to step inside. He had flown to Australia as one man and flown back another.

Henry's skin fitted so perfectly and he'd worn it so long, he barely remembered the man he'd been.

He had been surprised, therefore, to see William Holloway and an unfamiliar associate ringing his doorbell. And he had been horrified when, two days later, they came back. Holloway's companion had called Henry's name from the front garden, while waving about a tyre-iron like a chimpanzee.

Two days later there arrived in the post a mishandled matchbook, upon the inside flap of which a date and time had been inscribed in ballpoint ink. Henry had no doubt the matchbook was an invitation to join William Holloway on the given date.

At first, Henry was angry. Holloway's role in his retribution was intended to be utilitarian, of essentially secondary and emblematic importance. It was the police force he intended to publically degrade, by way of recompense for the iniquity with which it had treated him.

There was no better instrument than Holloway, a corrupted exemplar.

Henry regretted that it had gone so badly awry.

He had overplayed that particular hand, but it hardly mattered now. He was no longer angry. Quite the contrary. He was buoyed by Holloway's providential invitation; it seemed to be a kind of blessing granted to his own long-standing plans to visit the Caliburn Hotel.

He was so nervous and excited that his appetite had deserted him. But nevertheless he sat down to a balanced breakfast at 7.30, lunch at 12.30 and supper at 8.00.

Any good soldier would have done the same.

Twice a day for five days, he had read and reread Rex Dryden's autobiography, if it could be so called. Ten times, he searched for his own name in the index, or in the acknowledgements. Ten times, he was perplexed by its absence.

When he set the book down on the coffee table next to the sofa, it seemed to taunt him with his absence, his lack of import. He covered it with a clean tea towel, a souvenir of Cornwall. Even then, he could feel the scorch of the book's derision. He put it, still protectively wrapped in a tea towel, in the cupboard beneath the kitchen sink.

His private things were all over the house. There were private things in books and in cupboards; on computer hard drives; under floorboards; in the chest freezer in the garage. It took some time to gather about him those items he could. He drew great comfort from their proximity. There were other items he would have liked to add to the assembly, but they were larger and less accessible.

He went upstairs to his office, where he had installed a home network of five computers, desktop and portable. From each of these machines he disconnected the peripherals: printers, keyboards, scanners. Then, with a Swiss army knife and various degrees of difficulty, he disassembled each computer and removed their internal hard drives. Each of these he laid on a double-page spread from the *Sunday Telegraph*. He smashed each hard drive with several accurate blows from a ball-pin hammer.

He removed these shattered components to the bathroom sink. Over them, he emptied a tin of lighter fluid. He threw in a match. A flame erupted with a woof like a curious guard dog. Henry took a step back. The flames scorched the ceiling and threatened to set light to the transparent plastic shower curtain with the goldfish motif. Henry drew the curtain to one side and examined it to make sure it wasn't burning. It wasn't, although there arose from it a heady plasticky odour. When the flames had lowered somewhat, to dance on a bubbling mass of plastic and wire, Henry went back to his office.

It made him sad to see the spaces where his computers had been.

From various drawers and cupboards he removed handfuls of paperwork. They included some glossy 8 x 10 black-and-white photographs, some legal documents that related to the sale of Executive Solutions Ltd, carbon copies of repeatedly rejected job applications. These papers and others he stuffed into shoe boxes and Sainsbury's carrier bags, which he then taped closed. From other cupboards in other rooms he found and bagged several strips of photographic negatives, a large number of handwritten notebooks, some items of clothing, some jewellery. He went to the chest freezer in the garage and took from it a medallion of frozen, pale meat. The cutlet was wrapped in a heavily frosted zip-lock freezer bag. He gathered a small pile of VHS video cassettes, and from a drawer in the hallway table he removed a consumer model Motorola walkie-talkie.

All of these things, including the heavy computer monitors and eviscerated CPU units, he dumped in a pile on the tiled kitchen floor.

By then it was late in the evening and Henry was tired. He made a cup of cocoa and went to bed.

But in bed he thought about the book in the kitchen cupboard under the sink, and he couldn't sleep. He tossed and turned in his clean pyjamas.

In the morning, he took a chisel to the bathroom and tried to remove the melted remnants of the hard drives from the bathroom sink. He added what he could to the pile in the kitchen, but bits of plastic casing had sealed to the bowl, so that morning he shaved in the shower. He stood in the hot steam for many minutes until his stubble had softened. Then he washed his round face with Johnson's baby soap. He rinsed his cheeks and throat under the hot jet. Then he applied three drops of shaving oil to his palms and massaged the oil into his beard. He shaved his cheeks and upper lip and chin and throat until there was not a trace of bristle on his round, slightly jowly face, even when he ran his soft palms all over it.

That morning, he read the book again. This time he skipped straight to the section that covered Rex Dryden's experiences as leader of the Temple of Light. He trembled with rejection and rage. He was filled with the extravagant urge to punish.

After lunch, Henry gathered up armful after armful of his private things and carried them to the far end of the long garden. The medallion of meat had defrosted and the zip-lock freezer bag had gone damp and flaccid like a used prophylactic. He dropped everything in a pile. When the pile was complete, he tidied the edges of it with a garden rake. By then he was sweating, although the day was cold. He went back inside and treated himself to a long soak in a hot bath. When he had dried himself, he combed his hair into a neat side parting, with the help of a dollop of Brylcreem. Then he selected some clothes: pressed blue jeans; a checked shirt; a crew-neck, navy-blue sweater; a reversible beige windcheater. Hush Puppies.

He went to the garage for the eight-gallon petrol canister, which he lugged to the bottom of the garden. He glugged the petrol on to the pile of private materials, raising the canister higher as it emptied.

He watched the bonfire for several minutes, shielding his eyes from the spiralling embers that batted his head like moths. Then he turned and hurried back inside the house. He saw the neighbours' curtain twitch.

Inside, Henry looked around his house. It still smelled of new carpet, with a sharp undercurrent of burned plastic.

He dropped Dryden's book in the pedal bin. Then he went to the cupboard beneath the stairs and found the toolbox. Beneath the tenon saw and the hacksaw with the broken blade, the screwdrivers, the carpet knife, he found an oiled rag. He took out the rag and opened it. In the middle of it lay a 9-mm semi-automatic pistol. He wrapped the gun in a clean handkerchief and slipped it into the pocket of his windcheater.

In the garage, he threw the half-empty petrol canister in the boot of his Ford Mondeo. He made a mental note to refill it at the first opportunity. It would not do to run short at the crucial moment.

Outside, it was cold. He turned the engine over several times before the car would start.

III

Lenny had greatly enjoyed planning their encounter with Dryden.

The day of the *Hot Zombie Revue*'s penultimate show at Papa Doc's, he went to a dealer in Mayfair that retailed surveillance equipment to paranoid businessmen. He returned with three digital audio recorders shaped like pens and a tiny digital camcorder whose lens fitted through a buttonhole.

'The audio footage alone,' he told them, 'will be priceless.'

They called a minicab. It arrived twenty minutes late, then honked its horn urgently and impatiently on the doorstep, as if they were being inexcusably tardy.

There had been some discussion on how best to dress Holloway. It was important that nobody recognize him and he should therefore not stand out in any way. Although they were expecting a mixed crowd at the club, this might be difficult: Holloway would probably be the oldest person there. Equally, in order that Dryden took him seriously when finally they met, it was important that he dress soberly. So Holloway wore a charcoal-grey, single-breasted suit with a black polo neck and wire-rimmed spectacles with non-prescription lenses, which Lenny for some reason had stashed away in a drawer somewhere. Dressed like that in Islington, Lenny assured him, nobody would notice that he even existed – let alone suspect him of being the fiendish killer of Joanne Grayling. Lenny chose to wear the suit he'd worn in New Zealand, which he had still neglected to have cleaned or pressed. One of his skate-boarding shoes had split along the instep. He wore them without socks, and when he crossed his leg the knob of his ankle glowed like a night-light through the thin skin. Shepherd wore greasy blue jeans, and a washed-out American army-surplus jacket with dark olive stripes still visible on the breast.

The three of them squeezed on to the back seat of the mini-cab. The car stank of vomit and tallow and semen and unwashed clothes. The driver smelled like a palm that recently had stroked a wet dog.

They rode in silence. Holloway was reminded of an earlier journey: stripes of lamplight passing over them in modulated frequency; detritus on the street, human and otherwise; a snarl of traffic outside Finsbury Park tube station, angry horns being honked. The minicab driver cranked down his window and screamed at the driver of a car that had legitimately blocked them behind a red light. The other driver unfolded his middle finger, then looked away as if fascinated by the architecture of Rowan's Gym and Leisure Centre.

They stopped on the way. Lenny squeezed himself out of the car and ran across the road to buy himself some tobacco and a cold can of Coke for Holloway.

Back in the car, he said: 'You have to do something about that blood sugar thing you've got going.'

Holloway snapped the ringpull.

'Stress,' he said.

Shepherd said nothing. He rode in silence with his hands clasped in his lap.

He looked out of the window and watched north London scroll past. His eyes felt heavy and he was calm. It seemed like everything was over already. He experienced a surge of fondness for Lenny, as if he were already missing him. For Holloway he felt little. In fact, he didn't much like him. Alone in Shepherd's company, he seemed uptight and taciturn. Shepherd supposed he might well be, given the largely unspoken-of death that fluctuated like a mild charge between them. But still.

He mourned his lost idea of William Holloway. The William Holloway in his head had been an unmet friend, a kind of soulmate. And Lenny's easy friendship with Holloway irritated him. He wondered what the two of them had in common, what on earth they found to talk about – they always seemed to be talking.

Then he began to daydream that Lenny might be right: that the book and film rights for this disorderly sequence of error and misapprehension might in the end make them rich. He dreamed about becoming a celebrity.

He remembered being a boy, the holidays in Wales. The

sound of rain drumming on the roof of the caravan; the warm, wet calor gas smell. His first kiss. The fumbling loss of his virginity with a girl called Tina, whose family took the caravan three along. He rolled down her bikini top, made tight and twisted with sea water and sand. Her skinny white thighs rippled with gooseflesh and she smelled of seaweed and lotion.

He did not think of these things as belonging to another life.

The rotten stench on his father's breath in the weeks before he died. The barely animate skeleton on the hospital bed. His father had not become reconciled to death. He died angry and bitter. His corpse was like a bundle of twigs, something to be tossed on a bonfire at the foot of the garden.

He remembered the way Rachel ushered the children from the kitchen when he sat at the flour-smudged wooden table and tried to tear chunks of hair from his scalp because his father was in a box in the ground. He imagined him, quite still, gazing at the lid of his coffin. He remembered the terrible dreams that followed, the death and the sorrow that ejected him into wakefulness. He remembered what his doctors had said. What Rachel had said, who knew him so well. And he wondered how he came to be here, in this stinking car, in this disintegrating city with these men – trying to prove that a stranger had not committed a murder in order to prove that he had not, all those months ago, simply gone mad.

He looked sideways at Holloway. He was tensing and relaxing his jaw. The muscles rippled and clenched under the pale, delicate skin. And Shepherd didn't know any more.

He didn't understand what had brought them here.

Then he thought about the key under the plant pot outside

his house in Bristol, and the new bed in his old bedroom. He looked again at Lenny and Holloway. He felt something to which he could not put a name.

He reached under a spectacle lens and touched an eyelid. It flickered like the wings of a moth.

The cab pulled up outside Highbury and Islington tube station. Lenny paid the driver. No tip, because the driver smelled. They stood in the weak lamplight, their breath billowing in the cold. The door to Papa Doc's was sandwiched between a newsagent and a charity shop. The club broadcast its existence with a neon sign, an accrual of pasted billposters and two bored bouncers who stood with their hands clasped across their genitals. A good queue stretched down Holloway road. The punters were overwhelmingly male, mostly young, white, scruffy and middle-class, although there was a smattering of suits and goatee beards. These people Lenny called the Islington Curious.

They joined the back of the queue and shuffled forwards, hunched for warmth, their hands buried deep in their pockets. The bouncers allowed Holloway to enter after the most cursory of body searches, which was fortunate because he'd brought along his lock-knife. Lenny too walked straight in. This probably saved him some larger inconvenience, since various recording devices were secreted about his person. But the bouncers stepped back and looked at Shepherd with something like wary regard. He had their bulk, if not their stance and musculature.

Shepherd said: 'Hello,' and smiled tightly behind his beard.

They submitted him to a long and intimate search.

He found Holloway and Lenny waiting for him outside the box office, squeezing themselves against the wall while the queue of young men shuffled past.

'Come on, Jack,' said Lenny. 'Fuck have you been up to?'

'My name is Andrew,' said Shepherd, angrily.

The words touched Holloway like a live wire. He twitched erratically, jostling two dreadlocked punters, to whom he turned and tried to apologize.

'What did you say?' said Lenny.

'Nothing,' said Shepherd. He squeezed them back into the queue. He stooped almost double at the box office window.

'Three please,' he said.

Behind him, Lenny said to Holloway: 'Are you all right?'

Shepherd didn't hear Holloway's reply.

They passed the press of musty bodies outside the coat check and entered the club through a double swinging fire door. A mixing desk stood in the centre of stained, sticky wooden dance floor. Posters promoting ancient gigs were plastered over the available wall space. A bar extended along the far wall. It was illuminated white like a distress flare. The crowd pressed three deep, like scrabbling insects drawn to the light of a false moon. At the other end of the room was a stage and a battered lighting rig.

Lenny pushed in to the crowd at the bar, a £10 note clasped visibly in the fist he held above his head as if wading in deep waters. Shepherd noticed a similar display replicated up and down the bar, with no visible effect on the service. Since it seemed to convey no advantage, he wondered what the function of such a behaviour pattern might be. He resolved to ask Lenny when he got back. Lenny was certain to have an informed opinion.

Holloway was speaking to him.

He looked down and raised his eyebrows.

'I'm sorry?'

'What did you say?' said Holloway.

'What?' said Shepherd. 'When?'

'Just now. About your name.'

Shepherd wanted to hit him.

'Nothing,' he said.

'You told him to call you Andrew.'

'No I didn't.'

'Yes you did.'

'No I didn't.'

Lenny returned, clutching three plastic pint mugs to his chest. He had spilled lager over his jacket and down one leg.

Holloway supped chemical scum from the surface of his pint. The plastic glass was sticky with spilled lager.

Holloway looked at Lenny over the rim of his glass.

'Didn't he just say his name was Andrew?'

'Yeah,' said Lenny. He turned to face Shepherd. 'What was *that* all about?'

Shepherd looked at them both.

'Nothing,' he said.

'Well,' said Lenny. 'It was a bloody odd thing to say.'

Shepherd shrugged. He took a long draught of lager. Thin foam flecked his tangled moustache. Tiny bubbles refracted and popped in random sequence.

'I was joking.'

'Right,' said Lenny, dubiously. Supping on the lager, he shuffled left and right. He said: 'Good crowd.'

But Holloway wouldn't let it go.

'Is your name Andrew?'

'No,' said Shepherd. 'My name is Jack. As you well know.'

'Andrew what?' said Holloway urgently. 'Your name is Andrew what?'

Shepherd thrust his beard into Holloway's face. Holloway backed off a step. A strand or two of beard attached to Holloway's five o'clock shadow and shone red under the beer light.

'Stop it,' said Shepherd.

Holloway moistened his lower lip.

'Is your name Andrew?'

Shepherd clenched his teeth.

'I said *stop it.*'

'All right,' said Holloway. He held up his hand. 'All right. Sorry.'

He broke Shepherd's gaze and looked around the club. It was filling with students and the Islington Curious.

A shambling, indifferent man in a shapeless T-shirt took his place at the mixing desk. He put on a country and western compilation. Then he slipped a set of headphones over his ears and twiddled at the mixing desk to no noticeable effect. But he seemed pleased enough. He smiled privately and dutifully, like the pilot of a nuclear bomber.

For a few minutes, they made awkward conversation. Holloway kept snatching curious sidelong glances at Shepherd.

Lenny and Shepherd kept pretending not to notice. Then the lights dimmed. There was a smattering of applause. A few whoops bounced across the crowd like an inflatable ball.

The darkness hung there for a second. Then the curtain rose.

It revealed a backdrop on which was printed a truncated pyramid, topped with a human eye. The incomplete pyramid was enclosed in a net of stylized penises. From the urethra of each protruded a hand that grasped an object: a spear, a clock, a skull.

Top-and-tailing the image were the words: *The Hot Zombie Revue*.

Lenny whistled through his teeth. 'Jesus,' he said. 'That's the all-seeing eye. It's a Masonic thing – it's on the American dollar bill . . .'

He talked about it for a while, but nobody was listening.

By degrees, a vibration in the soles of their feet swelled into a shrieking, atonal symphony that went on, in darkness, for longer than seemed tolerable. It was combined with quick-cut visuals, projected on the pyramid backdrop. What at first seemed to be a Technicolor autopsy, with rich, glistening reds, revealed itself to be a gender-realignment operation shot in unsteady close-up: it was just possible to discern a penis being degloved before being sliced down the median, folded in on itself like a sock and tucked inside a hairy, ambiguous orifice. This was followed by the rapid flicker of war atrocities. The images passed too quickly for the eye to settle. They were followed by a looped clip of the grainy, over-colourized Zapruder film: Kennedy's head snapped back. Jackie clambered madly over the body. The car reversed: Kennedy's head snapped forward. His brains flew back in. Jackie crawled backwards like a lizard. The car froze, accelerated again. The head snapped back. Another blur of images; the face of a dead baby with opal eyes emerged from a halo of rubble: skeletal creatures in torn, stripy pyjamas: a black man hung from a noose. Horseback men in white shrouds. A burning Vietnamese child. Adverts for washing powder and perfume. Close-up of a porno actress feigning orgasm. Detail of tortured bodies. Burns. Chechnya. Kosovo. Genital mutilation. Whip stripes. A meat factory. A blood-smeared huntsman. Patty Hearst. Timothy McVeigh. Congenital birth defects. National flags. Lopped heads like pineapples on a Chinese road. David Koresh. Billowing smoke from the Branch Davidian compound. The Heaven's Gate website. Bill Gates.

The atonal squealing increased in volume. Holloway covered his ears. So did others, scattered through the bludgeoned crowd. Other young men mimed approval to one another. The screen flickered.

Lenny took a notebook and pen from his inside pocket. He wrote *MTV goes to Nuremberg* and showed the pad to Holloway and Shepherd. But Holloway and Shepherd still weren't paying him any attention.

The music fell away and Rex Dryden took the stage.

Lenny put away the notepad.

Dryden's triumphant deportment suggested he was prepared to receive rapturous applause which then didn't come. One or two punters clapped: there were some whistles and a couple of whoops. But mostly the audience stood in silent ranks before him.

He surveyed them. He wore a sober, single-breasted grey suit. A ring on the little finger of his left hand glinted under the lights.

He took the microphone.

'Please allow me to introduce myself,' he said. 'I was born on TV. Just like you, and just like Jackie, I got Kennedy all over me.'

Behind him, a close-up of Kennedy on the slab. A vaginal, black and crimson burrow through his skull.

Dryden did a half-turn and looked at the picture. Then he took the microphone from the stand and walked the stage. More images flickered behind him: Kennedy, alive and waving; Mussolini swinging from a lamp-post; Saddam Hussein in a jaunty Homburg with a feather in the band; Pol Pot: Muammar Qaddafi with his eyes rolled white; Jesus Christ; Peter Sutcliffe; Josef Stalin; the Reverend Jim Jones; Mao Tsetung.

'Look at these men,' said Dryden. 'All these good men. What do we know about them? What do they have in common?'

He stalked the stage like a polar bear.

'People believed in them,' he said. 'Some people thought they were God. Some still do. And some people thought they were the Devil. Some still do.' He paused, seemed to think. 'Let me ask you a question,' he said. 'How many of you in this room believe in God?'

He waited as if expectantly, his face extended as far forward as his stumpy neck would allow.

'Go on,' he said. 'Any believers here, raise your hand. We won't laugh.'

A ripple of nervous laughter.

Dryden feigned great surprise. He put a hand to his breast.
'*Nobody?*' he said, shocked. 'Not *one* of you?'

He mimed sadness. 'Goodness me,' he said, shaking his
head. He jutted out a fat lower lip. 'What does *that* say about
England in the twenty-first century?' He looked up. 'Well,' he
said. 'This evening is all *about* belief. I want to talk to you about
what you believe, and why you believe it. And I can't do that if
you don't know what belief is. Come on, now. Somebody here
must believe *something.*'

He shielded his eyes from the bright lights, put his foot on
an audio monitor and pretended to sweep the crowd with his
gaze.

'Nobody?' he said. 'Nobody here believes in *anything*? Don't
we have any revolutionary socialists? No free market libertarians?
No anti-vivisectionists? No pacifists? No anarchists? No racists?
Blimey,' he said, muttering into the microphone. 'Tough crowd.'

More nervous laughter.

'I'll tell you what.' He gathered the cable into a loop and
replaced the microphone in its stand. He put his hands behind
his back and leaned into it. Then he checked himself. He said:
'Fuck me. What am I like? Liam Gallagher?' He grinned at
the catcalling response from the audience and seemed for a
moment unrehearsed and natural. Then he collected himself.
He quietened the crowd with his hand. 'I'll tell you what,' he
said. 'What if we start the evening by introducing an unbeliever
to God? What about that?'

He scanned the close-ranked bodies.

Abruptly, the lights went up. The audience blinked.

'So,' said Dryden. 'Which of you unbelievers and heathens

believes in God the least? Which of you faithless young scum-bags needs salvation the most?'

Hands pointed at heads they did not belong to and names were called out. Friends jostled friends and nervous smiles became affably predatory.

'Ah,' said Dryden. 'Now then. That's more like it.' He put a finger to his lips and appeared to talk to himself.

He knew what he was doing. His gaze fell tantalizingly on those who clearly longed to get on stage, then passed over them. They whooped and yelled and screamed. He teased with a playful, lingering glance those who clearly were terrified he might ask them to get up there with him. Eventually, he selected from the audience a slim man with a shaved head, in combat trousers and an indigo denim jacket. The second volunteer was slouching, ambling, dreadlocked to his waist.

Dryden asked for a round of applause. The audience obliged. Dryden positioned the two young men on stage. He asked their names. The bald man was called Tim. The man with the dreadlocks was called Diesel.

'*Diesel?*' said Dryden. 'What kind of name is *Diesel?*'

Diesel was loose-necked and satisfied. He caught the eye of friends in the crowd and grinned.

Tim clicked his fingers nervously at his sides.

From the wings appeared two black-clad assistants. Each pushed a chromium trolley. Upon each trolley's four shelves were components that might have belonged to a stereo system, wired together at the rear. On the top shelf was a laptop computer and a spaghetti of wiring. The assistants lined up the shelves behind the volunteers, then they returned from off stage with a moulded plastic chair and a towel each. They placed the towels in the chairs and the chairs before the trolleys.

Dryden invited Tim and Diesel to sit. A pale woman with an extravagant head of curly red hair took the stage. She too was dressed in black, and held a clipboard. She kneeled at Tim's side and addressed him quietly and urgently. He nodded assent, took a biro from her hand and signed something on the clipboard. She repeated the procedure with Diesel.

Dryden said: 'This is Dr Fiona Wright. She's here to make sure I don't go astray and turn the dial up to eleven, or anything stupid like that.'

The doctor looked up from Diesel's side and smiled. Some in the crowd laughed, without quite knowing why.

Dryden went to one of the trolleys. He held the microphone like a television evangelist. He said: 'This is called a Transcranial Magnetic Stimulator. And no, I'm not making that up. This is a genuine piece of kit. We're paying through the nose to hire it. What it does is: it shoots a very precise, rapidly fluctuating magnetic field into a small patch of human brain tissue. Zap. The bit of brain that's been stimulated kicks into life, allowing people like Dr Wright here to learn what its function is.

'So, for instance – if I zapped your motor cortex, various muscles would contract, depending on exactly where I'd zapped you. You might have a little spasm in your little finger. Or your whole body might go into convulsion.

'If I zapped a cluster of cells called the septum – it's right in the middle of your brain,' he tapped the crown of his head with the microphone, '– you'd experience a burst of intense pleasure, like every orgasm you ever had, rolled into one and multiplied by your date of birth. Or so they tell me.'

More laughter from the audience. Diesel chuckled. Tim widened his eyes suggestively.

'Now, now,' said Dryden. 'None of that. We're here to a higher purpose.'

Tim made a disappointed pout. His eye sockets became shadows when he hung his head. The lights were dimming.

Now Dryden was half whispering into the microphone. 'This hold-up is for the boys to sign a clearance form. They could've done it backstage, but I wanted you to see that no jiggery-pokery is taking place. I've never met Tim, have I Tim?'

'No,' said Tim.

'Or Unleaded, here. Have I, Unleaded?'

'Diesel,' said Diesel.

'Sorry, Swampy,' said Dryden.

Laughter from the crowd. Diesel did a furtive wanker sign for the benefit of his mates.

'Now,' said Dryden. He tapped the side of his head, just above the ear, with the microphone. Amplified, the action had a percussive resonance. Dryden dropped his voice to a whisper. The grainy amplification made it insinuating and direction-less, like the wind through sand.

'This area of the brain,' he said, 'is called your temporal lobe. In a moment, these machines will fire a carefully calibrated burst of very intense magnetism into Tim and Swampy's tem-poral lobes. It won't take long, but we're going to need your complete silence for a few minutes. Can you do that? Just for one minute.'

On stage, the two volunteers sat in a spotlight. An assistant bundled two towels into sausages and placed them over their shoulders. Then they moved the trolleys into position. On top of each trolley, alongside the laptop computers, were two paddles. Each was about the size of a ping-pong bat. The paddles were joined like headphones and linked by a wire to one of the system's boxlike components. They were secured at both sides of each volunteer's head. The assistants encouraged Tim and Diesel to relax.

The doctor referred briefly to the computer screens. Then she checked the paddles.

She looked at Dryden and said: 'OK.'

Dryden looked at the audience.

'Quiet, please.'

He waited until there was silence.

The doctor pressed a key on each laptop. The trolleys began to emit a low, ascending electrical hum.

It didn't take long.

Tim barked a single laugh. His back went into spasm and he stiffened in the chair. His eyes rolled white. Spittle gathered at the corner of his mouth. Tendons stood in relief on his neck. He laughed again, rapturously, as at a great relief. Then he shouted:

My God!

He laughed again, exultantly. The laugh modulated into a joyful sob.

He began to weep. He held out his hands, as if beckoning something to him. He looked at the ceiling.

Meanwhile, Diesel shrieked and bucked in his chair. He

howled something that was not a word. He opened his eyes and glared at the crowd. Then he stood and ripped the paddles from his head.

The doctor and both assistants rushed to him. He was led off stage.

After a long minute, the doctor returned for Tim. She removed the paddles from his head. He beamed in pious bewilderment and followed her away.

Dryden hit each keyboard again. The hum died away.

The lights came halfway up.

Dryden took the microphone. Heavy breathing through his mouth, amplified. He pinned the crowd with his eyes.

Then he broke the spell. His voice seemed too loud.

He said: 'Don't worry about Tim and Diesel. They're all right. It happens sometimes.

'What happened was, Tim's temporal lobe was stimulated. So was Diesel's. As a result, Tim had an experience of the presence of God that was in every way as genuine and as powerful as that experienced by Saul on the road to Damascus. Except Tim knows it happened because we flicked a switch and stimulated the belief centre in his brain. It'll take him a while, but he'll get over it.

'As for Diesel, well. What can I say? It wasn't *God* that Diesel met.'

He held his breath, but he couldn't hold back the merriment. His cheeks swelled and he burst forth with a cackle. He clapped his hands. He took the microphone from the stand and walked the stage again.

'So,' he said, 'what happened in this room tonight? What does it say about us? How does it relate to what brings us here?

'I'll tell you. It describes Dryden's First Law: use the right tools in the right way, and people will believe anything you want them to.'

Holloway, Shepherd and Lenny had seen enough. They pushed through the crowd and the swinging fire doors, which were moist with condensed sweat and breath. They passed the lavatories and the coat check, the box office and the bored bouncers. They huddled on the corner of an arctic north London street. Taxis and minicabs breathed smoke into the dirty yellow darkness.

'That can't be legal,' said Shepherd.

'Like he'd care,' said Lenny.

Holloway stamped his feet against the cold

'Well,' he said. 'It might be bollocks, but it gave me the creeps.'

'Kid's stuff,' said Lenny.

'My arse,' said Holloway.

'Look,' said Lenny. 'He was probably using infrasound. It's easily done. A frequency of 18 or 19 hertz will produce feelings of unease and anxiety. Even panic. It's been the root cause of many a supposed haunting; busted electric fans, extractor fans, high winds in old window frames, resonating between 18 and 20 cycles per second. That sort of thing.

'A tiger roars at about 18 hertz before attacking. It's just at the edge of human hearing, so it's stuff you don't know you're hearing: but you still respond to it as a threat. You get scared: feel like you're being watched. Hunted. Funnily enough, the human eyeball has a resonant frequency of about 18 hertz: so infrasound can cause visual disturbance or hallucination as well. So people hear bad noises, and they see movement. From these clues, their mind creates a ghost. All clever enough, I suppose. But he's just *playing*. He's winding up those in the know.'

'Either that,' said Holloway. 'Or he paid two unemployed actors to put on funny hats and jump around making funny noises.'

'Fair point,' said Lenny. 'Whatever. Same difference.'

'Hardly.'

They had been standing on the corner, opposite the traffic lights. It was Holloway who turned up his collar and walked towards Upper Street. Shepherd and Lenny followed. Their steaming breath combined in the darkness above their heads.

Shepherd sniffed the air. He thought he could smell a bonfire.

'And who are those in the know?' said Holloway.

'People like me,' said Lenny. There was a certain light in his eyes. 'People who study this stuff.'

'What stuff?'

'Politics. Psychology. Parapsychology. Magic. Mind control.'

'Right,' said Holloway, somewhat dubiously.

'Seriously,' said Lenny. 'That was as close to black magic as I ever want to come.'

'Oh come *on*. It was Hammer House of Horror bollocks. He was like a stag-night hypnotist.'

They drew to a halt on the edge of the kerb. Lenny walked in excited circles. A nervous young couple, huddled in winter gear, crossed the road. A minicab beeped them. Lenny waved his hands as if ideas were crammed up and jamming behind his eyes.

'You're right,' he said. 'He *was* hypnotizing those people. All right, it was in the most basic way, but he was hypnotizing them. All those images. They meant nothing. They were just pictures he knew would appeal to young men with pretensions to nihilism. His target audience. They'll leave that club believing that somehow Dryden has *freed* them —'

They waited a long time for him to continue.

'He's doing it all again,' said Lenny. 'He's recruiting. Just to show us that he can.'

The Caliburn Hotel stood close to King's Cross station, about half an hour's cold, brisk walk from Highbury. Along Upper Street, the dark shop windows were arrayed with Christmas decorations. The bars were softly incandescent and crammed full of the fashionable young. Broken glass like cracked ice littered the paving stones outside the Angel. In the streets and squares behind King's Cross, it was darker and colder, like an Arctic night. Prostitutes huddled together for warmth under streetlights. Cars slowed but did not stop.

Anticipating a promised urban renewal that had yet to occur, the Caliburn was a members-only establishment renovated from three derelict town houses. Its door was an anonymous portal in the street. It was necessary to announce their arrival through an intercom set in the wall. With an angry buzz of the latch, they were admitted into a long, plain corridor with a black slate floor and halogen lamps set flush to the ceiling.

Reception was on the first floor. They walked through whispering, smoked-glass doors into a stark, modernist lobby.

The receptionist stood behind an asymmetric desk. Lenny announced himself and notified the receptionist of his appointment with Mr Dryden.

The receptionist referred to an LCD screen, tapped something into a keyboard.

'We're a bit early,' said Lenny.

The receptionist spoke without looking up.

'That's not a problem,' he said. 'Mr Dryden is expecting you in the bar. If you'd like to go through and wait?'

The bar was sumptuous and kitsch. Like a casino, it lacked windows. Perhaps in another incarnation it had been a gentlemen's games room. Close to the bar itself were arranged several tables and chairs constructed from luscious, vaguely erotic curves and undulations. The walls were lined with heavy, velvet sofas. Although there was room to comfortably accommodate perhaps forty people, tonight the bar was almost empty. It contained a smattering of the Islington Curious. They huddled over wine glasses, talked in hushed monotones.

Holloway, Lenny and Shepherd set some organically shaped, red chairs round a low, kidney-shaped table. A young waiter came and took their order.

As he rolled a cigarette, Lenny's hands shook.

Holloway met Shepherd's eyes. Shepherd glanced away.

Lenny lit the cigarette with a book of Caliburn Hotel, London matches.

The waiter brought their drinks to the table. He set each one down on a little paper doily with a scalloped edge. He set down a crackle-glazed, white ceramic bowl of peanuts and a crackle-glazed, black ceramic bowl of Bombay mix. Then he tucked the tray under his arm and went back to continue his conversation with the Australian barman. The Australian's accent but not his words carried across the muted room.

Holloway said: 'What time is it?'

Lenny glanced at his watch.

'Eleven. Just past.'

'What if he's early?'

'He won't be.'

'But what if he is?'

Lenny crushed the half-smoked cigarette in the clean pewter ashtray. He massaged his forehead above the eyes.

'Whatever,' he said. 'If you're uncomfortable, just – you know. Take your position.'

Holloway sipped his Coke. Musical tinkle of ice cubes.

'It won't take him long,' he said, 'to work out what you're doing.'

'Trust me,' said Lenny. 'It'll play. He's too interested in publicity to worry if we're genuine or not. He'll see what he wants to see: another opportunity to get himself in print. He's as subject to Dryden's First Law as the rest of us.'

Lenny made a sour face, as if the irony was acid in his stomach.

Holloway glanced again at the door.

'And what if Lincoln shows?'

Lenny said: 'For God's *sake*, Will. Relax.'

Holloway stood. He drained his Coke. Set the empty glass on the table. A slice of limp, pale lemon in its base, over the shrapnel of ice. He was perfectly calm.

'I'll just —' he said.

'You do that,' said Lenny. 'Whatever.'

Holloway went to the bar. He ordered another Coke from the Australian barman. He was pleased to see the barman wore a scrubby goatee beard on his chin and that his blond hair was in a ponytail. He hoped he was having a good time in London. He paid cash; tipped heavily, more than the price of the Coke. The barman bounced the coin in his fist and closed his fingers round it.

'Cheers, mate.'

Then Holloway seated himself in a far corner of the room, close to the fire doors in the corner. Somebody had left a newspaper on a nearby chair. He lifted and tried to read it. It was a *Daily Telegraph*.

He watched the door, in case someone entered who might be Henry Lincoln. He hoped he showed. There were questions to be asked that he had not discussed with Lenny.

He hoped he'd know him if he did arrive. He had only a mental image to go by. He toyed with the lock-knife in his pocket.

They had arranged to meet Dryden in the bar at 11.45. He was a little more than half an hour late. When the doors opened, Holloway was shaking with caffeine and sugar.

Dryden pushed the doors aside. The Islington Curious broke off their discussions for a moment and looked up.

Dryden saw Lenny from the doorway. He waved, then took his gloves off. Fiona Wright, the doctor who'd appeared on stage, accompanied him to the table. She wore a camel-coloured, ankle-length cashmere coat.

'Lenny, I take it,' said Dryden. He extended his hand. His cheeks were red with cold.

Lenny stood and shook his hand.

'Pleased to meet you.'

'And you. This is Fiona.'

'Pleased to meet you.'

'And you.'

She unbuckled the coat, removed it, folded it over the crook of an elbow.

Dryden's gaze fell on Shepherd. A grin split his face like an axe wound.

'*Mate*,' he said. 'Long time no see.'

Shepherd made himself smile. He half stood in the awkward chair and extended his hand.

'Yes,' he said.

Dryden's hand was strong and cold.

He seemed genuinely pleased to see Shepherd.

'How are you getting on?'

He unwound his scarf and took off his overcoat.

'Very well,' said Shepherd. 'Not so bad.'

'You look well,' said Dryden. 'So. What brings you along tonight?'

Lenny interjected.

'Mr Shepherd will also be contributing to the magazine.'

'Oh, right,' said Dryden. He grinned, and hung his folded coat over the back of the chair. 'They got to you, too, did they?'

'Yes,' said Shepherd.

He had an odd feeling. He glanced at the door as if somebody had walked in. But there was nobody there.

Falls

Dryden pulled back a chair. Fiona Wright thanked him and sat, hanging her coat over the back of the seat and setting her handbag down on the floor. Then Dryden hiked his trouser legs and took a seat beside her. The red velvet, upholstered chair encased his head like a throne.

He leaned forward, looked over his shoulder and lifted a hand to summon the waiter. He ordered them a round of drinks. Same again for Lenny and Shepherd.

The waiter sloped silently off.

Then Dryden said: 'So. Tell me again about this magazine.'

'It's called *Teflon Samizdat*,' said Lenny.

'Right,' said Dryden. 'Good name. Where does it come from?'

'What – the name? I made it up.'

'Right. And it's a —' He took from his pocket a much-folded copy of the press release Lenny had mocked up on the Macintosh. He held it up to the light. He squinted. 'It's a what what?'

'It's an Alternative Libertarian Manifesto,' said Lenny.

'Is it, indeed? And what's an alternative libertarian, when he's at home?'

Lenny forced a smile.

'*Teflon Samizdat* has a radical semiotic agenda,' he said.

'I see,' said Dryden.

He nodded encouragingly.

'— which is to expose the intellectual flaccidity of the so-called radical left and the so-called radical right.'

'What —' said Dryden. 'Every *month*?'

'Quarterly.'

Dryden was fighting a smile.

'Fair enough,' he said. Then he said: 'You don't *look* like a radical semiotician.'

'Well, that's sort of the *point*.'

'Steady on, son,' said Dryden. 'We haven't started yet.'

He boggled his eyes. Then, merrily, he held Lenny's gaze. Lenny looked away.

The drinks arrived.

'Right,' said Lenny. Across the room, he and Holloway shared a glance. Dryden didn't seem to notice. He sipped from his whiskey and ginger.

Lenny said: 'Shall we begin?'

He placed a Dictaphone on the table.

'Ready when you are,' said Dryden. He reached into his own pocket and set on the table a Dictaphone of the same make and model as Lenny's.

He savoured Lenny's expression.

He said: 'Nothing personal. This is a tip I picked up from Tony Benn, just to let you know what a terrible mistake it would be to misquote me. Legally, I mean. Not that you would, I know. It would upset your crusading agenda.'

Dryden and the doctor shared a glance. She picked up her wine and sipped. She looked away.

Lenny swallowed.

'Right,' he said. 'We saw the *Hot Zombie Revue* tonight.'

'Good stuff. Hope you enjoyed it.'

'I'm not sure *enjoyed* would be the right word.'

'Perhaps not. Did you find it stimulating?' He grinned. So many teeth. 'Semiotically.'

'Certainly it made me reflect.'

Dryden laughed.

'It did that, did it? It made you reflect? Well – I expect that's a compliment, coming from a radical semiotician.'

Lenny blushed. His voice was weak and he had to cough and start the sentence again.

'*It's a Wonderful Life*,' he said.

'What?' said Dryden.

'The Friends of George Bailey,' said Lenny.

Dryden tugged at his bristly grey throat.

He said: 'Is this a Dadaist interview? Or are we playing word association?'

Lenny swallowed and licked his lips. He said: 'The murderer of Joanne Grayling privately used various references to the 1947 Frank Capra film, *It's a Wonderful Life*. For example, his email address was bedford.falls. Bedford Falls is the name of the town that features in the story, from which the hero cannot escape. That hero is called George Bailey. It is a matter of public record that the killer of Joanne Grayling signed his communications, including those from bedford.falls, as "the Friends of George Bailey".'

Dryden's circular eyes widened to their full button circumference. His bit down on his lower lip. His beard was grey and bristly as a boar. One meaty hand squeezed at his thigh. He seemed to be waiting. He smiled. The smile faltered. Then it spread across his face again and he barked with laughter.

'The what of who did what?' he said.

Lenny repeated what he'd said, word for word.

Dryden looked from left to right. He said: 'What is this – like an Ali G thing? Candid Camera?' He half stood in the chair and looked around the room. 'Are you filming this, or something?' He sat down. He looked indulgent and beguiled. He waved his hand for Lenny to proceed. He said: 'I think I'd better let you go on with this.'

Lenny caught Holloway's eye and nodded. Holloway folded the second-hand *Daily Telegraph*, which he had been twisting in his hands like a dishrag. He wiped his palms on his thighs and began to make his way across the bar. He kept out of Dryden's line of vision.

'The kidnapper of Joanne Grayling —' Lenny began.

'The kidnapper of —?'

(Shepherd heard somebody say his name. It sounded like his father.

He looked to the door.)

'Joanne Grayling,' said Lenny. 'She was the victim of a murder that took place in Bristol earlier this year. Her mutilation had a certain cultic significance. Her whereabouts were successfully predicted by Mr Shepherd.'

Dryden's gaze went from Lenny to Shepherd.

'Successfully?' he said.

Shepherd looked away.

'It is also a matter of public record,' said Lenny, 'that the kidnapper of Joanne Grayling used the distinctive phrase "nowhere, forever" in his final communication to the Avon and Somerset Constabulary. To my knowledge, you have used this phrase twice: once, during a press conference shortly before Christmas, 1999. And once to my friend Mr Shepherd, shortly after you appeared together on —'

'Of course I've used it,' said Dryden. 'It's *my* phrase. I use it

all the time. But I don't have a *monopoly* on it. And I talk about
It's a Wonderful Life every night in my show. It's my favourite
film, for God's sake. It makes me cry. You'd know that, if you'd
stayed for the end.'

'We saw enough.'

'Enough for what?'

'Enough to confirm our suspicions.'

Dryden's voice had ridden up the scale.

'Suspicions of *what*?'

'In addition to emulating the murderous cultist, Jim Jones,
something you later claimed to have been a joke, you head a
secret, probably satanic cult, which seeks to emulate and sur-
pass the so-called Manson Family murders of the late 1960s.
These murders are seeped in your personal symbolism. It's yet
another matter of public record that in your Sussex base of
operations, you daily used *It's a Wonderful Life* to illustrate
your apocalyptic liturgy. For whatever reason, however iron-
ically you might claim it to be, *It's a Wonderful Life* is your
Helter Skelter; an allegory of Armageddon, of death and
rebirth. When you dispatched your acolyte or acolytes to rit-
ualistically slaughter the prostitute, Joanne Grayling, they
were instructed to use specific references to this text.
Additionally, you sought the symbolic, politically motivated
sacrifice of a pig, namely a police officer, namely Detective
Sergeant William Holloway.'

Dryden and the doctor exchanged looks. She widened her
eyes.

Dryden pursed his lips and exhaled.

He said: 'Is this what you mean by radical semiotics?' He sat back in his chair. His bristled double chin receded into his neck, revealing a fold of hairy flesh.

'Because fucking hell,' he said. 'It's really *good*.'

Lenny wiped his palms on his trousers.

He said: 'I'd like you to meet someone.'

Holloway took a forward step.

Dryden's line of vision was restricted by the high, curved back of his chair and he leaned ahead a notch. His eyes flicked up.

'Hello,' he said. 'Are you with us?'

Holloway shifted his weight.

'Yes,' he said.

'Right,' said Dryden. He stood and offered his hand. 'Hello, there. Take a seat. The more the merrier.'

Holloway looked at the hand. He took it in his. Shook it.

'Right,' he said.

That was the moment when he admitted to himself that Lenny was completely wrong.

A hot flush rose from his sternum, spread to his neck and ears. His face reddened, but it was dark and he imagined Dryden couldn't see. He pinched his nostrils and took a stealthy look round the bar. Nobody seemed to be paying them any attention.

'Are you going to take a seat?' Dryden asked him. 'You're welcome to. I don't think Salvador Dalí here is finished yet.'

Holloway couldn't meet Lenny's eye. He cast around, looking for a chair.

'Please do go on,' said Dryden. 'Don't stop now, whatever you do.'

Lenny said: 'Do you know who this man is?'

'No,' said Dryden. 'But I expect you're about to tell me. Is he a radical semiotician too?'

Holloway picked up a chair. It was unwieldy in his grip.

He was still trying to think of a reply when the door opened and a man entered the bar.

The man was perhaps fifty, with the bearing of a sitcom brigadeer. He was short, and wore his neat, dark hair – dyed? A wig? – in a precise side parting.

He walked quickly, unevenly, reaching inside his jacket with his right hand. In the other hand he carried a large petrol canister.

In a way, Shepherd had been expecting him.

He'd been prepared for the day when the dreams found him again.

He watched Lenny as he leaned over the kidney-shaped table, his hands clutching his knees, his face pale and his hair sticking up at all angles. He saw Rex Dryden perching like Buddha in his chair, laughing. Fiona Wright glancing from one to the other: William Holloway pausing in the act of lifting an absurd, overdesigned, high-backed chair with an awkward centre of gravity.

He knew the dreams had led them all to this moment.

He was content.

The man drew up to the table.

He was such an angry little man. He had a pale, moon face and his plump lips mashed venomously together. In his hand was a pistol.

Dryden looked up. His bright little eyes went briefly circular. On a cracked, rising inflection, he said: 'Henry?'

Holloway paused. He still held the chair.

He said: 'Derek?'

Holloway and Dryden looked at each other, then back at the little man with the gun.

Dryden half laughed, half swallowed.

'Henry,' he said. 'What are you *doing*?'

There was a long, still moment.

The hands of Lenny, Shepherd and Fiona fell to their laps. Their eyes were fixed on Henry. But his attention was monopolized by Dryden. He seemed hardly aware of their presence.

Henry kept the pistol at Dryden's chest and looked round the bar. He ran his tongue over his upper teeth. Looked back to Dryden. He had yet to speak.

While Henry surveyed the room, Lenny reached for the half-smoked roll-up that smouldered in the corner of his mouth. Henry jerked as if prodded. He turned and brought the gun to bear on Lenny. Its muzzle drew figure eights in the air.

Lenny held his hands at shoulder height.

He said: 'Steady on, Henry. Derek. Whatever.'

'Please keep still,' said Henry. He stared at Lenny. Then he said: 'Right,' and waved the gun between Lenny and Shepherd. 'You and you. Block the doorway with that sofa.'

Lenny and Shepherd stood gradually and uncertainly, as if on arthritic limbs. After a confirmatory nod from Holloway, they went to the wall and lifted one of the opulent velvet sofas. They hoisted it awkwardly and carried it towards the doorway.

Because Shepherd was taller and stronger than Lenny, they bore it at a steep angle.

'Wedge it firmly,' said Henry.

They dried their hands, then shoved and elbowed and heaved until the sofa was firmly wedged in the doorframe.

Then they took a step back and saw what they had done.

Because the door opened inwards, it would be necessary to remove the sofa before escaping from the room in that direction. And it was jammed in well. Two men would struggle to remove it. There were two further exits: one behind the bar, by which the barman and waiter entered and left, and a fire door in the dark, far corner. An EXIT sign glowed red in a box above it. But in order to reach either door, it would be necessary to cross the room without Henry noticing. That did not seem possible.

Henry scanned the bar. His tongue moistened his upper lip.

Holloway remained on his feet. He buttressed himself with the silly chair. Surprise and bewilderment had truncated his logical faculties. In those first seconds, he could not imagine how Derek Bliss had come to be there. Something was wrong: but for the moment Holloway was unable to articulate what it might be. He stared at Henry.

Then he turned. Keeping his weight on the chair, he reckoned the number of other people in the room. There were seven; six men and one woman, including the waiter and the barman. In the rich semi-darkness, their faces were blank with shock. They had watched in silent, passive disbelief as Lenny and Shepherd blocked the doorway.

Something in their helplessness galvanized him.

He said: 'Derek?'

His arms were shaking.

Henry looked at him. He frowned.

He said: 'Call me Henry. I'm not Derek any more.'

Holloway cupped his hands over his mouth. He could hear his breath, as through a respirator. He could not link the faint memory of a connection between the two names. Derek and Henry. But he knew he would. As soon as his mind cleared.

He said: 'OK. Henry. Is that right? Henry.'

'Yes. What do you want?'

'Let me speak to them.'

Henry said nothing.

'It'll keep them calm,' said Holloway. 'If they know I'm a police officer. If I let them know you're in absolute control.'

Henry's grin touched the corner of his eyes.

He made an indulgent face.

'Very well,' he said.

Holloway turned. He cleared his throat. The sound rang out, absurdly loud. Everyone looked at him.

He spoke slowly and clearly. He hoped he was projecting more authority than he felt.

'Everybody,' he said. 'Please listen. My name is Detective Sergeant William Holloway. I'm a police officer.' For a second he fought an implausible smile and he looked down, privately, at his shoes. 'Now,' he said. 'I know you're alarmed. But I'm going to ask you to remain calm. This man has not come here to hurt anybody. He and I have known each other for a long time. So please: remain calm. Let's all do as we're told. I'm sure this situation will resolve itself.'

Henry's smile seemed pinned to his eyes. He said: 'Tell them to disable their telephones and leave them on the bar. Then they can go and sit in the corner.'

Holloway told them. He watched as the perplexed, scared patrons moved in exaggerated slow motion, like a modern dance company, removing mobile telephones from their pockets, their briefcases: unsnapping batteries from their housing, then filing to the bar to set them down. When they had done so, Holloway told them to move to the far corner. They ducked their heads and moved as if expecting sniper fire from every direction.

Holloway waited until they were in place. Then he said: 'Now, I'm going to say it once more. It's imperative that you all remain absolutely calm, and absolutely silent. Do you understand me?'

He caught the eye of the Australian barman. On their behalf he nodded once.

'Right,' said Holloway. He turned to Henry.

'Derek,' he said. 'May I sit?'

'Yes,' said Henry. 'And call me Henry.'

'And will you join me? Henry.'

'I don't think so.'

'You'll be more comfortable.'

'No.'

'Then at least put down the gun.'

'I'll put down the gun when I choose to. You're not in command here.'

'Henry,' said Holloway, with empathic tenderness. He smiled like the Virgin Mary.

Henry's face knotted with rage.

He screamed: 'Shut up and sit down.'

Tiny beads of spittle left his lips and described falling-star parabolas.

Holloway shut up. He sat down. He pressed himself down on the sofa between Dryden and Fiona Wright. Their thighs nudged his. He drew consolation from their proximity. The feeling appeared to be reciprocated: when Holloway spoke, both Dryden and Wright encouragingly pressed their legs tighter to his.

Henry gestured to Lenny and Shepherd, propped up in the doorway, to join him. They sat on the floor and hugged their knees. They said nothing.

'Derek,' said Holloway. 'This is between you and me. Why not let these people go? Then you and I can talk this whole thing through in private.'

Henry looked down on Holloway with a blank stare.

He said: 'What do you mean?'

'You know what I mean,' said Holloway. 'We've got unfinished business.'

Henry frowned.

'We have nothing of the sort, ' he said. 'This has nothing to do with you. I don't even know why you came here. So sit still and shut up.'

Holloway sat heavily in his chair. He put his head to one side. He was about to speak: thought better of it. Sat back.

Henry said: 'You're not even a trained negotiator. You don't know what you're doing. You have no technique.' He pointed the gun at Dryden. 'Tell them what this is about,' he said.

'Henry,' said Dryden. 'I don't *know* what this is about.'

Henry's cheeks quivered.

'It's about *you*,' he said. 'You liar.'

Dryden sagged, as if punctured in the midriff. He rubbed a slow, broad palm over his bristling pate. He groaned. Then he put his head in his hands. He looked up. Spatulate fingers tugged at rheumy lower lids.

He said: 'Henry. Please.'

Henry cut him off.

'I won't be laughed at,' he said.

Dryden took this in.

He said: 'I wasn't laughing at you.'

'Don't open your mouth,' said Henry. 'The flies will escape.'

It seemed to Holloway that Henry was about to pull the trigger. He tensed. He clenched his teeth and buttocks and squeezed his fists. He tried to force himself to face the gun. But something inside him was stronger than his will, and he looked away.

There was a noise in his head.

'I'm going to give you a chance,' said Henry.

'I don't know what you mean,' said Dryden. He looked at Henry, then shook his head once, very slowly. He said: 'Please don't do anything stupid.'

Henry seemed to enjoy the mystified glances. He smiled. This time there was humour in it.

'It's better to light a candle than curse the darkness,' he said. He looked at Fiona and Holloway. 'You and you,' he said. 'Move.'

They left Dryden alone in the chair.

Henry jammed the gun into the waistband of his jeans. The weapon dug visibly into his belly. Still nobody moved. With a grimace of exertion, Henry bent at the knees and, keeping his back straight, hoisted the eight-gallon container to his chest. He supported its weight with one hand and unscrewed the lid with the other. He slipped the lid into his pocket. He took a step forward and, posed like a chubby swordsman, he rained petrol on Rex Dryden.

Dryden bellowed. Blinded, he threw himself at Henry. Henry side-stepped. Dryden's shin hit the table's edge. He flailed, then toppled to his knees. The table went with him. Glasses fell but didn't smash. They rolled around beneath Dryden as he crawled this way and that, apparently at random. He shouted that the petrol was burning his eyes.

Henry took advantage of Dryden's helplessness. He poured more petrol over his broad, hog's back.

Eventually, Dryden recovered some constraint. Still on his knees, he took a cotton handkerchief from his pocket and dabbed at his raw, cherry eyes. But by now Henry had drawn the pistol and retreated a few steps. Henry told Dryden to sit. Dryden stared at him for a long second. Then, with the stoic deliberation of a long-dominant silverback, he moved to the thronelike velvet chair.

Henry smiled at him.

'Who's laughing now?' he said.

Henry set the jerry can on the floor alongside him. Keeping his eye and the pistol on Dryden he bent at the knee, reached down and screwed the lid back on. Then he straightened. With his free hand, he dug into the hip pocket of his jeans. Between index finger and thumb, he removed a battered, glossy white matchbook.

On the inside flap, Holloway knew, he would see today's date inscribed in his own handwriting.

Holloway glanced at Lenny. He saw that Lenny too had recognized the matchbook.

Holloway rolled his eyes expressively. Lenny shrugged, as unsurprised as he was defeated.

Holloway looked behind him. The group of customers in the corner had drawn into a knot. They were still and watchful as birds on a wire.

Holloway looked away. He saw that he'd been spattered with petrol. He could feel it: cold, greasy, soaking into the weave of his jacket and trousers.

He noticed Fiona Wright examining her petrol-wet clothes. He caught her eye and tilted his jaw minutely upwards, a confected symbol of defiance. She answered with a tiny widening of the eyes.

Henry's gun remained directed at Dryden's head.

'Henry,' said Dryden. 'Please.'

His hands lay useless and heavy in his lap. He shuddered with the cold of evaporation.

Henry ignored him. He looked to Holloway and the others. He nodded his head, once, business-like.

'Right,' he said. 'Form a line.'

They hesitated. Exchanged glances. Henry hastened them with a wave of the pistol. With maladroit, crablike movements, they sidestepped and collided until they were roughly aligned: Holloway at one end, closest to Dryden. Then Lenny, Shepherd and Fiona.

Fiona's shoulder nudged Shepherd's elbow.

Gently, he reached out and lay his hand on her upper arm.

'Don't worry,' he said. 'Everything will be all right.'

She said: 'I wish I could believe you.'

Nevertheless, she was comforted by the quiet compassion in his voice. She wanted to wrap her arms around him, to hide like a toddler behind his legs.

'Believe me,' he said. 'I have a feeling.'

'You two,' said Henry. He waved the gun at them. 'Shut up. And move apart.'

Shepherd and Fiona shuffled a half-step away from each other. When Henry looked away, she reached out and brushed her fingertips along the back of his hand. He glanced at her. Nodded. A smile cracked his beard.

'Henry,' said Dryden. 'Please.'

Henry looked at him.

While he was distracted, Shepherd and Fiona edged closer together.

'Stop saying *please,* please,' said Henry. 'It won't get you anywhere. Here. Have these.'

With a flick of the wrist, he tossed the book of matches to Dryden.

On reflex, Dryden reached out and snatched them from the air.

Henry grinned.

'Very good,' he said. He adjusted his jacket, straightening it round the waist. 'Now,' he said. 'What I'm going to do is this. Starting with this four, I'm going to shoot everyone in the room.'

While Holloway, Lenny, Shepherd and Fiona remained contemptuously still, a squall passed over the hostages in the far corner. From Henry's vantage point, their horror was expressed in a series of jerks and spasms. He thought of battery hens. Or alarmed birds about to take flight.

He was forced to raise his voice over the clucking and squawking.

'Unless —' he said. He sounded like a committee chairman. '*Unless —*'

Soon enough he had calmed them. Then he could speak quietly again. He coughed into his fist. Took another moment to gather himself.

'Unless you set yourself alight,' he said to Rex Dryden.

This time, there came no squawking and no clucking. The silence in the room cramped like a muscle. Henry could feel the weight of many eyes on his shoulders. It was a good weight, assuring to the heart as the heft of something well-engineered was satisfying to the hand.

He felt their strength enter him.

Dryden looked up. He was the cracked remnant of a man. He said: 'What?'

He put three fingers to his lower lip, as if testing for blood.

Henry smiled with grim pity.

'I'm going to shoot everyone in the room,' he said. 'Unless you set yourself alight.'

Holloway needed human contact. He reached out and took Lenny's hand in his. Lenny squeezed back. Holloway swallowed. Lenny was a grey haze in the corner of his vision.

Dryden's eyes shone wet.

He said: 'Henry. You can't do this.'

Henry experienced a flash of anger. It passed through him. He looked with great tenderness upon Dryden's bowed head.

'But Rex,' he said. 'I'm doing it.'

He glanced pointedly at the matches in Dryden's hand. Then he looked at his wristwatch.

He said: 'You have twenty seconds to decide. Let's see if you have it in you to be a saviour.'

Dryden said: 'You of all people know I'm not that.'

The voice belonged to a scared old man.

'Well,' said Henry. 'I'm giving you a chance to be. Twenty seconds. From now.'

'Jesus Christ, Henry.'

'Eighteen seconds.'

'What do you want me to *say*?'

'I don't want you to *say* anything. Fourteen seconds.'

Dryden held out his hands.

'Do you want me to beg?'

'You can try —'

'Then I'm begging. *Please*, Henry.'

'— but it'll do you no good. Ten seconds.'

'Please.'

'Nine seconds.'

'I'll do anything you want.'

'You know what I want.'

'Except that. I can't do that. God, Henry. Please don't hurt those people.'

'It's in your power to save them. You have six seconds.'

'I can't. You know I can't do it. Nobody could do it.'

'I did it for you. Four seconds.'

Dryden balled his fists. He pounded at the petrol-soaked, velvet arms of the chair.

He bellowed: 'Henry, what do you *want?*'

'To let you know what it's like,' said Henry. 'You have two seconds. One.'

Henry lowered his wristwatch. He shook his head and looked sorrowfully down upon the crown of Rex Dryden's head.

He turned slightly and faced the four people lined up on his right. They were silent, drained of colour. Only their eyes moved, avoiding his: they were unable to meet Henry's level gaze. Hunched and timorous, they reminded him of a front page newspaper photograph, the prelude to an atrocity in newsprint. He wished he'd brought his camera.

Henry raised the pistol. He took a step forward. He was not a tall man. He reached up and rammed the pistol into Jack Shepherd's beard. He dug the muzzle into the hinge where jaw met skull.

Shepherd swallowed.

'Please don't,' he said.

Henry seemed to hesitate. Then he pulled the trigger once, and blew Shepherd's mouth off.

Shepherd whirled, loose-limbed, and slammed into the ground.

Lenny screamed. Then he stopped. He pressed two fists into his mouth and bit down on them.

In the periphery of his vision, Holloway could see the spasmodic twitching of Shepherd's hands and feet. He thought of a runner, warming up on a cold morning.

He was alerted by a fear-suppressed sobbing to Fiona inching towards them, closing the gap where Shepherd had stood.

She reached up and took Lenny's hand in hers; forced his fist away from his mouth. Holloway saw how violently Lenny trembled. He too reached out and took Lenny's hand. The three of them stood there, connected, blinking, staring ahead while Shepherd's heels drummed on the varnished wooden floor behind them.

Among the knot of patrons in the far corner, someone shrieked. It broke their stasis. Shouts of distress and spasmodic tics flitted among them, possessive as St Vitus Dance. Somebody had pissed himself. Henry saw his waving arms and the darker patch on the inside leg of his charcoal-grey suit. His lip curled and he looked away from them.

He saw that Holloway, Lenny and Fiona had kept their backs turned. Shepherd's corpse lay between the two groups, marking a line that could not be crossed.

Henry screamed at the patrons to shut up. He yelled himself hoarse. He waved the gun around. At some length, the customers fell quiet again. Their new, fragile hush was broken by intermittent, houndlike whimpering.

Dryden's fingers gripped the arms of the chair. Vaporous trails of petrol made him shimmer like a ghost. He sobbed through gritted teeth. His bright little eyes were twisted shut.

'Can you see God now?' Henry asked him. 'Or is it not God that you're seeing?'

Once again, Henry bent at the knees to lift the petrol canister. The pistol had cooled enough for him to jam it once again into the waistband of his jeans. Then he stepped forward and again drenched Dryden. Emptier now, the canister was lighter and more manageable.

Petrol rained on Dryden's lowered head and ran in twisting rivulets from the boney ridge of his brow.

Holloway stood closest to Dryden. He felt a cold mist on his cheek. He freed his hand from Lenny's grip and touched his face. Henry's glance flicked in his direction. Holloway became still. Henry looked away, and Holloway lowered the hand again. His fingertips were greasy with petrol. He wiped them clean on his lapel.

Then he slipped his hand into Lenny's jacket pocket.

Lenny understood. He glanced sideways and he shifted his position, to make it easier. But he could not meet Holloway's eye.

Henry set the canister on the floor. His hand was wet and slick, shining with spilled petrol. He wiped it on his thigh. Then he repositioned the pistol in his grip.

He said. 'You have fifteen seconds.'

Dryden screamed. He thumped at the arms of his chair.

He said: 'I won't do this.'

Henry shrugged.

'We did it for you,' he said. 'We took our lives for you.'

'Your lives weren't taken,' Dryden yelled.

'*Yes they were*,' Henry said. 'For your sake. Ten seconds. Do you know what that *felt* like?'

Dryden shouted: 'Jesus Holy fucking Christ.'

From Lenny's pocket, Holloway removed one of several books of Caliburn Hotel matches.

He put his hands behind his back, opened the flap and tore out a match. Because his hands were unsteady and the match wasn't easy to strike, he calmed himself by concentrating on the movement of Henry's lips.

'Seven,' said Henry.

With a sulphurous hiss, the match flared. Holloway cupped his hand. The flame burned him. His vision shimmered. He blinked. Set his teeth.

'Six,' said Henry.

Cupping the delicate flame in his blistering fingers, Holloway moved his hands to the front of his body.

'Four,' said Henry. 'Five.'

Perhaps alerted by movement in the corner of his eye, Dryden looked up.

He saw what was happening. He looked at Holloway. Holloway looked back. Dryden thought of a fox.

Then Holloway tossed the flickering match into his lap.

There was a noise like a door slamming. The hot blast caused Holloway to step back, shielding his face with his fore-arm. The thin skein of moisture was blasted from his eyes. He smelled petrol and singeing hair.

Dryden was screeching, trying to stand. The immediate, ferocious heat had fused his skin with the synthetic covering of the armchair. Bent at the waist, he flailed and screeched, a burning hunchback.

The sudden heat tripped the fire alarm. The hotel was filled with a shrill, two-note shrieking.

Finally, one of the customers broke free: the Australian barman made a run for the fire door. The others wavered, then, milling, chaotic, they stampeded in his wake.

Disorientated, Henry whirled about. His loss of control was sudden and total.

Holloway removed the lock-knife from his pocket.

Henry levelled the pistol at the panicking customers; at Lenny, at Fiona.

The automated sprinkler was activated.

Holloway stood for a moment in the spray of an artificial deluge. He brushed water from his eyes. Then he stepped forward and stabbed Henry in the neck.

'Jesus,' said Henry. He stumbled forward. Caught himself on a chair.

He turned to face Holloway. He looked baffled. He touched the knife.

Holloway put his face close to Henry's. For another bewildered moment, Henry thought they were going to kiss.

But they didn't kiss. Holloway bit Henry's nose off.

Henry screamed. It was lost in the two-note shrieking that surrounded them. He dropped the gun.

Holloway opened his mouth. Henry fell to his knees and buried his face in his hands. There issued a thick, slow welling between his fingers.

Holloway spat something into the fire. Wearing smeared clown's lips, he stooped to tug and worry the knife from Henry's neck.

One hand still cupping his face, Henry tried to crawl away.

Holloway stabbed him low in the back. Twice in the shoulder.

Henry collapsed and lay with his face resting on his forearm.

Holloway looked around and saw the room was on fire. Perhaps damaged or spent, the sprinkler system had deactivated.

He looked for a way out. Dryden had almost reached the door. His unextinguished body had set light to it, and with it the heavy wood and velvet sofa that Lenny and Shepherd had lodged in the frame.

Something in the sofa ignited. The blaze seemed to leap at him. Holloway put up his hands to shield his eyes and stumbled backwards several steps, into a low table.

Lenny rushed to catch him.

Holloway looked at himself. His right arm was burned. He looked down further and saw that his leg was burned too.

'What are you *doing* here?' he said to Lenny.

Lenny tugged at his sleeve.

'Leaving,' he said.

Holloway looked round the room. Everyone had gone.

Lenny grabbed Holloway's unburned left hand.

He said: 'Come on.'

But he seemed fearful, hesitant, as if Holloway was a rabid dog that might now turn on him.

Holloway nodded towards Henry, still breathing.

He said: 'No.'

'Let the fire do it.'

Holloway felt the strength go out of him.

'There might not be time.'

He had no idea how long they'd been here. But it seemed clear that the emergency services would be on their way. Somewhere in the forgotten world outside this burning room, the hotel was being evacuated. Bewildered guests milled over the pavements, asking each other what was going on. Perhaps by now, guests who'd escaped the bar would be joining them.

Perhaps the police were already assessing the situation according to the limited, contradictory, hysterical information available to them. Fire engines would be screaming in their direction. Ambulances.

Holloway shrugged Lenny off and hurried through islands of flame; drifting plumes of steam and black, oily smog. He grabbed the petrol canister. It was hot to the touch; left fume-filled and unattended for a few minutes more, it would probably detonate like a bomb. That would probably do the job he wanted. If there was time.

Lenny called his name.

Holloway's eyes stung. He stopped, and retched into his fist. Something was wrong with his lungs. He turned to face Lenny. The flames roared and flickered behind him. Smoke boiled and rolled above his head. The fire alarm howled.

He looked down at Henry Lincoln.

Lenny called out.

Just leave him.

Holloway shouted at Lenny not to watch.

Lenny didn't seem to hear.

With his toe, Holloway tipped Henry on to his back. He saw the cleft, bleeding hole where his nose had been. It was ragged and scalloped at the edge; the signature of Holloway's teeth. He watched the slow popping of lazy, rude bubbles, like a volcanic mud pool, that came and went with the rhythm of Henry's breathing.

Holloway drizzled petrol over Henry's face. Henry writhed and tried to jolt himself away. He made muffled grunting noises, like a snuffling pig.

Holloway stamped on his belly. Henry made a choking sound and bent at the waist. Holloway poured what remained of the petrol into his mouth. Henry gagged. He tried to vomit. Holloway shook the last drop from the canister, then threw it away.

He crouched to grab Henry's ankle. He recoiled at the touch of his skin. Then, with an exerted grunt, he began to drag Henry into the fire.

Henry became frenzied. He thrashed and kicked out. He grasped at furniture. When finally he closed his fist round the leg of a chair, Holloway stopped, bent, and stabbed at Henry's knuckles until he let go.

Stooped, the knife in his hands, Holloway looked up and saw Lenny's face.

The heat of the flames was like a palistrade. Lenny had retreated to the far side of the room. His edges were erased by the fumes and the steam and the shimmer of heat. He looked like a spectre. But he didn't leave. He stayed to bear witness on behalf of Jack Shepherd and Joanne Grayling.

Holloway's face was greasepaint-smeared with tears and soot and blood. He lifted the remains of his jacket over his head. Small blue flames licked over it like arcs of electricity. He could smell burning hair.

He grabbed Henry's ankle and pulled him further into the inferno.

Henry had contested every inch. Suddenly his movements became disorderly and erratic. He thumped and writhed and jolted. His ankle twisted from Holloway's grip.

Holloway looked out from under the jacket. He saw that

Henry's face was alight.

He stepped away.

He watched the lips peel back from Henry's teeth.

As Lenny advanced to meet him, Holloway threw his knife into the purifying heart of the flames and withdrew. The dense mantle of smoke was by now a low, boiling ceiling.

Lenny took his sleeve again.

'Come on,' he shouted.

Holloway was not ready to leave. As Lenny tugged at him, he hung back, staring into the flames.

Once, he thought he saw human movement. But it was probably the rapid play of light and shadow.

'You're burned,' said Lenny. His voice clear and distant.

Holloway realized the alarm had fallen silent.

He coughed. His chest felt restricted. He collapsed. Lenny took his weight.

The ceiling was on fire.

Holloway lay his arm across Lenny's shoulders. He looked down.

Together, they made for the fire door. It was a milky square in the far corner of the room, through which long ropes of grey smoke unbraided and scattered.

It took a long time to get there.

Part Four

The Visitors

I've been telling you to this day, without me life has no meaning. I'm the best friend you'll ever have.

The Revd Jim Jones, from his final address to his followers, Jonestown, Guyana, 18 November 1978

22

The ward room was quiet and bathed in a greenish half-light. Holloway lay on a metal-framed bed. He couldn't move.

From the acute fall of shadow, he knew there was a window somewhere in the room, looking on to the night outside. It might be any hospital in Britain. There was the sharp green odour of cut flowers, an aftertaste of disinfectant. Rubber wheels squeaked in the corridor outside.

He knew that time had passed. A dim glimmer in the upper corner was the butt end of a length of silver tinsel. Christmas had come and gone.

A nurse stood at the end of his bed. Perhaps she had woken him. He tried to speak, but there was a mask over his mouth. There were tubes in his throat and nose, his arm.

The nurse moved to the edge of the bed. She touched his forehead.

His eyes rolled white. He fell again.

The coma was a temporary death. He emerged slowly.

He seemed to remember visitors. But he must have been dreaming, because two of those visitors were Shepherd and Dryden. They stood in the doorway.

In the dream Holloway smiled.

Dryden and Shepherd looked sombre. They didn't speak. They stood at the foot of Holloway's bed. When he looked again, they'd gone.

He was visited by his aunt Grace. She smelled like the house in which she raised him, like sweet make-up and baking bread and fresh winter air. Her voice, when she spoke, had all the old strength. She lay a weightless hand on his forehead.

'Everything is all right,' she said. 'Don't worry. We come here first.'

In the dream he couldn't answer. He was distracted by the curtains, which he could see fluttering through her translucent body as if through a corrupted lens.

There were other people too. Ranks of dim figures lined up in the doorway and shuffled past his bed. But from those people, in the dream, he averted his eyes.

23

The winter had not passed before James Ireland came to Holloway's door.

Ireland wore a tweed suit in need of cleaning, a knitted tie. Scuffed brown brogues. Mustard-coloured socks pooled at skinny ankles.

By then, Holloway's lesser burns were healing well. The skin grafts on his arms and hands and shoulders and neck had taken. His eyebrows and lashes had grown back. But breathing remained difficult and a cylinder of oxygen was kept close to the bed.

He tired easily and slept many hours a day.

Although the doorway was quite high enough, Ireland stooped when he entered. It was a trick Holloway had often used. It suggested humility when none was felt.

Ireland stood at the end of Holloway's bed with his hands

behind his back. Holloway could see that he held a bulging carrier bag.

Ireland said: 'Well, well, well.'

Holloway had been helped into a sitting position. It was still difficult to speak.

He said: 'Hello, sir.'

Ireland turned and shut the door. He pulled a moulded plastic chair to the edge of the bed.

He said: 'How are you?'

'Better,' said Holloway.

His voice was a grainy rattle.

'And your leg?'

He tried to smile, but it felt rictal and ugly.

'It's a matter of time.'

'Quite,' said Ireland and glanced away.

He clapped his hands to break the mood.

'I nearly forgot,' he said. He reached into the carrier bag he'd brought along. 'I brought you some magazines. Are you able to read?'

'Yes,' said Holloway.

'Good, good,' said Ireland. 'I wasn't sure what to get. So I brought a selection.'

'That's very kind of you, sir.'

Ireland sat attentively straight as Holloway flicked through the magazines, feigning interest.

'Will,' he said at length, as if imparting a great secret. 'We're aware that you knew her. Joanne. We checked and cross-referenced every transaction into or out of her bank account. You must have known we'd do that. We know that on five different occasions, you transferred sums of money directly into that account. So we know you knew her, and it doesn't take Inspector Morse to guess what you were up to. All right? So why didn't you just say so? Why didn't you just come to me and tell me if this fucker was on your back?'

Because Derek Bliss, aka Henry Lincoln, was supposed to have died of a cardio-vascular accident in Australia five years before, it took some time to identify him. The connection might never have been made had a large bonfire in Henry Lincoln's garden not threatened to rage out of control, causing his neighbours to dial 999. When the bonfire was doused, a charred shoebox split and spilled its contents on to the sodden ashes amid the clothes and books and diaries and newspapers, the busted laptop computers and associated peripherals. The firefighters found a series of charred 8 x 10 photographs of what appeared to be a mutilated female corpse.

They called the police. The corpse in the photographs was later identified as that of Joanne Grayling.

Further items were found that related to her kidnapping and murder. As Ireland and Holloway spoke, the bagged and catalogued ashes were still being sifted.

Ireland knew that the day immediately prior to the murder of Joanne Grayling and his subsequent alleged theft of the ransom money, Holloway had gone to Leeds in search of Derek Bliss.

Indeed, as Henry Lincoln, Bliss had been interviewed in connection with Holloway's disappearance. So it seemed clear that Holloway knew who was responsible for kidnapping Joanne Grayling before that kidnapping became a murder.

Holloway needed to think. There were a great many lies to prepare. But he couldn't think. He didn't know where to begin.

Ireland looked upon him with deceptive eyes; moist and supplicant. Holloway knew the look. He'd seen it in other contexts. Or similar contexts, but from a different vantage point.

He was tired. He wished Ireland would leave. But Ireland hitched his trousers and crossed his legs; the action of a better-dressed man.

With that same deceptive tenderness, he searched Holloway's expression.

Then he said: 'If you don't let me help you, you'll go down for this.'

He removed his spectacles and pinched the bridge of his nose. Even Holloway began to suspect he might mean it. But only for a moment.

Holloway met Ireland's myopic gaze while he polished his spectacles with the tip of his tie.

Ireland breathed on a lens, held it up to the light.

He positioned the spectacles on the end of his long nose. Holloway could see his own reflection. It reminded him of a newspaper cartoon or a saucy picture postcard.

Ireland hung his head like a man come to deliver bad news. Outside, the spring wind carried the excited barking of a dog. Motes of dust span and shone in a shaft of sunlight.

He shifted in the chair.

'Tell me about Jack Shepherd,' he said.

He waited. He ran a hand through lank, thinning hair.

'Tell me who he was.'

The clock on the wall ticked through twenty seconds.

'I don't know,' said Holloway.

Fragments of teeth and shards of bone were found embedded in the walls and ceiling. But there was not enough left of Jack Shepherd's head to run a check against dental records.

Holloway closed his mind to the thought.

Ireland looked at him for a long time.

Then he leaned into Holloway's ear. He spoke through clenched teeth. 'Fuck you,' he said. 'Fuck you. Do you know what you've *done* to me?'

Holloway listened to the far-off dog. When he got out of here, he was going to get a dog. A Staffordshire bull terrier. Every morning, he would exercise it on the Downs. Eventually, when he'd regained his health, they would go running together along the Clifton Suspension Bridge. The dog would sleep at the foot of his bed. A muscular, triangular head on a low-slung, bow-legged, barrel torso.

Ireland's eye came closer to Holloway than a lover's. Holloway could see a crust of tiny yellow crystals rimming his eyelid. He could smell the delicate sweetness of his breath and the soap he'd shaved with, not well. The eggy patches on his lapel.

He stood. He brushed down his clothing.

'I'm not sure what'll happen next,' he said. 'But I suppose you're not going anywhere, are you?'

Holloway smiled with half his mouth.

'I'll be here,' he said.

24

On Easter Monday, Kate came to see him.

By then he was quite mobile and better able to enjoy the limited view from his window. Across the visitor's car park and past the corner of another wing of the hospital, he could see a green stripe of parkland. He spent several hours a day in physiotherapy, swimming gently in the warm, circular pool in the hospital basement. He walked using a treadmill on its lowest setting.

He was in ongoing conversation with a therapist and a groomed, predatory solicitor called Birkin.

Kate rapped on the door with the back of her hand.

Dot dot dot. Dash dash dash.

He looked up. He lay his book face-down on the bed.

The smile felt odd, spreading across his mouth.

'Oh,' he said. 'Hello, you.'

She paused in the doorway, like people do entering a church.

'Hello you, too,' she said.

He said: 'I wasn't expecting you.'

She frowned.

'Should I have called ahead? Are you tired?'

He dismissed the questions with a wave.

'I'm fine. I like your hair.'

She touched the side of her head with two fingertips.

She said: 'Caroline sends her love.'

'Right.' He nodded, or tried to: a spastic Prussian bow.

'She's going back to university. Next term.'

'Right,' he said. 'OK. Good. Great. How's whatshisname? Her boyfriend.'

'Ex-boyfriend. For the moment anyway. Robert. He's fine.'

'Well,' he said. 'He seemed nice. Very fond of Caroline.'

'Oh,' said Kate. 'He loves her. He adores her.'

'That's good,' he said, although he wondered.

He picked up the book again, but only to mark his page by folding down the corner. Then he closed the book and lay it on the bed next to him, in easy reach.

'She did come to see you,' said Kate.

'Oh,' he said. 'Right. I didn't know.'

'Several times. Before you woke up.'

'Nobody said.'

'She asked them not to.'

She put her handbag on the bed and unbuttoned her summer-weight jacket. It was darkly speckled with spring rain. She must have been caught in a shower between the car park and the hospital entrance. He had noticed it: several urgent spatters on the window, like the drumming fingers of passing schoolchildren.

'It upset her,' she said.

'I can't have been pretty.'

Kate faced him with the jacket hung neatly over her forearm.

'That's not what I meant.'

She lay the jacket temporarily along the foot of the bed, then leaned over and picked up Holloway's book. Without bothering to examine the title (it was *Captain Corelli's Mandolin*), she put it on the bedside cabinet, next to the empty vase. Stretching, she made an informal little groan of exertion.

Then she said: 'May I?'

He waved his good hand mock expansively.

'Please,' he said. 'Make yourself at home.'

She looked around the room, perhaps searching out Get Well Soon cards. There were two: one from Lenny and Eloise, a second from Fiona Wright.

Kate took the damp jacket from the foot of the bed and hung it on the back of the moulded plastic chair. She sat down and crossed her legs. She tapped her foot at the ankle.

Automatically, she reached out to pat his thigh. Then she stopped, withdrew the hand. She laced her fingers and clasped her hands in her lap.

She said: 'So. How are you?'

'Good,' he said. 'Getting there. You?'

'Good,' she said. 'Getting there.'

Their eyes met, locked. Broke free.

She smiled. She was facing the window. The low, fast-moving clouds passed across her corneas.

She leaned forward, made a face.

'Is it painful?'

'Not really. Well. Not any more. It hurts when the nerves grow back. My breathing could be better. But it'll come.'

'Right.'

She glanced at her lap.

She'd grown her hair. A lock of it fell across her face. A few strands adhered to her upper lip. She looked up.

She said: 'So. Any news?'

He looked out the window. The light reflected silver on the body of a distant, ascending aircraft.

He said: 'They know it wasn't me.'

She closed her eyes slowly and nodded once, a way of telling him she knew.

'Let's not talk about it,' he said.

He didn't want to lie to her. He knew that, if she asked too much, he would have to.

Without looking at her, he reached out a hand and she took it in hers. He watched her glance at the skin graft, glance away.

The skin of her hand was dry, a condition she always suffered during the winter months. He could smell a clean, cool moisturizer. Not the Oil of Ulay she'd used when they were together.

But they weren't together, and that brand name had changed.

'It's OK,' he said. 'It's OK.'

She squeezed his hand and let go.

'So,' she said. 'What happens next?'

'I don't know,' he said.

No charges had been brought, but he knew a case was being prepared. It was a logistically complex matter, involving several divisions and fragmentary evidence. He was prepared to be charged with the theft of the money. He had denied it. He was willing to do the time if necessary, but Birkin intended to use his record of poor mental health in mitigation. If he made a sufficiently convincing case that Holloway simply cracked under intolerable pressure, the CPS might choose not to prosecute.

Holloway didn't know what evidence had been left undestroyed on Bliss's bonfire. Nobody had mentioned David Bishop to him yet. Possibly no one would.

He said: 'I just have to wait and see.'

A long silence fell between them. A dark cloud passed over the pale sun. The room dimmed, then fluoresced with an abrupt, shadowless light so bright it seemed to hum like a wire.

When they spoke, it was at the same time.

He deferred to her, but it seemed she'd changed her mind about what to say.

With a flick of the hand, she brushed the fringe from her eyes. Holloway saw the ring on her third finger.

He swallowed.

'So,' he said. 'You took the plunge, then.'

She examined the ring as if she'd forgotten it was there.

'Yes,' she said. 'New Year. In Barbados.'

He smiled.

'Congratulations,' he said. 'And how is your husband?'

She smiled back at him. It was a good smile, happy and tender. It made him ache for all the years that had gone into it.

'Adrian's well,' she said. 'He sends his best wishes. He says get well soon.'

'Tell him I'm trying.'

She unlaced her hands and patted his knee.

'All right,' she said.

'He's good,' Holloway said. 'He's a good man.'

'I know.'

'Of course you do. And what about Dan?'

'His wife's ill,' said Kate. 'I think that's his main concern.'

'Yeah,' said Will. 'Of course.'

He didn't know what to do about Weatherell.

'Anyway,' she said. 'He's OK. He's fine. He knows about – your breakdown. Or whatever. He can't quite believe you thought he was to blame —'

'I don't think I did,' said Will. 'Not really.'

'No,' she said. 'Well.'

There was no polite way for him to break off the conversation. He could hardly pretend to have somewhere to go. But she knew him well. She stood, tucking a lock of hair behind an ear. She gathered her coat and handbag. She folded the coat over the crook of her arm.

She said: 'I still don't know what happened. Not really.'

He smiled.

'Nor do I,' he said. 'Not really.'

He remembered an optical illusion he'd seen as a child: a drawing of a young Victorian woman, seen in three-quarter profile, wearing a wide-brimmed hat adorned with an ostrich feather. On second glance, the drawing became a leering, hook-nosed witch seen in profile. Then the witch became a girl again. The drawing was both, but only one at a time. And when the eye was focusing, there came a second when it was neither.

She smiled.

She said: 'Even if you did know, you wouldn't tell anybody.'

A number of pillows were braced against the small of his back, supporting him.

He said: 'Would you mind?'

She helped him lean forward, and one by one she took the pillows out, punched them into shape and replaced them behind him. She helped him to lie back.

She fussed efficiently with the edges and folds of the bedding.

He said: 'Leave that. Don't worry.'

When she looked up, he saw she was about to cry.

He said: 'Come on, now. Come on.'

She wiped her nose with the back of her hand.

She said: 'I'm sorry.'

'It doesn't matter,' he said. 'Come on, now. Do I look that bad?'

She laughed and blew a bubble of snot from one nostril. She nodded and that made him laugh and that made her cry. She rooted around in her handbag. She took out a handkerchief and blew her nose.

He smiled. She laughed and sobbed at the same time.

Something had changed between them.

She sat again. She moistened a corner of the handkerchief and dabbed at her eyes. Then she took a mirror-compact from her bag and began to reapply her make-up.

He watched her. She held up the compact, tilted her head back and pulled a face, making a long O of her mouth. With a few deft sweeps of a brush shaped like a tiny fir tree, she applied mascara. She patted a sponge into the compact and applied foundation to her face in the proficient, business-like fashion he'd first seen more than twenty years ago, when she was only a girl.

Then, with quick, circular movements of her fingertips she blended the foundation along her jawline. She closed the compact in one hand – it made a convincing snap – then replaced it in the handbag. She took out a bottle of perfume and spritzed her wrists and neck. Applying perfume was something she always did after crying.

Looking at her now, he realized she probably didn't even know it.

She put the bottle of perfume back in the bag. The room had filled with a scented mist that caught the light from the window.

'Right,' she said. She brushed her skirt flat across her thighs, then stood.

She bent over to kiss his brow.

The perfume mist had settled on her hair.

She said: 'Look after yourself.'

'You, too,' he said.

'I'll see you soon,' she said. 'I'll bring Caroline.'

'OK,' he said. 'Give her my love.'

She nodded.

'Make sure you eat,' she said. 'Keep your strength up. Call us if you need anything.'

Us.

He kept his eyes open to see if she paused in the doorway. But their days of pausing in doorways were long gone, and that was OK. He listened to her footsteps echo in the corridor, grow fainter. He could have tapped their rhythm from memory. The thought offered a kind of contentment. He heard the squeak of the heavy, swinging doors. Their black rubber skirts brushed along the hospital lino.

Later, he sat on the edge of the bed and watched the green sliver of municipal park. It was just visible over the ranks of parked cars, whose roofs were still beaded with raindrops. The sunlight warmed his cheek. He heard cars on the nearby road. A distant radio.

He watched people. They strolled or walked, sometimes ran. They were too distant to see clearly. Sometimes they were accompanied by dogs: dark, fast-moving specks that buzzed like houseflies.

He thought about Jack Shepherd. He wondered if a man could dream his own death.

Sometimes, the events that brought him here seemed uncomplicated; everything linked to everything else in a clear sequence of cause and effect. Then his mind lost focus. Sequence and causation gave way to an older, chaotic pattern, at whose complexity he could only grasp, to whose arcane energies and unknown conjunctions he remained subordinate.

But sometimes those connections corroded and fell away, and all that remained was what had happened.

And then he was happy.